Rand's blue eyes gleamed. "So you're proposing to me?"

"I know that's typically a man's domain," Ginger replied.

He smiled. "You think I'd take my sweet time about it, is that it?"

He certainly took his sweet time about a lot of things. In bed, anyway. Ginger flushed, disturbed that the only way they knew each other all that well was sensually.

She waved off his assertion. "Don't know. Don't care." She stuck her hat back on her head. "I just want a ring on my finger before any more time elapses. So that by the time I'm showing and we have to start telling people I'm pregnant, we'll already be married, and it won't be such a big deal."

His eyes never left hers as he stood there in that very still way that he had. "Oh, it's a big deal, all right," he said in a low, soft voice that sent ribbons of sensation coasting down her spine.

TEXAS
★ COUNTRY LEGACY ★

THE BABY CONNECTION

Cathy Gillen Thacker

Ali Olson

Previously published as *The Texas Wildcatter's Baby* and *The Cowboy's Surprise Baby*

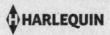

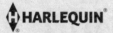

ISBN-13: 978-1-335-50010-6

Recycling programs for this product may not exist in your area.

Texas Country Legacy:
The Baby Connection
Copyright © 2020 by Harlequin Books S.A.

The Texas Wildcatter's Baby
First published in 2014. This edition published in 2020.
Copyright © 2014 by Cathy Gillen Thacker

The Cowboy's Surprise Baby
First published in 2018. This edition published in 2020.
Copyright © 2018 by Mary Olson

This edition published by arrangement with Harlequin Books S.A.

For questions and comments about the quality of this book, please contact us at CustomerService@Harlequin.com.

Harlequin Enterprises ULC
22 Adelaide St. West, 40th Floor
Toronto, Ontario M5H 4E3, Canada
www.Harlequin.com

Printed in U.S.A.

CONTENTS

The Texas Wildcatter's Baby   7
by Cathy Gillen Thacker

The Cowboy's Surprise Baby   243
by Ali Olson

Cathy Gillen Thacker is a married mother of three. She and her husband reside in North Carolina. Her stories have made numerous appearances on bestseller lists, but her best reward is knowing one of her books made someone's day a little brighter. A popular Harlequin author, she loves telling passionate stories with happy endings and thinks nothing beats a good romance and a hot cup of tea! Visit her at cathygillenthacker.com for information on her books, recipes and a list of her favorite things.

Books by Cathy Gillen Thacker

Harlequin Special Edition

Texas Legends: The McCabes

The Texas Cowboy's Quadruplets
His Baby Bargain
Their Inherited Triplets

Harlequin Western Romance

Texas Legends: The McCabes

The Texas Cowboy's Triplets
The Texas Cowboy's Baby Rescue

Texas Legacies: The Lockharts

A Texas Soldier's Family
A Texas Cowboy's Christmas
The Texas Valentine Twins
Wanted: Texas Daddy
A Texas Soldier's Christmas

Visit the Author Profile page at
Harlequin.com for more titles.

THE TEXAS WILDCATTER'S BABY

Cathy Gillen Thacker

Chapter 1

Whoever would have thought, Ginger Rollins wondered, that a tiny plus sign would have the power to forever change her life? But there it was. Bold as ever in the window of the testing device.

She sighed and stood, her knees wobbling as she paced the length of the nondescript hotel room she currently called home. Barely able to wrap her mind around the stunning news—she thought back to the rowdy town hall meeting in Summit, Texas, just six weeks ago. Where she'd locked eyes—and disputed ideas—with one tall, sexy, indomitable Texan.

If only her passionate arguing with Rand McCabe had ended there.

But no, as per usual whenever they met up, the two of them hadn't been able to call it quits when the meeting ended, and instead had taken their verbal clashing down the street to the establishment that stayed open the latest in that small mountain town. Equal parts pub, dance hall and pool parlor, the cavernous tavern was packed to the rafters with a singles-only event meant to take away the annual sting of Valentine's Day for the romantically unattached.

The band was loud, the company lively, the margaritas so strong you had to surrender your car keys and sign a pledge promising not to drink and drive to even get one.

If only, Ginger thought, she had stopped there, said a cool but firm good-night to Rand, and stuck to her usual ginger ale. Instead she had risen to the challenge of the ruggedly handsome environmentalist, and taken a seat beside him at the bar, where their disagreement had turned to laughter, their animosity to shameless flirting. Along with a host of others, they had closed the place down and taken the party bus back to her room at the Summit Inn.

The next thing Ginger knew sunlight had been streaming through the blinds. Her body still humming with the bone-deep satisfaction that was every bit as familiar to her as he was, she'd opened her eyes and groaned, aware it had happened. Again.

Only this time she had a scarlet heart with a broken arrow tattooed just below her shoulder. Rand had an exploding heart inked on *his* upper arm. And both of them were as naked as the day they were born. Ginger had moaned in dismay, because once again she'd felt way too exposed and vulnerable. "I don't believe this," she'd whispered to herself. *When would she ever learn*?

"Can't say I mind," a low masculine voice had drawled back.

Ginger winced. "Of course you don't mind," she'd muttered. He'd had a great time.

They both had.

"In fact, I don't think I've ever had a better Valentine's Day," he'd added.

As confident—and determined—as ever, Rand had turned his ruggedly handsome face and warm, strong body to hers. The stubble of morning beard, a shade darker than his rumpled mahogany hair, had lined his jaw. A sexy smile turned up the corners of his lips. But it was the compelling masculine intensity of his midnight-blue eyes when he'd admired her tousled hair and kiss-swollen lips that had really left her enthralled.

Damn him for reminding her just how right they were together. In bed anyway....

Ginger knew she should have said no when Rand's grin broadened and he'd reached for her again. Instead she'd given in to overwhelming desire and said yes to making love one last time.

To her relief, their coordinating tattoos hadn't been real. But apparently the consequences of their actions *had been*. And now, Ginger thought, on a fresh wave of emotion, she had to decide what to do before any more precious time elapsed.

Rand McCabe had collected eleven of the twelve soil samples he needed from in and around the Summit Creek bed when the pickup stopped just south of him. The door opened and an achingly familiar woman, with a mane of long copper-colored hair, stepped out into the warm spring sunshine.

A real looker, Ginger Rollins was dressed much like the last time he had seen her, in formfitting jeans, white

T-shirt and button-up Western vest. Her leather boots were thick and sturdy, meant for traversing hard-scrabble ground. Her stone suede hat had a rolled brim that spoke volumes about her sassy attitude.

And while Rand could not help but admire the sultry curves on her tall, statuesque frame, it was her pretty face, the pert, straight nose and soft, sensual lips that had haunted his dreams.

One more night together shouldn't have made all the difference.

But it had.

Perhaps that's why it bothered him more than usual that she'd been steadily avoiding his calls, texts and emails for the past six weeks, as was always the case after they hooked up....

His gut clenching with a mixture of impatience and anticipation, he watched Ginger stride toward him, her long legs eating up the ground. Slender shoulders squared, her chin held high, she moved with a smooth, effortless grace that made his heart jackhammer in his chest. Unfortunately there was no way of telling what she was thinking or feeling, given the sunglasses shading her dark green eyes. Figuring it best that he be standing when they faced off, Rand straightened to his full height. He set the soil sample in the bed of his truck. Inched off his leather gloves. Waited.

Her purposeful steps stopped just in front of him. Keenly aware that she owed him a big apology, for her usual lack of post-hooking-up etiquette, he looked at her expectantly.

Several long moments passed. Then she stuck her hands in the back pockets of her jeans and squared her shoulders again. Another beat of silence. Finally she said, "There's no other way to put this, so I'm just going to spit it out. I'm pregnant."

Pregnant. The word rolled around in his brain, refusing to compute. She was pregnant?

Ginger offered a weak smile, but did not take off her sunglasses. The silence between them stretched. Within him, anger and irritation surged. *After weeks of ignoring him, now this?* He took off his sunglasses, so she *could* see *his* eyes.

"Is this an April Fool's joke?" he demanded. Yet another way to torment him? If so, he wasn't laughing.

Every inch of her five-foot-eight-inch frame tensed. She let out a long, slow breath that first lifted then lowered her full shapely breasts. "Believe me, McCabe, I was as caught off-guard as you are."

He stared at her, still considering what to do and say next that wouldn't make the situation even more volatile.

Finally she took off her sunglasses.

To his surprise, she looked calm. Every emotional defense she had firmly in place. As though this whole speech was something she had rehearsed.

"Anyway." Ginger paused, appearing not to share the complex feelings roiling around inside him. "I thought I should tell you. Probably in person." She took another deep breath, suddenly looking oddly vulnerable. "So…" She gestured broadly, then started to pivot away from him.

Not about to let her run away from him again, especially now, he stopped her exodus with a light hand to her shoulder. Turned her slowly back to face him. "You're sure?" he asked quietly, searching her eyes, aware a sort of happy acceptance was beginning to crowd out the shock within him.

"Yes," she said softly, meeting his gaze for one long, telling moment that had them both—however briefly—on the same page. "When I first saw the plus sign in the indicator window, I was hoping it was a glitch in the home pregnancy test. Which is why—" She rummaged around in her back pocket, finally producing a folded piece of paper. "I saw a doctor over in Marfa and had a blood test and physical exam."

Her fingers brushed his briefly as she gave him the paper. It had her name and confidential patient information, all right, as well as lab results and the word "Positive." Under diagnosis, he saw "Pregnancy" listed, along with a projected due date of November sixth.

Their eyes met once again. Emotion shimmered between them as another long, awkward silence fell. He wasn't sure what she expected of him. Wasn't entirely sure what he felt, either. Except for the tiny hint of joy.

She assessed him with a long, level look and blurted, "Aren't you going to ask me if the baby is yours?"

Rand knew that would have been the logical response if their latest one-night stand had been with two people who were accustomed to having one-night stands. Neither of them was. That made her habitual running away from him—from the passion they shared—all the harder to understand and accept, given that their intermittent lovemaking had been ongoing for more than a year now.

"No."

Her green eyes glimmered with barely suppressed emotion. "Why not?"

"Because I don't have to, Ginger," he said. "I *know* it is."

Seeming vaguely insulted by his confidence, she squinted at him, then retorted, "How?"

Aggravated to find her still wanting to downplay what they'd experienced, which had been pretty spectacular, he returned, just as contentiously, "Because it was apparent from the very first time we ever went to bed together that you knew nothing about having a fling, and even less about turning an ongoing *series of flings* into a relationship."

She flushed. Guilty as charged. Shaking her head, she rasped, "We are such a bad match."

In certain ways, Rand conceded readily. In others… He couldn't disagree more. Because deep down, he had never felt anything like what he felt when he was with her. Nor—if his instincts were correct—had she. She was just too stubborn to admit it.

Sensing she was about ready to bolt, he let out a rough breath and stepped closer. "Well, given that we have a little one on the way, we're going to have to find a way to do better."

His gruff reminder brought a much needed dose of reality back to the situation.

"I agree," Ginger said. "Which is why," she continued resolutely, looking straight at him, "I'd like the two of us to make it official, at least for a while."

For once, Ginger noted, Rand McCabe had absolutely nothing to say. And that left her scrambling to put a halt to whatever confused notions he had. Hating how awkward this all felt, she lifted a cautioning hand. "Naturally, it won't be a real relationship."

Something flickered in his blue eyes then fled. "Naturally."

Trying not to think how attracted to him she was, she cleared her throat. "It'd be more like a business arrangement to get us through the birth."

And since they were both small business owners, she figured he would appreciate her matter-of-fact approach to their predicament. To her shock, however, it seemed to have done the opposite.

Still trying to get some sense of where she stood with him, Ginger let out a shaky breath and added, "Although there are obvious social advantages to being a 'family' while we await the birth of our baby…legally, it would also be easier."

He lifted a questioning brow, his gaze roving her head to toe.

Tingling everywhere his eyes had touched—and everywhere they hadn't—Ginger explained, "Under Texas law, a child born to a man and woman who are not married has no legal father. Conversely, if we're husband and wife when the baby is born, the child will automatically be yours in the eyes of the law. No additional paperwork will need to be done to establish paternity before we can put your name on our child's birth certificate."

"Looks like you've thought of everything," Rand said dryly.

Ginger had certainly tried. "It's all online. You can research it through the Texas attorney general's website, too."

Again, Rand merely nodded.

Frustrated he wasn't more forthcoming with his thoughts and feelings, she groaned. "Fortunately, we won't have to stay married too long." A little less than nine months, the way she figured it.

This time he moved closer. He stopped mere inches short of her. She inhaled the scent of soap and sun and man.

His blue eyes gleamed. "So you're proposing to me?"

Why did she suddenly feel as though that was a bad thing? "I know that's typically a man's domain."

He lowered his head, until they were nose to nose and she had no choice but to look into his eyes. "Uh, yeah!"

His gruff words were a direct hit to her carefully constructed defenses. Aware there were times when he made her feel very safe, and times—like now—when he made her feel very off-kilter, Ginger shrugged nonchalantly. "But I didn't want to wait for you to get around to it."

He smiled. "You think I'd take my sweet time about it, is that it?"

He certainly took his sweet time about a lot of things. In bed, anyway. Ginger flushed, disturbed that the only way they knew each other all that well, was sensually.

She waved off his assertion. "Don't know. Don't care." She moved to put her sunglasses back on, but stuffed them in her vest pocket instead. "I just want a ring on my finger before any more time elapses. So that by the time I'm showing and we have to start telling people I'm pregnant, we'll already be married, and it won't be such a big deal."

His eyes never left hers as he stood there in that utterly disarming way that he had. "Oh, it's a big deal, all right," he said in a low, soft voice that sent ribbons of sensation coasting down her spine.

She craned her neck to meet his gaze. "You know what I mean, McCabe. If we've already been hitched for three months or so before I have to start telling people

I'm expecting, then people aren't going to think much of it. It's going to be old news a lot faster than it otherwise would be."

"Or in other words—" his eyes never wavered from her face "—you don't want people to think we *had* to get married."

Determined to keep him at arm's length, Ginger fought the waves of sexual magnetism that always existed between them. "There's no such thing as having to get married in this day and age. But…"

He frowned. "There's always a caveat with you, isn't there?"

So what if there is? Ginger liked to be prepared for any eventuality, especially the bad stuff.

She stiffened her spine and plunged on. "Since the majority of the clients I want to put under contract are very traditional in their outlook, it makes sense for me—us—to be married. So that I will appear more…"

"Settled?"

She gave him a withering look before finally conceding, "Traditional, too."

Rand rubbed the flat of his palm across the nape of his neck. "Except for the fact that anyone who knows you at all kind of knows that you aren't conventional, Ginger. Not in the slightest."

True, she hadn't been. Until she'd realized they had a baby on the way. Knowing she had to provide for someone other than herself had changed everything. Made her yearn for as much stability as possible in her personal—and professional—life. Which included finding a way to land her first big contract as an independent oil woman, ASAP.

"Marrying you will show everyone that I'm finally

ready to settle down. That it's safe to trust my skill as a geologist, and to sign with me."

And that, in turn, would give their child the safe harbor he or she would need, even after she and Rand parted ways.

He sighed. "So this isn't just about the baby. It's about oil, too?"

Ginger nodded, as ready to be totally upfront about that as everything else. "The word on the street is that Summit County is going to lift their temporary moratorium on horizontal drilling any day now. When that happens, there's going to be a stampede of wildcatters trying to get landowners signed up."

"In particular Dot and Clancy Boerne."

A brief smile flickered across her face. "The fifty-thousand-acre Boerne ranch is where the most oil is expected to be."

"You think being pregnant and unmarried would eliminate you from the running?" he asked, sliding her a long, contemplative look.

In a word, yes. Ginger shrugged. "It's no secret that I've had an uphill battle trying to convince people to do business with me because I'm young, and female and a lot less experienced than some of the others vying for business."

He grinned, as if admiring her moxie. "And yet you persist."

He was darned right she did. "Just because wildcatting is still primarily a man's domain, doesn't mean it needs to stay that way."

Rand spoke with the respect of a son of the best lady wildcatter in the state of Texas, Josie Corbett-Wyatt McCabe. "Of course not."

"Furthermore, I've already demonstrated time after time I have a knack for coming up with drilling plans that get oil out of places that were previously considered inaccessible." Drilling plans that should have had her promoted at her previous job with Profitt Oil, if there had been any fairness involved. Which there hadn't been. "I just need a chance to show everyone what I can do now that I've ventured out on my own."

He rubbed the flat of his hand beneath his jaw. "Well, as long as you're confident…"

"I didn't expect you to cheer me on. Since all you want to do is *stop* people from drilling—"

"Irresponsibly," he interrupted, adding that important qualification. He had nothing against getting oil out of the ground, as long as it was done safely and with minimal environmental impact.

Ginger planted her hands on her hips, aware they were on the verge of yet another of their famously passionate arguments. "Well, I'm *not* irresponsible."

"And yet you're pregnant."

Ginger flushed. She should have known he would bring the conversation back to their lovemaking. He always did when they clashed, probably because he knew the topic got her even more worked up. "You get half the credit for that, cowboy. And it's not as though we didn't…"

"Use protection?" A hint of amusement filled his voice.

Ginger shook her head. "If the condom hadn't broken that one time…"

"There'd be no baby on the way."

No reason for them to be together now.

Another silence fell, this one slightly less combative.

Aware that if she wasn't careful she really would fall under his spell, Ginger stepped back and turned away. Needing a moment to pull herself together again, she swept off her hat and ran her fingers through her hair, doing her best to restore order to the tousled strands. For a long moment her gaze traversed the winding creek, fields of wildflowers and the granite mountains rising in the distance. With the blue sky overhead, and a warm breeze flowing over them, it really was a beautiful spring day. Quiet, too, since the Trans-Pecos region of far west Texas was not just rugged and vast, but sparsely populated.

But that, too, would change if what everyone was predicting, the oil boom that had already hit many other areas of the state, actually happened here in Summit County.

With a sigh, Ginger turned back to Rand. Realized all over again just how devastatingly handsome he was. As she finally met his eyes, she sensed she wasn't the only one feeling conflicted about everything that was going on. "Look. I know it goes against your grain, having to get hitched to me, even temporarily. That when the time comes for you to really settle down, you'll want someone a lot more…more…" She grasped for the right word.

He leaned forward and helped her out. "Demure?"

Irked, she narrowed her eyes at him and slapped her hat back on her head. "Whatever." Although to be truthful she couldn't imagine him with anyone else. "As far as you and I are concerned, however, this is only a temporary arrangement. One that can be undone as soon after the baby is born as possible."

"And in the meantime?"

Ginger shrugged. "We don't even have to live to-gether. Well, not really," she added hastily. "Especially if you end up working in another part of the state—"

"Not happening. I'm consulting in Summit County until the boom is over, same as you."

She had been afraid of that. "Then we'll get a place with separate bedrooms."

"Why?" He smirked in a way meant to infuriate. "We'll only end up in the same one."

"No. We. Won't. Sleeping together is what got us into this mess."

He rubbed his jaw with maddening nonchalance. "Keep dreaming, sweetheart." The corner of his mouth twitched in barely checked amusement. "That's one vow you'll never keep."

Flustered by his blatant delight at her frustration, Ginger shoved her hand through her hair. She didn't know why she let him get to her this way. "I don't know what it is about you and me that has us arguing every time we're around each other," she complained.

The wicked gleam in his eyes said *he* did.

"But right now," Ginger continued single-mindedly, "we need to focus on the least disruptive and most ex-pedient way to say our I Do's."

Rand looked no more eager to head home and in-volve their families than she did. "Right here in Sum-mit County is fine with me."

"Me, too," Ginger breathed, glad they were finally in concert about something. But then she felt the com-pelling pull of his gaze and her relief fizzled away. Steadfastly ignoring the shimmer of awareness sifting through her, she went back to her truck to collect the research she had already gathered, in preparation. Returning, she handed him his copy. "So here's the plan…."

Rand had never been one to let a woman take the lead. It just wasn't in his nature. However, he knew that Ginger was right; they needed to get married as quickly as possible. Otherwise, Ginger was likely to change her mind and bolt again. Only this time she'd be taking his unborn child with her.

So the two of them left the creek bed and went straight to the county clerk's office in Summit, Texas. They applied for a marriage license and made an appointment with a justice of the peace for as soon as the three-day waiting period expired.

"So I'll see you here Thursday at noon?" Ginger said on the courthouse steps after they had finished the paperwork.

Rand nodded. "You want to meet here? Or have me pick you up?"

"We can meet here."

He had figured she would say that. Although that, too, was going to have to change. Married people rode in the same vehicle, at least from time to time.

Pausing again, Ginger eyed him cautiously. "I'm just going to wear jeans…"

He shrugged. What did it matter since this wasn't a real marriage? "Okay."

"So no tie or anything," Ginger persisted.

He hooked his thumbs through the loops on either side of his fly. "Shirt and shoes optional, too?"

Flushing slightly, she told him archly, "You know what I mean."

He sure did. He rocked forward on his toes. "How about flowers? You want a corsage or anything?"

"Certainly not!" She appeared insulted at the thought.

He lowered his face until they were nose to nose. "You're bringing your own?"

She scoffed in disgust and stepped back in a drift of orange blossom perfume. "I'm not having any."

Of course she wasn't. Aware Ginger brought the *D* to *difficult,* Rand retorted, "Is everything about us—as a couple—going to be this nonsensical?"

"Ultra casual," she corrected. "And probably."

Rand could only imagine how their families were going to take to that. His parents didn't necessarily want everything to be fancy, but they did expect occasions such as weddings to be incredibly special. He'd only met Ginger's mother once—in passing—but Cordelia Rollins had struck him as the ultimate helicopter parent. And one who would definitely want a big elaborate wedding for her only daughter. *Not* a hasty elopement.

"All right, then," Rand said finally, making note not to adorn his new bride with any gift of a sentimental nature. "Good to know."

Ginger's hands flew to her hips. "You don't have to be so caustic."

As if he had started it. He let his gaze drift lazily over her before returning to her beautiful, emerald eyes. "You don't have to be so prickly," he shot back.

Her chin lifted in that all-too-familiar way. She sized him up for a long, thoughtful moment, then stepped a little closer. "Well, maybe it's a good thing you're so impossible."

He shortened the distance between them even more,

until only mere inches remained, then drawled, "And why, pray tell, is that?"

"Because then it won't be a surprise to anyone when we decide to go our separate ways a year from now."

"Or sooner," he allowed with a sigh, not seeing at that moment how they were going to make it one month as a married couple, much less all the way to their baby's birth.

"So... I'll see you Thursday?" she said finally.

He held her gaze, aware that for reasons he preferred not to examine *too* closely, he was looking forward to their next step every bit as much as *she* seemed to be openly dreading it. "At noon."

Her mouth twitching with satisfaction, she decreed, "I'll see you then," and sashayed off toward her pickup without a backward glance.

Chapter 2

True to her word, Ginger showed up on the courthouse steps Thursday at noon. In worn jeans, fancy Western boots, a white, lace-trimmed knit shirt and rose-colored vest, she looked pretty as a picture. "Ready?" she asked.

"As I'll ever be," Rand returned, more than ready to get the formality over with, too.

They walked into the courthouse, side by side. Only to promptly discover, to their mutual dismay, that all was not as it should be, after all.

"What do you mean we can't get married today?" Ginger lamented when they found out the justice of the peace set to conduct their ceremony was not even on the premises. "We made an appointment to get married at noon!"

"I know." The middle-aged court clerk swept a hand over his buzz-cut hair. "And believe me, the justice is sorry, but it can't be helped. It's a 'family' thing." Then he continued, a little lamely, "So if you all want the J.P. to marry you, you're going to have to reschedule…"

Not about to give up that easily, Rand asked, "Is there someone else who could perform the ceremony?"

"Not today. But…" The clerk studied the calendar on the computer in front of him. "The J.P. could fit you in a week from now, at three."

A week was too long to wait. Rand could see his bride-to-be thought so, too.

Ginger swung toward him, her body nudging his in the process. "What are we going to do?" she asked plaintively. "You told your parents you're coming to Laramie this evening to see them." She threw up her hands. "My mother is expecting me in San Angelo first thing tomorrow morning."

They hadn't told either of their families they weren't coming alone. That news, they had figured, could wait until they arrived, announced their "elopement" and introduced their new spouse, all in one fell swoop.

Aware she was sounding a little more emotional than usual—probably due to her pregnancy—Rand felt a surge of protectiveness rush through him. He gave Ginger's hand a brief, reassuring squeeze. "And we'll keep those promises," he said.

He dropped her hand and turned back to the clerk with a possible solution. "Do we have to get married in Summit County for our license to be valid?"

The beleaguered clerk perked up. "No, sir. Anywhere in the State of Texas is fine."

Rand thanked the clerk and they left the justice of the peace's office.

Ginger shot Rand a sidelong glance as they walked

toward the exit. Their footsteps echoed on the polished marble floors. "I gather you have a plan?" she asked.

"I do." He held the door for her, and accompanied her out into the midday heat of the spring day and down the broad limestone steps. "Even better, the place is sort of a McCabe family tradition. Which means—" he paused to give her a level look, hoping she would cooperate with him just this once "—it'll give our union an air of authenticity we probably wouldn't get any other way."

Although they hadn't talked about it, Ginger seemed to know what a hard sell their surprise elopement was going to be—for both families. Their eyes met and held once again. After a moment she took a deep breath, squared her slender shoulders and vowed softly, "Then I'm all-in."

At Rand's insistence, they would leave her truck behind and take his pickup for the drive north.

At Ginger's insistence, they phoned ahead to their destination, to make sure that Jeff-Paul Randall could marry them. The internet-certified minister slash business owner promised to be there when they arrived around five o'clock.

Relieved to have that arranged, Ginger climbed into the passenger seat of Rand's gray hybrid pickup and settled in beside the tall, broad-shouldered Texan.

Trying not to think about the fact he would soon be her husband, at least in name only, Ginger turned her attention to the rugged scenery. The creosote flats peppered with yucca and cholla cactus gradually gave way to elevations of higher rainfall, pinyon pine and scrub oak. Oil wells, cattle ranches and the occasional wind farm abounded, but towns were few and far between as they traversed the canyons, landed on Interstate 20 and gradually left the desert prairies and majestic mountains of the Trans-Pecos behind.

Rand said little during the four-and-a-half-hour drive. Ginger was quiet, too. In truth, there wasn't much to say. She just wanted the elopement to be over and done with. Although he didn't say as much, she was pretty sure Rand felt that way, too.

Finally they hit the outskirts of Laramie County. Minutes later they approached their destination: J.P. Randall's Bait and Tackle Shop. The squat, flat-roofed building with its peeling white paint was in the middle of nowhere, and just rundown enough to make it disreputable without being dangerous. Frequented by sportsmen and campers en route to Lake Laramie from the west, as well as people looking to fill up their gas tanks, or to be wed in a hurry, it was usually populated by a few cars and trucks.

Ginger knew, because she had stopped there herself a few times when in this part of the state. Never before, though, had she seen the establishment rimmed by three Laramie County Sheriff's Department squad cars. "I wonder what's going on."

Rand frowned. "The lights aren't flashing on the squad cars. Nothing is cordoned off by yellow tape…"

When Rand shrugged his broad shoulders, Ginger hitched in a breath. Masculine sinew strained against the soft chambray of his shirt, and she yearned to feel those smooth, rippled muscles beneath her fingertips….

"Maybe the deputies are just on a break," he said, snapping her out of her reverie.

"Maybe." Still, her feminine intuition told her it was more than that.

His expression serious, Rand pulled into the lot. The two of them got out of his pickup just as three men in khaki uniforms exited the shop. They grinned in recognition and Rand muttered a low curse as one of the men raised a hand in greeting. The other two deputies amiably followed suit.

Ginger pivoted to her husband-to-be.

So much for relative secrecy, she thought. "Obviously you know these men," she drawled. No surprise, in a rural county, where he had not only been born, but grown up.

Rand locked eyes on the approaching trio of law enforcement officers. A half smile tugged at the corners of his lips, yet his gaze remained wary. "Yep."

Her body tingling with a mixture of frustration and wariness, Ginger turned her attention back to the trio. All were about Rand's age, which meant early-to mid-thirties. All were well over six feet tall with fit, muscular physiques, all teemed with testosterone. But one of them was more similar to Rand than the other two. The badge on his chest said Deputy Colt McCabe.

It was all Ginger could do not to groan. "Tell me you're not related."

"Okay, we're not related," Rand repeated facetiously. *Except they clearly were.*

Deputy Colt McCabe slapped Rand on the back. "Hey, there, baby brother."

Rand braced, as if ready for more teasing. "Colt." The word was clipped and dry, yet oddly welcoming.

Colt McCabe's wicked smile broadened. He inclined his fine-looking head at Ginger and asked his brother, "Aren't you going to introduce us to your friend?"

Keeping his gaze trained on his older brother's, Rand angled his thumb at Ginger, as if they were no more than the most casual of acquaintances. A fact that for some unknown reason annoyed the heck out of her.

"This is Ginger Rollins." He turned, briefly catching her eye. Warning flashed in his expression. He, too, thought something was up, and wordlessly urged her to play along with whatever he said and did.

And really, Ginger thought, what choice did she have?

"Ginger," Rand continued with laudable politeness, "my brother Colt."

Colt tipped his Stetson in her direction. "Pleased to meet you."

Rand went on reluctantly. "This is Rio Vasquez." He nodded at the olive-skinned lawman, then the dark-haired man beside him. "And my cousin, Kyle McCabe."

Ginger shook all three deputies' hands in turn and uttered a cheerful greeting to each.

"So what brings the two of you to the bait shop?" Colt asked.

Ginger had a feeling, from the way Colt McCabe's eyes had initially been twinkling, that he already knew. So much for their plan of calling ahead to ensure there were no further delays.

Rand kept his poker face. "Nothing much," he told his older brother. "You?"

Colt's silence was answer enough.

Rio continued, in all seriousness, "We heard you have a marriage license in your possession that was issued in Summit County four days ago."

Rand pressed his fingers to his eyes and grimaced.

Wondering what her husband-to-be knew that she didn't, Ginger asked, "Is there a problem?"

All three deputies exchanged looks. "Mind if we take a look at it?" Kyle McCabe asked.

Unhappy that their marriage license might somehow be suspect, Ginger took it out of her handbag and handed it over. Kyle inspected it, then showed it to Vasquez and McCabe. All three shook their heads in silent remonstration.

"Just as we thought," Rio declared, eyes twinkling.

Kyle McCabe handed the license back to Ginger and said, "We're going to need the two of you to get back in your vehicle and follow us."

Whatever the joke, Rand was clearly not in the mood. He paused, as if weighing his options. "And if we don't?" he challenged.

Colt McCabe gave his younger brother another long, provoking look. "I think you can imagine," he retorted. "Sometimes it's just best to go along to get along, if you know what I mean."

"Go along with *what?*" Ginger asked.

Rand shoved a hand through his mahogany hair and muttered something under his breath that Ginger was just as glad not to be able to decipher. More meaning-laced looks passed between the four men.

Aware Rand seemed more exasperated and annoyed than concerned about whatever it was that was going on, Ginger knit her brow in consternation. "Is there something wrong with the marriage license?" Because if there was…

More looks. These seeming to tell Rand to keep her in the dark, at least for a little while longer.

Rand placed a protective hand at her back and turned

Ginger toward his truck. He leaned down, his warm breath brushing her ear and muttered, "We only wish that were all this was."

"You want to tell me what's really going on?" Ginger asked when the caravan had headed down the highway, in the opposite direction from which they'd come.

A mixture of resentment and resignation warred on his handsome face. "I'd rather not speculate," he said finally.

Okay. Next question. "Do we even have to go with them, then?" The three lawmen had made it clear, as they were getting in their patrol cars, that they weren't currently "on duty" with the sheriff's department. Colt had just gotten off shift, Rio hadn't yet started his and Kyle was on break. So, it was clear that whatever this was, it wasn't exactly official.

"No," Rand returned in a low voice. Having come to terms with their predicament, though, he was resigned to handling it with his usual good humor. "But we'd just be putting off until later what we may as well handle now."

Ginger rolled her eyes. "Well, that clears things up."

Rand reached over, put his hand on her knee and gave it a friendly squeeze. "Want my advice?"

Making no effort to hide her growing frustration, she plucked his hand from her leg as if it were an odious insect. "No, but I guess you're going to give it to me anyway."

Rand chuckled. "I suggest you relax and enjoy the peace and quiet, because it sure as heck won't last for long."

Turned out, Rand was right about that. The min-

ute they passed beneath the wrought-iron archway announcing the spread owned by Wade and Josie McCabe,
and headed down the tree-lined path to the big stone-
and-cedar ranch house, they saw the catering trucks and
the big white tents on the back lawn. Musicians were
already setting up. Acutely aware of their casual attire,
Ginger shot Rand a startled look. "Please tell me your
parents are having a party."

"It would appear so."

She added the important caveat, "One that *doesn't*
involve us."

"That, I can't say one way or another. I can tell you
all four of my brothers are already here. As well as…"

Ginger's face fell. She recognized the white Cadillac sedan with the vanity plate #1TXMOM. Her hand
flew to her throat. "Oh, no. My mother." A litany of
frustrated words followed.

Rand mirrored her feelings with a groan of his own
as the front door to the ranch house swung open and a
bevy of McCabes and Rollinses poured out.

Ginger's mother was dressed in a beaded knee-length
suit suitable for a mother of the bride. Perhaps because
they were the ones throwing the bash, Josie and Wade
were still in jeans, boots and loose-fitting cotton shirts.
All three parents looked as privately exasperated and
publicly determined as Rand and Ginger felt.

Rand and Ginger got out of the pickup, waved goodbye to the departing lawmen and met their families mid-
yard. "How did you find out?" Rand asked.

Josie McCabe scowled at her youngest son. "A re-
porter from the *Summit Journal-News* called me three
days ago to ask me how I felt about my environmentalist son marrying a rival lady wildcatter. From there

it was easy enough to find out a marriage license had been issued, so I called Cordelia Rollins to find out what she knew…"

Ginger's mom picked up where Josie left off. "And lo and behold, I knew nothing."

Wade added, "We all talked and decided if you two were going to get married, you were going to do it with friends and family present."

Josie nodded. "So I called the justice of the peace in Summit and asked him to hold off."

That explained the mysterious family matter that had kept the court official from marrying Rand and Ginger. "We already knew you were coming home this evening, so it was…well, not easy—" Josie frowned "—but possible, with Cordelia's help, to get a wedding set up here."

Rand quirked a brow. "What if we had canceled our trip north this evening?"

Josie shrugged. "I would have invented an emergency to get you here anyway."

"And what if we were already married when we got here?" Ginger asked her mother.

"Then you would have been married again, by a proper minister, in proper wedding clothes," Cordelia replied, shaking her head in reproach. "Honestly, Ginger, you are my only daughter. Were you really going to deny me the chance to see you pledge your love to the man of your dreams? Even if I haven't yet had the opportunity to even meet him, never mind give my blessing!"

If there was anything Ginger hated more than interference in her personal life, it was melodrama. "Well, as long as you put it that way," she quipped, raking a hand through her hair.

"You, too, young man," Josie scolded, stomping closer. "You know better!"

To Ginger's relief, she wasn't the only one taking exception to their public dressing down.

"Look," Rand was saying to his mother, "it's not as if I haven't done this once before. I had a proper wedding the first time around."

Rand had been married before? To whom? Ginger wondered, a tinge of jealousy trickling through her. But there was no time to delve into it. She could see that both mothers expected her, at least, to want the big, ultra-romantic wedding they had painstakingly organized, in lieu of the quick, no-frills elopement she and Rand had been hoping to have. Hence, Ginger had no choice but to set the record straight.

She sighed in exasperation. "I also had a big fancy wedding the first time." A fact her mother well knew. Consequently there was no need to go through that circus again. Even if the union she and Rand were planning had been a real marriage, which it wasn't.

Both mothers seemed stunned by the twin revelations.

Rand and Ginger turned to look at each other. Belatedly she realized she didn't know much about Rand, except how he felt about the environment and how great he was in bed. He knew very little about her, as well.

Abruptly aware they had overlooked a very important part of the marriage process, Ginger looked at Rand. "I think I need a moment alone with my, uh, fiancé."

"Good idea." Rand took Ginger by the arm and they headed down the driveway, not stopping until they were well out of earshot of everyone. Pivoting so no one would be able to read her lips, Ginger said ruefully, "We probably should have written a prenup."

Leave it to Ginger, Rand thought, taking in her soft, kissable lips and too vulnerable green eyes, to bring a highly emotional situation right back to cold, hard business. It was something she always did when she felt backed into a corner in any way. Something, in the end, that always drove him away.

Not this time. Not when she was carrying their child.

Aware all eyes were still likely upon them, Rand shrugged. "No time to do it tonight."

Ginger blinked up at him and raked her teeth across her lower lip. A pulse worked in her throat. "But we'll draw something up first chance we get?"

Rand nodded. As much as he would have preferred not to have to put themselves through that, Ginger had a point. It would make things simpler in the long run, if they put everything in writing well in advance of their divorce.

"In the meantime," Ginger continued practically, "in lieu of an actual marriage contract…how about a handshake deal?"

Cocking his head, he studied her face. "I'm listening."

"What's mine is mine, and what's yours is yours. There will be no community property gained during the union for us to quarrel about."

Her voice was calm enough, but he heard the steel-magnolia undertone. There would be no negotiating this or anything else in their union, at least as far as she was concerned.

He had a different idea.

Because he wasn't about to be pushed around by Ginger or any one else. "Everything regarding custody of our child will be equal, too."

This time she did not hesitate. "Right."

He relaxed in relief. "Okay, then." He tugged her in close and put one arm around her waist, shaking her other hand surreptitiously, in the age-old sign of a satisfactorily completed business deal. He whispered against her temple, "Let's do it."

"All right, you two!" Cordelia called from behind them. "Enough of that! We've got a wedding to put on!"

Once again, family interfered. Rand was escorted one way, Ginger another. A flurry of preparations followed.

Two hours later they were all together again, surrounded by two hundred of their closest family and friends.

This wasn't supposed to be anything more than a temporary legal formality, Rand thought in surprise. But standing next to the flower-strewed arbor in his parents' backyard, with a string quartet playing and his brother Colt stepping in to serve as best man, it sure felt like a real wedding. And, if the sweetly vulnerable look on Ginger's face as she floated down the aisle on her mother's arm was any indication, she was completely taken aback by the unexpected authenticity of the moment, too.

Colt teased Rand affectionately as Ginger neared. "I understand why you were in such a hurry to get a ring on her finger."

Ginger *was* beautiful, Rand thought, taking the opportunity to drink her in. Never more so than right now in her wedding finery.

The ivory-satin gown lovingly cupped her breasts, nipped in at her waist and left her arms and shoulders bare. The full skirt fell in a seductive swirl past her ankles. A sparkling tiara, attached to a short veil, was threaded through her upswept copper hair. As she neared him, her eyes met his. Held. As he took her hand in his, her delicate cheeks grew pink and her soft lips parted. Her chest rose as she took in a deep, enervating breath.

And then the ceremony began.

Ginger hadn't been this caught up in the ceremony the first time she'd been to the altar. To be feeling so breathless with excitement was…well, completely unprecedented, unexpected. And, she forced herself to admit, unrealistic. Yet, standing there with her hands clasped in Rand's large, capable palms, looking deeply into his midnight-blue eyes, she couldn't help but feel a little swept away.

Maybe it was the way he looked in that dark tuxedo, the striking contrast of the stark white shirt against the suntanned hue of his skin. Or how closely he had shaved, and the way his mahogany hair shone in the evening light. All she knew was that he smelled so damn good, like a sun-drenched forest just after a spring rain. That he felt so warm and was so tall and strong.

Maybe it was true, she thought, that women did instinctively search out the best specimen to father their children.

Right now, he seemed like the perfect mate.

To the point, it was easy to promise to have and to hold from this day forward.

At least, she added mentally, until the day their baby was born.

Then they'd see.

As she gazed into his eyes, she wondered if he was thinking the same thing.

That, too, would be reassuring. Because it would mean they might have all the trappings of a real marriage.

But "real" was, like this union, in the eye of the beholder.

The minister's voice rose, interrupting her thoughts. "What God has joined together, let no man put asunder." The reverend smiled broadly. "Rand, you may kiss your bride."

And heaven help them both, he did.

Chapter 3

But it wasn't just any generic end-of-the-wedding-ceremony-with-everybody-watching kind of kiss, Ginger thought in stunned amazement. It was a knock-your-shoes-off, make-you-tingle-from-head-to-toe embrace that weakened her knees. And had her surrendering to the warm, sure pressure of his mouth in a way she had never ever yielded before.

Not even to him. Not even during that fateful night when they'd made the baby she was carrying inside her.

This was something new. Something wonderful. Something suddenly and unexpectedly sanctioned.

And darn it all if Rand didn't take full advantage of the situation. Both arms wrapped around her, he brought her closer, until she was hanging on to him, soaking up everything about him—his strength, his scent, his warmth and tenderness. He was amazingly solid and real, so very masculine and persuasive. A low helpless sound escaped her throat, and Rand continued kissing her with the same quiet, unrelenting determination he channeled into everything that mattered to him. Until she mirrored his overwhelming need to make this mean more than it had. If only for this one moment in time. If only for the sake of their child…

Giving herself over to the marriage the way she had recklessly already given herself over to him, Ginger sighed again and curled her fingers into the fabric of his tuxedo jacket. Going up on tiptoe, she pressed hers breasts to the hardness of his chest and shifted her arms to his shoulders. His encircled her waist. And he brought her nearer still…claiming her as his woman, his wife. Just as she claimed him as her husband.

Rand hadn't intended to let the kiss take on a life of its own. Hadn't intended to turn Ginger—and himself—on to the degree that he had. Yet he couldn't say he was surprised. Whenever they were together, it was like putting a lit match to tinder. And that was something everyone who cared about them needed to see and understand. Because he knew if he and Ginger didn't want a heck of a lot of interference from family, needing—belatedly—to understand how and why they had come together in the first place, that they had some authenticating to do.

Problem was, he was beginning to want a whole lot more than a strictly-for-show kiss. He was beginning to want her alone. To want the hot, intense connection that blew all their impossible barriers away. But that couldn't happen right now, not with an audience surrounding them. It would have to wait until later. When they were alone. Celebrating their first official night together as man and wife.

Ginger moaned softly, trembling in his arms. Reluctantly, Rand lifted his head, looked into her misty green eyes and heard a cheer of approval from the guests.

His bride's acquiescence turned to a glare only he could see. Loving her display of fiery temper almost as much as her gorgeous copper hair, Rand grinned. He leaned forward, kissed her temple again and then held out his arm. She grasped it, just above the elbow, and motioned him down. She then whispered in his ear, "You're going to pay for that one."

Rand suspected he would.

He couldn't wait.

An exhausting few hours later the reception neared an end. Rand still looked incredibly handsome in his tux. Physically, Ginger was holding up, too. Emotionally was another matter. The strain of pretending to be every bit as ecstatic as they were expected to be had worn what felt like an enormous hole in her heart.

If any of this were real…

But it wasn't, Ginger reminded herself sternly.

And that meant she and Rand had to get out of there before they got any more caught up in the festivities, and what it was all supposed to mean to them. Or would have, had any of this happened the traditional way.

Predictably, Rand read her mind as they finished feeding each other bites of scrumptious wedding cake. He kissed her temple and murmured in her ear, "Ready to make a run for it?"

Ginger tried not to let her inner weariness show. "More than you know," she whispered back.

Two of Rand's brothers appeared at their side. "Don't forget the garter removal and the bouquet toss," Colt said, clapping Rand on the shoulder.

"Actually—" Rand winked "—I'm keeping that part private."

Ginger flushed at the sexy implication. Colt shook his head at his younger brother, grinning from ear to ear. She blushed all the more and flashed her groom a humorously reproving look. Now she *really* owed him.

Rand paused to wipe a smear of vanilla butter-cream frosting from the corner of her mouth, then kissed her lips gently. Excitement warred with the anticipation that had been building all night.

Feelings like this, Ginger knew, could be trouble. Feelings like this were what had gotten them into this mess in the first place. Rand seemed to intuit this, too. Unlike her, however, he didn't seem to mind.

"One last surprise." All three parents approached them. Along with Cordelia Rollins, Josie and Wade Mc-Cabe turned and gestured to the stretch limousine in the drive. "We arranged for a last-minute honeymoon, too."

Cordelia, who liked everything to be perfect, confessed fretfully, "Unfortunately, due to the short notice, we could only book you one night in the bridal suite at Lake Laramie Lodge. But if you'd like to stay on in a regular room, that's been set up, too."

Ginger and Rand shook their heads in unison. "Sorry, y'all," she told them, "but we're going to have to head back to Summit tomorrow."

Rand nodded. "We both have a lot of work to do."

Their parents looked disappointed for the two of them, but not surprised. One bouquet toss and a spirited goodbye later, and Ginger and Rand were cozily ensconced in the back of the limo. The glass divider was up, to allow them maximum privacy.

Sighing wearily, Ginger let her head fall back against the seat and she closed her eyes. Rand clasped her hand in his. "You okay?" he asked.

Was she? Ginger still felt that odd, unexpected emptiness in her heart. Telling herself it was just a reaction to all that had happened, she replied, "Yes. Just tired."

"Then we'll get you out of that dress and straight into bed."

That had her opening her eyes, turning her head.

Rand looked sheepish. "You know what I mean," he said.

Ginger did. And for that, she was grateful.

Rand—like the rest of the McCabe men—could be exceedingly gallant. She knew that side of him would come in handy when their baby was born.

Upon arrival, Rand and Ginger were whisked straight to the spacious suite on the top floor of the lodge. The thousand-foot space sported a living area, majestic bedroom and large spa-style bath. A big box of chocolates and a bottle of champagne on ice sat waiting, along with a sumptuous repast of fruit, bread and cheese. All in all, it was much too romantic, way too decadent and private, for comfort.

Ginger wondered how she was going to spend an entire night here, alone with Rand, and not do exactly what they had in the past…succumb.

"Would you like me to open the champagne for you?" the bellman asked cheerfully after setting their overnight bags down.

Rand declined the offer, then tipped the bellman, who promptly congratulated them again and headed out. Once they were finally alone, Rand looked her over, taking in every inch of her. "What's wrong?"

How about nearly everything? Ginger thought. Then, trying a diversionary tactic, said, "Did you ever wonder why our parents threw us a big lavish wedding instead of trying to stop us?"

Actually, Rand had given that a thought or two in the previous eight hours. Aware that Ginger still looked better than any woman had a right to look after the day they'd had, he locked the door and moved further into the room.

"My mom and dad know there's no dissuading me once I set my mind to something." He watched as Ginger attempted to work the tiara and veil out of her upswept hair. When it seemed she needed a hand, he stepped in to assist. While she stood stock-still, he found the pins and gently worked them free. Finished, he handed her the headdress. "What about your mom? Why was she so eager to see us get hitched?"

Ginger lifted her skirts, showing a flash of silk-clad ankle, and paused to toe off her high heels. Before Rand could help her, she eased off her satin garter, too, and dropped it onto the coffee table between them. Ignoring his look of comically exaggerated disappointment, she said, "My mom says her thirty-year marriage was the best thing that ever happened to her, and she wants me married to the love of my life, too."

Rand drank in the orange-blossom scent of her perfume. "How'd she feel about your divorce?"

Ginger sighed and went back to working the pins out of her hair. Finished, she ran her fingers through the silky copper mane and arranged the softly curling strands over her bare shoulders. "She wasn't pleased we were calling it quits. But she also knew Conrad and I weren't making each other happy. So in the end, she wanted what's best for me."

Ginger glided over to the bar, and poured herself a glass of ginger ale. "What about your parents?" She slanted him a curious look. "How did they feel about you getting divorced?"

Rand took off his bow tie, undid the first two buttons on his shirt and hooked his jacket onto the back of a chair. "I think they were relieved, given that it wasn't much of a marriage. It only lasted a month."

Ginger looked as if she thought his hasty divorce didn't bode well for the two of them, either. She sat on one end of the sofa and propped her stocking-clad feet on the table. "How come?"

Rand picked up the fruit plate and settled next to her on the sofa. He munched on a tart green grape.

"Turns out that Diandra expected access to my trust fund once the ring was on her finger."

Ginger leaned over and helped herself to a strawberry. "And you refused."

Rand turned to face her, balancing the plate on his bent knee. "That trust is my safety net, in case anything ever happens that leaves me unable to work." He draped his right arm along the back of the sofa. "I'm not going to live on it."

Ginger's brow furrowed. "Diandra didn't know that before you two said 'I Do'?"

Rand let out a mirthless laugh. "I had told her as much. She never thought I'd stick with it when we could have used it to live luxuriously. Anyway, as soon as she saw I was serious, she filed for divorce. When that didn't change my mind, she ended it for good."

Ginger made a soft sound he couldn't even begin to interpret. "How old were you?"

"Twenty-two."

Her eyes widened. "Wow."

"Yeah."

She tilted her head and took a longer look. "And since?"

Rand shrugged. "There's been my work, as an environmentalist. And you." She flushed in response. "So what about you?" He ate another grape. "How long were you married?"

She toyed with a wedge of peach and lifted it to her mouth. "Four years."

He watched her savor the juicy fruit. "What happened?"

She shrugged. "I realized Conrad was never going to take me seriously in a professional sense."

He sensed that was the least of it. Frustrated she wasn't being more forthcoming, he searched her eyes and pressed on. "You felt disrespected?"

"And then some. Plus..." She hesitated.

He waited.

She bit her lip. "I had the feeling deep down that something was missing between Conrad and me. Anyway, we split up two years ago. Got a quickie divorce. And all my mother's done since is try to talk me out of the oil business and into another marriage that will last."

Rand saw trouble ahead. "Uh-oh."

"Yeah." Ginger wrinkled her nose. "She won't be happy when this union ends in divorce, too, but that is a problem for another day. My task right now is to get some sleep, ASAP."

Rand couldn't argue that. She was pregnant, after all. It had been a very long day. "Need some help getting out of that dress?"

Looking lovelier than ever, she stood, pivoted and arched a delicate brow. "Really?"

"Hey." He lifted his hands in mock surrender. "Just offering."

"Mmm-hmm." Shaking her head, Ginger went over to the luggage stand and opened her overnight bag. Blinked, and blinked again. A litany of frustrated words followed.

"What?" Curious as to what had her so upset, Rand rose and sauntered over. Ginger held up a very sexy white negligee in one hand and a very feminine sundress, equally unlike her, in the other. Aside from that, and a handful of very brief satin-and-lace undies, another pair of shoes, an unopened package of pantyhose and a toiletries bag, there was nothing in the bag. Trying not to imagine what she would look like in all or none of the above, he quipped, "Not what you were expecting?"

"Obviously, someone—my mother, most likely—took out everything I had planned to wear tonight and tomorrow, and replaced it with all this."

Rand's grin turned into a hearty chuckle.

Blushing mightily, Ginger wagged a finger in his direction. "You laugh now. But this begs the question. What's in *your* overnight bag, cowboy?"

Ginger watched as a bemused Rand plucked out a pair of discrete black satin boxers, a razor, more cotton underwear, a starched button-down shirt, a pair of khakis and another pair of shoes.

"Who did yours?"

Rand pointed to the proper morning-after-the-wedding clothing. "Probably my mother." He caught sight of a gift bag stuck in a side pocket. The names of all four of his brothers were on the tag. "And then—" Rand groaned at the contents: a G-string with a big silver wedding bell on the front "—my siblings got into the act."

Next to that, was a big box of condoms.

Not, Ginger thought, that they would be needing those—even if she hadn't already been pregnant. She rolled her eyes. "Nice."

"Thoughtful," he agreed. Putting everything down but the provocative scrap of spandex, he asked, "Want me to try it on?"

Actually, yes, but that would lead to nothing but trouble. And they were in enough hot water as it was. So, instead, she gave him The Look.

Grin widening, he set it down. "I'm guessing that's a no."

He, however, did not look any the less discouraged. Trying not to think about what the mischievous light in his blue eyes portended, Ginger went back to studying the contents of her bag, then buried her face in her hands. "Well, now what are we going to do?" She had hoped to get two rooms somewhere and wear practical cotton pajamas to bed. Alone.

Beside her, Rand shook his head, looking just as distraught. "I don't know. We can't wear any of this."

He shrugged helplessly. "We'll just have to go to bed naked."

Ha! As if he could rope her into that! After the incredibly romantic evening they'd had? Even if it hadn't been their doing. "Nope. We won't. You know why? Because—" she disappeared into the bathroom and emerged victoriously with two thick white spa robes "—we have these!"

Rand stroked his jaw, looking ruggedly handsome as ever. He leaned close. Inhaling the scent of him, she realized he still smelled amazing. His expression amused, as if he knew where her thoughts kept wandering, he quipped, "Naked under that is good, too."

Ginger huffed in indignation. "I won't be naked."

His mouth quirked but he held his silence.

"I'll still have on my underwear." She felt the need to rush on. "Maybe my stockings, too." Just for good measure. With him around, she needed every bit of clothing she could get.

When he still said nothing, she turned her gaze back to his. He stood, legs braced apart, hands propped on his waist. "Now what are you thinking?"

His gaze trailed lazily over her before returning ever so slowly to her face. "I'm imagining what kind of frilly, sexy undies you do have on under that dress."

Squirming with embarrassment, Ginger caught a glimpse of herself in the mirror and saw her cheeks were a deep rose pink. "Well, you'll never know." Determined to keep him at arm's length, both emotionally and physically, Ginger swept into the large bath and shut the door behind her.

Unfortunately, she soon found out, Rand's playful attitude was the least of her problems.

"And here I thought you'd be down to your skivvies by now," Rand drawled when Ginger finally surrendered to the inevitable and opened the bathroom door. She swept into the suite, the skirt of her wedding gown rustling softly as she moved.

To her relief, he had done nothing more about undressing. And was, in fact, reclining on the king-size bed, hands clasped behind his head. His pleated white shirt was half unbuttoned. His cufflinks were off, the sleeves rolled up past his muscular forearms. He'd taken off his shoes, too.

Once again, his eyes caressed her. His gaze lingered on the cleavage spilling out of her fitted bodice, then drifted languidly over her waist, hips and thighs "You do look a mite skinnier now, though," he said after his long, slow perusal.

Wishing there was another option, Ginger moved toward him reluctantly. "It's because I took my petticoat off."

"Ah." Another pause and furrow of his dark brow. "What's a petticoat?"

"The froufrou thing that goes under my skirt to make it stand out. It's sort of like a half-slip for formal attire." She perched beside him on the bed, aware he hadn't moved a muscle. He looked turned on and frustrated.

She swallowed around the sudden dryness of her throat. "And you knew that, didn't you?"

One corner of his mouth lifted in a sensual smile. "I might not have. Only having brothers and all that."

Ginger recollected what she knew about the state's

most famously successful lady wildcatter. "But your mom…"

"Was a debutante in Dallas before she met and married my dad."

"And still goes to a party or two?" Ginger prompted.

Rand nodded proudly. "She does. Although she prefers jeans and boots and an oil rig to any black tie affair."

Ginger wiggled her toes, which were still aching from the hours spent in beautiful, impractical high heels. "I can second that."

Rand remained where he was. "So. What's your problem?" He had all the predatory watchfulness of a man in hot pursuit.

"I can't seem to get out of this dress," Ginger admitted reluctantly.

He appeared to mull that over. "You could sleep in it."

True, but…the fitted bodice was so snug. Ginger wrinkled her nose. "It wouldn't be very comfortable."

His grin turned wicked. "Ready to get naked, then?"

Heavens, no! "I just want you to undo the back of my dress. Please."

Kindness mixed with desire. He laid a hand across his heart. "Well of course I'll do my husbandly duty."

Not about to inquire what else that might entail, Ginger turned and reluctantly offered him her back.

Her pulse pounded as he shifted to the edge of the mattress and sat behind her. His bent knee just barely brushed the curve of her buttock. The sensation was exquisitely erotic and sensual. Shivering, Ginger shifted away from him.

He said nothing. Did nothing. She shot him an aggravated look over her shoulder. "Well?"

He lifted his broad shoulders in an affable shrug. "I was waiting on you to come back to me again."

They were close enough—too close—as it was. They did not need to have actual physical contact to accomplish this. She sucked in a tremulous breath. "Is everything between us going to be this difficult?"

At her irritable demand, a laugh escaped him. "I don't know. Is it?"

Groaning, she flounced back another inch. "Just undress me!"

His chuckle was warm and sexy, as if she had just given him the opening he needed. Not about to be seduced into thinking this was anything but a temporary business arrangement, Ginger clarified hotly, "You know what I mean."

"I do." His hands brushed the skin between her shoulder blades. He struggled with the triple row of close-set hooks at the top of her zipper. One by one, they eventually gave way.

Maddeningly, the zipper did not follow.

"Now what?" Ginger asked, finding the sudden stillness as excruciatingly erotic as his tender touch. Desire blossomed deep inside her.

Rand slid a hand between the fabric and her skin, his touch kindling her overwrought senses even more. "I just want to make sure…"

That she was spontaneously combusting from the inside out? Well, she was! "Rand, come on. Just do it!"

"Well, I sure hope no one can overhear us." Rand's voice took on his best needling aw-shucks tone. "Who knows what people might be thinking, us being in the bridal suite and all?"

Ginger groaned again at his clowning around and buried her face in her hands. Rand was doing what he always did when things got too intense between them. He used the combination of their mutual chemistry and his good humor to get her to relax. The trouble was, she didn't want to relax. Didn't want to let her guard down with him for one red-hot second.

Just like that, the zipper on her wedding gown came down, easy as you please. Cool air assaulted her spine.

Behind her, Rand sucked in his breath. And went very still.

Silk organza bodice pressed tightly against her breasts, Ginger pivoted to face him. "Now what's the holdup—?" she started to say. Then stopped at the expression on his face. She knew that look. All too well.

"I was right," he said. His blue eyes darkened as if he were imagining what the front view of her lace-and-satin bustier, garter belt and tiny panties would be. "Those are some mighty fancy underthings you've got on."

And some very elemental feelings they were both having, Ginger noted. "I think we should stop here," she said softly. Before they felt even more really and truly married than they did at this moment. Rand nodded, as if agreeing that things were getting way too complicated, way too fast.

"Probably should," he stated gruffly. "But…how about just one kiss?" Pulling her to him, he dropped his head low. His lips hovered just above hers, tempting…seducing. "It is our wedding night, after all."

Chapter 4

Knowing it was crazy to even pretend any of this could ever work out, Ginger started to pull back. Only to be brought slowly closer. "One kiss," Rand repeated. "That's all I'm asking."

And all, Ginger thought, she was prepared to give. But when his lips fit over hers, all rational thought went right out of her head. She moaned at the soft, sweet heat. The touch of his tongue to hers sent her even further over the edge. Pulse pounding, body trembling with need, she wrapped her arms around his neck and shifted even closer. Emotions soaring, she nestled the softness of her breasts into the sinewy hardness of his chest.

One kiss melded into another. And another.

The next thing Ginger knew, he was pulling her to her feet. Pushing her unzipped gown down. A circle of ivory satin puddled at her feet.

He paused to take her in; his eyes roving the full-
ness of her breasts, the nip of her waist and the swell
of her hips before sliding downward, along her thighs.
Clasping her to him, he kissed her cheek, the line of
her jaw, her throat. His lips toured the hollow of her
collarbone. Then, straightening slowly, his gaze raked
over her with startling possessiveness. Once again, he
enveloped her with his warm strength, seeming at that
moment to be fighting his own battle.

Tenderness emanated from him as first his fingertips and then his mouth caressed the uppermost curve
of her breast. His other hand slid down her back to her
hips, finding the delicate stretch of exposed skin between panty and garter belt. His breath was hot against
her skin, the lazy ministrations of his mouth giving her
a whole body shiver. She arched helplessly, wanting
him, wanting this, so much. Feeling wild and wanton,
she pressed her lips to his.

He held her face in his hands. "You are so beautiful."

When he kissed her and touched her like that, she felt
beautiful, inside and out. Thrilling at his touch, eager
to explore his body, too, she undid the remaining buttons and spread the edges of his shirt. His smooth skin
was delineated with hard ridges of muscle. Beneath her
questing fingers, she could feel the slow, fierce beating of his heart. The tantalizing traces of his aftershave
mingled with the clean fragrance of soap and the more
masculine scent unique to him. Needing, wanting, she
tangled her fingers in his hair, shimmied up against
him, closer yet. "You're breathtakingly gorgeous, too."

He laughed softly, his demeanor wickedly sensual,
his eyes dark with desire. "I'm glad you think so," he

murmured, "because at least for the time being, you're stuck with me."

That, she was, Ginger thought as he kissed her again, his lips warm and sure as his work-roughened palms slid over her, bypassing the barriers of satin and lace. Her nipples beaded against his palms. Lower still, moisture flowed. She trembled as he disrobed her, piece by tantalizing piece, kissing her slowly and seductively all the while.

Anxious for more, she undressed him, too. Kneading, stroking, caressing. And only when she was writhing with passion, did he lower her to the bed and stretch out beside her.

Ginger's eyes drifted shut as Rand parted her thighs and moved between them, creating ripples of yearning. She caught her breath as the sensations spread and pleasure flooded her in hot, irresistible waves, filling her with sensations unlike any she had ever known, and then there was no more holding back. He cupped her bottom and lifted her toward him, and took her slowly, sweetly.

Emotion overwhelming her, she wrapped her arms and legs around him, urging him on, taking him deeper and deeper. She gave him everything. He demanded more, as did she. And then there was nothing but the intense power of their connection that had them soaring, free, together, once again.

Rand felt Ginger's regret in the slight stiffening of her body, the way he always did as their passion ebbed and their breathing slowed. He wasn't surprised when she extricated herself and slipped from the bed.

The bathroom door shut softly behind her.

He lay there, listening to the water run, and then all fell silent. He supposed she was using the time to get herself together. He couldn't blame her. It had been one heck of a day, full of surprises. But in the end, they had achieved their goal, gotten married, and in the process, miraculously received the blessings of their families. Had this been a real marriage, they would have been over the moon with happiness.

But because this wasn't the usual union, they had to deal with that, and somehow find a way to make it all work.

Figuring she'd been hiding out long enough, Rand got out of bed, pulled on his boxer briefs and walked across the suite. He rapped on the door. "Ginger?"

No answer.

"You okay in there?"

Again, no answer.

Beginning to panic a little, he eased open the door. Ginger was wrapped in a thick white spa robe and seated on the plush stool. She had one arm on the marble vanity in front of her. Her head was nestled in the crook of her elbow and turned toward him. Her breathing was soft and even. As he neared her, he saw the tears dampening her cheeks.

He touched her shoulder. "Ginger…"

She shifted, sinking ever deeper into slumber, and mumbled something incoherent.

Whether she accepted it or not, she needed to be in bed. Rand said her name once more, and when she did not wake, lifted her in his arms. He carried her to the bed and put her gently down, then walked around to the other side and slid in beside her.

Clearly she had her regrets. Suddenly he did, too. But he gathered her close anyway and wrapped his arms around her.

"You're sure you want to do this today?" Rand asked the following afternoon.

They'd been on the go since early morning, managing not to talk about anything that had happened the day before, or how their wedding night had ended, at least for Ginger—in private tears and exhausted sleep. Rand, on the other hand, had lain awake most of the night, wondering how they were going to make this all work.

And not just in the public eye.

"I thought I'd made it clear that I do." Ginger's determination increased tenfold as his pickup approached Summit's historic downtown.

The four-and-a-half-hour drive from Lake Laramie to the Trans-Pecos area of Texas had done nothing but energize her. "We need to get this postnuptial agreement done."

Rand noted the vulnerability she had showed the day before had all but disappeared. And although he respected her strength, he resented the emotional distance she put between them every chance she got. He tightened his grip on the steering wheel.

"Agreed."

"But?"

He kept his eyes on the Main Street traffic. "I think it could wait until next week. Especially since it's just a formality."

Ginger adjusted her sunglasses on the bridge of her nose. "I never put off to tomorrow what can be done today."

Wasn't that the truth? Rand thought, parking the truck.

The two of them entered the brick building that housed Michelle Anderson-Garner's law office. The family law attorney, a willowy blonde in her late thirties, was waiting for them.

She took a seat opposite them in the conference room, and handed each a stack of forms and a pen.

"For this postnuptial agreement to be honored under Texas law, there must first be a full and fair disclosure of property and other financial aspects of each of your estates," she began. "So, basically, I need a detailed list of every asset and every debt each of you has, as well as any you may have accrued together. We can even go over who gets custody of the family pet, if you have one."

"What about kids?" Rand asked.

"Children are not covered under a prenuptual or postnuptial. Those issues are decided in family court."

"Can other issues be included in the postnup?" Ginger queried.

Michelle paused. "Such as?"

"Rand and I have agreed to run our marriage like a business."

"Okay…"

Ginger sat forward. "So I—we—were thinking of drawing up either a contract or bylaws that would detail how we are going to handle everything else."

Since when? Rand wondered, taken aback.

"That way," Ginger continued, "we wouldn't have to fight about things unnecessarily. We would already know how and where we're going to live, and so on."

Like most lawyers, Michelle had a remarkable ability to maintain a poker face. But even this, Rand noted, seemed to throw her for a loop. Not that he could blame the attorney. He'd come here under the impression they were only going to talk about financials.

Oblivious to the stunned reactions of the others in the room, Ginger carried on. "To be truly effective, our marriage contract should cover who is going to cook, or do laundry. Or, maybe we each should be on our own for these types of mundane chores."

Deciding as long as Ginger insisted on micromanaging all this, he might as well get what he wanted, too, Rand interjected casually, "The bylaws or marriage contract should also cover where we live. How many nights and days we can be apart at one time—or not be apart, as the case may be." He flashed Ginger a satisfied grin as his next idea hit. "Since both our jobs require travel, maybe we should stipulate that we at least take jobs in the same county."

Ginger's brow furrowed. Clearly she hadn't expected him to speak much at this meeting, if at all.

"Obviously we still have some things to work out..." she said.

"Privately," Rand added curtly. "And yes, we do."

Her spine stiffening, Ginger turned back to Michelle. "The point is, Rand and I have both already been divorced once. Neither relationship ended amicably, probably because we both went into those unions too naively. We're determined not to make the same mistake again." Ginger squared her shoulders. "Which is why we want to work all this out now."

Having absorbed everything his wife had said, the attorney turned her attention to Rand. Clearly, Michelle wanted to know where he stood.

"I don't want to spend all my time with Ginger fighting," he admitted. "So if it will help to work out all this stuff now, then I'm all in."

Ginger expected the meeting would last for at least another hour. Instead, Rand suddenly thanked Michelle and promised to make another appointment as soon as they had all the information ready for her to peruse.

Their attorney thought that was a good idea. It would save them on their legal fees, as she was billing them at her hourly rate.

Ginger did not want to pay more than she had to, for services. So she thanked Michelle and rose, too.

Moments later she and Rand were walking out into the spring sunshine. He had been in a mood all day. Quiet and brooding. He kept looking at her, too.

That was probably because he'd apparently had to carry her to bed the night before, when she'd fallen asleep in the bathroom. That was no surprise. In the past few weeks she had been falling asleep more readily and more often than usual. It was, she had learned, a symptom of pregnancy in the first trimester.

Her overabundance of emotions, too. Which was why, she guessed, she had gotten all weepy after they'd made love the night before.

Part of it, of course, was the fact it was their wedding night that wasn't really a wedding night. At least not in the genuine traditional sense. And the other part was that, if things were different, she could easily see herself falling in love with him.

And she knew she couldn't let that happen.

Not when the two of them had such different outlooks on life.

Aware he was studying her, in that same careful analytical way, Ginger asked the first question that came to mind. "Why did you cut that meeting short?"

"Because clearly we have some talking to do, and I didn't want to do it in front of anyone else. Besides—" he pushed an errant strand of hair from her cheek "—it's been a long couple of days, and you're looking a little worn around the edges."

Ginger made an unappreciative face. "Thanks."

"You're also pr—"

She touched her finger to his lips before he could finish saying the word.

He stopped, his lips pressed evocatively against her index finger.

Aware this was as close to a kiss as she wanted to get, now or at any other time in the future, Ginger swiftly dropped her tingling hand and stepped back.

Still holding her gaze with a wickedly sensual one of his own, Rand continued. "I figured you could use a little nap before we combine places."

Lovely. He was bossing her around. Again.

Ginger propped her hands on her hips. "Is this how it's going to be? You're going to 'little lady' me every chance you get?"

Rand cupped her elbow and guided her toward his truck. "If you mean look out for your best interests…"

"I mean treat me like some hapless female who doesn't have enough sense to do anything without your interference."

He opened the passenger-side door. "Women in your situation need sleep."

"How do you know?" She took in the day's growth of beard on his ruggedly chiseled face. It seemed impossible that he could be more handsome now, in khakis and a button-down shirt, than he had been in a tuxedo the night before, but he was.

Rand shrugged; the happy gleam in his eyes at odds with his solemn tone. "I've been reading up on it since you told me you were carrying my child."

Wow...that certainly was unexpected. But putting a romantic spin on this could only lead to more trouble.

"Well, there's no reason to get all worked up about it." Ginger put her right foot on the running board, grabbed the handle above the window and swung herself gracefully up into the passenger seat. "It's just a temporary medical condition, easily managed by me."

Rand circled around and slid behind the wheel. "Well, too bad, then." He turned to smile at her. "Because you're going to have me looking out for both of you whether you want me there or not."

Ginger glared at him. He regarded her steadily and calmly in return. Okay, maybe she was being a tad overemotional. Again. Whether she wanted to admit it or not, the thought of a nice cozy bed and comfy nap pillow was enticing. But that would come later, when she had finished the tasks she had to do in the meantime.

Ginger released a beleaguered breath. "So where are we going to live?"

"Whoa!" Rand chuckled as he fit his key in the ignition. "You're actually agreeing to share space with me?"

Ginger flushed self-consciously. "Everyone will expect it."

"So that's the only reason you want to reside under the same roof?"

"Truthfully? Yes, it is."

Another silence fell, this one taut with a different kind of tension.

Rand turned the air-conditioning on high. "The closest available rental home is fifty miles away."

Somehow she wasn't surprised he had checked into that. When it came to getting her under his roof—and back into his bed—he was always thinking ahead. "Not good when we're talking mountain terrain." The commute to Summit and back could be an hour or more each way, every day.

Rand draped his arm across the back of the seat. "I do still have my cottage at the Red Sage guest ranch. I've been renting it by the week for the past four months."

Ginger had to admit it would be roomier—and less intimate—than the hotel room where she'd been staying. "Okay."

In less than an hour they'd packed her stuff and checked her out of the Summit Inn. She followed him in her truck out to the Red Sage.

Twenty-five minutes outside of Summit, the guest ranch encompassed twenty-nine-thousand acres of juniper and ponderosa-pine forest, wildflower-strewed meadows, red-rock canyon and stately mountains. The sprawling century-old ranch house was located at the end of a blacktop road half a mile from the rural highway. The three-dozen cottages surrounded a large party barn, where weddings and receptions were often held. Campsites were located near the end of the private hiking and biking trails.

Rand parked in front of Cottage 12. The one-story building had clapboard siding, red shutters and door, and a sloping slate-gray roof. Ginger situated her truck beside his.

Both got out. "There's a complimentary breakfast buffet every morning in the main house. Otherwise we're on our own for meals. There's also a coin laundry and an ice and vending machine area."

He opened the door to the cottage and led the way inside. The front appeared to be one large room sporting a small galley kitchen and combination dining room–living area with a fireplace. Behind it was a bathroom and one bedroom just large enough to house a queen-size bed, tall bureau and a nightstand. Behind that was a small porch with a slow-moving fan overhead. Screened for privacy with latticework and attractive landscaping that featured native shrubs and flowering plants, there was an old-fashioned porch swing meant for two, a comfy-looking chaise longue and two small side tables.

All together, the cottage encompassed about seven hundred square feet, the size of a normal one-bedroom apartment.

Ginger looked at the bed. There was no way she and her six-foot-plus husband could sleep in it without touching. And touching led to...

She *really* had to stop fixating on that.

"What do you think about us getting two cottages, side by side?" she asked casually as she walked back into the safety of the main living area.

Rand followed her. Evidently not at all surprised by her question, he shrugged his broad shoulders. "It'd be a good way to convince people we're not really married, if that's what you're aiming to do."

Ginger sighed.

There were two wing chairs and a love seat in the living room; no sofa large enough to sleep on. She raked a hand through her hair, trying not to think how cozy and romantic this all would be under other circumstances. Now it just felt much too small and close. "I suppose a roll-away bed is out of the question, then?"

He nodded; a solid wall of masculine determination. "Completely."

The sensuality in his gaze had her heartbeat picking up, big time.

"It's not as if we haven't shared a mattress before," Rand pointed out, hovering closer to her.

Ginger suddenly felt as if the air had been sucked out of her lungs. "I know."

His gaze narrowed. "But…?"

Ginger swallowed, and pushed the wealth of erotic memories away. Just because they had recklessly made love the night before did not mean they would be doing so again. She wet her lips and said bluntly, "I was hoping to keep this on business terms."

He remained stoic. Not protesting. Not agreeing. Not…anything.

Wishing she knew more about what their immediate future held, she finally relented. "But… I guess this will do." *It would have to.*

Slowly the tension eased from his tall, ruggedly handsome frame. He offered a reassuring smile, his victorious attitude evident. "Let's get the rest of your stuff in. Then I'll go over to the front office and let Claire McPherson, the manager, know we're newlyweds and you'll be staying here with me. And I'll get you a key."

Settling in was easy, Ginger thought. Making this temporary union of theirs a success, while keeping her pregnancy hidden, would not be as simple.

Chapter 5

Rand had known sharing quarters with Ginger would be challenging. However, he hadn't expected her to be so contrary about every little thing.

"You don't have to leave all your things in the suitcases," he told her. "You can unpack."

Ginger struggled to fit her bags into her half of the closet. It wasn't an easy fit and took another hard shove to shut the door.

He lounged against the lone bureau, arms crossed in front of him.

Scowling, Ginger grabbed her handbag and perched on the edge of the bed. A curtain of copper hair fell across one shoulder as she pulled out a notepad and pen.

"What are you doing?" he asked.

Ginger scribbled. "Adding another requirement for our marriage contract." She paused to look up at him. "No unsolicited advice."

He let out a conciliatory breath. "Sorry. I wasn't trying to boss you around. I just wanted you to feel welcome here, like this was your place now, too." Given the fact that a week-by-week rental was the closest either of them got to an actual home these days, she had to concede.

Abruptly her shoulders lost their rigid tilt. Her expression softened, too. "So we're in agreement about this?"

"Yes." He gave her a level look and did his best to reassure her. "There will definitely not be any bossing each other around."

Her lips curved into a smile. "Good. Because I don't want to waste time arguing with you."

"I don't want to argue with you, either," he said quietly. Their gazes remained locked. Intimacy followed. As was always the case, though, before they could take their relationship one step further, something inevitably got in the way. His cell phone rang and it was followed shortly thereafter by the ring on hers.

Ginger stepped outside to answer the call.

Rand stayed in the cottage and listened to his caller. "That's great news!" he exclaimed. "Yes. I'll be there." He severed the connection.

Seconds later Ginger stepped inside. "The county's moratorium on horizontal drilling has just been lifted," she announced joyfully. She came closer in a drift of floral and citrus perfume. "Dot and Clancy Boerne are having a meeting at their ranch this evening."

Uh-oh, Rand thought. "I know."

Ginger paused. "You were invited?"

He nodded, aware they had hit the first professional

hurdle in their marriage. "The Boernes have asked me to analyze the environmental impact of all the proposals from wildcat drilling operations."

Ginger's jaw took on the stubborn tilt he knew so well. "Well, you can't do that."

"Why not?"

"Because I'm bidding on that work!" she snapped.

More than that, Rand knew, she was counting on winning the contract to launch her career as an independent oil woman.

Ginger continued hotly, "You're going to have to recuse yourself."

Rand had to draw the line somewhere. He figured it may as well be here. Especially since she was the one who was actually carrying their child, and hence would eventually be out of commission, at least for a short time. "How about *you* recuse yourself?"

More temper flared. "I'm not letting this opportunity go, Rand."

He shrugged, knowing she would receive income from this project only if she won it, whereas his fees were guaranteed. "I gave the Boernes my word I would thoroughly review every proposal to let them know the risks. I will be operating with a panel of three others. I've been working with them and many others in the county for months now, to ensure land and interests are protected. I'm not backing out."

Ginger strode farther away. "Well, neither am I."

He studied her, clearly disappointed. He had hoped she would be more reasonable. Clearly this wasn't the case. "Then I suggest," he said mildly, "that you accept this is just the way it's going to be."

* * *

Had the complications ended there, it would have been a tough but not ultimately insurmountable problem, Ginger thought.

Unfortunately when they got to the meeting at the Boerne ranch, and saw who else was in attendance, she realized her woes were just beginning.

Not only did she have her new husband looking over her shoulder in a professional sense, she apparently had her new mother-in-law interested in acquiring the work, too. Because Josie Corbett-Wyatt McCabe—the current head of Wyatt Drilling—sauntered onto Dot and Clancy Boerne's lawn just as the meeting was about to begin and took a seat on the opposite side of the large outdoor gathering.

Feeling like a player in a minor league team, who had just had a major league player show up and push her out of her long-coveted spot, Ginger turned to Rand in shock. "Did you know your mom was coming tonight?"

"No." He stared at his mother, clearly ticked off.

Josie stared back at her son, giving no quarter, either.

As far as Rand's mother was concerned, Ginger noted, this was business, pure and simple. Family connections did not enter into it.

Ginger couldn't help but admire that about Josie. She felt that way, too. It was only Rand who seemed to think they should make exceptions.

Before she had a chance to think about the best way to handle what was bound to be an uncomfortable situation, yet another man joined the hundred-plus oil people on the lawn.

As their eyes locked, it was all Ginger could do not to groan out loud. Not him, too.

Rand took in the latest arrival's air of cool detachment. Unlike most of the other oil folk there that evening, clad in jeans, boots and work shirts, the VP from the midsize oil company wore designer jeans, a trendy sport coat and a tie.

Tensing, Rand leaned down to murmur in her ear, "Do you two know each other?"

"Kind of."

Rand waited.

"He's my ex-husband. Conrad Profitt."

Rand blinked in a way that let her know he could hardly believe his ears. Which wasn't surprising, she supposed. Since they had only referred to their exes by their first names, he had no way of putting two and two together until now.

"Your first husband was the heir apparent of Profitt Oil?" he asked in stunned amazement.

"Yep."

Another pause. "Did you know he was going to be here tonight?"

"Nope." Ginger took in Conrad's pompous, self-congratulatory air. Could this situation get any more complicated?

Meanwhile their hosts called the meeting to order. The brawny, white-haired rancher stepped to the make-shift-podium, while his petite and pretty wife passed out folders to all the guests. Clearly ready to get on with it, Clancy Boerne began. "We asked you all here tonight because we want to give you a chance to recover the oil on our property. The deadline for submitting drilling plans, cost estimates and proposed oil-lease terms is three weeks from this evening."

Next, Clancy introduced the three experts on seismic mapping, directional drilling and recovery performance that he and his wife had hired to help them sift through the proposals.

Finally he introduced the fourth and last member of their advisory panel—the lone environmentalist in the group. Clancy smiled. "You all know Rand McCabe. He's been working closely with the county commissioners and many of the ranchers in the area to help us protect our properties. Rand will vet the proposals, from an environmental standpoint, and report back to us on any insufficiencies and dangers.

"My wife, our attorney and I will go over the results of both that and the independent financial and engineering analysis. The top ten bidders will then be asked to further explain and/or defend their proposals in a question-and-answer session at our attorney's office. The panel of three experts will assist us in the questioning, and another comprehensive analysis will be completed. After that point, we'll decide which outfit to use and notify everyone by telephone a few days later."

Conrad Profitt raised his hand and asked sagely, "Does anyone else see a problem with Rand McCabe vetting his own mother's bid?"

Ginger turned to look at her ex-husband, not surprised Conrad was already crying foul. Whenever her ex felt he couldn't win on his own, which was most of the time, he used whatever device he could to level the playing field. In this case the hint of familial impropriety.

At the podium, Boerne scoffed at the concern. "The only one who should have a problem with Rand being involved is Josie Corbett-Wyatt McCabe—since she's had her son interfere in more of her drilling projects than she can probably count."

Everyone chuckled, knowing that truer words had never been spoken. The rift in the McCabe clan over *that* long-standing issue was legend. Turns out, Rand was as cautious as his mother was fearless.

Another independent oilman promptly raised his hand. "What about Rand's new wife, Ginger Rollins?" he demanded. "You telling me McCabe's going to be as hard on her as everyone else, them being newlyweds and all?"

Rand's expression remained impassive, while Ginger grimaced. She hadn't wanted her new marriage to come up tonight at all, at least not in a business sense.

Meanwhile, Ginger's ex stared at her in astonishment. Clearly, Profitt hadn't heard.

Nor had most of the people there.

Figuring any defense should come from her, Ginger stood and addressed the crowd. "I guarantee you that Rand will be as tough on me as he is on everyone else."

Despite her avowal, skepticism abounded.

Dot Boerne took the floor. "We're going to have the names on all the bids redacted by our oil-and-gas attorney before we see the proposals. Rand and the other advisors will not have access to that information, either. The winning semifinal bids will be chosen strictly on the merits of ingenuity, environmental safety and cost."

"What about the final round?" someone asked.

Dot said, "Obviously, we'll know who we are dealing with then, since we'll expect all the executives and field experts from the various companies to be at the Q and A sessions."

Clancy Boerne added that in the end he and Dot

would choose the company they were most comfortable with.

More questions followed. Eventually the meeting concluded.

Conrad ambled over to Ginger and Rand. She couldn't be sure, but she thought her ex's head of meticulously groomed brown hair might be thinning a tad.

Her ex-husband stuck out his hand to Rand. "It appears congratulations are in order."

"They are." Rand amenably shook the oil tycoon's hand, then stepped back and put a proprietary arm around Ginger's shoulders, tugging her close to his side.

Still flummoxed, Conrad turned his full attention back to his ex-wife. "I had no idea you were serious about anyone."

"Nor should you have since we haven't spoken in— what? Two years?"

Conrad's smile broadened. "We should remedy that," he said.

Ginger had an idea what her ex-husband wanted, and it wasn't friendship. "I disagree." She turned to Rand, deriving comfort from his muscular warmth despite herself. She slipped her arm around his waist and looked up at her new husband adoringly. "You ready to go, sweetheart?"

Taking her hint, Rand smiled. "I sure am, honeybunch." Still holding Ginger protectively close, he pivoted and gave Ginger's ex a two-fingered salute. "Nice to meet you, Profitt."

They walked off, arm in arm, only to be stopped again several steps later. Everyone, it seemed, wanted to talk about their newly married state. More questions and congratulations followed. Finally they made their way to the rows of cars and trucks parked along the lane that led to the ranch house.

To Ginger's chagrin, Josie McCabe was waiting next to her pickup, her manner all business. Ginger sighed. The last thing she wanted to discuss with her new mother-in-law was the cutthroat competition ahead.

Rand paused beside Josie's canary-yellow truck. He looked as tense and irritable as Ginger felt, although for more complicated familial reasons. "Since when have you been interested in drilling in Summit County?" he asked his mother.

Josie sent her youngest son a look of reproach. "Since they came out with the massive improvements in horizontal drilling technology last fall. I knew there had been problems in the past when that method of oil recovery was tried here. I also knew, with the amount of oil beneath the ground, that it would be only a matter of time before it commenced again, safely this time." She turned slightly, leveling them both with her sturdy gaze. "I've always intended to be in on the ground floor of the boom in Summit County."

And yet her son remained unconvinced. "I've never seen you here, going ranch to ranch, like everyone else," Rand said.

Josie shrugged. "I came down last summer, ahead of everyone else, and made my connections then."

Of course, Ginger thought. A lady wildcatter as successful as Josie McCabe would not let an opportunity like this one go unexplored. "Which is why you were invited to hear the Boernes' stipulations on the bid process for their ranch." Because Josie had already laid the groundwork.

Josie nodded. "Luckily, I'd heard the rumors the moratorium was about to be lifted. So I was already here."

"And yet you didn't say anything, when you saw us yesterday, about coming back to Summit," Rand persisted, clearly unhappy. "Even when you knew that Ginger and I were returning today."

Josie's gaze narrowed with maternal rebuke. "I didn't want you to think I planned to interfere in your marriage. Because I don't. And I didn't think it was a good idea for us to be arguing business on your wedding day."

"It's not a good idea for family to be arguing, period," Ginger put in.

Never mind hovering around each other, under difficult circumstances, such as these.

"I agree." Josie straightened, her manner brisk. "That is why I think *you* should recuse yourself, Rand. Let some other environmental impact engineer advise the residents of Summit County."

Ginger looked at Josie, surprised and relieved to find them so like-minded. "That's exactly what I told him," she blurted.

Although that still left her and her new mother-in-law angling for the very same work, which wasn't a good situation, either.

Rand harrumphed. "I'm not bowing out unless both of you also remove yourselves from the bidding process. And I don't see that happening." He paused, giving Ginger and Josie a hard, assessing look. "Do you?"

Rand expected Ginger to give him the silent treatment once they settled in his pickup. Instead she turned to him and asked, "Do you know what is in the fridge back at the cottage? I didn't have a chance to look."

He sighed. "Condiments and beverages, mostly."

She glanced at her watch. "The grocery store in Summit is open until ten. Do you mind if we stop there before we head back to Red Sage?"

Rand's mood brightened. This was the first thing she'd done that was the slightest bit domestic, and he liked seeing this side of her. "Sure. No problem."

While he drove, she plucked the notepad and pen from her bag and made a list. She tore it in two as they headed inside. "If we each take a basket, it will be faster."

And, Rand noted, they needed to be quick since they only had fifteen minutes until closing. It took every moment of that to get the items she had assigned him. When they met up at the line, the clerk rang up the items, he paid, and Ginger bagged.

Only when they got back to the cottage did he have a chance to really see what they had purchased. Steak, chicken, ground beef. Lots of fresh produce and fruit. Cereal. Milk. Juice. Several kinds of flour and sugar, spices and other baking items. Eggs.

"You planning to cook?"

"Are you?"

He lifted an affable shoulder. "I can grill."

"Well, I can do everything else."

"Sounds like a plan," he said cheerfully.

Ginger finished putting the refrigerator items away, then picked up the lone bag of chocolate sandwich cookies and a gallon of milk, and carried them, along with a glass, to the dining table.

She disappeared for a moment. He heard her hauling her suitcase out of the closet. More activity followed, then she came out with a bottle of prenatal vitamins in her hand. "Doctor's orders," she explained as she sank onto a chair and kicked off her shoes.

Rand moved to join her at the table. "Actually, there's something I've been meaning to ask you…" He cleared his throat, feeling oddly out of sorts. "Have you had any morning sickness yet?"

"Thankfully…no. I'm hoping to dodge that bullet altogether. I have friends who have been green around the gills for their entire pregnancy, and that would put a definite crimp in my work schedule." Relaxing with a mixture of fatigue and relief, Ginger poured herself a tall glass of milk, downed a vitamin and then opened the bag of cookies.

Brow furrowing, she studied the interior of the package.

"Is there a problem?"

"I'm deciding how many to eat."

He loved the fact she was, and probably always would be on some level, a total mystery to him. He also loved how cute she looked when she was mildly perplexed. He sauntered closer. "Are we rationing them?"

She wrinkled her nose and returned, in the same deadpan tone, "If I had as many as I wanted, I'd eat the whole package in one sitting."

Rand laughed, not surprised she was greedy when it came to pure pleasure. So was he. He pulled out a chair, turned it around, sank onto it and folded his arms along the back. "So how many are you going to partake in, then?"

While she considered, Ginger let out a sexy little sigh. "Mmm. Two is too little, six is too much, even though there are six in the individual snack packs they sell." Her luscious lower lip pushed out in a delectable pout. She squinted, still thinking, and finally said, "Probably four." Decision made, she took four from the center row of the package.

Rand took four, too, from the same row, leaving complete rows on either side of the pillaged one. "I haven't had these in a while." He got up to get a glass for himself.

"Me, either. But I got to thinking about them while we were waiting for the meeting to start." She opened up a cookie and licked the vanilla cream out of the middle.

Rand nearly groaned.

The milk he was pouring splashed over the rim. Ignoring the hardness pressing against his fly, he grabbed a dishcloth and mopped up the mess. Returning to the table, he sat opposite her. "Is it your first craving?"

Ginger made a face, clearly resenting his question. "Hey." She lifted a staying hand. "I'm trying not to be a cliché."

Rand watched, his mouth dry, as she dunked a chocolate circle into the milk, swished it around delicately, and then popped the soggy confection into her mouth.

"You could never be a cliché." Unbearably sexy and sensual, yes.

Oblivious to the ardent nature of his thoughts, and the growing hardness of his lower body, she shot him a skeptical look and sighed. "You say that now…"

He meant it now. She was without a doubt the most fascinating and infuriating woman he had ever met. The woman he wanted most to bed…with or without his wedding ring on her finger.

Ginger sighed and broke open another chocolate sandwich cookie. "But when my mother finds out…"

He studied the troubled sheen to her dark green eyes, the slight tremble of her lower lip. "You think your mom will be happy about the baby?" he asked softly.

Ginger groaned. "Over the moon." She patted Rand on the hand, then stood. Finished with her snack, she headed for the bedroom. "And that, 'honeybunch,'" she drawled over her shoulder, mocking his earlier faux endearment, "is when the trouble starts."

Rand had no idea what Ginger meant by any of that. But sensing she needed her space, he let her have her privacy, only heading for bed when he was certain she was sound asleep.

When he woke the next morning, a little after dawn, she was already up. Papers, computer, maps spread all over the living area of their cottage.

She was still in her pajamas, glossy hair knotted on top of her head, a mug of decaf coffee in her hand. A pan of cold oatmeal was on the stove. "You know there's a free breakfast buffet at the main house every morning," he reminded her.

She nodded.

"We could go over together."

She barely looked up from the mounds of data she was studying. "No time." She flashed a wan, distracted smile. "You go ahead. And don't come into my temporary office. I don't want you looking at any of my plans until the Boernes ask you to do so."

He lifted a palm. "Firewall. I swear."

"Good."

Rand went to breakfast, ate and brought her something back.

She looked at the plate he carried in stunned amazement.

"In case you get hungry later."

For a second she looked longingly at the quiche and fruit salad, then went right back to what she had been doing. "Thanks, that looks really good. Mind putting it the fridge?"

"No problem."

Aware he had his own appointments to keep that day, he headed out, only to come in contact with an attractive fifty-something brunette in their front yard. She was dressed in oversize denim work clothes and engineer-style boots. A backpack laptop case slung over one sturdy shoulder, her hands were filled with rolled-up maps.

Rand paused to tip his hat. "Maria Gonzales, I presume?" He recalled Ginger mentioning the previous night that her drilling partner, a happily married woman with three teenage sons, would be here every day, working with her. And this woman sure fit the bill.

Dark eyes twinkled. "And you must be the never-stops-working-either Rand McCabe—the guy who finally got Ginger to settle down again."

Rand didn't know about that. His new wife still seemed to have both feet as far out the door as she could get, without raising any more eyebrows than they already had.

Maria put her maps down long enough to shake Rand's hand. "I never thought I'd see the day, but I'm glad I am. Ginger needs a big strong hunk of burnin' love like you to spice up her life." She winked. "And the fact you're doing it with wedding rings on your fingers is even better."

Ginger appeared in the doorway. Her elegant cheekbones were highlighted with a rosy-pink flush. "Rand and I may be hitched—"

Temporarily, he could see that his new wife wanted to add, but wisely didn't, lest she blow their cover.

"—but that doesn't mean anything important about our lives is going to change," Ginger finished, stubborn as ever.

The long-married Maria chuckled, picked up her maps and turned back to Rand. "I see you've both still got some 'adjusting' to do," she teased.

Rand nodded, and just for the fun of it, hauled Ginger to him for a long, sexy, off-to-work kiss. "Uh-huh, and I'm aiming to help my beloved do just that." He lowered his head and, ignoring Ginger's soft gasp of surprise, pressed a hand to her spine and staked his claim with another steamy liplock.

Clearly shaken, Ginger broke off the kiss. Temper only he could see glittering in her dark green eyes, she flattened her hand across his chest and gave him a playful nudge, meant to throw off their audience. "Fun as this has been," she feigned sweetly, "it's time you went to task on something else."

"What could be more important for a still-honeymooning couple than this?" Rand bantered back. He grinned, and just for the hell of it, he kissed his wife again, even *more* passionately this time. Her flush turned even deeper but there was no denying the subtle shift and surrender of her supple body, nestled against his. Eventually though, knowing they both had much to do, he let her go. "See you later," he said. And heard only Ginger's huff of embarrassment, and Maria's laughter, as he strolled on down the walk.

When Rand returned that evening, he expected to find Ginger and Maria still hard at work. Instead Maria's van was gone and there was a familiar white Cadillac in front of their cottage with the license plate #1TXMOM, and a small U-Haul behind it.

Beside it was a yellow pickup with the vanity plate WILDCAT.

Rand stared at the vehicles in shock. Had Ginger known about any of this? If so, she hadn't said anything about expecting either of their mothers to come by.

He cut the ignition, got out and headed for the front door. He did not know what was going on, but he sure as heck was going to find out.

Chapter 6

"Mom, please…" Ginger's tired voice floated out the open cottage window.

Rand tensed at Cordelia's reply.

"Honey, I'm sorry, but I have to be honest with you. I do not want to see you make the same mistakes that you made in your first marriage." There was a long pause. "And from the looks of things, you've started your second marriage off on the wrong foot, too."

"I really think," he heard his mother interrupt kindly, "that all is not what it may seem."

Figuring enough had been said, Rand walked through the front door.

Ginger was standing in front of the workstation she had made for herself, her hair still damp from the shower and coiled in a loose messy knot on top of her head. She was clad in one of his blue chambray shirts and a pair of her comfortable-looking khaki cargo pants and socks. She wore no makeup but looked sexy as all get-out, just the same.

Rand nodded at the three women. "Nice to see everyone." He strode straight toward Ginger, took her in his arms and gave her the kind of kiss you would expect two people who were still technically in the honeymoon phase of their relationship, to give each other; the kind of kiss he had tried to give her that very morning.

This once, Ginger did not resist the open display of their passion. Maybe because she was as eager for respite from the familial scrutiny as he was.

Finished, Rand lifted his head. He caught the plea for help in her green eyes, then turned back to their mothers.

"So, what did I interrupt?" he asked.

Josie spoke first. "Cordelia called me while she was driving down, for directions to the place where you were staying. Since I just took a cottage here, I agreed to meet up with her in Summit and lead her out to the Red Sage." She grimaced. "Unfortunately, there are no more cottages to be had. Hotel rooms, either, at the moment. Which is why I walked down to offer Cordelia lodging in my cottage this evening."

Rand had to hand it to his mother. She might be a thorn in his side at times, but she also knew when to come to the rescue.

Ginger looked at Rand. "I also told Mom she could spend the night with us."

"But I don't think it's a good idea to impose on newlyweds," Cordelia told him demurely, "so I accepted Josie's invitation."

Thanks, Mom, Rand thought, telegraphing her a

grateful look. "How long are you staying?" he asked his new mother-in-law.

"Just this evening. I have to be back at work the day after tomorrow, but I wanted you and Ginger to have all the wedding gifts that have poured in for you."

Ginger smiled pointedly at Rand. "I tried to tell Mom we don't need any of those things at the moment…"

"And I told my daughter," Cordelia explained, "that all the gifts will help her to properly set up housekeeping, wherever the two of you end up."

Rand looked out the window. The U-Haul trailer attached to Cordelia's Cadillac looked small, but he knew from experience just how much the 5 x 8 compartment could hold.

"But not to worry. I've already sent thank-you notes for the two of you, too."

Rand blinked in surprise.

"Mom thinks of *everything*," Ginger allowed tightly.

Cordelia caught the irritation underlying her daughter's too bright tone, and swung back to her only child. She propped her bejeweled hands on her hips. "You're telling me that you and Rand would have had time to do that in the next month?"

Actually, Rand thought, they wouldn't have.

"Those notes had to go out," Cordelia huffed.

"And we thank you for it," Rand said. If this was an example of Cordelia's usual helicopter parenting, no wonder Ginger was so flummoxed.

With an even brighter smile, Josie tried to push things along. "Back to the U-Haul."

Rand jumped in before the situation deteriorated further, suggesting, "How about I do the heavy lifting and bring everything in?"

Cordelia beamed. "You're such a dear."

"I'll go with you." His mother followed him outside and down the short stone path to the vehicles. Together, they walked around the Cadillac and opened up the trailer. It was packed to the gills. As was, apparently, the trunk and interior of Cordelia's Cadillac. Some of the gifts were still in shipping boxes, others just the store packaging. Rand handed one of the smaller boxes, marked Fragile, to his mother. "So what was going on back there before I walked in?" he asked casually.

Josie gestured for him to hand her one more. "Mother-daughter squabble."

The distressed look on Ginger's face said it had been much more. Rand took a large, heavy box marked Cookware. "Who was winning?" he mused.

Boxes balanced under her chin, Josie pivoted and headed up the walk. "Who do you think?"

As they neared the open window, Rand could hear female voices rising inside the cottage once again. He said, "I wouldn't count Ginger out."

"I'm not." A new respect laced Josie's low tone.

Their eyes meeting, they paused on the sidewalk. "Do me a favor?" Rand asked.

His mom nodded, amenable.

"Do whatever you have to do to divert Cordelia so I have time to talk to Ginger alone."

"You're sure you want to go out for dinner this evening?" Cordelia asked a good twenty minutes later when all the boxed wedding gifts had been brought inside and stacked together in neat rows on the screened-in porch. It was the only place in the small abode where they could even hope to be out of the way.

With a smile, Rand jumped in to persuade her. "It will be a chance for the four of us to get to know each other better."

"But we'll need to get cleaned up first," Josie commented, linking her arm through Cordelia's. "So let's walk down to my cottage." She smiled. "We'll stop by the office on the way, and speak to them about bringing in a roll-away bed."

"I noticed a Help Wanted sign in the window, when I drove in." Cordelia sounded worried. "Is the service here substandard, because of that?"

Rand caught his mother's most patient smile as the two women exited and shut the screen door behind them. "I believe that posting has to do with the party barn operation," Josie replied as their voices faded. "But we can certainly talk to Claire McPherson…"

Finally silence fell. The spring breeze blew through the open windows. Ginger looked at Rand, then the overwhelming amount of cardboard boxes, and let out a groan. "I don't have time to mess with any of this."

Nor should she have to, Rand thought.

He sat next to her on the love seat and took her hand in his. "It's not that big a deal. We'll take whatever you need out of them and put the rest in storage."

"When? I still have work to do tonight."

As did he.

He patted her arm. "Look, the gifts are fine where they are now, on the porch. We'll get to them when we get to it."

"I suppose that'll work…for now." Still looking distraught, Ginger ran her fingers through her damp hair. "I wasn't planning to go out to dinner."

Nor was he. He'd been hoping to have a night alone

with his new bride, maybe figure out a way to get her back into his arms, wanting to make love with him again.

He pushed aside his own selfish desires. "It's just one evening. You heard your mother—she's leaving in the morning." The two of them could deal with it. Especially if a good "performance" this evening appeased Cordelia and hence kept her from trying to "help" even more.

Another long, discouraged look. Ginger plucked the hair dryer from her suitcase, plugged it in and began blowing the residual dampness from the gleaming copper strands.

Enjoying the sight of her getting ready to go out, something he wasn't usually treated to, he perched on the edge of the bed and watched.

Ginger bent from the waist. As she ran the dryer over the underside of her hair, her shirt gaped in front, giving him a very nice view of cleavage and lace.

Rand felt himself hardening again. A perpetual state of affairs…

"She's trying to control my life," Ginger complained, pouting as she switched off the hair dryer.

Rand shrugged and stood to ease the pressure. "So don't let her." He walked around, willing the blood pooling low to dissipate.

"Easier said than done." Ginger shook her head. "You have no idea how smothering Mom can be, when she thinks—erroneously, I might add—that I desperately need her assistance." Wearily she went to the closet. Her large suitcase was open, the clothes inside a rumpled mess. Her hair tumbled over her shoulders as she studied the choices, then finally plucked out a white knit shirt and a relaxed-fit navy cardigan.

Rand ambled closer, offering a sexy wink. "Not going to wear my shirt?" He ran a finger down her cheek.

Ginger flushed and stepped back, her hand flying to the buttons. "Sorry about that."

Hungrily, he watched her undo one button, then another and another, as she swiftly undressed.

Suddenly she wasn't the only one wishing they didn't have plans for dinner out.

Unable to help himself, he moved close enough to see the shadowy valley between her soft, luscious breasts. Aware her spirits still needed bolstering, he bent and kissed the silky skin of her temple before giving her shoulder a reassuring squeeze. "Don't apologize. I like the way you look in it."

As elusive as ever, she danced away, slipped the shirt off and tossed it at him. He caught it and lifted it to his face. It was warm and soft and smelled the way she did—fresh out of the shower—like orange blossom and shampoo and woman. Figuring there was no need to let any of that go to waste, when he needed a clean shirt, anyway, Rand removed the shirt he was wearing and slipped on the one she had been wearing.

Grinning despite herself, she shook her head at him. "Our mothers are going to know what you just did."

"So?" He waggled his eyebrows. "I don't mind sharing everything with you." *Including and especially a bed.*

Her mood improving, Ginger chuckled as she pulled the knit shirt over her head and then worked her arms through the sleeves. Her breasts, which seemed to get fuller every day now, were spilling out of the lacy bra. She tugged the white fabric down over her ribs, started to tuck it into the snug waistband of her otherwise loose-fitting cargo pants, then brought the shirt tail back out again to hide the slow but subtle changes in her slender body. She put the navy cardigan on and began buttoning.

"I really am sorry. I didn't mean to confiscate your wardrobe. But I was in the middle of a wardrobe crisis when I heard the knock at the door, and I still needed a shirt, so I grabbed the first oversize thing I saw."

"Which happened to be my shirt."

Ginger picked up her makeup bag and carried it to the bathroom mirror. "It's big enough to hide the very beginning of a baby bump."

He lounged against the portal, making a careful survey of her still-slender body, and watching her apply a thin layer of moisturizer to her freshly scrubbed face. "No one can tell you're pregnant." Even he was having trouble discerning the changes. And he'd made an art out of studying every delicious inch of her, even before they'd hit the sheets that very first time.

She flattened her free hand against her tummy and checked out her profile in the mirror with a worried frown. "Yet."

Rand picked up his electric razor. Figuring he might as well get rid of the day's stubble, he ran it over his jaw. Finished, he reached for his toothbrush. "When do you want to tell our families?"

Ginger rooted through her cosmetics bag. "Not until it's so apparent we have no choice."

Fascinated, he watched her finish putting on her makeup. The process was quick; the results subtle but pretty. "I take it having your mom show up like this was not a happy surprise?"

Ginger put on a layer of gloss, then smacked her lips together. Finished, she reached for a pair of earrings and threaded them through her pierced lobes. The golden oil wells dangled sexily. "You see how my mom is reacting, and all we are is married?"

Rand nodded, aware the ultimate helicopter parent in Cordelia seemed to be operating on full speed.

Ginger shook her head miserably. "There's no telling how much she'll want to interfere when she finds out her first—and probably only—grandchild is on the way."

To Ginger's relief, the first half of dinner with their mothers went well. Josie and Rand kept the conversation squarely on things they could all agree upon, but eventually Ginger's mom brought the focus back to where she wanted it. The state of Ginger's new marriage.

"Honey, I don't mean to interfere—"

Famous last words, Ginger thought, bracing herself.

"—but I really think you ought to forget trying to get your own business going, and go to work for someone else. Or better yet, not work at all while the two of you get settled into a new routine."

"We're already settled," Ginger said.

Rand nodded. "I'm happy."

He certainly *looked* happy, Ginger thought, then quickly warned herself not to get too excited, given the fact that he was just living up to familial expectations, same as she.

With another smile of encouragement, Cordelia pushed on. "The point is, marriage is an adjustment and the newlywed phase is something to be savored, not rushed through blindly. Don't you agree, Josie?"

Put on the spot, Rand's mother paused. "I think Rand and Ginger know better than we do what they need, Cordelia."

"Still—" Cordelia ran a spoon through the frosting on her coconut cake "—it never hurts to take the time to get every detail set up properly."

Unable to stop herself, Ginger cut in. "We've already done that, Mom."

As always, Rand seemed to know where she was going almost before she did.

He gave her a look that advised her not to continue, but Ginger knew there was only one way to quiet her mother. "That's why Rand and I saw a lawyer about drawing up both a postnup, to cover the financials, and a marriage contract, to cover everything else that could possibly cause us problems down the line. Because neither of us has any intention of leaving anything to chance."

"Well, I have to hand it to you," Rand told Ginger an hour later, after they had returned to the Red Sage guest ranch, said good-night to the moms and retired to their "honeymoon" cottage. "You took mild parental concern to DEFCON levels of wariness, in a flash."

Glad the dinner was over, Ginger paused to toe off her boots. "It wasn't that bad."

Rand hunted around in the fridge and pulled out a bottle of beer, left over from his "bachelor" days. He twisted off the cap and sauntered closer. "Ah, yeah, it was. Especially when you referenced your list and told them what was on the agenda for the marriage contract so far."

Ginger looked longingly at the icy brew, then frowned and headed for the cabinet. Ignoring his contemplative gaze, she revealed, "My mother already thinks I'm completely misguided." She twisted the cap off the bottle she had hidden behind the coffee cups and shook a prenatal vitamin into her hand.

Rand lounged against the kitchen counter and watched her pour a glass of milk. "And now she knows for sure?"

Ginger rolled her eyes at his teasing. She didn't know how he did it, but her new husband could always coax a smile from her, even under the most trying of circumstances.

"Your mother didn't say much about it." She paused to swallow her vitamin, then made a face and went for a chocolate sandwich cookie, as per usual, to kill the lingering iron taste of the supplement.

Rand admitted this was so with a tilt of his handsome head, then took another swig of beer. He wiped his mouth with the back of his hand. "That's because she was in shock."

Ginger studied Rand over the rim of her glass, curious now. "Your family doesn't believe in prenups?" She would think, with their wealth and influence, it would be a no-brainer.

Rand watched her eat another cookie, just for the heck of it. It had been a stressful evening, after all.

"McCabes believe in marrying for love." He moved closer, lifted his finger and wiped a drop of milk from the corner of her lip before ever so slowly lowering his hand and stepping back. "And a love that is strong enough to compel one of us to hitch our wagon to someone else's for the rest of our lives also requires a huge amount of trust. On everyone's part."

Tingling from his light, tender touch, Ginger shrugged and drained her glass. "Maybe that's the case under usual circumstances," she acknowledged. "But when all's said and done in *our* situation, they'll be thankful we've gone to the trouble to put everything in writing ahead of time."

After taking another slow, thoughtful sip of beer, Rand looked her over. "You're talking about our inevitable split?"

Ginger nodded. It was what they had agreed upon, what they both knew would happen. Yet to her surprise, she couldn't help feeling a little discomfited about it, too.

Rand wasn't surprised to see Ginger go right back to work that evening. He was a little annoyed by the continual chirping of her cell phone. Finally, around midnight, she shut it off. "Who keeps calling?"

Ginger grinned and reached for The List. She added No Monitoring Each Other's Calls to the marriage contract must-haves. Then sat back, her expression baiting. "You really want to know?"

Did he? And if so, what did that say about him?

He took a chair, set it a distance from her work area and lowered himself into it. "Yeah," he said, deciding to go with his gut, and satisfy his curiosity no matter how it looked. "I do."

"Three were texts from my mother."

"Everything okay?"

"She wants to have a private talk before she leaves

in the morning about the ins and outs of being a good wife."

Ginger got up and stretched.

Somewhere in the course of the evening, she had changed into a pair of loose-fitting, pink-and-white-striped cotton pajamas. Her hair had been put up in a loose and messy knot on top of her head. Sexy copper tendrils curled against her nape and brushed at her temple and cheeks.

Rand stayed where he was with effort. "She's serious?"

Another sigh. Another slow, feline stretch. "Oh, yes." Her rueful smile upped his pulse. "My mom completely doted on my father. Her whole life revolved around making him happy, and when I was younger, taking care of me. She could anticipate our needs before we even knew what they were."

Ginger and Cordelia did not seem to be on the same page these days, Rand noted. "What happened to change that?"

Ginger stood feet apart, hands clasped behind her. She bent down, so her face was at her knees, and stretched the kinks out gently. "My dad died when I was a senior in high school. Massive heart attack. He was out on a rig on the Gulf, doing geological studies for a customer. He was dead before they could get him airlifted to a hospital on shore."

Rand could see how much that had hurt—and how much she did not want him to go to her and hold her right now. "I'm sorry," he said softly.

"Yeah." Briefly, sadness crossed her face. "It was tough. I still miss him to this day. Anyway, my mom was beside herself with grief. To make matters worse,

I was leaving for Texas A&M that same summer. She asked me not to go, to skip a year and stay home in San Angelo with her, but I knew if I did, she'd never even begin to move on with her life. So I made the decision to go off to college anyway."

Rand noted the complex mixture of emotions on Ginger's face. Grief. Resentment. Most of all, she bore the look she had when she felt smothered with attention or pushed into a corner. "I'm guessing Cordelia didn't take it well?"

"She started driving up to see me a couple of times a week. Always, a surprise."

Rand recalled how much he had wanted independence in his first heady college days. "You resented it?"

Ginger nodded sharply. "Everyone was making fun of me, and I felt…suffocated. I was missing my dad, too, but I also needed to be on my own. Anyway, we had a big blow-up during fall break. I went off with a friend, rather than go home, and she was devastated. But I just… I couldn't take it. Our family doctor referred Mom to a grief support group and a therapist, and she eventually realized she had to have more in her life and went back to work as a party planner."

Impressed, Rand said, "No wonder she did such a good job with our surprise wedding."

Ginger smiled in agreement, and then went quiet.

"You really think Cordelia's going to be a problem for us?" he asked.

Ginger raked her teeth across her lower lip. "I hope not."

"But?" Rand persisted when she didn't go on.

Ginger lounged next to him against the counter. "Any time my mom senses I'm in a dilemma—or even at risk of *getting* in trouble—she starts becoming over-involved in my life again." She winced. "She says she just can't help it."

Rand tucked an errant strand of hair behind her ear. "You think she senses something is up with us, other than what we've told everyone?"

Ginger shook her head. She pivoted to face him, and as she moved, the notch collar of her pajama top crinkled, giving him a nice view of the uppermost curve of one lovely breast. "I think she wants to believe you're the love of my life, and vice versa, and that our impetuousness grew out of the passion we have for each other."

Rand had the idea that his mother, a real romantic at heart, had erroneously come to the same conclusion.

Ginger moved away again, taking with her the seductive glimpse of her breast. "My mom doesn't want us to lose sight of that…um…'passion' in all the drudgery and domesticity of day-to-day living, so she's trying to help me—us—keep our focus on what's important during our honeymoon phase."

Rand knew the one thing he did not need was any help remembering to covet his wife. That was an ever-present constant that had him physically uncomfortable whenever they were alone. "But you still want Cordelia to give you your space."

"Heck, yes!"

Rand wanted that, too. Otherwise, he would never have the time and opportunity to convince Ginger to make love with him again.

And again.

Ginger's brow furrowed as if she sensed the libidinous nature of his thoughts. "What are you thinking?" she demanded.

Already concocting his path to greater marital happiness, Rand grinned. "That for all our sakes, it's time you and I do a little more convincing."

Chapter 7

"They're coming," Ginger announced as she stepped away from the window.

Rand held out his arms. Ginger went into them, and began kissing him passionately, just as they had planned.

It was supposed to be a staged kiss. Purely a means to an end. But, as always, the moment his lips touched hers, she felt a lightning bolt of desire soar through her. All coherent thought fled. Her only focus was the soft persuasive warmth of his mouth on hers, the strength in the arms around her and the hardness of his body pressed against hers.

A delicate cough sounded behind them.

Her blush of embarrassment all too real, Ginger turned to see their mothers standing on the other side of the screen door.

Rand flashed an unrepentant grin at both their moms. "Sorry." He shrugged. "Newlyweds."

Josie gave them an assessing glance that spoke volumes about the doubts she was privately having. "So we see," she said dryly.

Rand held the door open and ushered both women inside.

Cordelia admired the stand mixer, toaster and espresso maker they had set out on the counter. A nice set of cookware was sitting on top of the stove, ready to be put away. More boxes were opened. Meanwhile, Ginger's real work was nowhere in sight.

"You have been busy!" Cordelia beamed her approval.

Ginger nodded. "I realized you're right, Mom. I do need to pay more attention to making Rand happy."

Rand laced his hand around Ginger's waist. "And I need to make sure my beautiful bride has everything she wants and needs." He squeezed her affectionately, and kissed the top of her head. "Otherwise," he mused, "what's the point of being married?"

To their delight, Cordelia bought their ruse, hook, line and sinker—maybe because she was seeing what she wanted to see.

Rand's mother, though, was not such an easy sell.

"You want to tell me what's really going on?" Josie asked when she caught up with Rand in Summit later that day.

Rand paused, just outside city hall. "I'm happier than I've ever been." The moment he spoke the words, he knew they were true.

"That, I can see. But I still think you and Ginger aren't telling us everything."

Rand shrugged. Waited.

Josie continued. "You're sure there's nothing else you want to tell me?"

He did. And he didn't. Finding out he was having a child—and with Ginger, to boot—was the best news he ever could have gotten. Part of him wanted to tell the world; the rest knew just how fragile his relationship with his new wife was. He didn't want to do or to say anything to put their growing closeness in jeopardy. Rand gestured amiably. "Nothing I can think of."

"Mmm-hmm."

Figuring now was the time to be frank about other matters, however, Rand continued. "Look, Mom, I know how much you love all your sons."

"I really do."

"I also know you've managed to let go of my brothers."

"Just not you?"

He smiled indulgently. "You worry when we're not happy."

"You got that right."

"But it's really not necessary. I'm a grown man. I can solve my own problems."

The tears his mom hadn't shed at his wedding to Ginger suddenly misted Josie's eyes. She squeezed his hand, said thickly, "Just so you know if you ever need advice or comfort you can still come to me."

A lump suddenly in his throat, too, Rand hugged her warmly. "Thanks, Mom. But you've got nothing to worry about."

And for the rest of the two weeks that followed, all

went as smoothly as he had promised. Ginger worked nonstop on her proposal, Maria Gonzales by her side much of the time.

He met with many of the landowners in the area, who were interested in exploring their options, but—like Dot and Clancy Boerne—wanted to hire him to ensure their property was protected from an environmental stand-point. And it was only three days before the bids were due to be turned in, that conflict arose.

Ginger was just putting the finishing touches on the computer model of the drilling plan she had engineered for the Boernes when a knock sounded at her cottage door. She looked up from her computer and frowned at the person standing on the other side of the screen door. This, she thought, was what she got for leaving the main door open to let in the warm spring breeze.

"Got a minute?" Conrad asked.

Ginger knew that coolly calculating look. She turned away from her ex-husband, wondering yet again how she ever could have thought herself in love with him. "No."

"Give me five minutes of your time and I'll stop pestering you."

Ginger rose to unlock the door. But only because she knew Conrad would persist until he said what he had come to say. She ushered him inside, but left the main door open. Then stood contentiously between him and the oil-recovery plan she and Maria were going to submit.

Conrad removed his hat, slapped it against his thigh, and ran a hand through his thinning hair. "You're still ticked off at me, aren't you?"

Once again, he was dressed in a sport coat, designer jeans and tie. And of course shiny rattlesnake-skin boots that ran into the thousands of dollars. "Actually, I'm not." Truth was, she didn't really care what Conrad did, as long as she didn't have to see or hear from him. Not that this had been much of an issue thus far, given how acrimoniously the two of them had parted.

Looking slightly uncomfortable standing there, hat in hand, her ex-husband regarded her somberly. "The company made a mistake not taking you seriously."

Of course they had.

"Frankly, we should have done whatever was necessary back then to retain you," he continued.

Now, it was all beginning to make sense....

To succeed in the oil business, a person had to be good at mapping geologic strata and identifying mineral deposits, acquiring the land, and/or designing, supervising and completing major drilling projects. The best CEOs were talented in all three areas.

Conrad was a good land man. He had a knack for being able to talk to people and sign them up. However he struggled mightily in the other two areas. A fact his multitalented father had worried about, since Conrad would never be able to take his place at the helm unless the board of directors backed Conrad. And the board wouldn't do that unless Conrad had proved himself on a big project, which he had yet to do.

Ginger regarded her ex sagely. "Would you still be saying this if one of your top competitors *hadn't* struck oil in Ochiltree County, using a very similar strategy to the one I proposed?"

Conrad flashed his most persuasive smile. "The point is, Ginger, you had the right approach all along.

My dad and I, and the rest of the VPs, were just too thickheaded and set in our ways to realize it."

"Okay." Ginger shrugged. She had some idea what this mea culpa was costing her egocentric ex. "Apology accepted."

Conrad eased closer and continued his pitch. "Profitt Oil wants you back, as VP of domestic exploration."

"That's a pretty big promotion."

He nodded, serious. "And this time, my father and I will personally see to it that we follow your drilling plans, starting with the bid for the Boerne ranch."

She knew they would, if Conrad could somehow take credit for it. But it no longer mattered. It hadn't for a long time.

She turned him down with a look, then ushered him toward the door. "Thanks for stopping by."

He dug in his heels. "Come on, Ginger. For once in your life, be reasonable! You know you haven't got a chance in hell of winning the bidding frenzy over the Boerne deal. Or any other worthwhile oil lease in this neck of the woods, for that matter!" His beseeching smile turned ugly. "Your drilling partner, Maria Gonzales, may have a stellar reputation, but you're too new at this, your resources as a fledgling independent too slim. The midsize companies and well-established wildcatters are going to get all the work."

Maybe so, but not for lack of trying on her part, Ginger thought stubbornly.

Glad that Maria—who was beginning to feel a little nervous about their chances of winning the job, too— had missed Conrad's confidence-busting speech, she said, "And here I thought you just showed up to flatter me." She opened the door, and pushed Conrad through it, right into Rand's imposing form.

Her current husband looked about as pleased as her former husband.

Rand scowled at Conrad. "I believe the lady asked you to leave."

Conrad took another few steps away from Ginger, then turned. "You don't have to run through the entire trust fund your dad left you to prove yourself," he told her. "You have other options, Ginger. At least you would if you weren't too foolish to consider them."

"That's not why I'm doing this!" Ginger retorted. She pivoted away from both men and stormed back inside.

In her wake, low voices rumbled unpleasantly on the stoop. One set of heavy male footsteps headed away from the screen door, the other walked in. Rand took a moment to look her over, head to toe.

Resisting the urge to throw herself into his arms, and let him hold her for as long as he wanted this time, Ginger stayed where she was.

Although she had gotten over her ex's betrayal and her divorce a long time ago, she still felt frustrated, as well as a little embarrassed, by all the time she had wasted when she was with Conrad.

"You okay?" he asked quietly.

Taking a deep breath, she nodded. Her days of trying to win a man's respect were over. He either gave it to her or he didn't.

Squinting, Rand stepped a little closer to her. "How long was Profitt here?"

Ginger turned and hazarded a glance at her computer. "Any time at all is too long."

Silence fell as Rand waited for a more complete answer.

Her body warming as much as if he had actually touched her, Ginger finally replied, "Five minutes, maybe less." She pivoted toward Rand and studied him in return, wondering if that was a hint of jealousy—or wariness—in his blue eyes.

Knowing she probably would have felt the same if she'd caught him in a tête-à-tête with his ex, she asked, "How much did you hear?"

"Enough to know Conrad and his colleagues dismissed your drilling strategies out of hand when the two of you were working together."

She winced. "While pretending to take me seriously." That humiliation hurt the most.

"What made you realize he wasn't sincere?" The expression on his handsome face gentling, Rand stepped behind her and massaged the tense muscles between shoulder and spine.

The expert ministrations of his fingers was heavenly. Ginger shut her eyes and leaned into his soothing touch. She hadn't realized until that second how tense she was.

She released a contented sigh, then forced herself to continue relating the heartbreaking details of her past.

"I was checking my work mail on our home computer one day, and stumbled on an email between my ex and his father. His dad wanted to know when Conrad was going to convince me to quit working and get serious about producing some heirs to the family dynasty. Conrad had apparently promised his father it would be soon, but it wasn't soon enough for Conrad Senior's agenda. He urged his son in no uncertain terms to just get on with it, and bribe me with whatever he had to, to make it happen.

"Conrad wrote back and said he and I didn't work that way. And that he had the utmost confidence that I *would* come around eventually, but not until I got the oil business out of my system. Hence, Conrad wanted to keep humoring me a little while longer. Until I got fed up with constantly falling flat on my face and decided to quit and make babies."

Rand made a dissenting sound as he worked his way down to her waist, relaxing every taut sinew in his path. Reveling in his tender touch, Ginger shifted to allow him greater access. A little more of this wouldn't hurt, she told herself. After all, it wasn't as if they were making love. Besides, if she was this tense, wouldn't that mean their baby was tense, also?

"I gather you confronted your husband?" Rand asked eventually, kneading her lower back.

So relaxed now her knees were getting a little wobbly, Ginger nodded. "Conrad admitted he had never wanted me to work after we were married. He felt one career was enough for any couple."

Rand took her hand and guided her over to the love seat. His tone a husky murmur, he ventured, "You disagreed."

Ginger sank into the thick comfortable cushions. She watched as Rand took a seat beside her. Idly, she took his hand in hers and gave it a brief appreciative squeeze. "I saw what not having something of her own, to give her life purpose, did to my mother, over time. How much happier she was when she started working again and had a life outside of mine. I didn't want to travel the path she did." Ginger paused and bit her lip. "And I still don't."

"So what *do* you want?" he asked gently.

She turned her gaze to his. "I want it all. Satisfying career, family." *Love.* "And if I can't have that," *as she fully expected she probably would not, in the end,* "then I want to know I will always be able to support myself and my baby. That I don't need anyone else to do so." *Or,* she added silently, *anyone else to make me feel happy and complete. I want to do that on my own.*

Rand continued to study her thoughtfully. He kept her hand in his when she would have let his go. "First of all, it's *our* baby," he corrected her finally, his expression kind. "And you don't ever have to worry about having money to raise our child safely and comfortably because I will more than see to that."

Guilt flared in Ginger. Belatedly she realized how selfish she had just sounded.

Rand paused, his gaze roving her flushed cheeks. "Second, you'd have more of a nest egg if you held on to your inheritance from your dad and went to work for someone else."

Ginger knew that, too. She extricated her hand from his and stood. "But I wouldn't be independent, Rand. And for me—" she paused, looking intently into his eyes "—independence is key."

"It's going to rain tonight."

Ginger looked up from the geological maps she had spread out over the dining table to see her husband framed in the doorway. Looking relaxed and still full of energy, he had one broad shoulder braced against the frame.

She'd spent so much time weighing the data and trying to pull together a coherent package that would not only address all potential problems, but recommend the best way to get the recovery factor above forty percent, that she was feeling a little woozy. And worn out.

"Why are you telling me?" Ginger asked, confused.

It wasn't as if she was outside or had been for days. Rand was the only one who had been going out to meet with clients. Her work was right here.

He inclined his head toward the screened-in back porch. The sun had set hours ago. Through the open slider between bedroom and porch she could hear the soothing sounds of cicadas and nightingales. The faint scent of wildflowers and the barbecue someone had cooked for dinner lingered in the cool mountain air. "I thought you might want to do something about the rest of the boxes your mother brought us."

She blinked. Sometimes he had the strangest timing. "You're asking me to unpack the rest of our wedding gifts? Now?" When she was just two and a half more days away from having to turn in the biggest proposal of her life?

He shook his head, but gallant as ever, stayed far enough away not to be able to get even a glimpse of the confidential data she was working on. "I'm *asking* if I can move your belongings."

Hadn't they already gone over this at the time they were delivered? "You can't bring them into the living area. Or I won't have room to work. And if we put them in the bedroom—"

He guessed where she was going with this. "We won't have anywhere to sleep."

"Right."

"But if we leave them on the back porch and the storms are even half as fierce as what the weather bureau is predicting, they will get soaked through. That is why I talked to Claire. She said there's room in one of the storage areas behind the party barn, and offered to let us temporarily stash the stuff there for a nominal fee."

Ginger couldn't say she would mind. She had missed being able to sit on the swing on their back porch. Plus, it would be good to take a little break from her work.

She set down her pen and rose. "I'll help you carry them over there."

He put out an arm to block her way. "No. You won't."

Now he was telling her what to do? Trying not to think how long it had been since they had made love, or even really kissed, she propped her hands on her hips. "They're *our* boxes."

"And you're—" At her raised brow, he stopped to censure himself appropriately. "In no condition to be lugging heavy stuff around."

Ginger scoffed. Telling herself that she was glad Rand accepted her continued work and fatigue-related rebuffs, and had not gone all-out to put the moves on her, she joined him on the back porch. Then ambled close enough to whisper, "I'm pregnant, not disabled."

And he, she was pretty sure, was just biding his time. Waiting, the way he always did, until the tension built to the point she couldn't—wouldn't—say no.

Oblivious to the amorous nature of her thoughts, he narrowed his gaze. "You can hold the doors for me. That's it."

Their gazes clashed as strongly as their wills.

"I mean it, Ginger," he persisted in a tone that brooked no dissent.

She thought about arguing. Then wearily gave it up. She could tell this was one battle she wouldn't win.

Aware it felt oddly nice to be fussed over and protected this way—by him—she shrugged as if it did not matter to her either way. "Suit yourself."

He grinned, victorious.

Which in turn made her regret giving in so easily.

But a concession was a concession, so the next fifteen minutes were spent with Rand lugging the collection of wedding gifts outside, while Ginger facilitated his efforts and held the doors open for him. When Rand had fit all the boxes into the bed of his truck, they both climbed into the cab. Rand stretched his arm along the top of her seat as he backed out of the space. "Michelle's office telephoned me today."

Ginger nodded, admitting, "I got a call, too." She just hadn't had the time or inclination to return it.

"They want us to schedule the next appointment so they can get working on the postnup and marriage contract for us." He drove slowly past the Red Sage party barn where a fiftieth wedding anniversary gala was under way.

Trying not to think how happy the partying group looked, or to wonder if and when she would ever have something that incredible to celebrate, Ginger turned her attention forward once again. She did not need to feel wistful.

"When do you want to go?"

Pushing aside her sudden wave of matrimonial loneliness, Ginger looked through the windshield. "When I have time." Why hadn't Rand made more of an effort to get her into his arms again? Usually he was tireless in his pursuit of her. At least when she let him anywhere near her...

He shot her a sidelong glance, seeming to be thinking about a lot more than their current conversation. "Which will be?" With an aggravated frown, he attempted to pin her down.

"I'm not sure. A few weeks maybe." Honestly, she continued, "I really want to get through the Q and A part of the bidding process first." Assuming she made it to the semifinal stage, as she hoped she would.

Rand nodded briefly in understanding. "I'll be too busy to meet with her again until after that's done, too."

Wondering if she should be in more of a hurry to get the postnup done, Ginger fell silent.

Rand parked the truck in front of the door of the storage facility and cut the engine. "Your mother called me."

Uh-oh. Ginger slid out of her seat, circled around to the back and opened the tailgate. "What about?"

Rand loaded boxes onto the dolly he had borrowed from Claire. "Well, first of all, she asked if you were cooking for me."

Ginger stifled a groan. "And what did you tell her?" Nothing, she hoped, that would prompt Cordelia to run right down there and help out again.

Dramatically, Rand parsed his words. "That it was more of a mutual effort, with me grilling..."

"And me pouring prepared salads and cut up fruit into bowls?"

He squinted, thinking. "I *may* have made it sound a lot more labor-intensive than that."

Ginger let loose another mental oath. "She probably didn't believe you."

"She does seem to know you pretty well," he said. Ginger rolled her eyes. So she hadn't exactly been pulling her fair share of the domestic duties. She planned to make it up when he was the one working all the extra hours, vetting the proposals.

They put the first load into the corner of the storage room, then returned for a second.

"What else did my mother say?" Ginger asked curiously.

Strong muscles bunching beneath the smooth cotton fabric of his shirt, Rand lifted several heavy boxes onto the dolly. "She wanted to know why you weren't returning any of her calls."

Ginger tensed, indignant. She defended herself hotly. "I did talk to her, once. And I texted her several times."

"Apparently, that's not good enough to set her mind at ease." Rand angled a thumb at his chest and ventured lightly, "So unless you want *me* playing Twenty Questions with your mom…"

Ginger most certainly did not. She laid a staying hand on his arm. "I'll take care of it."

His muscle warmed beneath her palm, but he made no effort to disengage. Kindly he said, "She sounded worried."

Ginger knew that was true, but that wasn't her fault, either. She turned away from Rand's gentle regard and marched on down the path. "There's no reason to be. My mom knows I'm so swamped with work right now I barely have time to eat and sleep. I also told her I'd call her when I got my bid in."

"Okay, okay." Rand rolled the second load to the storage area. "No need to shoot the messenger."

Ginger winced, aware she had sounded more than a little irritated, and in fact, was moody nearly all the time now. She wanted to say it was all pregnancy hormones, but deep inside, she knew it was more than that. It was loneliness and frustration, yearning and indecisiveness. The need to be with him; the even more fierce need to keep him away. Most of all she worried about falling in love with him, only to have her heart broken— irreparably—later on.

Because the truth was, he hadn't asked for any of this. She was the one who had proposed. She was the one who had needed to be married for business and professional reasons. He was only here because of the baby. Their baby. And as much as the reckless side of her wanted to see where all this could possibly lead, the honorable side of her refused to trap him into anything other than what they had agreed upon.

"Sorry," she huffed reluctantly.

"Yeah? Well…" He paused next to her, took her chin in hand, and lowered his face to hers, seeming at that moment to have none of her inner ambivalence. "You should be," he teased.

Their eyes met again.

She wanted to tell him to go away even as she ached for him to come even closer. He chuckled wickedly in return. Then his lips pressed against hers in a kiss that was as shockingly intimate as it was unexpected. Sweet, fierce need spiraled through her, arrowing straight from her brain to her heart, to the part of her housing the baby she carried deep inside her.

Ginger moaned, glad he had finally taken the incentive she'd been wishing he would. Yet scared, too. "Damn you," she whispered. "Damn this." *Damn my too vulnerable heart.*

He cupped her face in both hands and brushed his lips over hers. "Damn everything but this," he countered with a smile.

To her regret, another, even steamier clinch followed.

Unable to fight the yearning any more than she was able to resist him, Ginger went up on tiptoe, wound her arms around his shoulders, and brought his lips ever closer. She kissed him again, deeper, slower, more persistently.

He groaned, every inch of him going all hot and hard and male, while she turned soft and feminine and surrendering. His hands slid down to cup the small of her back and fold her tightly against him.

She reveled in his tenderness and the need pouring out of him.

And still he kissed her, again and again and again. Until both of them were panting, trembling for more. And it was only then that Rand pulled back, suddenly in control once again. "As much as I'd like to finish this here and now..." he said roughly.

Ginger knew. They couldn't. Nipples aching, she pulled away from him once again. "Saved by propriety," she quipped with an ease she couldn't begin to feel.

"Temporarily." He walked back to the truck and began unloading what was left. Swiftly. Decisively. One box after another and another...

Ginger used the time to pull herself together and admire the ruggedly beautiful landscape. The thick dark clouds overhead obscured the stars and the moon, and even the rugged mountaintops in the distance. The air seemed to get cooler and damper with every second that passed.

As Rand carried in the last box, big fat raindrops splattered their clothes and the tops of their heads. Hurriedly, they locked up and ran for the truck. They'd hoped to beat the storm, but by the time they got back to their cottage just a few minutes later, rain was falling in thick, heavy sheets.

"I don't have an umbrella so we can either sit here or make a run for it," Rand said from the cab of the truck.

Making a run for it meant getting drenched, head to toe. Waiting it out meant sitting in the truck with the windows steaming up and the rain pounding all around them. And that could only lead to one thing...

Aware she felt far too vulnerable and needy as it was, without bringing sex into the mix once again, Ginger reached for the door handle. In an effort to keep temptation at a minimum, she kept her glance averted. "I don't know about you but I'm making a run for it."

She leaped out into the pouring rain. He was right behind her.

They vaulted into the cottage, clothes plastered to their bodies. Passion pulsed between them, unmet. Ginger sucked in a deep breath. "I'm going to change and then get back to work."

He gave her a long assessing look, knowing what that meant as well as she did. A brief flash of disappointment flickered in his eyes. "Not even a small break?"

Ginger shook her head. As much as she wanted to while away the night in his arms, she couldn't let either of them go down that path. "I still have a lot of proofreading and polishing to do. But I will call Michelle's office tomorrow and get our next appointment set up for the postnup. Because our attorney is right, we do need to get that done." Before their situation got any more complicated than it already was.

Chapter 8

Eight hours later Rand lay in bed alone, watching the early morning light stream in through the edges of the window blinds. As usual, Ginger had slipped out of bed just before dawn, grabbed a robe and headed for the shower. He remained where he was, fighting the ever-present physical frustration that came with sleeping with but not making love to Ginger.

He shouldn't have been surprised. His wife had said at the outset this was to be strictly for business, a marriage in name only. Like a fool, he hadn't expected the hands-off-each-other dictate to last. But with the exception of their wedding night lovemaking and a few passionate kisses, it had.

The man in him wanted to seduce her right back into his arms. The husband in him knew that would be almost as big a mistake as marrying her on strictly her terms.

The question was, how did he get them out of this quandary without pushing her even further away? He was still searching for a solution when he heard the water shut off. Rustling sounds followed. Then Ginger stepped out of the bathroom, her hair wrapped in a towel, her body clad in a thick knee-length terry-cloth robe, the pajamas she'd been wearing in hand.

Rand watched her go to the suitcases she still refused to unpack, and rummage through them. Usually, she quickly found what she needed. This time, she didn't, and a soft string of unpleasantries followed.

He smiled, watching her search for the second time. With another beleaguered oath, she stomped over to the bureau where his clothes were stored. Once there, she paused to look hesitantly over her shoulder. He closed his eyes in time to feign continued sleep. Relaxing, she turned her back to him once again, reached into the top drawer and pulled out a pair of his cotton briefs. She nestled them briefly in her hands, appearing to mull over her options, then tiptoed back toward the bathroom.

What was she up to now? Rand didn't know, but he damn sure intended to find out. "Mind telling me where you're going with those?"

A startled Ginger bumped into the wall, then swung back to face him. Rand sat up and switched on the bedside lamp.

They both squinted at the sudden infusion of light. As his eyes adjusted, he saw the pink flooding her cheeks. "I need some clean underwear."

"What's wrong with yours?"

"It's all dirty, and I haven't had time to go to the laundry."

"So you thought you'd wear mine?" he asked wryly.

"It's preferable to going commando, but if you object…"

Imagining that, he grinned.

She heaved an exasperated sigh. "Please tell me you'll let me borrow these just for today."

The thought of her in his boxer briefs brought all sorts of erotic images to mind. "Depends. Can I see you in them?"

She gave him the kind of look a teacher gave a class clown who was acting up. "What do you think?" she retorted.

Best not to go there. "I think we probably should get some laundry done."

Her lower lip shot out. "I'll get around to it as soon as I get my proposal in."

To prevent a stampede all bidders had been given a time slot to hand-deliver their proposals. "How close are you to finishing?"

"We're going to give it one more read-through, and then take it the print shop this afternoon."

"And once that's done?"

She shrugged. "We turn it in and wait."

On pins and needles, it seemed.

She regarded him warily. "When do you and the rest of the panel start the review process?"

"Monday, in the Boernes' attorney's office." Where every drilling plan would be under lock and key, the panel's work under the purview of the managing oil-and-gas attorney, until the semifinal winners were eventually declared.

Ginger groaned and sat on the foot of the bed, his briefs still clutched in her hand. "This whole process is going to take forever."

Breaking down her resistance was what was taking forever.

He caught her by the waist and tugged her toward him. "And there's only one way to make the time go by as quickly as possible." He bussed her temple. "Stay busy together."

"Somehow, this wasn't what I thought you meant this morning," Ginger drawled hours later as the two of them sorted through piles of dirty clothes in the guest ranch laundry. It was after 10:00 p.m., and they were the only two people in the large square room. Which was a good thing, given how many loads they had to do.

"You thought our clothes were going to wash themselves?"

She sent him a droll look.

"Wait." He snapped his fingers as his next idea hit. "You mean you wanted to do this all by yourself? You, being the wife, after all."

Ginger tried not to think how ruggedly handsome he was, with his mahogany hair all rumpled, the shadow of evening beard lining his face. She tossed one of his socks at his head. "You are so funny."

He caught it with one hand. "You mean you want *me* to do it all?"

She dropped her silky delicates into a machine, out of view. "Tempting. But…no."

His gaze roved over her. "Then what do you want?"

Besides the walls between us to stay firmly in place?

Ginger wondered. "Us both to do our own laundry," she said firmly.

He sauntered close enough she could smell his brisk, woodsy cologne. "No mingling of the underpants, hmm?"

Warmth climbed from her chest and neck into her face. "Or anything else."

"Easier said than done, given that you're still in my skivvies," he teased.

Her chin lifted. "How do you know?"

"Lucky guess."

His lucky guess was right. A palpable silence fell. She fit her denim jeans into three different machines, and his filled up four. Their shirts went into several more. Her delicates took up yet another machine. His cotton garments the last.

Ginger opened up several rolls of quarters, and together they went down the line, adding money, then detergent and softener. Once all the cycles were selected, they went back to idly roaming the long, brightly lit room. Ginger could tell from the way Rand was looking at her he was thinking about kissing her again. She was wanting, thinking the same. And yet she knew if they succumbed to passion yet again, their marriage would feel like more than a temporary arrangement. And that could be dangerous in so many ways....

Her phone vibrated. Ginger looked at the caller-ID screen, pushed Ignore and put it back in the holder at her waist. "Your mom again?" Rand asked.

"Ex-husband. He's been calling and leaving messages nonstop since he stopped by the other day."

Rand's brow furrowed. "Have you spoken with him?"

"No. Because I know what Conrad wants, and he thinks if he keeps pestering me, he'll get it." She sighed.

"But he won't?"

"Not a chance in this world, no matter what happens next. There's no way I will ever work for him or his father again, and one day soon, he will realize that."

"Good for you," Rand said proudly. He squeezed her hand. "Because you're worth more than the Profitts will ever know."

When he looked at her that way, he certainly made her feel valuable. "Thanks," Ginger whispered.

Rand squeezed her hand again, then let her go.

Regretting the sudden absence of physical contact, Ginger took a seat on one of the plastic chairs next to the windows. The fatigue of a few very long weeks overwhelming her, she closed her eyes and let her head fall back. Stifling a yawn, she felt rather than saw Rand drop down beside her. He slipped an arm around her shoulders and leaned to murmur in her ear, "You know, you can go on back to the cottage and go to bed, if you like. I'll stay and finish here."

Ginger was tempted. Yet, because she knew how much of a slacker she had been on the domestic front since they had married, dutifully protested anyway. "Thanks, but I have to do my jeans my way."

That meant eschewing the dryers and hanging them to dry, so the denim would expand with the weight of the water rather than shrink.

Luckily for them, the bathroom shower rod would support half a dozen of her blue jeans. The Adirondack-style furniture and the swing on the screened-in porch would handle another seven.

By the time they had everything laid out, the clothes

in the electric dryers were finished. Ginger helped Rand stuff the clean, warm clothing into plastic baskets and mesh laundry bags. Together, they heaped them into her truck, drove back to their cottage and carried everything inside. Aware it was close to midnight, Ginger yawned again. Rand turned her in the direction of the bedroom. "You're going to bed," he said, the warmth of his hands on her shoulders.

Ginger hated being bossed around, even as she melted at his tender touch. She arched a brow. "Must I remind you that you are not the boss of me?"

He paused. "Must I remind you that you're now sleeping for two? And you have a proposal to turn in tomorrow morning? I presume you want to be fresh and rested for that?"

Ginger wanted to stand her ground. However, her body, her business and the baby nestled deep inside her had other ideas. So, for once, she let her husband call the shots and headed for the bed. Too worn out to look for a clean pair of pajamas, she slipped off her jeans and crawled beneath the covers.

The moment her head hit the pillow, oblivion claimed her.

Ginger woke hours later to the familiar sound of her mother's voice. "My maternal instinct told me something was wrong!" Cordelia said. "And this mess just proves it!"

"Actually," Rand returned mildly, "the only thing it shows is that neither Ginger nor I are all that great at being domestic."

"Well, someone needs to be, and in most cases, it's the wife!" Cordelia returned.

With a muffled oath, Ginger lifted her head. Unfortunately for her, the door separating the bedroom from the living area was wide open. Catching sight of her, Cordelia swept toward her.

"It's nine o'clock. What are you still doing in bed? Are you feeling all right?"

Ginger sat up in a panic. "I'm supposed to be at the Boernes' attorney's office at eleven!"

"I was just coming in to wake you," Rand said.

"You shouldn't have let me sleep so late." Throwing back the covers, she climbed out of bed and dashed into the bathroom. The jeans hanging on the rod were still pretty wet.

Her mom was right behind her. "What happened here? Were half the dryers all broken? It looks like a laundry room exploded. Not to mention the piles of wrinkled clothing out in the living room."

Ginger followed her mother's glance. It was an apt description.

"I didn't get as far as I might have with the folding," Rand said lamely.

Apparently not. Which would not have mattered had her mother not been here, looking on disapprovingly, her gaze intimating that Ginger was well on the way to botching yet another marriage, due to her lack of domestic instincts.

Trying not to think about how much more the demise of this relationship was going to hurt than her first one had, Ginger tested the jeans on the back porch. They were nearly as damp as the ones in the bathroom.

The denims she'd had on the day before had a big coffee stain across one thigh. That would have been okay, if she hadn't had an important business meeting to attend.

As intuitive as ever, Rand guessed the direction of her thoughts.

"Want me to toss a pair in the dryer?" he asked.

Ginger hated to accept yet another favor, but had no choice. "If you wouldn't mind, I'd really appreciate it."

"Since when do you line-dry all your jeans?" Cordelia interjected.

"Since I—" *found myself pregnant and unable to fit in practically everything I own* "—married an environmentalist," Ginger said as she searched through the piles of clean wrinkled clothes for two towels.

"Well, I guess that's good for the harmony of the marriage," Cordelia allowed, sniffing as she held up a horribly wrinkled shirt.

Normally, Ginger wouldn't ask, but she was desperate. She turned to her mom. "Do you want to iron something for me?"

Cordelia smiled, happy to be needed. "Absolutely. Afterward, I'll put away the food I brought you."

Ginger rummaged through the piles and plucked out a white knit shirt, and an embroidered cotton vest. "Everything you need, including the spray starch, is in the coat closet. I've got to hit the shower or I'll be late."

Both women sprang to action.

Unfortunately, Ginger's problems didn't end there.

Rand returned with a pair of jeans that was warm and soft—and way too tight. Ginger had to lie on the bed and even then she could hardly shimmy them on. She was still struggling to pull up the zipper when he eased open the door ever so slightly and let himself into the bedroom, ironed clothing in one hand, an oversize stainless-steel travel mug hiding her prenatal vitamins in the other.

"Oh, my heavens," Ginger said, looking at the mug. "Tell me she didn't see."

He whispered in her ear, "Only because I happened to think of it and got there first."

Ginger breathed a huge sigh of relief. "Thank goodness."

Smiling at her tenderly, Rand kept a firm grip on the mug and handed over the ironed garments. "Your mother asked me to bring these to you."

Ginger looked at the clock. It was now ten minutes after ten. She had to leave in seven minutes if she wanted to make it to her appointment on time. Worse, she was beginning to feel vaguely nauseous.

"You look a little green," Rand observed.

Ginger lifted a hand. "Don't say that." To the baby inside her, she whispered, struggling to her feet, "And don't you do this to me!" Not now. Not today…

Rand assisted her the rest of the way to her feet. He looked down at the booty-tight denim. "Are you going to be able to get those snapped?"

Obviously not. She gave him a lethal glare, then took the knit shirt and slipped it over her head. It was as bad as the jeans, showing her burgeoning waistline, and illustrating her inability to snap or fully zip her jeans.

Five minutes left.

Nausea rising.

Ginger took a deep breath, closed her eyes and forced herself to calm down. This shirt wasn't going to work. She went to the closet and selected a tan-colored twill shirt. "Mind if I borrow this?"

"Help yourself."

She slipped it on and put the unbuttoned vest over that. Luckily, the last hole on her belt worked, and it was enough to hold her unzipped pants up on her hips. The oversize man's shirt looked kind of cute, in a tunic-length-shirt sort of way. And it matched nicely with her tapestry-print brown, tan and indigo cotton vest.

She ran a comb quickly through her still-damp copper hair, twisted it into a businesslike knot low on the nape of her neck and slapped her suede cowgirl hat on her head. Grabbing her briefcase, she headed for the door.

"Where are you meeting Maria?" Rand asked.

"In town, outside the lawyer's office."

"Wait—what happened to the shirt I ironed for you?" her mother asked in confusion.

"Wardrobe crisis. Changed my mind!" she replied, and kept right on walking.

"It's some sort of wildcatter superstition." Behind her, Rand explained in his casual, charming tone, "Ginger thinks wearing a piece of my clothing gives her good luck. Who's to say it doesn't?"

Who indeed? Ginger thought.

"I hope it goes well!" her mother rushed to call after her.

"Thanks," Ginger said over her shoulder to both Rand and her mom. The way her day was going thus far, she would need every ounce of luck she could get.

Dot and Clancy Boerne were at their attorney's office as the bidders dropped off their proposals. The gregarious couple not only thanked everyone for participating, they took the time to chat a little, as well. With Maria, the focus was on her family and three teenage sons, and what it was like for a woman to manage a mostly male drilling crew.

With Ginger, the focus was the change in her marital status. "So how are things on the home front?" Dot asked.

"Good," she said automatically, a little surprised to realize it was true. Despite the stress of trying to make everything work, she was happier and more content than she had been in a long time. Of course a lot of that could be due to the baby she and Rand were secretly expecting, too.

"Glad to hear that," Clancy said cheerfully.

Dot added, "The first few weeks or months can be harder than anyone expects, due to the adjustments required."

Sensing some reassurance was needed to keep her fledgling company firmly in the running, Ginger said, "Rand and I know that. It's why we've taken a very practical approach to everything on the domestic front."

"Dividing chores evenly, I guess?" Clancy mused.

"Actually, we're trying to keep our lives as close to what they were as possible. Rand and I are very independent at heart. We respect and appreciate that about each other."

Catching Dot and Clancy's look of surprise, Maria grinned and, playfully elbowing Ginger, threw in her two cents. "I've seen the two lovebirds together enough to vouch for that. They're crazy about each other."

Dot smiled approvingly and turned her attention back to Ginger. "The important thing is that you and Rand have realized you belong together and have taken steps to make a lasting commitment to one another, the same way Maria has with her family. That shows a laudable maturity and the kind of personal stability Clancy and I look for in all our business partners."

Meaning what? Ginger wondered, upset. That she wouldn't be in the running if she hadn't married Rand?

Chapter 9

Ginger was still thinking about the conversation she'd had with the Boernes as she drove back to the Red Sage.

Rand's pickup was gone. So was her mother's sedan. Glad to have a moment alone, she parked and went inside.

The living area of the cottage was pretty much as she'd left it, with unfinished laundry everywhere. The refrigerator, freezer and cupboards were different, however. They were packed with homemade varieties of all her favorite foods. And some of what she now knew were Rand's, as well.

Tears of gratitude blurring her eyes, Ginger reached for her phone. She called her mom to thank her, and this time it was she who got no answer.

She grabbed a couple granola bars and drank a glass of milk. She knew she should start folding and putting away her portion of the laundry, but instead headed right back to bed, shucking her too tight blue jeans as she went.

She climbed beneath the covers, telling herself she'd just rest for a few minutes. The next thing she knew she was waking from one of the soundest, most gratifying slumbers of her life. It was dark outside. Rand was in the living room, sitting on the love seat. But that wasn't the only thing that was different, she noticed as she struggled to sit up. Not by a long shot.

Still yawning and rubbing her eyes, she walked out to join him. Shirttail out, boots off, he looked relaxed and casual.

Noting how the soft blue of his shirt brought out the darker blue of his eyes, she asked, "What time is it?"

He looked at his watch. "Nine o'clock."

That meant she'd been asleep nine hours.

Seeming to realize where her thoughts were going, he patted the seat beside him and said gently, "You were tired."

She certainly must have been. Realizing she was clad in nothing but his shirt—which came to mid-thigh— the unbuttoned vest, and a pair of boot socks, she sat beside him on the small two-cushion sofa and continued to look around at the unusually neat and orderly space. They'd been married for weeks now, and being here with him like this was still a pleasurable assault to her system. "Did you do all this?"

His mouth quirked. "Your mother folded, ironed and organized all our laundry. I assembled the shelving system she insisted we needed. And then we both put everything away."

Ginger blinked in amazement. How was it that he

worked so well with her mother while she and Cordelia could barely have a civil conversation these days?
"While I was sleeping."

Rand shrugged, as if it was no big deal. His glance
fell to her bare thigh, then returned to her eyes. "Your
mom knows how to be quiet, as do I."

Her skin tingling where his glance had been, she
rose gracefully and walked back into the bedroom.
She switched on a light and studied the contents of the
closet. It looked the way Ginger's closet had when she
was growing up, and her mom had still been in charge
of Ginger's life, a fact that was simultaneously comforting and disturbing. Ginger sighed. "She also unpacked
my suitcases."

Rand nodded, appearing as relieved about that as her
mother probably had been. "Yeah, although given that
your toiletries were all in our bathroom and you'd gone
through most of the clothing that was in there already,
there wasn't a heck of a lot to do there."

Ginger reached for a pair of once loose-fitting but
now snug jersey pajama pants and tugged them on over
her bare legs. She swung around, feeling trapped and
restless once again. "Where are my suitcases?"

Rand draped his arm along the back of the love seat.
"With mine, in the storage area, next to the boxes."

"And where's my mom?"

"She was able to get a room at the Summit Inn in
town this time. Said she was staying for at least a couple of days."

Days in which, Ginger suspected, the advice on how
to live happily married ever after would be free flowing.

Perceptive as ever, Rand leaned forward, hands
clasped between his spread knees. "Look, I get that
she's a little over-involved, but your mom means well."

Ginger sniffed. "That doesn't make her interference in our home life any easier to take."

Rand moved lithely to his feet and walked toward her. "She said that she wants us to have the best possible start to our marriage. Her way of facilitating that is to create some sort of utopian honeymoon segue into married life. My mom's way is to give us space, and believe me, that's not easy for her."

Ginger walked to the kitchen. Aware she was hungry but didn't yet know what she wanted, she poured herself a glass of milk. "What do you mean?"

Rand slouched against the counter, arms folded in front of him. "In the past, her instinct has always been to rush in and offer her advice whenever she thinks me or my four brothers are making a big mistake. It's caused problems with all of us, in the past. The fact she's not doing it now, coupled with how much your mom is doing, just shows me how much both our families really want our marriage to work."

And that was a problem, too. "I guess I didn't consider the devastation second divorces for each of us would have on our parents."

Abruptly, Rand looked disturbed about that, too.

Sipping her milk, Ginger forced herself to take comfort where she could. "But our families will be happy about the baby, even if they're not happy about our eventual split. And over time, anyway, they're bound to appreciate our commitment to bringing up our baby together, as friends."

For Rand, that was no longer enough, although it had sounded good at the outset. There was something about living together as a married couple that made them feel like husband and wife, as well. And made him want more from the arrangement than he was currently getting. More sex, more intimacy, more closeness of every kind.

Silence fell between them as Ginger drained her glass and set it aside. Her hair was loose and wild tonight, the rest of her sleep-rumpled and vulnerable. She was heart-stoppingly beautiful to him, and sometimes just looking at her made his chest ache.

Misreading his pensiveness, she went still. "I know you're tempted to shout the news. Sometimes I am, too, but we're not telling anyone yet."

He ran his finger down the curve of her shoulder, and was rewarded with a whole body shudder. "Because of the bid."

Ginger lifted her chin. "I don't want to lose out on this opportunity because anyone thinks I won't be able to do the work while pregnant."

"They wouldn't necessarily think that." Rand looked at her for a satisfyingly long moment. "My mom worked during all five of her pregnancies right up until the due dates. Any leave she took was after she gave birth."

She inhaled deeply. "She's definitely a role model, and one I intend to emulate. But given what Dot said to me today when I turned in the bid with Maria… I'm not taking any chances."

Ginger filled him in on what had transpired.

Color blooming in her cheeks, she ambled back to the love seat and sank onto it once again. The mountain air streaming in through the open windows was a little chilly, evidenced by the delicious imprint of her nipples against her shirt. She shivered as she glanced over at the stack of papers. "What are you looking at?"

He handed her the folder he'd been perusing when she'd walked in. Ignoring the rigid hardness of his body, he walked over to close the nearest window. He brought a cream-colored fleece throw—another of her mother's homey touches—and draped it across her shoulders. Sinking down beside her, he said, "Those are sales brochures from Summit Realty. Your mom thinks we really ought to consider buying a place."

"That would be the way to go if we planned on being together indefinitely. Since we don't…" Ginger met his eyes and shook her head. "Fiscally, it doesn't make sense. You know that as well as I do."

Rand narrowed his gaze. "Living with a baby in a weekly rental doesn't make sense, either."

Ginger seemed to know they couldn't continue like this. However, to his frustration, that didn't mean she was in any particular rush to figure everything out right this minute, either.

"Can we talk about this later?" Her stomach rumbling, she jumped to her feet and went to the kitchen. "Because I'm starving."

Enjoying the view, he stayed where he was. "At last, something we can agree upon."

She made a soft sound of exasperation, opened the freezer and quickly located one of her mother's homemade meals. "Have you had dinner?" She tossed the words over her shoulder.

"I was waiting for you to wake up."

His shirt rode up slightly in the back, the rumpled hem clinging seductively to the soft jersey covering her buttocks, as she studied the contents of the fridge. "Do you like beef chili?"

I'd rather have you. He let his gaze drift over the

delectable, feminine slope of her backside. "So much I can eat it cold out of a can."

Ginger whirled toward him, the curves of her breasts pressing against the cotton fabric of his shirt. "Well, hopefully, we can do better than that."

Hopefully, once dinner was over, they could do a *lot* better than that...

He propped both legs on the coffee table and stretched his arms out along the back of the love seat, content to watch her putter around the small kitchen. Looking pretty and sexy in her usual, determined way, Ginger opened up the fridge once again. She pulled out grated cheddar, sour cream and pickled jalapeños. "What about Frito pie?"

His fingers itched to touch the silky copper hair drifting over her shoulders. "I eat it every chance I get."

"Me, too." Oblivious to how hot and frustrated he was beginning to feel, Ginger sorted through the dry goods in the cupboards. "Oh, no."

Concerned, he rose and headed toward her. "What's the matter?"

She swung back to him, hands planted on her slender hips. "We don't have any corn chips."

Normally, Rand noted, the lack of any one culinary ingredient was not cause for concern with the woman he'd married. Most of the time, Ginger seemed practically ambivalent about the food she was consuming. But at this particular moment, she looked incredibly distraught. And that could only mean one thing...

He peered at her curiously, both amused and delighted. "Is this your second craving?" The chocolate sandwich cookies with the vanilla cream centers had been her first.

"Don't be silly." Flushing, she waved off the allegation and resumed her determined search of the cupboards. "You know I've been sailing through this pregnancy."

She rummaged around for the travel mug she usually stuck in the very back of the cabinet. Realizing it was time for her to take her prenatal vitamin, Rand held up a staying hand and went to retrieve the bottle hidden in his laptop carrier.

"I also know you've been sipping ginger ale and eating saltine crackers like nobody's business."

He handed her the mug he'd spirited away, and she sent him a grateful look. Probably because his quick thinking that morning had managed to keep her über-organizing mother from finding Ginger's prescription vitamins, thereby preventing her from discovering why it was the two of them had married so hastily.

Ginger shrugged. "They do the trick."

Cocking his head, he studied her for a long moment. What else had she been holding back from him? "So you *have* been nauseated."

"Just a little bit every now and then. I haven't actually thrown up."

"That's good."

"Tell me about it."

Aware he wanted her to confide more than that in him, he edged near enough to drink in her womanly scent. "Have you had any other cravings?"

She filled a glass with milk, stirred in a little chocolate syrup and swallowed a prenatal vitamin. "I never said this was one."

He folded his arms. Waited.

And was rewarded with a blush and an almost smile.

She lifted both her hands in grudging self-defense. "Okay, if it will make you happy, yes! I *have* been wanting Frito pie made with my mom's chili for weeks now." She shrugged off his amused laugh and bent to find a saucepan in the cupboard. "But that happens to me anyway when I've gone too long without some really fine home cooking. It happens to everyone."

She paused to dump the frozen block of homemade chili in the saucepan, and set it on the stove. "That's why the subliminal messaging in TV food commercials is so successful." She turned the burner on medium heat, then put on the lid, and pivoted back to him. "Once you see a hamburger with everything, you can't rest until you actually have one."

Leaning close, he ran a thumb over her cheek and needled her playfully, "If you *like* hamburgers. I don't imagine the messaging works on you if you don't."

She grinned at his teasing, the way she always did, and tilted her face up to his. "You know what I mean. Furthermore—" she jabbed her thumb at the valley between her soft, luscious breasts "—*I'd* be perfectly happy eating our chili without anything but cheddar cheese and sour cream and jalapeños."

Except she wouldn't, Rand thought, when she'd had her heart set on Frito pie. And they both knew it. Ginger was the kind of woman who wanted *what* she wanted *when* she wanted it. Just like he wanted what he wanted—which, at the moment, was mostly…her.

Oblivious to the licentious direction of his thoughts, she looked at the clock, realizing, as did he, that the grocery stores in the area were all closed until morning. She scowled. "Do not make me feel silly about this."

"Wouldn't think of it." Aware this was one problem he could actually solve, he headed for the door.

"Where are you going?" He tempted her with an easy grin, admiring anew the way his shirt gently outlined her breasts. The changes in her body were subtle but incredibly erotic. "Off to save the day, of course."

Rand was back fifteen minutes later, grinning as though he had just won the lottery, two single-serving packages of Fritos in hand.

Ginger tore her glance from the handsome contours of his face, and pretended to be busy at the stove. "Where'd you go?"

He sauntered closer, with exaggerated chivalry. "My mom's cottage. She didn't have any Fritos, unfortunately, nor did any of the other guests in adjacent cottages."

Mortified that he'd been reduced to begging for corn chips at ten-thirty at night, Ginger covered her face with her hand. "Tell me you're kidding me."

He shifted even closer, his voice low and sexy. "I kid you not." She peered at him through spread fingers, aware she had never been this fussed over by any man. "So who *did* have them?"

"Heath and Claire."

The proprietors of the Red Sage guest ranch.

He slouched against the counter next to her, legs crossed at the ankle, hands on either side of him. "I figured they've got kids in elementary who take lunches to school. And what goes better with sandwiches and fruit than chips? So seeing their lights were still on downstairs, I went over to the main house and explained the situation—"

Ginger tore her gaze from his rock-solid chest and abs. "You told them that I was—"

He lifted a hand to her face, gently touching her cheek, and flashed her a crooked smile. "Celebrating the completion of one of your work deadlines. We were all set for Frito pie, only to find out we were fresh out of corn chips. They were happy to give me what they had, although they refused to take cash for it, so we'll have to replenish their stock tomorrow."

Ginger paused, still not sure whether she wanted to kiss or scold him. And still the chili bubbled on, filling the cottage with its fragrant spicy smell.

Aware she was still tingling from his brief sensual touch, she took a deep breath. "You're sure they didn't guess we were expecting?"

Rand shrugged and wrapped his arm around her shoulders. "They didn't appear to."

"Or worse, think we were being ridiculous?"

He kissed her temple, cheerful as ever. "We are newlyweds."

"Newlywed professionals in our early thirties," Ginger corrected, telling herself not to read anything into the easy affection in his eyes. "Who should be beyond such silliness."

Rand paused thoughtfully. "What's the real problem here?"

"I just don't want to appear frivolous when I'm trying so hard to get people to take me seriously."

"First of all," he said, taking down two stoneware bowls from the cabinet, "no one who knows you thinks you are the least bit ditzy, on any level." He opened up two packets of chips, and poured them into the bottom of each bowl, then ladled a generous amount of beef chili over top. "Everyone knows how serious and hard-working you are in every respect. But you're still entitled to enjoy yourself."

Aware if she were truthful, there was only one way she really wanted to enjoy herself—in his arms, in their bed—Ginger added a healthy sprinkling of cheddar, some fresh chopped tomato, several jalapeño slices and a dollop of sour cream to the fare. "Believe me, I wish I could spend a lot more time having fun than I have lately."

But Ginger wasn't sure even that was a good idea.

They carried their dinner out onto the back porch and sat side by side on the porch swing. The evening was breezy and cool, with a full moon and stars shining above. Enjoying the time alone with his wife, Rand slanted her a curious glance. "If you want to have more fun, why don't you take more time to relax?"

Ginger carefully gathered all the ingredients on her spoon. She lifted the steamy concoction to her lips, blew lightly across the top. For a moment she savored the incredible mix of flavor and texture. Rand did the same. From the look on his face, he found the dish as deliciously satisfying as she did.

Finally she allowed, "I can't afford to goof off when I have so much riding on the drilling rights to this particular oil lease."

"Maybe too much," Rand decreed candidly, reminding her with a frown that as important and potentially lucrative as the Boerne lease was, securing it was just *one* job.

There would certainly be other opportunities down the line.

"Since you've only really pursued the one property here, why not start vying for leases in some of the other up-and-coming areas, outside of Marfa or Fort Stockton—where I don't already have contracts to do the environmental screening—from here on out?" Where there would be no conflict of interest between them? Or her and his mother's company, for that matter?

"If you want to work in those areas, I give you my word that I won't," Rand assured her. "And in the interest of family harmony, I'll get my mother's company to avoid bidding in that area, too."

Her expression both reflective and conflicted, Ginger ate a little more, then took a sip of her milk. "I can't afford to do that."

"Why not?"

She raked her spoon through the center of her chili, mixing the melted cheddar and sour cream. Finally she muttered, "I guess it's not as if you won't find out soon enough anyway." She pushed a jalapeño pepper to the side, took another bite, sighed. "I have enough money in the trust fund I got from my dad to pay Maria and her drilling crew to work under my direction for thirty days, but that's it." Her lips flattened. "We either get a viable flow out of the shale deposits the first time out, or I'm done here."

"Maria's company couldn't pick up the slack?"

"She's on as much of a shoestring budget as I am. And she has a weekly payroll to meet. She can only afford to work for jobs and people that pay as they go."

"So you're stuck. This one job, and that's it."

"Yep."

Taking a long swallow of beer, he studied her quietly. She looked stressed and worried again, none of which was any better for their baby than it was for her. "And it has to be the Boerne lease?" Where the competition was exceptionally fierce. "No other property in the area will do?"

She inhaled deeply. "The satellite imagery, soil samples, and even the 'creekology' or lay of the creek beds on the Boerne land are all incredibly positive. I've walked that ranch. I can't explain it except to say that I know in my gut that particular strata of rock is going to produce vast amounts of oil. The other properties in this area might or might not."

Rand's mother and grandfather had the same innate talent for scouting out the big energy fields. It was a God-given sixth sense few had, and all wanted. If Ginger had it, too, she was more like his wildcatter family than she realized.

"The challenge will be to get the oil out safely," she continued soberly, "with as little disruption and damage as possible to the existing ranch."

Rand knew Ginger was talented enough to do that, too. The big question was, who would the Boernes select? And how would Ginger react if all she had done thus far was for naught? Would she renege on what she'd said so far, take her ex up on his offer and go back to work for Profitt Oil?

Ginger put her empty dish aside. Shivering in the damp evening air, she curled up next to him on the swing. "I've spent months courting Dot and Clancy. I've thrown all my research and testing budget at this one project. I don't have enough money to all over again. If I don't land this bid with the Boernes, then I'm going to have to call it quits and go back to working for someone else again."

Rand put his dishes aside, too. He sat back, wrapped an arm around her shoulders and pulled her into the curve of his body. He leaned over and pressed a tender kiss on the top of her head. "And you don't want to do that," he ventured.

Ginger continued staring stubbornly at the shield of trees on the other side of the screen. "I want the freedom to pick the jobs that are right for me. And our child. The only way I'll really be able to do that is if I'm my own boss."

Another silence fell.

Rand inhaled the familiar soap and shampoo scent of her hair and skin. "Then I hope, at the end of the day, the Boernes pick you."

Ginger tilted her head to look at him. Wistfulness and something else he couldn't quite read gleamed in her pretty green eyes. "You mean that," she acknowledged softly.

Rand nodded. "I've already got plenty of work in Summit County. If you're awarded this lease, more will follow. That would be good for you, good for our baby, good for us." He threaded his hand through her hair. "And speaking of that, you know what else would be good for us?"

Ginger caught her breath. "I have a feeling you're going to show me."

It was all the invitation Rand needed. "You're right. I am."

Chapter 10

Rand shifted Ginger over onto his lap, so she was straddling him, and then pivoted himself to the center of the swing. Hardly believing how good she felt against him, her breasts pressed against his chest, her inner thighs cupping the outside of his, he tipped her face up to his and kissed her long and wet and deep. Kissed her until she fisted both hands in his hair and quivered. "Rand." She whimpered for more as he slid his hands beneath her shirt, ghosted lovingly over her ribs. "What are you doing?"

He found what he was looking for, the soft, warm swell of breasts, the hard jut of her nipples pressing against the center of his palm. She moaned again at the erotic sensations he dispensed, grinding against him.

Chuckling affectionately, he went on a little tour, kissing, unbuttoning and unfastening. Until her shirt was off, and then so was her bra. And God help him if she wasn't the most beautiful woman he had ever seen in his entire life.

He bent his head to kiss the tight, puckered tip. Savored the moment as she caught his head in both her hands and held it there. Taking her nipple into his mouth, he quipped, "I'm helping you have a little fun."

Her head was back, her eyes closed, as he worshiped one breast, then the other. She moaned again when he eased a hand beneath the waistband of her pants and found the most feminine part of her. "This isn't fun," she gasped, her hips rocking helplessly. "It's sex." Eyes still closed, she shivered in delight, still having enough moxie to protest, "Which happens to be what got us into trouble in the first place!"

Rand recalled all too well the recreational activities they had shared on Valentine's Day. And the satisfying surrender that had followed... Memories that fueled his fantasies to this day.

Gripping her hips in the way he knew she really liked, he moved her back and forth across his lap, kissing her passionately until she writhed with pleasure and kissed him back. Finally, when she was soft and warm and eager, he lifted his head long enough to stare into her eyes. "I don't know about you, but I kind of like the trouble we're in."

She didn't respond...she didn't have to. He could see how she felt even if she wouldn't yet actually say so.

Shifting her off his lap, and onto the center of the swing, he dropped to his knees. Her green eyes softened all the more and her breath caught as he stripped the rest of her bare and tenderly worshiped the quivering inner skin of her thighs, her navel.

Another moan wrenched from her lips. "Spoken like a man."

Determined to make her concede it was foolish to stay away from each other physically, the way they had been trying to do, he left a trail of kisses over her lower abdomen, her silky-wet center. Aware he wanted every part of her, he murmured, "You can fib all you want, but I know you want me, too."

She leaned forward, took his head in her hands and kissed him back in the way he'd been wishing for. "How?" she demanded, stubborn as ever.

"By this." He touched her erect nipples. Moved lower still, to the dampness between her thighs. "And this." He moved his fingers in the way she liked, until she pulsated. "And this."

"So I'm weak…" She arched against him pliantly, still kissing him. "At least," she whispered, "where you're concerned…"

He moved her hand to the proof of his desire, wanting, needing her to feel what she did to him, too. "Then that makes two of us," he told her gruffly, "because I can't resist you, either…."

Ginger knew she could have let Rand possess her then. They would have both climaxed, and could have called it a night. But she didn't want it to be over, didn't want him having all the fun. All the control. So she stripped him naked, too. Made him take a turn on the swing while she found new and inventive ways to pleasure him. And only when he put his hands beneath her bottom and tugged her to him, did she straddle him again. Only when he kissed her with the passion that had been so sorely missing from their married life, did he fill her with one smooth stroke, pressing into her with such perfection that she cried out from the sheer pleasure of it. Only then did she let him send her spiraling again, and only then, when she was at the pinnacle of desire, did he follow.

To their mutual pleasure, the aftershocks were as potent as their lovemaking had been. Letting them know that once again they had risked it all. Just to be together again.

Trembling, Ginger clung to Rand.

She couldn't believe she had done this. Again. Let her heart get miles ahead of her head, let them risk such disappointment. But she had. Worse, she wasn't sure what she was going to do about it.

Because getting this close to each other—and they were becoming more enraptured with every passing moment—was not part of their original agreement.

Ginger was still in bed the next morning, nibbling on a saltine and taking long slow breaths in through her nose and releasing out through her mouth, when Rand strolled in.

As usual, he had hit the complimentary daily breakfast buffet at the main house, and had thoughtfully brought something back for her. This morning, it was spinach and artichoke quiche, fruit compote and a decaf latte. He set the repast on the night table beside her bed.

The aroma, pleasant as it was, sent her severely challenged equilibrium even closer to the edge.

Looking sexy as ever in a T-shirt and jeans, Rand sat on the edge of their bed. "Your mom called. She wants us to have dinner with her this evening."

Reminding herself that she had successfully battled

the malady thus far, Ginger struggled to contain her nausea. "Just us, or is your mom invited, too?"

"It'll be the four of us."

She wiped a bead of sweat from her temple. "This is starting to be a regular thing. Although I'm not so sure it's a good thing."

Her mother was too nosey; his mom too observant and astute.

He grinned in agreement and offered her a hand. The moment Ginger sat all the way up she knew she was in trouble. She shoved him out of the way and, hand to her mouth, ran for the bathroom.

By the time she finished, tears were streaming from her eyes. Afraid to venture too far from the commode, she sank down on the cool tile. Rand knelt beside her. He placed a cold wet towel on the back of her neck, and handed her another for her face.

"So much for jalapeños," Ginger joked weakly in an effort to cover her humiliation.

He shoved the damp hair from her forehead, agreeing gently, "So much for morning sickness…."

Amen to that, Ginger thought. What a horrible way to start the day.

He slid her another tender look, then rose and returned a second later with a glass of ice water and lemon slices. "That's supposed to help."

"Reading up again?" She took a cautious sip.

He gently helped her to her feet. "I like to be prepared for whatever comes my way. And since you admitted you'd been feeling nauseated the last few weeks…"

Ginger paused at the sink to brush her teeth and rinse with a mint-flavored mouthwash. With his arm around her waist, she made her way back to bed. She sank onto the rumpled sheets, wishing she hadn't just disgraced herself in front of him. Talk about sexy...

She was glad he was there anyway. Just having him near made her feel better. She let her gaze drift over every ruggedly handsome inch of him. "You're too gallant for your own good. You know that?"

The faint hint of a smile curved of his lips. "What can I say?" He covered the back of her hand with his. "It's a family trait all the McCabe men share." His grip was warm and comforting. Sighing inwardly, Ginger turned her palm over, so she could hold on to him.

The moment drew out.

Another inscrutable look. A tantalizing grin.

Her nipples peaked. "You can't possibly be thinking what I think you're thinking," she accused.

But he was.

"See?" His voice was low and a little rough. He kissed the back of her hand, the inside of her wrist. "I'm not so gentlemanly, after all. Especially when this is one of our rare mutual days off." He worked his way up to her elbow. "Besides, what better way to get that newlywed glow going before we see the two moms?"

She stared down at the sight of his lips on her skin. Their lovemaking the night before had been enough to have her falling in love with him. Another bout might make it last forever.

And the vows that bound them together were not the everlasting kind.

Determined to protect both of them, from as much hurt and disappointment as possible, Ginger curled a hand around his biceps. "Actually, there is something else that needs to be done before we see our mothers."

Intrigued, he lifted a brow and gestured for her to continue.

"We need to finish drawing up the terms of our marriage contract." It was only half done and at this rate, they'd never be ready for their next meeting with the family law attorney.

Her suggestion had the effect of a bucket of cold water poured over his head. His expression went from playful to recalcitrant, just like that. "You really want to do that today?" Before they ended up making love again?

"Yes, I do. So…." Resolutely, she tossed back the covers, went to the fridge, came back with their half-finished list and a pen. "Let's get started."

"What have the two of you been doing today?" Cordelia asked when Rand and Ginger met up with the two moms at the Summit Inn.

"Working on our postnup," Ginger said.

Cordelia and Josie exchanged glances rife with maternal concern.

Not wanting to get into that again, Ginger asked the moms the same question.

Josie said, "Preparing for the Q and A session with the Boernes. I know we haven't won anything yet—"

But she expected her company to win. Ginger expected Wyatt Drilling to make it to the semifinals, too. Everyone did.

"It just makes sense to be prepared," his mom finished.

Abruptly, Ginger wondered if she should have been doing the same instead of just waiting around for the announcement. She hadn't been worried about the Q and A; to date, she'd spent so long engineering her oil-recovery plan she knew the facts of her proposal inside and out. Maria was equally prepared to discuss the actual drilling process.

Ready to learn from one of the best, however, since she now had access to Texas's most famous lady wildcatter, Ginger looked at Josie. "If you don't mind my asking, how do you get ready for that?"

"I have someone on my team grill me."

Ginger's mom looked at her. "I could do that for you," Cordelia offered.

"That would be fine, Mom. But I really need to get someone who knows the ins and outs of oil exploration. Like Maria, my drilling partner."

"Oh." Cordelia briefly looked hurt. Her next idea hit just as suddenly. "Rand can't do it?" she asked with all the tenacity of a veteran helicopter mom.

Ginger shook her head. "There's a firewall between us. We can't discuss the bids."

Josie conceded, "I can't help her, either, since my company is competing against hers."

Cordelia turned back to her daughter. "Maybe you should take this as a sign, then, and just drop out."

"No!" Rand, Ginger and Josie all said in unison.

Ginger knew her mom meant well; that didn't necessarily help. "I've gone too far for that, Mom," she explained with as much patience as she could muster. "Now, what did you want to tell us this evening?"

"Actually, it's what I'd like to show you. So if you don't mind coming along for the ride—" Cordelia ushered them all into her Cadillac.

"I have to tell you, I have really fallen in love with

this little town," Cordelia said as she drove to a Craftsman-style home on Oak Street.

Ginger immediately recognized it as one of the homes in the Realtor brochures Rand had been perusing the evening before. Except now there was a "sold" sticker across the front of the yard sign.

Cordelia parked in the driveway and got out. "Let's go in, shall we?"

Ginger had a sinking feeling. "Mom." Ignoring Rand and Josie McCabe's perplexed expressions, she dug in her heels. "What did you do?"

Cordelia waved her hand dismissively. "I want you to see the inside first."

Feeling a migraine coming on, Ginger pressed her hands to her head. "Tell me you didn't buy this for us as some sort of an over-the-top wedding gift."

Cordelia affirmed, "I didn't buy it for you."

Ginger's whole body sagged in relief.

The older woman turned the key in the lock and opened the door onto one of the nicest interiors Ginger had ever seen. She turned with a smile, announcing, "I bought it for me."

Rand had no idea what to say. Nor, if their expressions were any indication, did his mother or his wife.

"You bought this home," Josie repeated to Cordelia, as if saying the words out loud would somehow shed light on the situation.

Cordelia walked through the spacious, well-lit rooms. "Initially, I wanted a place to stay when I'm in town, visiting." She turned, admiring the sunny yellow walls and gleaming wood floors. "Then I thought about how far the drive was between San Angelo and

Summit, a good four hours under the best of circumstances, sometimes a lot more. And the fact that there are no easy commuter flights between the two places. So I decided I would move here instead."

Ginger stared at her mother, all the color draining from her face. "Tell me you didn't quit your job."

"I quit my job."

Josie's hand flew to her heart.

At least his mom knew what a mistake this was, Rand thought wryly.

"But only because I got one here," a beaming Cordelia continued.

"Where?"

"With Claire McPherson—at the Red Sage guest ranch."

Coincidentally, Rand thought, where he and Ginger were now living.

"Apparently, they're short-staffed for events in their party barn. And with the busy summer season coming up, she was delighted to have me on board."

Ginger slumped down on the staircase. She looked so wobbly, Rand sat beside her and put his arm around her.

"What about your house in San Angelo?" she asked.

Cordelia shrugged. "I put it on the market. Since it's in such good shape and I priced it reasonably, it won't take long to sell."

An uncomfortable silence fell.

Ginger stared at her mother in abject misery. "You realize I haven't actually won any work here yet, Mom."

Unperturbed, Cordelia walked over to a window and adjusted the shade, so even more light poured into the room. "You will, honey. But even if you don't, it's my understanding that Rand has plenty of work."

Ginger stiffened and got to her feet. "What does that have to do with me?"

It was Cordelia's turn to look annoyed. She sent her only child a chastising look. "Plenty, since you're his wife, and part of being his spouse is creating a warm and loving home for him."

Rand rose. He hated to be in the middle of this, but since his name had been mentioned, he had no choice. "Ginger's been doing fine on that score," he said easily.

"Really?" Cordelia spun toward him. "You forget. I've seen the way the two of you have been living."

Ginger huffed. "So?"

Cordelia stepped forward, her hands knotted at her sides. "How many home-cooked meals has she prepared for the two of you? Has she prepared even one?"

Rand nodded, making no effort to disguise his pleasure. "We had chili with all the fixin's last night," he announced.

"Chili that I made and brought to you," Cordelia corrected. "Had I not..."

"Food isn't the issue here," Josie interrupted her.

Cordelia sniffed and folded her arms in front of her. "Really? I beg to differ."

"Rand and Ginger's privacy is," Josie asserted.

The two mothers-in-law stared at each other in stony silence.

"And to that end—" Rand interjected.

"I think everyone should back off," Ginger put in. Her expression distraught, she headed blindly for the door.

"Believe me, I would—" Cordelia cut her off at the threshold "—if I thought you were coming even close to meeting your husband's needs. Don't you see? Your marriage to Rand will fail as surely as your first failed, if you don't put your husband first!"

Rand wrapped his arms around his wife's shoulders. "Our marriage will fail if we don't put each other first," he corrected her. Able to see Ginger was at her limit, which in his view was understandable, he continued mildly, "And to that end, I think Ginger and I should take a rain check on dinner this evening."

Sagging with relief, Rand's mother quickly added, "Actually, I'm feeling rather tired, too."

Cordelia glared at Josie in disbelief. "You're siding with them?"

The lady wildcatter shrugged her shoulders in abject surrender. "I'm not siding with anyone. I'm just saying we all need a time-out."

"Amen to that," Ginger muttered beneath her breath.

They all looked at each other. It seemed everyone was in agreement except Cordelia. "I'll drive you back, then," she said stiffly. She ushered everyone outside onto the front porch and locked the door behind them.

The two older women headed for the car, but Ginger hung back. "Rand and I are going to walk."

Cordelia started to argue, then stopped. "Suit yourself," she said. Face rigid with hurt and disapproval, she got in the car with Josie and drove off.

Silence fell between Rand and Ginger. He was glad his wife had opted to walk back to their vehicle, which was still parked at the Summit Inn. They needed time alone. It was a pleasant spring evening. And the distance wasn't all that far.

Ginger raked her hands through her hair. She shook her head in disbelief. "What a nightmare."

Rand took her hand in his, gave it a reassuring

squeeze. "I guess you weren't kidding when you said your mom was a helicopter parent. Up to now, I thought it was kind of cute, the way she kept butting in, trying to help."

Her eyes glittered with frustration. "And now?"

He shrugged. "Frankly, it's a little scary, realizing she could drop everything to follow us to a job site."

Ginger leaned into Rand's touch. "She pulled herself together once, when she reacted like this, after my dad died. I'm sure she can do it again."

Figuring she needed more than simple hand-holding, Rand tugged her against his chest and wrapped his arms around her. "And in the meantime?" he asked, feeling the rapid beat of her heart.

Ginger blew out a weary breath and turned tortured eyes up to his. "We brace ourselves for even more interference."

How are you doing?" Josie asked Rand several days later when she ran into him outside city hall.

"Okay," he said. Given the fact he had been locked in the Boernes' attorney's office for at least twelve hours every day with the other members of the independent review board, evaluating all the proposals and red-flagging any potential problems, for the upcoming Q and A sessions.

"And Ginger? How has she been?"

Not as well, Rand admitted silently. She was on pins and needles as she waited to find out whether she would advance to the semifinal round or be eliminated. But he figured his mom knew that.

"Are she and Cordelia still on the outs?" Josie prodded.

"Pretty much, yeah."

Josie waited, sensing there was more. Needing to unburden himself to someone, Rand continued, "The day after Cordelia told us about the move to Summit, she came over to the cottage to apologize."

Josie paused. "What's wrong with that?"

Rand rubbed at the tense muscles in the back of his neck. "Cordelia also dropped off a binder of favorite family recipes."

His mom winced. "Let me guess. Ginger hasn't been near a stove since."

He nodded. "Not that this is necessarily a problem except that Ginger hasn't wanted *me* to cook anything for us, either. Instead she asks me to bring takeout for both of us every night on my way back from town."

Rand had humored Ginger, like countless expectant dads before him, because she was hormonal and totally stressed out. However, the "not cooking anything on principle" was beginning to get old. Especially when they had a freezer full of homemade dinners.

Rand studied his mom. "You understand where Ginger is coming from, don't you?"

Josie nodded. "This is a very tough business to break into, for anyone."

Rand remembered that little bit of family history. "But you made it happen anyway."

"Over both my parents' objections, since my dad thought the oil business was no place for a woman and my mother wanted me to be part of Dallas society."

Rand smiled, still not really able to envision his tomboy mother making her official debut to the social elite in a white gown and gloves, although he had seen the photos that proved she had indeed endured what she had considered the ultimate in public humiliation. "You quit that, too."

"Not until after my debutante years." Josie sighed. "And not without enduring a lot of quarreling with both my parents. Ginger is a strong, smart, independent woman, Rand. She'll figure out a way to handle Cordelia, same as you and you brothers have all found ways to deal with me when I've meddled in your lives."

Rand was glad his mother had finally backed off. It helped, not having to bicker with her, too. It also helped being able to come to her with his problems, at least when it came to understanding women. "What should I do in the meantime?"

"Be there for Ginger. But don't, under any conditions, try to tell her what to do."

That, Rand already knew. "And when it comes to Cordelia?"

Josie paused, thinking. "I'm not sure how successful I'll be, but I'll try to get Cordelia to ease up a little."

"I'd appreciate it. Ginger's got enough on her plate right now without dealing with her mom's disapproval."

Josie started to say something, then stopped. She gave him an odd look, but still didn't say what was on her mind. Finally she asked instead, "How is Ginger's preparation going for the Q and A sessions?"

Rand tensed. "She won't say." But Rand had a feeling, given the way his new wife had been walking around the cottage, scowling and muttering to herself when she and Maria weren't rehearsing together, not all that well.

Finally he admitted, "I'm trying to give Ginger the space she needs."

Josie nodded approvingly. "I'm sure she appreciates it."

Did she? It was hard to tell. All Rand knew for certain was that Cordelia's criticism of her daughter's ability to participate in an effective marriage had put a damper on his relationship with Ginger. He wasn't sure how to get them back on solid footing. He only knew that it wouldn't happen until Ginger found out whether she had won—or lost—the biggest business opportunity of her life.

When Rand walked in Monday evening Ginger was going through all the line-dried denim in her closet. He had missed her, during the hours he had been around, but there was no telling from her expression whether or not she had missed him.

Glad to be home again, nevertheless, he went to her side, watching as she tersely checked out one label, then another, and another. "Wardrobe crisis?"

Her lips twisted unhappily. "Something like that."

The shirt she had borrowed from him clearly wasn't the problem. She looked pretty and ultra-casual in the oversize light green button-up.

In no hurry to go anywhere, he lounged against the bureau, arms crossed at his chest. Steadfastly ignoring his presence, she shucked off the pair of paisley pajama pants she'd been wearing and pulled on a pair of denim. To her visible frustration, there was no way they would come even close to zipping. With a muttered oath, she took off the pants and tried another pair to the same result.

"Maybe you should buy some maternity clothes," Rand offered casually.

She sent him an irascible look and shook her head. "It's way too soon for that."

Rand didn't really see what the big deal was. Yes, her waistline was thickening, but only because their baby was growing inside her.

Ginger sat on the edge of the bed, the long tails of his shirt covering her bare thighs. "I am going to have to buy larger clothes, though."

"Want me to go with you?"

She flashed him a droll look. "To do what? Hold my purse?"

Rand shrugged. "Or get sizes for you, or whatever."

Not above doing what had to be done to get to spend more time with her, and perhaps regain some of their previous closeness and make love again, Rand used what leverage he had. "If you want people to think our relationship is as authentic as our skills in the field, we're going to have to be seen together at least some of the time. Otherwise, people are going to start to wonder what's going on with us."

That got her. "Okay, fine." Ginger vaulted to her feet and put on a pair of sexy black yoga pants with a roll top that ended several inches below her navel. "As long as we get dinner in town before we come back here."

Rand shrugged. "Fine with me." He could use a good meal and some quality time with his new bride.

Together, they headed for Summit, and once there, went straight to Callahan Mercantile & Feed, an old-fashioned general store that carried everything from camping gear to authentic Western wear.

Rand accompanied her inside. "So what are you looking for?"

She headed for the shelves of ladies' jeans and

plucked up several different sizes. "Loose-fitting, practical work clothes." She handed him a stack of different
styles and sizes, then moved on to the cotton vests and
men's twill shirts. Satisfied she had enough to try on,
she found a unisex fitting room located in the middle
of the clothing area. The look in her eyes said she did
not want him to come in with her, so he waited outside
the locked door.

And then waited. And waited. And waited.

Wondering what was going on in there, and hoping she wasn't starting to feel sick again, he moved
closer. "Ginger? Everything okay in there?" No answer.
"Honey?" he prompted, a little louder.

Hannah Callahan Daugherty, the proprietress of the
mercantile, appeared at his side. Married and a mother
herself, the slender brunette flashed an easy-going
smile. "How's it going?"

Rand wished to heck he knew. "I'm a little concerned
about my wife," he confessed.

A huff sounded from behind solid oak. "Oh, for
heaven's sake!" The dressing room door slid open
slightly and Ginger reached for him. "Just come in,"
she ordered, exasperated.

Mindful of the soft, feminine hand suddenly fisted
in his shirtfront, Rand shrugged good-naturedly.
"Women!"

Hannah laughed and moved off. "Just let me know if
you need anything," she said over her shoulder.

Ginger tugged Rand the rest of the way inside. As
he had feared, her eyes were red and glistening with
tears. "Must you make everything such a big deal?"
she snapped. He wasn't the one who had locked himself in here, crying.

"What's the problem?" he asked quietly, as calm as she was emotional.

She plucked at the sides of her jeans, which seemed to comfortably fit her thickening waistline but overwhelm everything else. Her lower lip trembling, she whispered back, "I look like I'm wearing jodhpurs, that's what. But I can't go down a size, because if I do, they won't fit me in the waist and I won't be able to get them zipped."

Rand eyed the pile of discarded garments. It certainly seemed as though she had been busy while he'd cooled his heels. "What about the other styles?"

Ginger threw up her hands. "They're even worse. I either can't get them on…or I can and the tummy on them sticks out a mile, making me look a lot more—" She gestured comically as if outlining the belly of a whale. "Than I already am," she finished finally.

Rand knew when he was in over his head. "Want me to call Hannah in?" Surely the storekeeper would know how to get a better fit.

"No!"

He leaned close enough to her ear, then dared ask, "Want me to take you to a maternity store up in Fort Stockton?"

Her glare turned lethal. "How do you know where the closest one is?"

Damn, she was pretty when she was agitated. He shrugged. "Same as always. I researched it online." He paused to smooth a lock of silky copper hair from her face. Tenderly, he tucked it behind her ear, then murmured, "You could always order something off the internet."

"There's no time for that. I have to find something to

wear right now, that I won't look ridiculous in." Moisture flooded her green eyes. She dashed away her tears with her knuckles, before they could fall.

He tried to simultaneously problem-solve and tease her out of her dejected mood. "You could borrow a pair of my jeans, the same way you do my shirts. Because those probably would work, since they're just sort of straight up and down." He illustrated with his hands. "Instead of all nipped in or curvy."

It had been a shot in the dark, born of sheer desperation.

Ginger's eyes lit up.

She let out a low, delighted laugh and palmed the center of his chest. "Out of the mouths of the unenlightened," she blurted.

Grabbing her phone, she quickly looked up the measurements on the pants she'd been wearing. He helped her convert them to men's sizing.

An hour later they left the store. Ginger had half a dozen pairs of men's jeans, a few men's shirts and a couple new ladies' vests—in a larger size, to accommodate her blossoming breasts—bundled together in a mercantile shopping bag.

She was wearing a new pair of men's jeans, too. "Feel better now?" Rand asked, winding a protective arm around her waist.

Ginger leaned into him briefly, looking happier and more relaxed than he had seen her in days. "Much. I should have gone for the 'Southwestern' Annie Hall slash Katherine Hepburn style of dressing much earlier."

He tucked her in closer to his side, predicting, "You'll have people talking."

"But it will be about why I'm suddenly electing to wear all men's clothing."

Her triumph was as much an aphrodisiac as her temper. In fact, everything about her got his engine running.

"And you'll say...?"

She winked. "That I would have done it a whole lot sooner if I had only known how much more comfortable guy's clothes were than gal's."

Rand grinned, glad she had solved her problem, and would be able to get through the next few weeks, or months, comfortably. Playfully he tweaked her nose. "So, back to the dinner you promised me..." His stomach was growling hungrily. As was hers.

She slanted him her usual feisty look. "We're having pizza. And I'm paying."

"Works for me." Matter of fact, anytime he was with her, anywhere he was with her, worked for him.

They paused to lock her new clothes in his pickup, then walked down Main Street. They were nearly to Salvio's Pizza Place when they saw Maria standing in front of the fire station, where her truck was parked. Conrad was standing next to her, and they were talking. It didn't appear to be a particularly pleasant conversation.

"What do you think that's about?" Rand asked.

Ginger looked pained. "I don't know."

His protective instincts kicked into high gear. "Want me to intervene?"

"No. Maria has three teenage sons, a husband who is not always known for his work ethic and a crew of roughnecks working for her. She can handle Conrad the same way she does all the rest."

They watched as Maria shook her head firmly and walked past Conrad, who still seemed to be pleading his case, even after Maria got in behind the wheel.

"Well, whatever he wanted, he didn't get it," Ginger observed when Conrad got in his vehicle and drove away, too.

Rand let out a low sound of agreement. "At least he's not still bothering you."

Briefly, guilt flashed across Ginger's face, but she recovered quickly as they continued down the street. Then she paused, presumably to look at the menu posted in the window. "Actually, Conrad is still texting and calling and emailing me, every day, telling me it's not too late. I can still come back to Profitt Oil."

Rand had assumed that had all stopped, and was dismayed to find it was still ongoing. Although he did understand why Profitt would be loathe to let Ginger slip out of his life. Rand felt the same way.

He leaned a shoulder against the glass. "What do you say to him?" he asked, curious.

Ginger made a noncommittal sound. "Nothing. I already answered him once, in person. There's no reason to do so again. Eventually he'll get the message."

Rand hoped that was so.

Ginger rocked forward on the heels of her boots and studied him thoughtfully. "You're not jealous, are you?"

He lifted his brow. "Should I be?"

Chapter 11

What did it mean if Rand was jealous? Ginger wondered, trying not to read too much into his droll retort. Especially if he wasn't the kind of guy to ever get jealous?

"No, of course there is no reason for you to be even the tiniest bit jealous." Although she knew she was playing with fire, feminine devilry made her pursue the issue. She narrowed her gaze. "Why on earth would you be, anyway?" It wasn't as if her ex had anything on the incredible man in front of her. Rand was not only ruggedly sexy in that all-man-to-her-woman way. He was funny and charming to boot.

Still not looking all that concerned, he shrugged. "Because I don't want my wife being pursued by another man."

Admiring his confidence, she reiterated, "Well, you

don't have to worry about that. The only man I want is you." Realizing belatedly how that sounded, she wrinkled her nose. She hadn't meant to be so possessive, either. "You know what I mean," she added hastily.

He met her gaze, the corners of his mouth barely turning up, and waited for her to continue.

Reluctantly she did. "I mean, we're married. And hence, exclusive."

"Anything else?" He studied her, his expression inscrutable.

Actually there was. But Ginger didn't want to get into that now, didn't want to open herself up to hurt. "Yes. I'm starving." She let her glance fall discretely to her tummy, then stood on tiptoe to whisper into his ear, "And I'm pretty sure you-know-who is, too."

As always, the mention of the baby they were having united them in a common cause.

"So what are we waiting for?" He brushed a kiss to her cheek, then, hand to her waist, ushered her inside the pizza restaurant. They settled in a cozy booth in the back, and placed their order.

As Ginger had expected, their dinner was delicious. And Rand was a charming dinner companion. They finished off the pizza and salad, then lingered over a huge slice of cheesecake, topped with fresh blueberries, strawberries and whipped cream.

Aware she'd eaten her half of the shared dessert, and maybe a little more, Ginger put a hand to her tummy and groaned. "I have a feeling I'm going to regret this."

He chuckled. "You'll be fine."

He took out his wallet and put his card on the receipt tray. The waitress took off with it before Ginger could stop her.

She frowned at Rand. "Hey, I'm supposed to pay!"

He shook his head, as intent on being in charge as ever. "Really can't let you do that…"

Why did he always have to be such a man?

"Then I'm just going to owe you."

His eyes twinkled. He seemed more than ready for whatever she sent his way.

"That sounds fine." He leaned over and kissed her slowly, lingeringly on the lips. "More than fine, actually."

Ginger hadn't meant to respond, but when he dipped his head and kissed her again, even more evocatively this time, she found herself kissing him back, just as sweetly.

When he finally moved away, a round of applause followed.

Ginger flushed at the reaction of their audience. Rand smiled even more wickedly, and then moved to kiss her again. "Playing Mr. Newlywed to the hilt, aren't you?" she commented when they finally pulled apart.

His eyes darkened emotionally. "I'm definitely starting something."

She knew he was.

She just wasn't sure where it would lead.

Where she *wanted* it to lead.

They were quiet on the drive home. Taking advantage of the blessed silence, Ginger turned her attention to the passing scenery and mulled over ways to keep the expectations they'd started their union with intact.

And only when they had turned into the lane leading to their cottage at the Red Sage, did she finally turn to him and speak what was on her mind.

"Do you think we should add sex to our marriage contract?"

* * *

Rand had to hand it to Ginger. Just when he thought he was beginning to understand her, she went and laid something like that on him. "I don't know." He cut the motor on his truck.

The spring evening was pleasantly warm and serene. The sun was setting, against a backdrop of granite mountains in a blue-gray sky. Closer to the cottages, well-tended beds of red sage and a collection of other wildflowers and natives grasses bloomed.

"Do you really think we need to do that?"

Ginger inhaled a deep breath. She seemed apprehensive again. "Well…maybe." She shrugged and released the catch on her seat belt, then sat back against the seat. "It's clear we still desire each other."

He wondered if she had any idea how cute she looked in men's clothing. Or how much he wanted to unbutton her shirt right now.

"And always will."

The stubborn tilt was back to her pretty chin. "We don't know that."

Body hardening, he watched her exit the cab, her movements as graceful and feminine as the rest of her.

She reached around to open the rear passenger door. She stuck her head in, and continued her argument determinedly. "My body is going to change, and that may change the way you feel about having sex with me."

"You're probably right." Ignoring her quick look of surprise, he circled around his truck to help carry her shopping bags inside. He set them down and watched as she closed the door behind him. "Probably, as time goes along, I'm going to want to make love to you even more."

Her rosy lips took on an even more mutinous twist. "I'm serious!"

He walked around, shutting the blinds one by one, while she paused to take off her boots, then turned on the lamps, lighting the cottage with a soft, romantic glow.

If she needed reassurance, he was here to give it. "So am I." He caught her against him and stroked her hair with the palm of his hand. "You're only...what? Three months along? And already your breasts are full and luscious and spilling out of the cups of your bra."

She moaned. "Rand."

He moved around behind her until there was no space between them, nothing but pleasure. "Your tummy has this intriguing little slope." He ran his hand sensually over the baby bump.

She shuddered in response and her eyes drifted closed.

He pressed a smile into the softness of her hair. "And your thighs. I don't think they've ever been this silky." His hand slid between them. "Or the most delectable part of you, so..." He unzipped her jeans and slid his hand inside. "Wet."

She throbbed at the tender stroking of his palm. "That's because pregnancy fills me full of hormones."

"That's part of it," he murmured, turning her to face him.

"What's the rest?"

Rand tugged her jeans and panties off, and lifted her onto the counter. Body aching with the need to claim her, he stepped between her spread thighs. Their glances met. He imagined what it would be like to be with her, like this, not just until their baby was born, but forever.

"It's basic chemistry." He undid the buttons of her shirt and lavished the curve of her cheek, the lobe of her ear, her throat, with his lips and the tip of his tongue. She quivered; her full, voluptuous breasts taut against the sheer fabric of her bra. "Whenever we're around each other for any time at all, I want you, and you want me."

She caught her breath. "But…"

He threaded his hands through her hair. "No buts, Ginger. It's true." And proceeded to kiss her, again and again, until she was as hungry for him as he was for her. His head got a little lighter, his body got harder. And still their mouths meshed as he consumed what little resistance remained.

Ginger kept trying to keep her feelings out of it. This was just sex, fueled by a million different things. Except the one thing that counted. The one thing that could have made them last forever. *Love.* He hadn't mentioned it. She didn't dare. Because she knew if she let herself fall for Rand in that way, there would be no turning back. She'd want him in a way he had never been prepared to give, and that would ruin everything.

So she forced herself to concentrate only on the warmth of his touch and the urgency of his body. Desperate to feel the heat of him surrounding her and filling her body, she ordered brusquely, "Undress. I mean it, Rand. Now."

Instead he tugged off her shirt, her bra.

And brought her right back against him.

The nakedness of her inner thighs brushed against the sturdy fabric of his denim. His lips lightly moved against hers, and he kissed her until she felt her soul stripped bare. Tongue plunging into her mouth, hands moving upward to claim her breasts.

Again and again they exchanged wet, hot, hungry kisses and she welcomed him in, welcomed him with everything she had.

Catching his head between her hands as he worshiped her breasts, her thighs.

Bringing her to the edge of the counter and holding her there…plunging her into passion, then sweet rapture, as a violent shudder racked her entire body.

She tangled her hands in the silky hair at his nape, bringing him upward, forcing his mouth back to hers. And then, finally, his boots and jeans did go. And so did his briefs and his shirt. He stood there, in all his naked glory, wanting her as much as she wanted him. She appreciated all the gorgeous male muscle and whorls of dark silky hair lingering over his navel, his thighs and the most masculine part of him, before returning her gaze back to his.

He smiled.

"Ready whenever you are."

He laughed. And crushed her to him. She ached with the need to be filled, and yearned with the desire to be loved. "Now, please," she whispered.

His eyes softened. "With pleasure."

She braced her hands on his shoulders. He lifted her toward him, and up slightly, against him. Their joining was everything she wanted, everything she dreamed. She gave herself over to him, to this, the marriage she'd never imagined possible. And for one long moment, as their bodies exalted and their hearts sang, she let herself imagine that maybe…just maybe…their relationship might last.

* * *

Rand went to sleep with Ginger wrapped snugly in his arms and woke at two in the morning, alone. Concerned she might be feeling ill again, he went in search of his wife. She was curled up on the love seat, a blanket across her lap, oblivious to everything but the laptop computer in front of her. He stood framed in the doorway, for a moment just taking in his new wife.

The softness of her breasts, pushed against her pale blue pajama top. Her long copper hair, tousled from sleep...her fair cheeks still bearing the glow of their recent lovemaking. She was intent on whatever she was studying on-screen, her dreamy concentration only adding to the gentle contentment that seemed to radiate from her these days. Pregnancy agreed with her. So did marriage, though he doubted he could get her to admit that. Yet.

She turned, spying him in the doorway.

He smiled, and glad for any excuse to be near her, sauntered closer. "Can't sleep?"

"Checking my email."

He went to the fridge and poured them each a glass of milk. He closed the fridge with his foot. "I thought the Boernes weren't supposed to notify the semifinal winners until tomorrow morning."

"They're not."

"Then…" He settled beside her. "You're looking at cribs?"

Their fingers brushed as she accepted the glass he gave her. "And baby clothes. And furniture. I was trying to get an idea of what it was going to cost to outfit a nursery."

She moved the cursor to the bar along the top of the

screen that showed him the other webpages she had been perusing.

"You're getting excited."

She admitted as much with a nod. "Aren't you?"

"I am. But I also know you need your sleep."

She gave him the look she always gave when anyone tried to tell her what to do, think, feel… "Uh-huh."

He grinned at her decided lack of enthusiasm. Figuring he knew just how to get her where she should be, however, he waited until they'd both finished their milk. Wordlessly he set the glasses and laptop aside, stood and swept her into his arms.

"We're not making love again," she warned.

He carried her to the bed. "I know."

But they did make love. And this time they slept, wrapped in each other's arms, until eight the next morning.

Ginger was the first to stir. She lifted her head, looked at the clock and groaned. "I forgot to set my alarm."

Aware how hard she'd been working, he kissed her brow, then eased from the bed. "Sleep in."

"I can't." But then Ginger sighed and snuggled deeper into her pillow. "Maybe just five more minutes…"

She was fast asleep by the time he was dressed.

Whistling, Rand headed for the buffet, figuring he would surprise her with breakfast in bed. He was halfway to the main house when he saw Cordelia's white Cadillac parked in front of the guest ranch office, his mother moving hurriedly inside. He had no idea what was going on, and honestly, didn't think he *wanted* to know. But when he passed the open windows, Cordelia's sweet, plaintive voice floated out to him. "I think we should do it, Josie. I think it would help."

His mother argued back. "More likely, Cordelia, it will make things worse."

And "worse," Rand knew, was something that they did not need.

Not when his marriage to Ginger was finally become as real as it needed to be. He took a detour into the building, bypassed the reception area and walked into the party-planning suite.

Cordelia was dressed in an elegant business suit.

His mother wore jeans.

Both were poring over a lot of pale pink and light blue party stuff. Wondering what the hell was up, he asked, "What's going on?"

"Nothing," both women said in unison, stepping in front of the stacks on Cordelia's desk.

The way the two moms were blushing guiltily and wouldn't quite look him in the eye said a lot. None of it good, Rand thought. He pointed to a cardboard cutout of a stork carrying a bundle that said, Good News Is Coming Soon! He grimaced. "Tell me this doesn't have anything to do with me and Ginger."

Another telltale silence. Rand took a hard, assessing look at his mother, then another at Cordelia. He shoved a hand through his hair and exhaled wearily. He couldn't say how or why, but… "You know. Don't you?"

For a second no one said anything, no one moved. The two women seemed to know they were being presumptuous. Finally, Cordelia threw up her hands and looked at him as if he were the idiot in the room. "Of course we know. Your mother and I both knew the moment we saw you and Ginger together on your wedding day. The way she was glowing and you were strutting around like a proud papa to be!"

His mom added informatively, "An even bigger clue to us was the fact you were getting married at all, never mind so quickly, when you had both told everyone after your divorces that you were never walking down the aisle again."

Rand scowled. "If it was so obvious, why didn't you say anything to us then?" he demanded.

His mother sighed. "Because we didn't want to deter you from doing the right thing for your baby."

"And because I knew the moment I saw you with my daughter that you were the man she's been waiting her entire life to meet and fall in love with," Cordelia said.

Except he and Ginger weren't "in love" with each other, Rand thought. Not yet. Maybe not ever. And, as long as they stayed as happy as they had been the night before, he was beginning to be okay with that, too.

He shook his head, as if that would clear it, then went back to what the two women had been quarreling about when he entered. "So why were you arguing?"

Cordelia stiffened. "I want us to throw you and Ginger a surprise baby shower in the party barn."

"Not gonna happen," Rand decreed. "In fact, no more surprises of any kind."

Josie folded her arms. "I told you he wouldn't like it, Cordelia."

"Ginger won't, either," Rand added.

"Why not?" Ginger's mom argued. "You can't tell me my daughter's not happy about having your baby!"

Of course Ginger was happy; they both were—that went without saying. It was a new life. A part of him. A part of her. What was there not to be happy about?

"She doesn't want anyone to know because she's worried they will hold it against her when it comes to business," Rand explained.

"And she's right to think that way." Josie backed up his claim. "Wildcatting is still largely a man's domain. There are a lot of people who don't want women on job sites period, never mind pregnant women."

"You faced the same discrimination?" Cordelia asked her, looking thoughtful.

Josie nodded. "Naturally, I worked around it, just as Ginger's doing." She reached over and squeezed Cordelia's arm. "I know you mean well. We all do. But you and I have to step back and give these two lovebirds the time and space they need."

"And that means," Rand concurred, "Ginger's 'news' is hers to tell whenever and however she sees fit."

Cordelia studied him with a mother's keen eye. "You really adore my daughter, don't you?"

Rand nodded. More than anyone would ever know. "So you'll do what I ask?" He looked at both mothers. "And pretend you don't know?"

Josie and Cordelia nodded in unison.

That settled, Rand headed over to the main house. He filled a to-go platter for them to share, then circled back to the cottage.

As he expected, Ginger was awake. She had a broad smile on her face.

Rand set their breakfast on the dining table. "What's going on?"

She pointed to her computer screen. "Maria and I made the semifinals—that's what! We drew Slot 9 on the Q and A sessions tomorrow!"

"That's wonderful." He crossed the room and wrapped his arms around her.

Ginger hugged him back. "Of course it's not just me." She babbled on, reaching for the can of ginger ale she'd been sipping. "Profitt Oil and your mother's company were chosen, too. But this is great. I'm officially in the running."

"Good thing I brought you some breakfast, then." He winked.

She put a tentative hand to her tummy. "Thanks, but…" She took another small sip of soda. "I think it's just going to be saltine crackers and soda for now." She rose, already in high gear. "I've got to call Maria. Get a shower. Prep for the Q and A!"

The rest of the morning went swiftly.

By noon, Rand had received a phone call, too.

Not sure how *his* news would go over, he went to find Ginger, who was sitting on the back porch, running through her data. She took one look at him and sat back in her chair. "What's wrong?"

Reluctantly he filled her in. "Dot and Clancy have asked me to sit in on the Q and A sessions."

Her brow furrowed. "I thought only three independent geologists were going to do that."

"Initially, that was the plan. Now they want an environmental engineer there to handle any issues that may arise. And since I've already vetted all the proposed drilling plans…"

She considered that with her usual cool professionalism. "Makes sense."

"Are you okay with this?" She'd worked so hard. He didn't want to do anything that could possibly throw her off her game. And having him in the room could distract her.

Ginger pushed a hand through her hair. "Would it matter if I wasn't? You've already refused to recuse yourself once."

He'd since had time to regret that. "For this round, the identities of the participants won't be hidden, unlike the way they were in the initial proposal review."

She studied him, as if wondering why he was even asking her this. "Is this new attitude of yours because we put sex back on the table? And you don't want us to take it off again?"

It was deeper than that.

Not sure she should hear that now, though, when her attention should be solely on the oil lease she was trying to acquire, he merely shrugged. "Let's just say I'm very invested in keeping peace in our family." *As well as continuing to make love to you every chance we get.* "So if this is going to make you uncomfortable in any way…"

Abruptly she looked vaguely insulted, almost irked. "No. I want you there," she responded quickly, then paused, struggling to explain. "I feel better when you are around. Safer. And I know that's odd. Not to mention totally out of character for me. Let's chalk it up to a pregnancy thing, okay?"

Damn but she was cute when she was hormonal.

Chuckling, Rand took her in his arms. "I like being with you, too."

Ginger spent the rest of the day alternately feeling very confident and very anxious. To the point she was considering her options when Rand ambled in at dinnertime, carrying takeout from the local barbecue.

His gaze drifted over her. "Still can't get hold of Maria?"

Ginger brought plates, silverware and napkins to the table. "I've emailed, texted and called her repeatedly all day."

Rand filled two glasses with water and ice. "Is it possible she's on a job?"

"No." Ginger sat opposite him. "The one she and her crew were working ended late last week."

His gaze swept her thoroughly. "Maybe Maria hasn't checked her messages."

"Maybe."

He reached across the table and took her hand. "I'm sure she'll check them tonight."

Ginger hadn't felt the need to lean on a man in a long time. She felt it now. "You're right. I'm being paranoid." Deliberately, she shook off her low mood. "Maria's probably just been prepping, same as me."

He opened the paper bags and set the containers of mesquite-smoked chicken, potato salad, green beans, slaw and peach cobbler on the table.

"Looks good."

He grinned, already loading their plates. "Got to have you strong and fit for tomorrow."

Smiling, Ginger took two bites and put her fork down.

Concern lit his gaze. As always, he knew the second it hit. "Morning sickness?"

Deliberately she took a deep breath and willed the nausea away. "Or evening."

Rand took his cell phone out of his shirt pocket. "Want me to call your OB-GYN?"

The sight of him reacting like a parody of an expectant dad made her heart sing. "No. I see her next week. I'll talk to her then, if it doesn't improve." Beginning to feel a tiny bit better, Ginger leaned toward him. "You should go with me. Meet her. I mean," she added hastily, suddenly wondering if she was asking too much, "if you can."

His smile deepened. "Of course I can."

They resumed dining. Rand ate with the hearty appetite one expected of a man his size. Ginger tried her best, but still couldn't really eat anything. Finally she pushed back her chair, knowing if she didn't get away from the sight and smell of the deliciously prepared food soon...

Rand joined her as they carried their dishes to the sink. He laid a comforting hand at her back. "Can I do something for you? Make you some chamomile tea or something?"

"No. But don't worry... I'll be okay." Ginger swallowed hard. With the tips of her fingers, she blotted the perspiration dampening her hairline. "I haven't actually thrown up since that one time. I've always been able to work through it."

Determined this would not be the exception to the rule—bad enough he'd seen her hugging the toilet bowl once—she walked out onto the back porch. A nice breeze was sifting through the screens, and the mountain air was cool and bracing. She truly appreciated the beautiful scenery as the peaceful evening descended. Gradually, her pulse rate slowed. Her stomach settled.

Able to see she was finally feeling better, Rand laced

an arm around her shoulders. "I'm really proud of you, you know."

The funny thing was, she was proud of him, too. Ginger turned toward him. The fronts of their bodies touched as she tilted her face up to his. She loved it when he held her like this. So tenderly and protectively. "About the job?"

He sifted a hand lovingly through her hair. "The way you handle everything that comes your way."

She splayed trembling hands across the solid warmth of his chest. "I don't know about that," she confessed. "I'm feeling pretty nervous right now."

He wrapped his arms around her, gathered her closer yet. "You're going to do fine."

He said it with such conviction she could almost believe him. She leaned her head on his shoulder and let him hold her. "Just keep saying that."

Keep making all my dreams come true.

Chapter 12

Ginger stared at Maria the following morning, feeling as if the rug had just been pulled out from beneath her. "What do you mean you can't work with me on the Boerne lease?"

"I'm sorry. I really am." Maria wrung her hands. "But I have to do what's best for my family and my crew. The job I've been offered is a one-year gig. Guaranteed. Even if we were to win, which..." Doubt crept into her voice. "You know how stiff this competition is..."

Ginger thought about what she and Rand had seen in Summit the evening before. "Did Conrad have anything to do with this?" she asked furiously.

Maria shook her head. "He made me an offer. I turned him down flat, same as you. This gig came from the Southwestern Oil Company late last night."

A reputable midsize firm, not involved in the bidding in Summit County.

"Part of the deal was I start today."

Ginger held up her hand. "I understand." And the hell of it was, she did. Having a family changed everything.

"I'm sorry, Ginger. Really I am." Maria pivoted and hurried down the sidewalk to her truck.

Ginger stood there, watching numbly as her ex-drilling partner drove away.

Rand came up behind her. "What are you going to do?"

Good question. "At the moment? Try not to lose my breakfast." Ginger whirled and went back inside the cottage.

Only a step behind her, Rand stood just inside the front door. Ginger stared at him. Although she wasn't scheduled to appear until much later in the day, he had to be there within the hour. "Don't you have to be going?" she snapped.

"If you need me…"

She lifted a hand. "I'll be fine. Really." Hand to his shoulder, Ginger pushed her husband out the door.

He hesitated on the other side of the threshold. "Call me if you need me."

Ginger nodded. But they both knew she wouldn't. Like it or not, this was something she had to figure out for herself.

Hours later, she was still struggling with the recent turn of events.

She drove into town, fighting morning sickness every step of the way. Aware it was Conrad's turn to defend his company's proposal, she avoided the lawyer's office where the meetings were being held, and stopped by the pharmacy instead. Sweat gathered at her hairline as she perused the aisles.

As always happened when she wanted to appear incognito, a clerk appeared at her side. "Are you feeling all right? You look a little green."

No surprise—she felt awful. Ginger took another deep, enervating breath. "I was looking for some spearmint lozenges or lemon drops."

"They're with the candy." She led Ginger two aisles over and gave her a sympathetic smile. "If you need anything else, let me know."

Ginger nodded. She picked up one package of each, another bottle of chilled ginger ale and a sports drink containing electrolytes.

She paid for her purchases and went back out to her truck, drove to the park down the street from the attorney's office and sat, with the windows open, letting the spring breeze blow over her. Eyes closed, she breathed in through her nose, out through her mouth. Until finally the symptoms subsided.

Eventually, Ginger opened her eyes. Another disaster averted. Now all she had to do was get through the Q and A.

Rand knew the moment Ginger walked into the conference room to face the Boernes, their attorney and the four-member panel that she was in a bad way.

He doubted anyone else knew what was wrong, thanks to the cheerful smile she had plastered on her face.

Unfortunately, given what he had already heard that day, he knew her dismay was only going to get worse.

Dot Boerne began. "First of all, Ginger, we want you

to know that Clancy and I loved your proposal. You came up with a drilling plan that was not only the most cost-effective of all the proposals we received, but did not disturb the parts of our land we hold most dear."

Ginger smiled. "I'm glad you liked it."

"Unfortunately we understand that you've had some bad news. That your drilling partner, Maria Gonzales, has dropped out of the competition and taken her crew to another job."

For a moment Ginger looked taken aback. Recovering, she squared her shoulders and pushed on with her usual confidence. "That's true, but I know I can find replacement workers who are just as talented."

Clancy Boerne grinned and nodded approvingly. "In fact, you've already done so, haven't you?"

Ginger blinked. Clearly, Rand thought, she didn't know what Boerne was talking about.

The older gentleman continued. "Profitt Oil has offered to step in. And given that you've worked for them in the past—"

"Where did you hear this?" Ginger interrupted pleasantly.

"Conrad mentioned it when his team was in here earlier today."

Rand watched as Ginger nodded, her expression grave. "I'm sorry you were given that information. It's incorrect. Yes, I was asked to go back to work for the company, but I have refused, and will continue to do so."

Rand relaxed in relief.

"Then…?" Dot persisted.

"I still want to do the job, but it's going to mean finding another crew…"

The Boernes nodded their understanding, but they weren't happy. More questions followed. Though it was clear by the time the Q and A session ended that Ginger had lost whatever edge she had walked in with.

Rand followed her outside during the brief break that followed.

Hands on her hips, she glared at him. "You knew?"

He nodded. "There was no way I could warn you."

Briefly, hurt and dismay flickered in her eyes. She looked ready to break into a string of roughneck-ready words. "Of course you couldn't."

Rand kept his physical distance. "Your ex-husband is a horse's behind, but I still have a job to do here, and I have to be fair."

Ginger nodded, then pivoted sharply and headed for her truck. Rand followed, hard on her heels, his urge to protect her stronger than ever. "Where are you going?"

She jerked open the driver's door, threw her briefcase in and climbed behind the wheel. "Exactly where you'd think. To find my no good ex-husband and give him a piece of my mind!" She drove off.

Torn between his duty to hear the last Q and A of the day—which happened to involve his mother's company—or see to his wife, Rand went back inside. The choice was easy. "Sorry about this, but my wife needs me," he said frankly and without apology. "You all are going to have to carry on without me."

It didn't take long for Ginger to spot Conrad's Porsche. It was in front of the steakhouse on Main Street. She parked her truck and went inside. Conrad was seated at the bar, bourbon in hand. He had a smug, happy look on his face.

Although she was still fighting waves of ever-increasing nausea, she was determined to have this out with him here and now.

She tapped him on the shoulder and he slowly turned around. "Hey, darlin'…" His voice was slurred. It was as if he, too, knew he had lost his bid for the Boerne oil lease.

"Were you responsible for Maria getting a job with another oil company?"

Conrad squinted thoughtfully, as a garlicky smell Ginger might have appreciated under any other circumstances floated in from the dining room.

Her ex took another sip of bourbon as she swallowed and tried not to breathe in. "I might have mentioned to a colleague or two that she was awfully good—had to be if she were going to partner up with you—and relatively inexpensive, too. Compared to some of the other outfits around."

Conrad's needling smile deepened, as did the resentment in his gaze. "I also might have mentioned there was a very narrow window, in which to steal her away from all this Boerne ranch business. Why?" He chuckled mirthlessly, his wounded ego showing. "Did your friend back out on you? Let you down, the way you let me down? Or…wait. Have you come here to beg my forgiveness in front of all these people, so I'll bail you out of the mess you're in?"

Ginger's fists knotted at her sides. It was all she could do not to punch him in the face. "You conniving, mean-spirited snake…"

Conrad set his glass down and rose slowly. "It was a mistake to tell the Boernes that you would never under any circumstances work with me or anyone at Profitt Oil again."

His bourbon-scented breath was even more unpleasant than the garlicky smell. Ginger reeled backward. "How c-could you…?" she sputtered.

Conrad raised his cell phone. "Because their attorney telephoned me to verify, as soon as you left the room," he said, leaning in, his low voice turning even uglier.

With effort, Ginger held her ground. "So what?"

"So now it's my turn to ruin your business prospects," Conrad threatened.

Without warning, Rand came up behind Ginger and stepped protectively in beside her.

His timing stank.

Unaware that the last thing she wanted—or needed—at that particular moment was to have her husband come in to fight her battles for her, Rand put a gentle hand on Ginger's waist. Furiously, she shook off his touch. The people in the bar, which were mostly oil men, began to chuckle.

"I've got this," Ginger hissed as yet another wave of smells—this time some sort of pan-seared fish—wafted in from the dining room.

Muscle working convulsively in his jaw, Rand stayed exactly where he was, but did not attempt to touch her again.

Determined to further the show they were now putting on for everyone in the steakhouse bar, Conrad tilted his head in a mocking manner. "Well, isn't that sweet. Looks like the little woman—or should I say wife?—has emasculated you, too."

More chuckles. A gasp. And a swift, shouted prediction of trouble to come.

"But then, that's what you do, isn't it, darlin'?" Conrad turned back to Ginger. "You marry a man with great oil company connections and you use him to try to get into the executive ranks. Only in this case, the oil company you have your eye on eventually running is helmed by a woman. So you probably think your master plan will be even easier to execute."

No one who knew Josie Corbett-Wyatt McCabe would ever think the female wildcatter was able to be pushed around.

Ginger shook her head vehemently. "I never wanted to take over Profitt Oil," she informed everyone in the room.

"Really? 'Cause it seems like you did a pretty good job of showing me up within the company, when you were my wife. And then when my father and I finally understood your game, you divorced me and lassoed him." Conrad pointed to Rand.

Aware her husband was holding on to his own temper by the slightest of threads, Ginger retorted, "That's not why I married Rand."

"Yeah?" Conrad downed the rest of his drink, then followed it with a short, resentful laugh. He leered at her. "Then why did you marry him in such a great big hurry if it wasn't to somehow influence what happened from here on out? Are you going to tell me you love him? 'Cause I don't buy it. There's something else going on here."

There was. But Ginger couldn't reveal it, not with the Boerne decision still hanging in the balance. Sickness overwhelmed her as another wave of assorted food smells assaulted her. Aware she was about to embarrass them all, she told Conrad grimly, "You're a jerk, you know that?"

And then, unable to fight it a second longer, she leaned over and threw up all over his fancy rattlesnake boots.

The problem with throwing up, after two entire days of trying not to throw up, was that Ginger couldn't seem to stop. Even after her stomach was emptied, the dry heaves continued.

That was how she ended up in the emergency room cubicle at Summit hospital, with Rand at her side, slowly but surely easing her humiliation and making sure she got everything she needed.

Two bags of IV fluids and some anti-nausea medicine later, she was finally able to catch her breath and turn her attention to the loving man beside her.

She wasn't the only one who looked as though they had just been through hell. Rand's usual calm was shattered, his expression turbulent, his jaw tight.

Ginger met his eyes. "Sorry I let it get that far."

"Probably no sorrier than Conrad's boots."

His joke broke the tension, and she laughed. "Somehow I have the feeling my ex is not going to be bothering us again."

Rand's eyes glittered with humor. "Probably not."

Their gazes meshed. Ginger squeezed Rand's hand.

"I know what I said earlier, but the truth is, I'm glad you were there. It helped, knowing you had my back."

"Even if you didn't want me to actually step in and defend you?"

Ginger nodded.

Tenderness radiated from him. "I'm glad I was there, too." He tightened his fingers on her.

Another heartfelt moment passed.

A nurse, who had been standing there quietly waiting, shook her head and muttered, "Lovebirds." With a wink of approval, she exited and promptly returned with the E.R. doctor, Thad Garner.

The nurse wheeled the ultrasound closer to Ginger's gurney as Dr. Garner asked, "You two heard the baby's heartbeat yet?"

Rand and Ginger shook their heads.

"Well, you're in for a treat." The doctor smiled as the nurse spread gel across Ginger's tummy, switched on the machine, then handed him the wand. On the television screen, they saw what looked like liquid moving waves. Then, as he continued moving the wand over Ginger's belly, the shape of a tiny baby appeared. It was one thing to know you were pregnant via test results— it was another to actually see your little one nestled snugly in your womb. Ginger gasped in amazement. Head, body, fingers, toes… All were there.

Tears of happiness flooded Ginger's eyes. Wonder filled her heart. And then the sound. *Th-thump. Th-thump. Th-thump.* Their baby's steady, strong heartbeat echoed through the room.

"It's too early to tell if it is a boy or a girl yet…" Dr. Garner said cheerfully. He grinned at the emotional parents-to-be. "But all looks good." He printed out a photo for them, then handed it over. Rand and Ginger perused it together joyously.

Dr. Garner continued, more seriously, "But we need to do something about the nausea, so that you don't get this sick again, because hyperemesis is definitely not good for the baby. I talked to your OB-GYN over in Marfa. We agreed you need to take it easy for a few days. And we're sending you home with some anti-nausea medication, to take as needed. It will make you sleepy, so don't drive or operate heavy machinery while you're on it, okay?"

They nodded and thanked the doctor. He slipped out. The nurse removed the IV from Ginger's arm, and Ginger was free to dress. She looked at Rand gratefully. "You've been really great today, you know that?" Tears misted her vision.

"Hey." Gazing down at her tenderly, he traced a thumb beneath her eye and kissed her cheek. "That's what husbands are for."

They didn't talk much on the drive back to the cottage. The medication had indeed made Ginger sleepy, and she dozed most of the way. She was so wobbly upon arrival that Rand picked her up and carried her through the door to their cottage, and all the way to their bed.

Some of their neighbors saw and chuckled.

Ginger moaned and rested her head against his broad chest. "They probably think it's some honeymoon thing."

Rand grinned. "Yet another benefit to being married." He set her down gently, then went to help her ease off her boots. "Pajamas now? Or later?"

"Actually…"

He waited.

Ginger pushed herself up on her elbows. "You're not going to believe it, but… I'm actually hungry."

Rand sat beside her. He aimed to please. "What do you want?"

Ginger grunted in frustration and rested her head on

her bent knees. "What do I want? Or what can I have?" They were two different things.

He kissed the top of her head. "The first."

Ginger tested her steadiness, and found, now that she'd been sitting up a minute, she felt a lot better. "Well…" She squinted, thinking. "I'd kill for my mother's homemade chicken noodle soup."

Rand rose. "I could ask her to make some."

Ginger caught his wrist before he could spring into action. "No. I can't push my mom away for being too intrusive one moment and then summon her at the first sign of trouble. It's not fair."

Rand scrubbed a hand across his jaw. "I don't think she would see it that way. I think she'd be grateful to help."

Ginger went to the bureau and pulled out a pair of loose-fitting cotton pajamas. "That's the problem. Once my mom starts, she doesn't know how to stop helping."

"And that's the only reason you don't want your mom here, because she's been too pushy in the past?"

Leave it to her husband to see even her most closely guarded anxiety. Reluctantly, Ginger admitted to herself that the being-too-close-for-comfort thing with her mom sometimes went both ways. Deciding on impulse that she wanted a shower, too, Ginger got out a clean towel and washcloth, and stashed them in the bathroom.

"If I were to see my mom right now, I think the fact I'm pregnant would come spilling out. And I don't want to tell our families that way. I want it to be a totally happy occasion, with everyone we love gathered together."

Their glances met in the bathroom mirror. "Kind of

like the engagement-party-slash-wedding announce-ment we missed?"

"Yeah." She paused, studying him, too. "Do you get that?" She knew it was sort of corny.

"I do." He lingered nearby while she brushed her teeth. "We may not have started out our marriage in the most orthodox way, but we can publicly start out the pregnancy in a way that mirrors the joy we feel."

Ginger blotted her mouth. "And it's only a few more days. Once the Boernes make a decision—" and she knew what her immediate work future held "—then you and I can start thinking about how and when we're going to tell people our 'news.'"

Rand was just hanging up the phone when Ginger came out of the bathroom fifteen minutes later. She was clad in her favorite pair of loose-fitting pink-and-white-striped pajamas that buttoned up the front. She had a white towel wrapped around her head, and her feet were bare. She still looked tired, but her color was better and she seemed to be moving more energetically.

"Who was on the phone?" Ginger asked, settling in a corner of the love seat.

"Our moms."

She paused in the act of unwinding the towel from her hair. "They heard?" Her cheeks turned a little pinker.

Noting how good she smelled—like the citrusy soap and shampoo she used—Rand sat beside her.

"Everyone in town heard."

She groaned and covered her face with her hands. "What did you say?"

"The same thing I plan to tell everyone—that your

illness was a combination of exhaustion, stress and dietary indiscretion."

Ginger worked a comb through her hair. "That sounds ladylike."

"Doesn't it?" He winked and they exchanged grins. "Anyway," Rand pushed on seriously, "they both know you're fine." *And that the baby is fine, too.* He cleared his throat. "And the doctor said you needed rest. So back to what we were discussing before you showered— what you're going to eat tonight. I say we do what your mother suggested and refer to the list of acceptable foods the E.R. doctor gave us on discharge and figure it out on our own."

Ginger did a double take. "Whoa. Wait. Cordelia actually said that?"

Rand nodded. He'd been surprised, too. "With a great deal of difficulty, but yes, she did allude to the fact that I'm your husband and I need to start helping you with things like this, and vice versa, if we are ever to be the kind of team—"

Rand stopped in midsentence, swore mentally, aware he had almost said, *The kind of team our baby is going to need us to be.*

Ginger finished combing the tangles from her hair. "What?" She prodded him to finish. "What did my mom say?"

Knowing now was not the time to add to his wife's stress, by letting her know he had already confirmed their happy news to their moms without her knowledge, he said instead, "The kind of team that all good marriages are. Or something like that. It was a little…"

"Preachy?"

He winced diplomatically. "That's not the word I would use."

Ginger laughed and rolled her eyes. "Well, my mom is right, on this, and probably many other things, as well, loathe as I am to admit it. You and I do need to figure this out on our own." She rose once more.

Aware she was supposed to be resting, he blocked her way to the kitchen. "But what you want is chicken noodle soup?" Gentle hand to her arm, he guided her right back to their bed.

Ginger shrugged, sighed and obediently climbed beneath the covers. "It's what I always have when I've been sick."

Good to know. "Then chicken noodle soup it will be." He brought in a sleeve of crackers and some ginger ale in the meantime. "I thought about making toast…"

"You're right." She smiled at him. "Better to be safe than sorry."

His heart going out to her, Rand kissed her forehead and then headed back to the kitchen to see about rustling up some of the soup she craved.

While Rand searched the cupboards for a can of soup, Ginger ate a couple of crackers, took a sip of ginger ale, then lay back against the pillows and closed her eyes. It had been a long few weeks… Before she knew it, she was fast asleep.

She awakened several hours later to the most delicious smell.

For a moment she was back home in her childhood bed, her mom in the next room, and the most wonderful sense of well-being came over her.

And then she became aware of her wedding ring, and

she remembered how she had come to be in this situation. And the tears that had been held back burst free and rained down, full-force. And that was, of course, when Rand walked in, looking handsome as ever. "Hey." He took her in his arms and held her until the storm passed. "You haven't even tasted my soup yet...."

She cupped his face. His skin was warm and his evening stubble rasped against her palms. "You made me soup?"

"I asked your mom for the recipe and she was kind enough to email it to me."

"That's it? My mom just sent it to you? She didn't offer to make it for us or insist on running over?"

Rand gave a slow shake of his head. He turned his face into her palm, and brushed his lips across the center. "No, she just told me how to make it, and I have."

He left again and Ginger fell silent. Had she finally gotten through to Cordelia, after all these years of enduring her smothering ways? Or was there some other reason her mom was suddenly more hands-off than usual?

Her husband returned, tray in hand. "Although," he cautioned cheerfully, "no guaranteeing the results. I'm a griller, not a soup maker."

Ginger sat up against the pillows. "I'm sure it will be great."

"Well, I cheated. I didn't make the noodles from scratch. I used store-bought." He pulled up a chair, flipped it around and sank onto it.

Once he'd fit the tray across her lap, Ginger dug her spoon into the rich golden broth, redolent with carrots, celery, chunks of white chicken and plump egg noodles. She blew lightly, then lifted the spoon to her lips. "Where did you get them?"

Rand's eyes roved over her lovingly. He appeared to like what he was seeing despite the fact her hair was sleep-rumpled and still damp. "My mom. She was still in town, having dinner with her team. So she stopped at the grocery on the way home and dropped the stuff off."

Ginger took a bite, then another. The soup was just what she needed. She smiled. "That was nice of her."

"It was."

Another pause. "Was she mad at you for skipping out of her Q and A?"

Mad at me? "No." Rand sobered. "Everyone understood. When a man's wife needs him, the man goes. End of discussion."

Her throat tightened a little. "You don't think that she thinks I was trying to undercut her in any way? Professionally or otherwise? By not having you there to back her and her team up, if need be—"

"Or disagree with them," Rand interjected. "No. My mom didn't mind. Although, as it turned out, there weren't any environmental issues for most of the semifinalists, since pretty much everything had already been covered in my initial analysis and environmental impact reports. Basically, any competitor with problems on that score didn't make the cut."

Relieved, Ginger ate more soup. "So when will the Boernes decide?" she asked eventually.

"They are going to take two or three days to confer, then they will let everyone know one way or another with a phone call from their attorney. Which, as it turns out, is a good thing for you—" he flashed her a heart-stopping grin "—since you and our baby are supposed to spend the next few days resting." He hesitated, still scrutinizing her. "So? How is the soup?"

"Really good," she decreed.

Blue eyes narrowed. "But not as good as your mother's?"

Of course he would put her on the spot. Knowing it was some kind of test—that he wanted to see if she would lie—she eventually sighed and said, "It's not better or worse, it's just different." She spooned up the last of his soup, savoring every bite. "Homemade egg noodles taste different than store-bought."

"Next time," he promised, rising to take the tray from her.

As soon as he'd set it safely aside, Ginger grabbed him by the front of his shirt. Grinning, she hauled him against her. "*This time* is great." She raked her fingers through his dark rumpled hair, not sure what she would have done this past month without him. Not wanting to find out, either.

"Just in case I haven't made myself clear." She matched his wickedly sensual look with one of her own. "You've been a wonderful husband, a wonderful father-to-be, a wonderful everything…."

His mouth quirked and she brought him nearer still, intending only to share a quick, easy kiss. Her plan went awry the moment their mouths meshed.

He cupped his hand at the back of her head and kissed her again, slowly and masterfully. Helpless against the tidal wave of feelings, she gave herself up to his embrace.

His arms came around her as he joined her on the bed, threw back the covers, and stretched out beside her. He dropped his head and kissed her again until she moaned, until the point of breathlessness. Her body was humming with need. "Rand," she whispered, wanting the safety and heaven only he could provide.

Briefly he lifted his head. "Is that a yes?"

She laughed and trailed her tongue across the powerful curve of his shoulder. "Heck, yeah."

He grinned. Taking in a sharp breath, he threaded his hands through her hair and tipped her head up to kiss her.

The make-out session continued, as hot and heavy as ever. Impatient, they rolled onto their sides, facing each other. Still kissing, caressing. Her hands slid to his fly, unsnapping, unzipping. His fingertips slid beneath her pajama top, tracing the round shape of her breasts, the shadowy valley between, before finally finding and caressing the tight tips. An arrow of desire shot through her. Lower still, she was so wet. And still, they kissed and touched, stripped each other naked, and then they kissed again, until they gasped in tandem pleasure. Not satisfied with her shaky moan, he slid down her body. Nestled between her thighs.

She writhed against him in exquisite torture. She caught his head. "Now, Rand…" She wanted him inside her.

Rand knew their culmination would be better if he took his time. He also knew there was much, much more he wanted to give. So he simply smiled and went on a little tour. The flat of her belly, the indention of her navel, the insides of her thighs. Then lower still, kissing and caressing her until she was clutching at him, making soft little whimpers for more. He demanded everything of her, until she willingly gave it, and the distance that sometimes cropped up between them, completely faded.

And still he kissed and fondled, and let her ardent response seduce him, heart and soul. He blazed a trail over her sensitive spots, giving her exactly what she wanted and needed, until she arched and cried out.

"Now, you," she insisted.

And as it turned out, he couldn't deny her that, either. Heart racing, he lifted her on top of him, eager for mutual gratification. Slowly, gently, he guided her onto him. She raised herself up a little, wrapped her hand around him, and took him deep. Their eyes met as they moved in perfect synchrony. And then they kissed again, his thumb sliding over the spot where they joined. She came again, which he liked, because it meant she felt so much…he felt so much…and he immediately followed her. Satisfaction roared through them and, still trembling, she pressed her face to his throat.

Aware of everything that had changed between them—and all that, to his frustration, still hadn't—he continued to hold her close. She clung to him, murmuring her pleasure, and eventually sliding right back into sleep. A deeper contentment—coupled with a soul-deep worry—followed. And as he held her, Rand couldn't help but think of the look on his wife's face back in the steakhouse bar.

For a moment when publicly pressed about why she had married him, she'd had that deer-caught-in-the-headlights look.

Rand hoped she didn't feel as trapped as it had momentarily seemed. Because the truth was, their marriage was the best thing that had ever happened to him. He hoped by the time their baby was born, she would feel the same way.

Chapter 13

The following evening Rand walked in the door and did a double take. His gaze swept the nicely set table and cottage living area. Both were neat as a pin. He followed his nose and headed straight for the stove. "What's all this?" He peeked at the chicken roasting in the oven.

Proud of her handiwork, Ginger flashed him a sassy look and brought out a salad from the fridge. "What do you think it is?" She shook the bottle of homemade vinaigrette and poured it over the mixture of fresh raspberries, almonds and spinach leaves, then carried it to the table.

Pleasure lit his face. "You're cooking dinner for me?"

Ginger winked and went back to fill the serving platter. "I know. Amazing, isn't it?"

He washed up and helped her carry everything to

the table. He paused to hold out her chair for her. "You were supposed to be resting."

Ginger wrinkled her nose. "For me, this *is* resting."

Smiling affectionately, he sat opposite her. "That's probably true."

"And we do have to eat," she noted as they filled their plates with tender slices of chicken and roasted root vegetables. "So what better than food I've prepared for us?"

"Did I bring the right woman home from the hospital?"

Ginger grinned. "Funny."

"Really. All kidding aside, what's going on?" Sobering, he paused to search her face. "Did you find out you won the bid?"

Tension stiffened her spine. "No. There's no news on that front."

"Then…?" He met her gaze and the air seemed to crackle around them.

Ginger had promised herself that even though their situation was changing due to the baby, they would not have to alter anything about themselves. When the truth was, they had already begun to change, for the better. Aware they were on the brink of some sort of mutual epiphany, she shrugged. "I thought about everything you've done for me since we got married. All the food you've brought in, the laundry you pretty much finished by yourself, not to mention going clothes shopping with me and bolstering my spirits."

"And the sex," he interjected, his eyes gleaming mischievously. He lifted her wrist to his lips and tenderly kissed the inside. "Don't forget the great sex."

Tingling with need, Ginger returned his flirtatious glance. "There's no way I'm forgetting the great sex.

Not. A. Single. Minute. Of. It." She punctuated each word with evocative meaning.

He grinned and leaned across the table to kiss her on the mouth. "Exactly what I want to hear."

When they eventually pulled apart and went back to enjoying their meal, Ginger continued. "I'm serious, though. I think you've been a much better husband to me than I've been a wife to you." She felt guilty about it.

"That's not true. You're carrying my baby."

"Our baby," Ginger corrected thickly.

And it was a part of her and a part of him and a precious symbol of all their life would one day be…

"You're right." Rand's glance drifted over her barely discernible baby bump. "It's *our* baby." Contentment flowed between them as their eyes met.

Their serious mood intensifying, Rand bared his soul. "You've also made me realize there's a lot more to life than work and causes."

Ginger relaxed, realizing she wasn't the only one who was being transformed. "Such as?"

"Home. Family." He started to say what Ginger thought might have been "love" then changed it to simply, "All this."

Ginger rose to clear the table and retrieve the dessert she had made. Over her shoulder she said, "I do like our life together."

He caught up with her at the kitchen sink and took her in his arms. "Me, too." His mouth hovered over hers, and they kissed.

When they came up for air, she said, "Chocolate cake…"

"Sounds good." He undid the first several buttons on her shirt. "But it can definitely wait."

She closed her eyes and sighed as his lips made an evocative tour of her throat, collarbone and the sensitive spot behind her ear. Hands clutching his shoulders, she caught him with a kiss on the jaw. "We've so begun to think alike."

He lifted his head and captured her gaze. "Which, in this instance, is a very good thing."

Rand swept her up into his arms and carried her into the bedroom. Ever so gently, he let her down beside the bed. Toed off his boots. Removed his socks. Reaching up behind him, he tugged his shirt over his head in one very smooth, easy motion. Her mouth went dry at the sight of him in just a pair of low-slung jeans.

Her eyes roamed his satin-smooth skin and strong muscle. "Keep going."

His lips quirked. The jeans went. So did the boxer briefs.

Oh, my.

His breath rasped. "Now you."

Eyes holding his, she undressed slowly. One by one, everything came off. Shirt. Bra. Socks. Jeans. Panties. His heated gaze made a slow, thorough tour of her.

"We're good?"

He grinned. "So good."

The next thing she knew, he had pulled her against him. She loved the feel of him even as she loved the ragged groan she wrenched from his chest. Her hands were everywhere. So were his. Their kisses were long, languid, passionate and sweet.

Breathing erratically, they landed on top of the covers. He palmed her breasts. She clutched his biceps and arched up into him. And still they kissed and kissed. Already cradled by her open thighs, he slid into her. She cried out, shuddering in pleasure. And then there was nothing but the two of them, this moment, their future beckoning as powerfully as their present. His strokes were strong and slow, making her groan, making her want. She quivered and trembled against him, letting him know how very much she needed the oblivion and wonder he offered.

"Now, Rand, please..."

He gripped her hips. "You first..." His raspy declaration was all it took. Her body exploded in sensation, and as she came, she took him along with her, their locked gazes as steadfast as their hearts.

An hour and one more lovemaking session later, they were cozily ensconced on the screened-in porch. Clad in pajamas, eating slices of chocolate cake and scoops of homemade vanilla ice cream. He bussed the top of her head. "You are an amazing chef."

"Thank you." She grinned and kissed him back.

He savored the very last bite. "This is, without a doubt, the best dessert I have ever eaten."

Seizing the opportunity, Ginger playfully feigned affront. "That's the one thing I didn't actually make."

Rand went still. Bemused by the way he constantly felt he had to protect her tender feelings, Ginger chuckled. "Actually, I made that, too."

Let off the hook, he gave her a chiding look, then kissed the bridge of her nose. "And she jokes, too."

Finished with their desserts, they set their plates aside and cuddled together on the porch swing. Aware she needed to unburden herself to someone, and she wanted that someone to be her husband, Ginger eventually admitted what had been nagging at her all day. "I think I'm going to lose the bid."

Rand lifted a dissenting brow. "First of all, you haven't lost it yet," he reminded her. "But, *if* you do, it'll be because of—"

Ginger jumped in to list all the mitigating factors. "Maria's defection, not to mention the fact that I don't have the skill set to build an entire wildcatting company from scratch." Exhaling, she turned her troubled gaze to his. "Because if I did, let's face it, I never would have allowed my ex to sabotage me the way he did."

Rand pushed the swing into a lazy comforting rhythm, as matter-of-fact as ever. "For the record, I didn't see that coming, either."

But that wasn't all that was bothering her. She studied Rand, wanting his reaction to this, too. "The point is, if Dot and Clancy don't choose me to do the drilling on their land, I'm going to have to make a decision whether to pursue another job with someone else. Or—" and this, she knew, was even trickier "—hold off looking for something else until after the baby comes."

Rand shifted her onto his lap. "You know I'll support you in whatever you do. Especially if you find you really like being a mom and—" he squinted, waiting for her reaction "—want to take time off to have another baby, too."

His words were a shock, all right. Ginger put her arms around his shoulders. "Whoa. *What?*"

"Well…" Mischief lit his midnight-blue eyes. "Sometimes it's good to get all the baby-making out of the way at once, if you're planning on resuming a career, and/or you want to give a child a sibling close in age, so they'll have a playmate growing up."

His logic was both convoluted and oddly reasonable. Trying not to get too caught up in the fantasy of what it would be like to have a real long-lasting family with Rand, instead of the temporary situation they had both agreed upon at the outset of their marriage, Ginger bit her lip. "That was the one thing I always lamented, not having a brother or a sister."

He rubbed his thumb across the curve of her lower lip. "I always wanted a sister, but after five boys, mom and dad said they were done."

She grinned wryly. "I imagine their hands were pretty full." With five sons, all as handsome and smart and full of life as Rand.

He shook his head, remembering what appeared to have been a fun-filled childhood. "You have no idea." He cleared his throat and regarded her with choirboy innocence. "Anyway, if you decide you want to do this again, I want to go on record here as saying I'm all in."

Ginger shifted, feeling the resurgence of his desire—and hers. "All in?" she teased.

His laugh was low and seductive. "Most definitely all in."

Aware what would happen if they continued to be that close, Ginger slid off his lap and carried their dishes to the kitchen. "Don't you think that would be a problem?" she said over her shoulder. "I mean, if we were to do that, we wouldn't be married by then. According to our agreement, we'd be divorced."

He stepped in to help with the dishes. "We could always get married again. Or stay married and put it in our infamous contract."

Ginger nudged him with her shoulder. "Hey, that contract is going to save us a lot of grief over the years."

His hands encircled her hips, and he turned her to face him. "If we ever finish it."

Ginger shivered in the night air coming through the open windows. "We'll finish it," she promised.

He combed his fingers through her hair. "You really think so?"

"I know so," she returned softly. Because she really wanted this temporary marriage of theirs to work. And even though she knew they were getting ahead of themselves, turning the practical arrangement into an increasingly romantic one, she still wanted them to succeed. Not just as parents, but on every level.

Ginger didn't know whether it was the loneliness of the cottage after Rand had gone off to work, or the thought of waiting another day before finding out which company had won the lucrative bid...or just the fact she was pregnant. All she knew was that she missed her mom and needed to see her. And there was, Ginger knew, only one cure for that.

So just before lunch, she went over to the Red Sage business office. Her mom was in the party planning suite, looking as pretty and personable as ever. She paused in the doorway, aware her mother still had every reason to be irked with her. "Got a minute?"

"Always." Cordelia put aside the stack of invitations she had been working on. She perused Ginger with her usual mixture of affection and worry, then finally said, "You look good."

Ginger felt good.

Accepting her mom's wordless invitation, she sauntered in to take a seat on the other side of her mother's desk. Ginger smiled, suddenly wishing she could break down and tell her mom everything that had been going on. She wanted to tell her how hormonal and nauseated and overjoyed and overwhelmed she had felt the past three months. But she couldn't. Not when she and Rand had decided they would tell their families about the baby, all at once.

Aware her mother was still perusing her closely, Ginger shrugged. "I guess I've got that honeymoon glow."

"That must be it," Cordelia mused in return.

"Well, that and some extra sleep the past day or so," Ginger couldn't resist adding.

Another sharp-eyed maternal glance. "Over your stomach upset?" she asked gently.

Ginger nodded, comforted to know her mother still cared. "Which brings me to my next point. I wanted to thank you for giving Rand your famous chicken noodle soup recipe."

Cordelia's eyes lit up. "How did it turn out?"

"Good." She smiled back, then felt obliged to admit, "Well, not as good as yours, but it was still very comforting."

Cordelia interjected, "It's the thought that counts."

"Yes, it is." Ginger sighed, knowing that Rand wasn't the only one who deserved better from her. Still looking her mom in the eye, she pushed on, "I want to apologize. I haven't been very cordial to you, as of late."

Cordelia lifted a delicate hand. "You had reason to be annoyed with me," she said. "I shouldn't have just quit my job and taken one here without speaking with you first."

Ginger rose and moved closer. She leaned against the desk, needing to be near. "That's the thing, Mom. I was wrong about that, too. You don't need to ask me for permission to do what you want to do, any more than I need to ask you. We're both grown women. We can make our own decisions."

Cordelia stood and embraced Ginger in a warm, heartfelt hug. "I just want you to be happy."

Relieved to no longer be quarreling, Ginger hugged her mom back. "I am, Mom." For the first time, in a really long time. "I really am."

Cordelia squeezed her hand. "I know, honey. I see that in you and Rand. And that makes me feel like I can go on with my own life in a way I really haven't been since your dad died."

Ginger blinked. "Are you trying to tell me you're dating again?"

"I'm trying to tell you I'm going to start." She smiled serenely. "Seeing you with Rand has reminded me what it's like to be in love with someone, really in love, and what it means to make that leap of faith, and share your life with that person."

Was that how they looked to others? Ginger wondered, astonished.

Cordelia told her, "I want to be married again and have a fuller, more satisfying life. And seeing you with your new husband is what's convinced me to do so."

"She thinks we're in love," Ginger told Rand over dinner that same night.

He studied her, as if not getting the guilt they should both feel.

"We both know that love never entered into our decision to marry," Ginger pointed out.

Another inscrutable look. Another long, thoughtful pause. "That's true." He frowned. "But—"

Ginger's cell phone rang. It was the notification she had been waiting on. She swallowed and picked it up, her hand trembling with apprehension. "Ginger Rollins." She listened, her spirits sinking like a stone. "Yes. I understand." She ignored Rand's concerned look, then managed to say, "Thank you. I appreciate that." She closed her phone, not the least bit consoled to discover her bid had come in fourth overall. "I didn't land the job. Your mother's company did."

"I'm sorry."

"Me, too," Ginger admitted. Had she not been married and expecting a baby, she probably would have been devastated. "But if it wasn't me," she said, determined to be a good sport despite the setback, "I'm glad it was her."

A knock sounded on the door. Josie McCabe was on the other side of the screen. Squaring her shoulders, Ginger smiled at her mother-in-law and motioned her in. "Congratulations."

Rand glared at his mom in exasperation.

"Couldn't you have given Ginger a little time to lick her wounds?" he demanded.

Josie came forward briskly, businesslike as ever. "No, I couldn't. I need to ask Ginger what I've been wanting to ask her for weeks. I want you to come to work for my company. And I want you to work with me on the Boerne project. And, Rand, I want you to come to work for me, too."

Rand gave his mother a wary look. There was an undercurrent between them that Ginger could not decipher, but clearly something was going on between them.

"Why?" Rand asked tersely.

Josie gave Rand an enigmatic look back. One that

confirmed there was something else going on, some other reason besides Ginger's and Rand's business acumen.

Josie lifted a hand, index finger up. "Because Wyatt Drilling has always been a family company, handed down to me from my dad." Her finger count went to two. "You are the only one of my children who is remotely interested in the oil business on any level." She raised a third finger. "I think having an environmentalist on board to advise us on each and every project is a good idea. And four—" she made the appropriate gesture "—I think the three of us working together to run this company will be a very good thing."

Josie's smile encompassed both Ginger and Rand. "I don't expect an answer right away. I know you have to think about it, but when you are ready to sit down and hammer out the details, let me know, and we'll do it."

"I don't appreciate the timing, Mom," Rand told her rather brusquely.

Josie gave Rand another telltale look that seemed to speak volumes. "Just think about it," she said as she headed out the door.

When they were alone again, Ginger asked, "Did you have any idea that was coming?"

Rand helped her clear the table. "None."

Aware she hadn't had this nagging sense of being deliberately excluded in a familial tiff since she'd been married to Conrad, Ginger put a pot of decaf coffee on to brew. "Well, it doesn't make sense to me," she ruminated, still wondering what Rand—and Josie— weren't telling her.

"Why would your mom be in such a rush to have us both working with her?"

Rand shrugged and averted his gaze. "You're a tough, talented competitor. She probably doesn't want anyone else to hire you."

There was still something missing. Ginger continued pacing. "I mean, it would make sense why she'd want to bring me into the family company as soon as possible if she knew about the baby. But there's no way she could know about that. Unless…" Ginger studied the peculiar expression on Rand's face. "Did you tell her?"

A long, reluctant pause followed. "I didn't have to," he conceded finally. "She and your mother had already figured it out."

The news was like a bucket of ice water poured over her head. *"When?"*

He barely looked at her. "From the moment they saw us on our wedding day. They saw how you were glowing. Noticed how fast and determinedly we were getting hitched—despite the fact we had both vowed after our divorces that we would never say 'I Do' to anyone again." He spread his hands wide, as if it were no big deal. "And they figured it out."

"And told you."

He gave her a longer, narrow look. "No. I walked in on them arguing about whether or not to throw us a surprise baby shower a week or so ago."

Lovely. "And didn't see fit to tell me? *Any* of you?"

"Your mother wanted to confront you." His eyes remained steady on hers. "I forbade it."

"Why?"

Frustration turned the corners of his lips. With the tone of a man who was never expected to explain himself, he returned, "Because you were already fighting morning sickness and under so much stress at work. I didn't want you to end up in the hospital."

Ginger huffed. "Which I did anyway."

"Unfortunately."

Ginger stared at him, wondering how everything could turn so awful, so fast. Hands knotted at her sides, she moved closer. "So all this time, the three of you were—what?—humoring me."

He glared down at her, said mildly, "Protecting you. And yes, we were."

Tears misted her eyes. "At your insistence," she clarified.

His jaw set. "It's my job, as your husband."

She spun away from him, overcome with a horrible sense of déjà vu. "It's your job to tell me the truth!" she cried.

"And I am."

"Now!"

Another silence fell, even more fraught with tension than the last. There was suddenly so much wrong with their situation, Ginger didn't know where to start. Her gaze jerked back up to his eyes.

She supposed the best place to start was where the trouble began. "I can't accept your mother's job offer."

Acting as if this were all hormones again, instead of a fundamental breakdown in their relationship, he stared at her in weary resignation. "Why not?"

Ginger went back to what had upset her at the end of her conversation with her own mother that day. The willful deception that had paved the way for the entire past month. "Because," she sighed, irritated she had to explain this to him, too, "your mother just asked because she thinks our marriage is a real one."

His expression grew stonier.

"I mean, she does, doesn't she?" Ginger persisted. "You didn't tell our mothers *that part* without me, did you?"

"No, of course not."

"So they think we've made a real, lifetime commitment to each other?"

"I assume so, yes."

"Then we have to set the record straight," she reiterated, going back to what she'd been trying to tell him over dinner. "And explain to them that our marriage is nothing but a temporary arrangement for business reasons."

He folded his arms across his chest. "What if I want it to be more than that?"

Tension knotted her gut. In an effort to gain control, she returned to her usual businesslike attitude. "You know our agreement," she told him.

And she knew her promise to *herself,* to never again be in a relationship where she was humored and betrayed, the way she'd been in her first marriage.

Rand stood his ground. "I know our *initial* agreement."

Meaning what? The fact they'd become closer gave him license to do whatever he pleased as far as she was concerned? "Our marriage is not a forever kind of thing," she reminded him stubbornly, refusing to delude herself into believing otherwise.

His face took on a brooding expression. "You're saying you still want a divorce as soon as we have the baby?"

Did she? In a perfect world, no. But he had more than proved this wasn't utopia. Not even close. She had to be practical. If she stayed, he would break her heart. And maybe their baby's heart, too. Swallowing the lump in her throat, Ginger ran a weary hand through her hair. "I'm saying I'm tired of the pretense. I don't want to walk around every day feeling like a liar. Because that's not who I am. And it's not who you are, either, Rand." That much she knew.

He exhaled roughly, looking as ticked off as she felt. "You're right about that."

Their anguished glances meshed and held. "Then you understand we have to tell our parents the truth about why we really got married, that we were never as wildly and passionately in love as we pretended."

He lifted a brow, challenging, "Or ever will be for that matter?"

Ginger didn't know what to say to that.

In the end it didn't matter.

Rand simply looked at her, a world of hurt and disappointment in his eyes. "Point made," he said quietly.

And then he walked out.

Chapter 14

"And that's it?" Michelle asked from across the law firm conference table two days later, her expression inscrutable. "Rand just grabbed his laptop and left?"

Ginger nodded and settled even deeper into her chair, aware she hadn't felt this miserable in her entire life. "I haven't seen or heard from him since. Hence, I wanted to let you know we would be coming to you for a marriage dissolution instead of a marriage contract."

Suddenly she paused. "You don't look surprised." Ginger had half expected the happily married attorney to give her a lecture on sticking with it and seeing the problems through. Instead, Michelle was calmly making notes on the yellow legal pad in front of her.

"So what was it like before the big blow-up the two of you had?" Michelle asked.

"Great, actually," Ginger admitted, a little mystified

about that, too. How was it that things had gone from so wonderful, to so bad, that quickly?

Calmly, Michelle continued to take notes. "You were working on the terms of your marriage contract?"

Ginger nodded. "Trying to anticipate—and solve— any problems that could possibly come up in the future. Not that there were many in the present. We just naturally seemed to click as roommates. And lovers."

Wow, had they ever clicked as lovers, she amended silently.

"But then what happened in the bedroom had never been the issue between us," she continued, aware she needed a sounding board, and the quietly analytical attorney in front of her was as good as any. "That was good from start to finish."

Michelle looked up. "And Rand seemed happy then, too?"

"Very. I mean, I'd never seen him so relaxed and… content, I guess. Before we hooked up, he was always using his passion to fight for one environmental issue or another. Then, when we realized the baby was on the way, everything sort of changed." She sighed. "Our focus shifted more to each other and making things work than on either of our business goals. And once that happened…everything just seemed to fall into place."

"Even when you had small differences of opinion on the actual terms of the marriage contract, the two of you were trying to hammer out?"

"That's correct." Ginger exhaled. "As furious as I was with him over not telling me that our mothers knew we were expecting a baby, I never thought he'd decide to end things just like that." Ginger studied the levelheaded family law lawyer. "But you're not at all surprised, are you?"

Michelle put her pen down. "You want me to be frank?"

"I do."

"You and Rand were and are the exception to the rule."

"In what way?"

"Most people enter into marriage thinking it's going to be some fantastic fairytale. They don't understand—or want to understand—what you and Rand intuited from the get-go. That marriage *is* a business, albeit a very personal one."

Ginger blinked, still listening intently.

"In either situation, you first decide to throw in together. Then you draw up the contract. When, how, where you're going to proceed. The day you get married compares to the day you go to the secretary of state to actually register your new business."

Ginger reflected on the official legal start to their new venture. "That was an incredibly happy moment."

Michelle smiled. "It is for everyone because it's the beginning of the honeymoon period."

That had been wonderful, too.

"But then the real work begins." Michelle sobered. "Bylaws for the business—or in your case, the actual terms of the postnup and marriage contract—are drawn up. And let me tell you, no one ever agrees about those. It's always a difficult process. There are always subtle but significant differences of opinion. In business, quarrels concern how much to spend on advertising or how much staff to hire…"

She cleared her throat. "However, in marriage, it's

usually an emotional issue, such as whether or not you should quit pretending to be in love and tell your families the real reason you got married when you did. Or whether Rand should have told you the moms had guessed you were pregnant, instead of moving to protect you the way he thought was right in that moment."

It was clear Ginger and Rand had serious disagreements about those issues. But also true that their quarrel didn't seem as significant today as it had when it had occurred.

Ginger studied the happily married woman opposite her. "You're saying I should cut Rand some slack?"

Because Rand's gallantry is one of the things I love best about him? One of the things I've come to count on the most?

The savvy attorney smiled knowledgeably. "I'm saying that whether in business or marriage, everyone always plans for when things go wrong." She paused to let her words sink in. "No one ever plans for what happens when everything goes *right*."

"So it's true?" Josie said to Rand when he tracked her down at the Boerne ranch two days after her visit to the cottage. He could see that surveying and staking was already under way. "You're ending another marriage?"

Rand scowled at his mother. "I was hoping you'd give me some tender loving care."

"Nope. Fresh out of that."

"Seriously?" he quipped.

Josie looked him squarely in the eye. "I'm not going to sugarcoat it for you, son. You're being an idiot."

Rand followed his mother over to her pickup. "She's not ever going to love me, Mom."

Josie grabbed a couple of bottles of electrolyte drinks from the cooler, and handed one to him. "Do you love her?"

What difference did it make? Rand wondered as he worked the cap off and took a long, thirsty swallow.

His mom quenched her thirst, too, then continued looking at him the way she had when he'd brought home a note from school saying he had misbehaved in some fashion. She had always wanted an explanation from him first, before passing judgment. She wanted one now, too.

Rand exhaled in frustration. "We were supposed to see our family law attorney today to hammer out the final details of our postnup and marriage contract. The appointment was made weeks ago."

"Okay. And…?"

"Ginger sent me a text saying she was planning to attend without me, and that when she was there she was going to let Michelle know where things stood."

"Which is where?"

"I don't know. Over?"

Josie arched a brow. "Shouldn't you be asking her that instead of me?"

"As you know, she's pregnant."

"So?" his mom asked.

"I don't want to argue with her. Or upset her."

Josie rolled her eyes. "And she couldn't possibly be upset now, with the two of you not speaking to each other."

Rand returned the sarcasm with equal vigor. "Is there a point to this cockeyed lecture?"

An indignant sniff. "I want to know why you aren't at that meeting, too."

"Because I do not want to go over there and be put in a position where I have to defend myself for doing what was right in the first place."

"I see. So, bottom line, you're afraid Ginger might disagree with you in front of the attorney, and hurt your feelings?"

Why did his mother persist in misunderstanding the entire situation, as well as his motives? "Because I'm—"

"Afraid?"

"—pretty damn sure that Ginger is going to want to continue our marriage only as a means to an end. And while I might have thought it was an acceptable idea in the first place, I don't anymore. Hence, I'm not going to pretend everything is right as rain, and drag out a union that is bound to end in another colossal failure." Sighing roughly, he raked a hand through his hair. "I'm not like you and Dad and my brothers. I'm not good at figuring out who to spend the rest of my life with, Mom."

His outburst was met with thoughtful silence. Finally his mom tilted her head and probed gently. "I'm interested. How did you come to that particular conclusion?"

Rand grimaced. "Easy. I married one woman who wanted me to give her everything money could buy."

"And when you didn't, that marriage ended, rightly so. Although had you asked me, I would have told you from the get-go she was a fortune-hunter."

Rand turned a glance skyward and pleaded for patience. When he finally had it, he looked back at his mother. "Then I married a second woman—"

"Who doesn't want your money or even any sort of family nepotism when it comes to her career, either."

Rand paused to decipher that. "Ginger turned you down?"

Josie nodded. "In an email. She said as much as she would love to work with and learn from me, she couldn't in good conscience accept a job offered her only because of family connections that were going to end anyway."

His spirits plummeted yet again. "Did you disagree with her? Try to get her to change her mind?"

"No."

He squinted. "Why not, if you believe in her?"

His mother let out a reluctant breath. "Because Ginger is right. If you two don't work this out, she would never be happy working with me."

So much for the pep talk he'd wanted, even if it had been as off-base as the rest of his life. He folded his arms in front of him. "Well, we're not going to work it out."

Another contemplative pause. "What makes you so sure of that?"

Same reason as always. "Because Ginger's elusive to the core."

"Independent to a fault." Josie helped heap on the criticism.

"She's never going to let me give her anything," Rand railed. "Not commitment or security or—" He stopped.

His mother smiled and, guessing exactly where he'd been going with that rant, delivered her final blow.

"Love?"

Ginger was back at the cottage, trying to figure out what her next step was going to be, when a knock sounded at the door.

Rand stood on the other side of the screen door.

He looked resolute. Handsome. Serious.

Her heart turned over in her chest at the sight of him standing there, clad in one of the button-down Oxford-cloth shirts she had once enjoyed wearing so much.

"Hey," she said softly before she could stop herself or think of a better opening to what she wanted and needed to say.

He smiled at her and, lips set stubbornly, opened the door and strode inside the honeymoon cottage where they'd begun their married life. Languorously, he crossed to her side. "How did your appointment with Michelle go?"

It was a simple question. Packed with emotion, beneath the masculine reserve.

She let her glance caress the long muscular legs, encased in soft faded denim, his equally worn boots. Remembering how much she loved every part of his strong, tall body, she returned her gaze upward, over the hard musculature of his chest and neck, to his face.

She took a bolstering breath. "I wanted to talk to you about that." Wanted to do a lot of things, in fact.

Another flicker of indiscernible emotion appeared in his midnight-blue eyes. He came closer, wrapped an arm around her waist, then put a silencing finger to her lips and said gruffly, "First, I need to say a few things."

Ginger splayed her hands across his chest. "Okay."

He looked at her with sincerity and regret. "I haven't been honest with you. So in a way, you're right. I have disrespected you this whole time by not leveling with you."

It helped to have him admit that, even as the knowledge filled her with fear. Ignoring the sudden wobbliness of her knees, Ginger urged, "Go on."

"I know what I said about it being only a temporary, heat-of-the-moment kind of thing the first time we landed in bed together."

She had pretended the same.

"But the truth is," Rand confided hoarsely, gazing into her eyes, "I never wanted a no-strings, easygoing affair with you. I was just humoring you, and telling you what I thought you wanted to hear."

Her heart clenched. "As a means to an end."

"Maybe." He paused, reflecting. A mixture of mischief and irony turned up the corners of his lips. "Because I did want to see you again and I figured downplaying what had happened between us was the only way that was going to happen."

His deadpan humor was infectious. "You're probably right about that," Ginger returned dryly. She'd been shaken to the core by the intensity of the passion they'd felt. Still was.

Rand tenderly cupped her face in his large hands. "But mostly it was because I let my pride and my fear of failing at another relationship get in the way."

Ginger tipped her head up to his. "I've been apprehensive about putting myself out there again, too. Which is," she explained, "the only reason I ever considered a continuous string of one-night stands with you. Because I was afraid to look any more forward than the moment we were in."

"But the truth is—" he admitted, his voice a sexy rumble "—from the very first time I set eyes on you, I knew in my gut that I was never going to be satisfied with that. I'm a one-and-only-one-woman kind of a man. And the one woman I want in my life is you, Ginger Rollins-McCabe."

Tears slipped down her cheeks as she thought about how much time they had lost, how abandoned she'd felt the past couple of days. "Then why didn't you tell me?"

He searched her face with quiet intensity. "Because I knew how much you prized your independence."

"Maybe not so much anymore."

He shushed her again. "I'm not finished." His voice caught. "You've got to let me get this out."

Her throat aching with pent-up emotion, she nodded.

"I don't want to end our marriage," he said, flattening a hand on her spine and bringing her closer. "And it's not because we're likely to be taken more seriously in business if we stay hitched, or because it's what our families want, or even more importantly, because a two-parent home will be good for our baby...or any other children we may also choose to have—"

She grinned at the realization he was thinking ahead, again.

"It's because there is no other woman in the entire world for me. It's because," he continued in a gruffly tender tone that lit her soul on fire, "you bring a joy and a contentment and an excitement to my life in a way that no one ever has before. I love you, Ginger Rollins, with all my heart." He bent his head and kissed her sweetly. "And I have from the first moment we hooked up."

The last few pieces of her broken heart mended at the realization they'd been on the same track all this time, they'd just been too stubborn and too wary to admit it.

Ginger kissed him back. "That's good to hear." She was crying in earnest now, so happy she felt she would burst. She wreathed her arms about his neck and went up on tiptoe, getting closer yet. She slid her fingers through his hair, wanting, needing, so much. But needing to give back, too. Her breath caught in a little hiccup. "Because I've learned a lot the past couple days, too."

Rand listened intently, seeming to know that she had a lot to get off her chest, too. Bolstered, she told him with quiet honesty, "I thought if we ran our marriage with the levelheaded efficiency a good business utilizes, that we could somehow protect ourselves from any future disappointments. But I know now, that's not true. Every facet of life is messy and emotional." Her lips trembled. "In the end, all the ups and downs and working things out, is what makes a relationship so strong. The struggle to get it right is what makes us grow, and I very much want to grow old with you."

She tilted her face upward and kissed him again; he returned the caress just as lovingly. Then, with a contented laugh, she pulled back long enough to admit, "Which is why, I've now realized, I could never quite bring myself to finish that darn marriage contract. Because I sensed our life together was always going to be a work in progress. That we'd always be able to find a better, fairer, more loving way to do things. And that the day we ever declared ourselves 'perfect'—"

"Was probably the day to go back to the drawing board?" he teased.

Ginger's low chuckle mingled with his. "I haven't said it, up till now, but I'm saying it today with all my heart and soul. I love you, Rand McCabe." And to prove it, she kissed him yet again, even more passionately this time.

"I love you, too." Rand hugged her fiercely, then buried his face in her hair. "So much."

They clung together, bound by so much more than marriage vows and a baby on the way. "So we're good?" Ginger murmured as the gladness in her heart grew by leaps and bounds.

"More than good," he decreed firmly. "Ecstatic."

Epilogue

Six months later...

"So what do you think?" Ginger asked, scrutinizing the newly hung sign. "Did it turn out the way you imagined?"

Rand appraised the bronze placard hanging from the curlicued metal arm just above the door: Rollins & McCabe, Environmentally Sound Oil Exploration. He turned to her and grinned. "It's exactly the way I imagined it. No," he corrected, pausing to kiss her tenderly, "it's even better than I thought it ever could be."

"I know what you mean." Ginger rubbed her swollen belly as the two of them walked inside the office that housed their consulting business. The four-room space on Main Street, in Summit, Texas, was outfitted with a reception area, an office for each of them and a conference room. "We've already accrued quite a client list."

Ginger contracted out her services and engineered petroleum drilling plans for clients. Rand did the environmental impact reports, and made sure their client's interests were protected, in terms of their land. Companies like Wyatt Drilling and other small-to-midsize oil companies brought in the teams of roughnecks and did the actual oil exploration and recovery. It was an arrangement that worked well for everyone, and gave Rand and Ginger the freedom and independence they both wanted.

They hadn't ruled out the possibility of one day joining Josie McCabe, at Wyatt Drilling, but for now this setup suited them all just fine.

"How are you feeling?" Rand asked.

Ginger stretched some of the tightness from her spine, felt the baby kick in response, feisty as ever. "I'm fine."

Rand lifted a questioning brow, reading her as expertly as ever.

Reluctantly, Ginger relented and told him the rest. "My back hurts. It's been aching all afternoon." Aware it was time for them to call it quits for the day, she reached over and turned off her computer.

"Then why didn't you say so?"

"Because I feel like all I do is complain about— Ouch!" She paused.

Panic warred with the excitement on his handsome face. "Is it time?"

Ginger wished. She was so tired of being pregnant, tired of feeling hot and bulky and continually hormonal and out of sorts. Although Rand kept insisting she had never looked lovelier…

Patiently, she circled around to join him. "Not for a few more days. You know th— Ouch!" She grabbed hold of the edge of the desk and doubled over in pain.

"You're in labor."

Was she?

The tight rubber band of pressure circling her entire midriff said, yes, this was indeed a contraction. But one contraction, as she'd found out the hard way, did not mean she was in labor.

She relaxed as the sensation passed. Feeling a little foolish, she straightened. Rand hovered protectively close, ready to spring into action the moment she said the word. Their eyes met and she shook her head. "I don't want to go to the hospital." She moaned, remembering the excitement, followed swiftly by humiliation and letdown. "The false alarm we had last week was embarrassing enough." She'd been so sure. They both had. Only…

Rand wrapped a comforting arm around her shoulders. He kissed the top of her head. "It happens a lot. And you know what the OB staff said. Better safe than sorry…"

Ginger remembered. Still… She turned to kiss Rand's chin. "We can wait a little bit. Time the contractions and then—"

Without warning, she felt something running down her leg. More pressure. More liquid. All of it puddling mysteriously at her feet.

Rand looked at her feet, then at her face, then back at the floor. He seemed as stunned and overjoyed as she felt. "Your water just broke, didn't it?"

Ginger laughed to cover the onslaught of fierce building pain. "I knew all those birthing classes we've taken and that internet research you've been doing would come in handy," she panted.

"I'll get the suitcase," he said quickly.

Wincing, Ginger grabbed his biceps and held on tight. "It's already in the pickup," she huffed.

"Then I'll get the truck."

Again, Ginger shook her head. "How about we both walk to the parking lot together?"

"You're sure?" He was already locking up with one hand, phoning the obstetrician with the other.

"Positive," Ginger said, for once happy to cede over all control to her adorable husband. She leaned against him when he wrapped his arm around her, savoring his warmth and his strength. "I want you by my side every step of the way."

And he was. Through the short drive to the hospital, the check-in, the labor and the birth. The doctor even let Rand do the honors and cut the umbilical cord.

It was only when they were situated in the mother-baby suite that the three of them were alone again. Ginger in the bed, Rand next to her, their precious little baby girl, happily fed, and cuddled against their chests. They looked down at her gorgeous halo of Rollins-red hair and McCabe-blue eyes. She had Ginger's nose and Rand's stubborn chin. And was seriously, the most beautiful baby that either Rand or Ginger had ever seen.

They snuggled contentedly as the newborn finally drifted off to sleep. "So it's official?" Ginger whispered to Rand. "We're going to name our little darlin' Jasmine Josie Cordelia McCabe?"

He grinned tenderly, pausing to kiss both momma and baby. "We are."

"Our mothers are going to like that."

"They sure are." ·

Ready to share their excitement, Ginger smiled. "So what do you say we conference-call both our families and introduce them, via Skype, to our first—"

"But not last—"

"—child."

Rand got the laptop and set up the camera and microphone. "Of course, we don't have to decide the exact number of kids right now. We have all the time in the world to work on—" he waggled his brows suggestively "—that."

Ginger couldn't wait to make love with him again.

"That's what I like about you," she teased. "Always thinking ahead." *Always taking every opportunity to love me, and let me love you back.*

They kissed again. Hearts bursting with joy, they called their families to give them the happy news.

* * * * *

Ali Olson is a longtime resident of Las Vegas, Nevada, where she has been teaching English at the high school and college level for the past seven years. Ali has found a passion for writing sexy romance novels, both contemporary and historical, and is enthusiastic about her newly discovered career. She loves reading, writing and traveling with her husband and constant companion, Joe. She appreciates hearing from readers. Write to her at authoraliolson.com.

Books by Ali Olson

Harlequin Western Romance

Spring Valley, Texas

The Bull Rider's Twin Trouble
The Cowboy's Surprise Baby

Harlequin Blaze

Her Sexy Vegas Cowboy
Her Sexy Texas Cowboy

Visit the Author Profile page at
Harlequin.com for more titles.

THE COWBOY'S SURPRISE BABY

Ali Olson

To peanut butter and jelly sandwiches. You got me through the most nauseous moments of this pregnancy and thus were instrumental to the completion of this book.

Chapter 1

Amy McNeal stepped through the sliding glass doors into the cool autumn air of Texas and breathed it in greedily, ignoring the smell of the exhaust fumes from the waiting cars. After two months in Northern Africa in summer, any temperature below blistering was a refreshing change.

As she walked toward the line of vehicles moving at a snail's pace through the pickup area, her phone started buzzing inside her large travel purse. Amy shifted the suit bag she was carrying to her left hand and dug through the purse with her right, then pulled out her phone and tapped it to answer the call. "Hey! I'm almost at the pickup location," she said.

"I know. I can see you. You better hurry or I'll need to loop around again," answered her brother from the other end.

She looked along the line of cars, trying to peer through the windows for a familiar face. "I don't see you. A little help?"

"I'm in the black truck," he told her.

She rolled her eyes. "This is Texas, Brock. I'm looking at about six black trucks."

"You know, maybe I'll just leave you to find your own way home, if you're going to be like that," he said, but she could hear the smile in his voice and knew she wasn't actually in any danger of being left at the curb.

"Look right. I'm waving out the window," he said.

She spotted him, fifty feet farther along. "I see you! Wait there and I'll be over in a second," she told him.

Amy dropped her phone back into her purse and strode quickly through the crowd of people waiting with their luggage along the curb. When she got to her brother's car, a man in an orange vest was telling him he needed to keep moving, that he wasn't allowed to wait there. "I'm here!" she said breathlessly, slinging her backpack off and into the truck bed, then hopping into the passenger seat.

With a little wave to the airport employee, she settled into her seat and Brock steered them out and away from the airport. "You know we get in trouble here if we sit idling at the curb, right?"

Amy shook her head. "I always forget about how many rules there are in America."

Brock raised an eyebrow and glanced at his sister from the corner of his eye. "If you came home more often, you know, you might remember them."

Amy crossed her arms and turned toward Brock. "You've been back in Spring Valley for two months and already you're starting to sound like Ma," she commented.

"She misses you," he told her, sending a small stab of guilt through her. "It's good to have you back."

Amy gave her brother a smile. "It's good to see you, Brock."

"You're back for the whole month, huh?"

Amy nodded. "I had to be here for my big brother's wedding."

There was a moment of silence, and she knew Brock was waiting for her to say what had happened that made her decide to change her plans and come home so early, rather than just for the weekend of the ceremony. Up until the day before, that had been the plan. But she wasn't ready to explain the events of the last couple weeks, so she stayed silent.

After waiting a few more moments for her to add anything else, Brock said, "Well, I'm glad you'll be around. Be careful, though. You might find yourself deciding to settle down in Spring Valley, regardless of your plans."

Amy snorted. There were at least two very good reasons she would be leaving Spring Valley again. One was her lucrative career as a travel writer, and the other was a handsome cowboy with cornflower-blue eyes. She had some loose ends to tie up with said cowboy, but that didn't mean she'd be sticking around afterward. She was here to set things straight, not make herself miserable. Or him, for that matter.

"Hey, it happens," Brock said defensively.

"Speaking of settling down, how's your fiancée doing?" Amy asked, both because she was interested and because she wanted to change the subject.

Brock looked for a second like he might not accept the topic shift, then gave her a wide grin she didn't remember ever seeing on his face before Cassie came into his life. "She's great, Zach and Carter are great, the ranch is—"

"Great?" Amy said for him.

"Really, really great," he said, nodding, his smile even wider, if that was possible.

"So you don't miss bull riding at all?" she asked, wondering if he'd really given up the rodeo circuit without a qualm.

Brock shook his head decisively. "Not one bit. Giving that up was one of the best decisions I've ever made, and it gives me more time around the people I love. With the wedding, the ranch and twin boys, time is one thing that always seems to be in short supply."

Amy wasn't sure if she believed that Brock didn't miss the rodeo circuit at least a little, but he seemed sincere, so she just had to assume that when he lost his heart, he lost his mind a little, too.

She could remember the rush of riding a horse in the ring, hearing the shouts of the fans, like it was yesterday instead of a decade ago. She had only made it to junior rodeo before dropping out, but that didn't mean it wasn't still a part of her life.

Even after all this time, she still sometimes watched videos of rodeos on her computer when she felt particularly homesick.

But Brock had given it up without a backward glance. Because of love.

Amy had already warned her brother once about the danger of falling in love, so she didn't say anything now. Still, it worried her. What if it didn't work out for him?

She didn't want him to go through that pain. She knew what it felt like to have her whole imagined future with someone come crumbling down around her, and she worried about her brother experiencing the same thing.

Sure, Cassie was wonderful—and they were committing to marriage, after all—but sometimes people who might be perfect for each other still didn't end up together.

"You okay?" Brock asked, breaking into her thoughts.

Amy swallowed the old hurt that was threatening to break the surface and put on a smile. "I'm fine."

For now, at least. After she talked to Jack, though, who knew?

Jack Stuart ran a brush through the chestnut mare's coat, enjoying the feeling of calm it created in him. No matter what else was going on, he could always find some peace around horses. Right this minute, he needed it.

"Any idea how long she'll be around?" he asked his brother.

Tom shrugged his shoulders, not seeming to notice his brother's sudden edginess. "I'm guessing the whole month, up until the wedding. Brock said it was the longest she'd been home since she left for college."

Jack didn't want to tip off his brother about how interested he was, but he couldn't help it. He needed to know everything his brother knew. "Did he say anything else?"

How is she?

Is she seeing anyone?

Does she still think about me after all these years?

"Nope, just that she was coming to town for a bit all of a sudden. The boys tackled him right after, and you know how they are. Had to tell him everything that had happened at their lessons."

Jack didn't say anything, trying to bite off his disappointment that he couldn't learn any more.

"I'm surprised the twins are still coming here at all, to be honest. What with Brock's parents owning a riding school and Brock himself able enough to teach them. Not that I'm complaining of course—we can sure use the business," Tom said, his mind drifting off to other topics besides Amy. "I really think it's only to give those two lovebirds some time alone. Have you seen them together? Don't know if I've ever known two people to be more infatuated with one another."

Oh, Jack did. His older brother had been too busy at college to remember how Jack and Amy had been senior year of high school. Tom knew they'd dated, but not that they'd been in love. Jack and Amy had been planning a life together. Family, careers, everything.

Then, the summer after they graduated, she went off to a university thousands of miles away despite all their plans together, without a word of explanation. He didn't know what had changed or why she decided not to talk to him again. He just knew it still hurt.

And here was his chance to talk to her, hear her side of it, and finally put it all behind him.

As he and Tom left the barn and walked through the twilight toward his childhood home, he felt the itch to get in his truck and drive straight over to see Amy. He would be there in less than five minutes.

The urge almost made him veer toward the side of the house, but he managed to keep himself in check. If she had just gotten home, she was spending time with her family. Not the best time to drive up and demand an explanation.

No, he could wait until tomorrow, Jack told himself.

"Mom loves that you're going to be home for a good long while, you know," Tom said as they neared the house.

Jack could see his mother moving around the kitchen, and he felt a pang of guilt over his desire to drive over to see Amy without a word of explanation to anyone. His mother had likely been cooking up a storm while they were out with the horses.

Jack glanced at his brother, whose mouth was set in a thin line. He knew that Tom was worried about their mother and the ranch she'd lived on for so many years, and that Jack being home wasn't the godsend their mother thought it was, if only because it brought a halt to any extra cash Jack brought in from riding in rodeos.

Tom hadn't been kidding when he'd said they could use any extra business their little riding school could get. As the town had shrunk over the years, so had the number of students they could count on coming to learn to ride. After their father died and Tom moved back to pick up the slack, it had only gotten worse; and Jack knew Tom felt that it was his failings as an instructor that was causing the trouble, despite anything Jack said to the contrary.

Jack hated that he had no idea what he could do about all that. Up until last week he'd tried to help by sending home what he could from his earnings on the circuit, but even that never seemed to be enough. He was sure he could become a real champion if the cards fell right, and then they could stop worrying so much, but for that he needed a great partner and a whole lot of luck—two things that hadn't seemed to come his way lately.

His old partner was decent, but since he broke his leg and decided to call it quits, Jack wasn't sure what he'd do. No partner, no rodeos. No rodeos, no money.

He loved being home on the ranch he hoped to run one day, but now he needed to find someone to rope with. It was the type of decision that could make or break his career. All that on his plate, and now there was Tom to help, too. It was a tall order.

And now he had Amy McNeal to think about. His stay in Spring Valley was already getting much more complicated than he'd expected just a few days ago.

As the sun dipped behind the mountains ringing Spring Valley, Amy lowered herself carefully from Brock's truck until her feet were planted securely on the gravel driveway of their parents' old sprawling ranch house. The last time she'd come home, she'd fallen and twisted her ankle badly doing that very thing, and she wasn't about to go through that again. If Cassie, who was a doctor and lived next door, hadn't taken care of her, she might have ended up missing her departure flight last time.

Amy turned her attention from her feet to the group of people standing on the front porch. Cassie was already there, with her twin sons, and Ma and Pop, all happy to see her. Amy felt a twinge of homesickness, which was silly. She *was* home, after all.

Cassie, Brock's fiancée, came down and gave Amy a tight hug. Even though they had only met up a couple times during Amy's last stay, and that was when she was still just the neighbor, Cassie had been kind and friendly from the start.

"How's your ankle?" she asked the moment she and Amy broke apart.

"Good, most of the time. Just gives me the odd twinge if I step down wrong," Amy said, glad to have a doctor in the family.

Cassie nodded sympathetically, but it was clear there wasn't much to be done about it. Just another sign that she wasn't in her teens anymore.

The cool evening breeze ruffled Amy's hair, and she wished she had a jacket. Living out of a backpack for years, she'd learned to just buy occasional items as she needed them, and she certainly hadn't needed anything heavier than a light sweater in nearly a year, following the summer and staying on tropical islands or in deserts.

She might need to buy a coat. But for the time being, she would just borrow something from her mother, however grandmotherly her Ma's wardrobe was—and it had been since she'd adopted Amy, if the pictures were any indication.

Ma herself rushed forward and pulled Amy into a tight hug, and Amy felt her heart swell with the feeling of home. As much as she avoided Spring Valley, she missed it, and the people. "Hi, Ma," she said, hoping the older woman wasn't going to cry.

Ma was a tough lady, but she never could understand why Amy was gone so much, and it hurt Amy to see the toll it took on her. To avoid it, Amy rummaged in her bag and pulled out two packages, handing one to Ma and the other to Cassie. "They're some different spices and a grinder," she explained.

Cassie thanked her, but Ma looked skeptical. "Smell

them and give them a shot," Amy said, sure her adopted mother would manage to make something magical and somehow still completely Southern with them.

Then Amy turned to her soon-to-be nephews. "I brought y'all spices, too!" she told them.

"You did?" Carter asked, not sounding too enthused at the idea.

"No. I want to be your favorite aunt, and I have some catching up to do, so I brought you fez hats and drums," she said, pulling out the items and handing them to the boys.

Zach immediately began giggling to see the funny little hat on his brother, and they both started hitting the drums enthusiastically. Brock appeared at Amy's elbow. "Drums? Really?" he asked his little sister.

Amy shrugged. "There were some really cool knives I considered getting them. This seemed like the better choice."

Brock and Cassie winced at the noise. "I'm not so sure about that," Brock commented.

Cassie whispered quickly to Zach and Carter, and they both ran over to Amy, giving her a big hug. "Thanks, Aunt Amy," they said in unison.

Amy nodded to them, fighting tears. She didn't want to admit how much it twisted her heart to be around these two sweet boys. They reminded her too much of truths she didn't like to think about.

"Time to get inside," Ma said, ushering everyone through the door. "Dinner's ready and will start getting cold any minute."

Amy, thankful for the interruption, followed the rest of them inside after giving Pop a quick hug. She only paused at the door for a second, looking in the direction of Stuart Ranch, and wondering what her life would be like if things had been just a little different.

Suddenly, she wished she was on a plane to Panama. Or Indonesia. Heck, Idaho would work. Anywhere, so long as it was a couple thousand miles from the painful memories that were threatening to come back to the surface now that she was here.

But those painful memories were the reason she was here, so she bit back the desire to flee and walked inside her childhood home, closing the door behind her.

Amy soon found herself sitting down at her parents' table, already piled high with Ma's famous cooking. "So, update me on what's going on with everyone," she said, hoping talk would keep her mind from wandering back toward Stuart Ranch.

"Pop's working himself too hard fixing the barn when he could just let me do it. Or hire someone," Brock began as they all began filling their plates.

Pop cut into Brock's scolding. "I'm not so old I can't lift a hammer, Brock," he said around his mustache. "And the horses will appreciate it, which is good for the riding school."

Pop had always been such a strong, consistent force in her life that it was hard for Amy to imagine him ever slowing down, but she could see that Brock was concerned. Still, he didn't seem willing to push the topic any further than he already had.

"Speaking of riding," Brock said, pointing to the twins, "these two have been doing a great job learning to ride and care for horses."

Zach and Carter beamed. "Mr. Stuart says we're naturals," Carter declared.

Amy about choked on her water. "Stuart?" she asked in between coughs.

Brock nodded, looking proud. "Tom Stuart's taken over the school since his father passed a year ago. The boys go there twice a week."

Amy's heart started again. She hadn't known the boys were going to the Stuarts', and hearing the name out of the blue like that had done more to her than she liked to admit. She suddenly hoped to heaven that Jack was still out on the circuit. Maybe he would even be gone the entire month she was there, and she could board her plane to Thailand after the wedding and just forget about her resolution to speak to him, which seemed awfully daunting now that she was home.

Brock gestured to her with his fork. "Jack's back in town right now, too. Weren't you two an item for a while in high school?"

Amy felt her heart jolt again at the sound of his name. Of course, Brock had been on the rodeo circuit when they'd started dating. He didn't know how serious their relationship had been, didn't know that his name cut through her like a knife.

But Ma and Pop knew some of it. Pop stood, clearing his throat, and all the attention turned to him. "I just want to thank y'all for being here. It does an old man good to see so many people he loves around the table together."

There was a round of "hear, hear!" and a lifting of glasses, and then Pop sat back down. "Now, stop with the chatter and get to eatin'. I don't plan on having leftovers," Ma added.

With that, they tucked in, eating heartily. Amy didn't look at Brock, in case he decided to start up the conversation again. She did, however, risk a glance at Pop, who was looking at her with concern. Amy gave him a little nod of thanks, then turned her eyes back to the plate in front of her.

Jack Stuart was in town right this minute, just a few miles away. When she'd bought her ticket to come home, she had hoped he would be, but now…

The mix of emotions he evoked was too much to analyze. All she knew for sure was that she couldn't run and hide any longer, and she needed to be prepared to talk to him. Tell him the truth.

Amy awoke long before sunrise, her internal clock still not quite on Texas time. Once awake, her mind immediately turned to Jack, her stomach twisting. She lay in bed wondering if he already knew she was home, if he would decide to confront her about her disappearance after graduation, or if she would be the one to seek him out. And if she could force herself to actually do so.

She knew that her eighteen-year-old self hadn't handled things particularly well, and she still felt guilt rise in her when she thought of the messages he had left, asking her to please call him and tell him why she hadn't talked to him, why she had just left without saying goodbye.

She had listened to each one over and over again, torturing herself just so she could hear his voice, but she hadn't had the nerve to call him back, to talk to him, to explain why she'd gone away.

She was stronger now, though. She had made the decision to come clean to him, and she *could* handle it, however difficult it might seem. After all, their relationship had been a long time ago. About a decade now.

Shouldn't that be long enough to wipe away everything that had happened between them?

She knew, though, that it hadn't been long enough for her.

Amy sighed and pulled herself out of bed, determined to get her mind off her high school sweetheart.

For an hour, she struggled to write an article about her experiences in the Sahara Desert, but the camels and tribesmen and women felt impossible to capture in words when her brain was so full of other things so much closer to home.

Finally, frustrated, she turned from her laptop and paced the length of her small childhood bedroom, trying to get her mind to settle down and focus. She felt too closed in to think properly—that was the problem, she told herself.

Amy could see that the sky had lightened enough for the world outside her window to be more than just a swath of darkness, and she determined that it would be best to get out of this tiny room. Her eyes landed on her old tan Stetson, hanging on one of her bedposts, just where she would always put it after a ride, and she smiled.

In a couple of minutes, her hair was falling down her back underneath a battered cowboy hat, and she had thrown on her jeans. With her old cowboy boots in one hand, she sneaked quietly down the stairs in just her socks, hoping not to wake anyone.

Once she was standing outside and the back door was shut behind her, she slid her feet into her boots and walked quickly toward the barn, feeling like a younger version of herself. When she reached it, it took no time at all to slip inside and find her old tack in its place against the wall. Pa had taken good care of it while she was gone.

The smell of hay and the nickering of horses surrounded her and was a soothing presence, and for a moment she stood there, feeling the supple leather of her saddle and remembering old times when she wanted nothing more than to live on a ranch and ride in rodeos. And marry Jack.

She turned from the saddle, wishing she could turn from her thoughts as easily, and walked along the row of horses. Since the family ran a riding school, there was no shortage of animals to ride, but she still looked over them all, telling herself she wasn't looking for Bandit.

Bandit had been her horse back in the day, a beautiful black stallion with white freckled markings on his nose, and when he died during her first year of college, she'd cried long and hard. It still sent a pang through her heart to think of him, and she knew she would always wonder if he'd felt abandoned when she moved so far away.

Bandit wasn't there, of course, and she looked over the horses once again, this time seeing them as they were, and not what they weren't. A feisty-looking mare, dark brown, butted Amy with her nose, stopping her in her tracks. When Amy looked the animal in the eyes, she knew they'd get along just fine.

Amy saddled up the mare, whose name she didn't know, and walked her out of the barn. In the early-morning light, the mare's coat shone a deep bronze, and Amy patted her. "What do you say we go for a ride, girl?" she asked.

The horse snorted and pulled her head up quickly, almost as if she was nodding. Amy grinned at her and mounted the animal, settling into the saddle as if she'd only been riding the day before. With that, the two were off around the property, getting to know each other.

For a few minutes, Amy was content to ride at a walking pace as she accustomed herself to the mare's gait. Once she was comfortable, though, she started to feel antsy. The lingering anxiety was still there, nagging at the back of her mind, and she decided to do what she'd always done to clear her mind in the old days: outrun her thoughts. Amy turned the mare toward the fence line, and in a few seconds they were through a small gate and onto a trail that wound its way through the trees that bordered her parents' property.

Soon Amy and the mare were moving at a quick trot along the footpath. Amy leaned close to the mare's neck as she reveled in the familiar feeling. She must have traveled along this trail hundreds of times when she was in high school, exercising the horses and leading children from her father's riding school along the path.

When they broke through the last of the trees into an open field, Amy urged the horse to go faster, and they streaked through the short grass at a run, hurtling along until they reached a dirt road. The feel of her hair streaming behind her as the cool wind slapped her face gave Amy more joy than she remembered feeling in a long time. When they slowed, she took in a deep breath and shivered with the cold.

By that time the sky was full of light, and Amy knew it was probably time to get back. She turned the mare to walk along the road, back toward the ranch.

Amy was still breathing hard, her heart pounding, when she saw something that made it beat even harder.

A few hundred yards up the road was a truck, a cowboy leaning against it and watching her.

She knew the truck and the cowboy so well, she recognized them immediately, even though it had been a decade since she'd seen either one. How many times had she looked up from a ride to see that cowboy leaning just that way on that beat-up old truck?

Without any guidance, the horse continued walking toward the ranch, bringing Amy closer and closer to Jack Stuart. She couldn't bring herself to look away from him, and he kept his eyes locked on hers.

This was it. She'd promised herself she would do this, and now the time had come. Amy took a long, calming breath.

After what felt like an eternity, the mare was only a few feet from the truck. Amy pulled on the reins and the horse stopped and waited to be told what to do next. Amy wished someone would tell her what she should do, too, but she knew she'd need to figure it out for herself.

Jack moved away from the truck and came closer, stroking the horse's muzzle, still keeping his eyes on Amy. For a long moment, they stared at one another, only a foot of space between them.

If her heart hadn't been beating so hard, it might have stopped at the sight of Jack so close. He looked a little older, but he was still handsome as ever, his wavy dark hair playing around his ears in the breeze. And his eyes, that same light blue that haunted her dreams, bored into her.

She couldn't think of what to say. *Hi* seemed silly, with all the unanswered questions and years standing between them.

"I heard you were in town," Jack said, breaking the silence at last.

Amy nodded, not taking her eyes off his. "For a month."

"I was on my way to your house when I saw you two."

She wasn't sure what to say to that. Had it brought up old memories for him, too?

"I'd like to talk, Amy," he said, his voice sounding strained.

Was he hurt, or angry, or both? It was hard to tell exactly how he felt from the way he clenched his jaw, but it was enough to make it clear that he hadn't forgotten about what had happened between them all those years ago.

And now it was time to explain. As much as she wanted to run away again, she wasn't going to. The mare snorted and shifted beneath her, as if she could feel Amy's roil of emotions.

Her eyes began to sting with the tears of all the years she'd missed with him because of the hand fate had dealt her.

Chapter 2

Jack hated what seeing her did to his heart. She had dumped him—even worse, just avoided him—yet when he looked at her all he wanted to do was pull her into his arms. The moment he'd seen her as he was driving along, her blond hair flying along behind her just like it did when she rode junior rodeo in high school, it was like the last decade had never happened.

It was even worse when she looked down at him from her perch on the horse, her green eyes sparkling with tears. He couldn't meet them and keep his distance. He turned his eyes to the truck. "How about we sit for a few minutes?" he asked, lowering the tailgate of his truck.

It would be warmer in the cab, but he knew Amy would want to keep close to the horse. Besides, he didn't think he could be in that small a space with her and keep his wits about him. As it was, he already felt claustrophobic despite the wide-open sky and the large animal between them.

Amy swung herself off the horse, wincing when she dropped her weight onto one foot, and if he'd been any closer, he would have automatically put his arms on her waist to steady her. He was almost glad for the distance between them, since he wasn't sure what touching her would do to him. "Are you okay?" he asked.

She nodded. "Twisted my ankle a while back, and it still gives me trouble sometimes."

Jack almost said something, anything, to keep the conversation away from the tough stuff, but he kept his mouth shut. It was finally time to talk about what had happened between them.

Amy seemed to think the same thing, because she walked over and sat down on the tailgate, reins in her hand, and sighed. "For what it's worth, I'm sorry. About not calling you," she said, her voice quieter, softer than he remembered ever hearing it before. "I was a coward not to talk to you about what was going on."

He waited while she took a deep breath, and for a brief moment he considered stopping her right there. If whatever she was going to say took a decade to come out, maybe he didn't want to hear it. Maybe, if she never said anything, they could just start where they'd left off...

He brushed away the crazy idea. He needed to know.

"A few days after graduation, while you were gone on your family trip, I went to the doctor."

His mind filled with possibilities, some of them terrifying, though none of them made sense. Was she sick? If she had been ill for the last decade, she certainly didn't show it. She looked as beautiful as she had at seventeen, even more so, with the air of confidence she seemed to exude now, even when she was near tears.

Had she gotten pregnant? That seemed like an odd reason for her to run from him, since she would have known, even at that young age, that he would be more than happy to raise a child with her. They had been talking about having a family together nearly the entire time they were together.

His mind flitted back to illness. What if she *was* sick? Deathly sick? And he didn't know?

He waited, the pit of his stomach tense, for what the doctor might have told her that had made her disappear from his life.

"I found out that I can't have kids, Jack. Ever. I left because you deserved to be with someone who could give you the family you've always wanted."

Jack felt a combination of pain and relief. He turned to look carefully at Amy. "But you're not sick or anything?" he asked.

"Except for not being able to have children, I'm fine—"

"It's *you* I cared about, Amy, not whether or not you can make babies. Hell, you're adopted. You know better than anyone that there are other options, if we wanted kids."

Jack had never felt so relieved, yet at the same time he was sad for all the years together they had lost. Sure, he'd wanted kids, but this was Amy. What he'd always wanted, more than anything, was *her*.

Amy still looked somber. "You say that now, Jack, and I know you would've said that then, but the years would have gone by and you'd have wished we could have children. *Your* children. Even if you didn't, I'd always wonder if you did. I didn't want that to fester underneath the surface, ruining our relationship."

"So you left?" Jack asked, searching her face.

Amy looked away from his eyes. She seemed embarrassed. "I couldn't break up with you. I know I never would've been able to make myself say the words to you. And since I couldn't let myself stay with you, leaving felt like my only option. I'm sorry for doing that to you, Jack. I was a coward. You deserved better."

At last, a great weight disappeared from Jack's shoulders. After years of wondering, at least he knew the answers to all his unanswered questions. Now there still seemed to be one question left: Where did he go from there?

Amy sat on the tailgate, chilled by the early-morning breeze and by her own thoughts. She waited for him to say something that would give her a clue as to what he was thinking. If he despised her cowardice, wanted nothing to do with her, she deserved it. She wouldn't run from it anymore. She patted the mare's soft muzzle absentmindedly, waiting.

Finally, he spoke. "We should get your horse back to the barn," he said, hopping off the tailgate and holding out his hand to her. "How about we walk there? I can come back for the truck."

She was speechless for a moment. The unexpected friendliness, the opening of a door she thought long closed, surprised her. When she took his hand, however, its warmth and steadiness rushed through her, and the spark of recognition and comfort that flowed through the link made her smile. Her hand felt right nestled in his, like they had never been apart.

"Your hands are freezing," Jack commented, pressing hers in both of his.

She was warmed by more than his palms as he helped her stand, and their fingers lingered together for an extra moment before he let go to close his tailgate and pull his keys from the ignition.

They began walking side by side toward her parents' ranch along the road, the mare walking along behind them and occasionally batting Amy with her nose, as if anxious to move faster. Amy, though, wasn't in any rush to finish the half mile or so walk. She didn't want this intimate moment to be over too quickly.

"I can't believe you still have that old truck," she told Jack, glancing back at the vehicle parked beside the field. "After all the times it broke down in high school, I never would have imagined it would last so long."

"I had to put a lot of work into it over the years, and it still has a few quirks," Jack said, giving her a sidelong smile that went straight to her heart, "but I've loved it since I was a teenager. I could never just give up on it."

Amy blushed, feeling the words resonate through her, sure he was talking about more than just the truck.

But no. Even if they did, the facts of the situation had not changed. She still couldn't have children, and he still deserved the chance to find a woman who could give him the family he'd always wanted.

He had the chance, and it seems he never took it, she thought to herself. She couldn't stop the heat from blossoming in her chest. It turned to ice as she put back up the walls she'd built around her heart in the past few days. She knew now better than ever that she couldn't let herself get carried away with a man. Even if it was Jack.

He stopped walking and turned toward her, and she

did the same. Suddenly, she felt as if he was much too close, and at the same time too far away, and she longed to move closer. To touch his lips with hers. She took a step back.

She was sure the feel of their lips, their bodies, together would also be on the list of things that hadn't changed, and it scared her.

"Will you go out with me tonight?" he asked, his voice low and deep.

The word *yes* was on her tongue, but Amy balked. She couldn't let them fall right back into the relationship she'd run away from, could she? What about all that had happened since? Would there just be too much between them? And she had no idea who he was now. He could be every bit as despicable as Armand, the person she least wanted to think about.

Jack seemed to realize her indecision, because he turned and started walking toward her house again. After a moment, she pulled herself out of her shock and hustled to catch up with him. When he spoke, he sounded lighthearted, confident. Exactly the Jack she knew from high school. "How about this—we go out tonight just to get to know each other. We start fresh. No expectations. No baggage. No past. Just us, two twentysomethings who met while I was out for a drive and you were going for a ride on your horse."

She had to smile at his antics. "No past? So you saw a random woman riding a horse in the middle of nowhere and stopped to ask her out?"

His eyes danced with laughter. "When you put it like that, it doesn't sound so great. How about I was driving along when I saw a beautiful woman and a beautiful horse, and I felt compelled to speak to her. The woman, not the horse."

Amy wasn't sure if she was amused or panicked. For a moment he sounded just like Armand. Charming, flattering…but this was *Jack*. He was being sincere.

Wasn't he?

They grew quiet and walked a little longer, until her childhood home appeared down the street.

"So I'll pick you up tonight at seven?" he said, his voice serious as he turned toward her again.

Amy nodded, though a large part of her yelled that it was too much, too soon. Jack's face lit with a smile, and he turned his attention back to the house that loomed before them. She was glad he wasn't looking at her any longer, so he wouldn't see just how torn and confused she was.

She tried to tell herself she was being stupid, worrying over nothing. She'd known Jack almost as long as she'd been alive. Armand was—well, he was a blip on the radar of her life, not worth thinking about. So she would just stop.

The likelihood of that was so far-fetched that Amy couldn't stop a snort from escaping.

"What're you thinking about over there?" Jack asked, the gleam in his eye making him so devilishly handsome she wasn't sure if she wanted to kiss him or run away.

"That wasn't me, that was the horse," she said, turning away so he wouldn't see the flow of emotions she couldn't control.

He snorted skeptically in response, and she felt the tension inside her break as a laugh broke from her throat. She'd forgotten how easily he could make her laugh, regardless of her mood. She had missed that.

They arrived at the house, and even though the mare was pulling Amy toward the barn, she couldn't pull herself away from Jack, as if something magnetic about him forced her to stay close to him now that she'd found him again.

He looked in her eyes again, making her stomach drop somewhere near her toes. "Seven, right?" he asked.

The note of insecurity in his voice sent a pang through her heart. It reminded her again of how much she must have hurt him. She nodded. "Seven."

He leaned forward and brushed his lips against hers, sending a shock wave of hormones rushing through her body. Her mind recoiled at the feeling, and she almost called the date off right then and there. The idea of being vulnerable again so soon, even with Jack, made her more than nervous.

Jack seemed to realize he'd crossed the line. He tilted his hat and said, "I don't normally kiss ladies I just met. I assure you, I'll be a perfect gentleman on our date."

He turned back toward the road and began walking away, but she wasn't ready for him to disappear. Not quite yet.

"You haven't even asked my name," she called to him, desperate to see his face again for a few more seconds.

He looked at her with a smile and bowed. "Where are my manners? Name's Jack, miss. And you are…?" he asked.

God, he was so cute she could hardly speak. "Amelia. Friends call me Amy."

"Amelia," he repeated, as if tasting the word, and

she felt such an overwhelming urge to kiss him she was glad he was already several feet away.

Reluctantly, she started toward the barn, following the horse's insistent pull. Before she could get too far, though, she realized something. "This is all I have to wear for a date," she said to his retreating figure, raising her voice so he would hear and gesturing toward her jeans and old T-shirt. "I've been living out of a backpack in the African desert for the past year."

He just smiled at her again. "Sounds like you'll have some mighty interesting stories to tell me at dinner, miss. You can just wear that," he said, eyeing her carefully. "I like the cowgirl look."

Before she could say anything in response, Jack had chuckled and waved. "See you at seven," he called as he turned away a final time.

Once he was gone, she spun toward the barn and practically ran the rest of the way, making the horse move quickly to keep up. Even so, Amy was unable to outrun her thoughts.

What was the matter with her? Jack was *not* Armand. He wasn't the type of guy to seduce her and manipulate her into falling for him. He wasn't a selfish liar. He was Jack.

Still, she couldn't seem to stop herself from panicking every time he said something sweet or she felt desire rise up.

She knew she was still hurting from what she'd been through, and that it was far too soon to go on a date with Jack. She knew she should've said no. But it was too late now, and a part of her wanted so badly to be with him again, to feel his arms around her. To be safe and secure.

She was going on a date. That was all there was to it. They would talk and eat and get to know each other again. And maybe, maybe she would be able to convince herself that everything that had happened in Morocco was in the past.

As she brushed down the mare, Amy went over the morning's events once more in her head. Jack was just as attractive as always, that was for sure, but in high school he'd seemed a little more…happy-go-lucky, she supposed. He had always seemed happy, as if life smiled upon him. There was something careworn about him now.

She fervently hoped that she wasn't the one to change that about him.

She shook her head at the irony of that thought, since it was just that part of his nature that had been one of the reasons she had run instead of talking to him. She'd been worried he would convince her that the doctors were wrong and they could have exactly the life they'd planned because it was the life he *wanted*, dammit, and everything always worked out the way he wanted.

And she had known all those years ago that if she talked to him she would cave, give in to the hope even when she knew the odds, and it had made her a coward.

But now—

"I saw Jack Stuart walking you home," Pop said from behind Amy, startling her out of her thoughts.

He came up beside her and pet the horse she was grooming, but said nothing else. Just waited.

Amy nodded. "He spotted me while I was out riding. We had a good talk."

Pop said nothing, but she could tell by the slight curve of his mustache that he was pleased. He didn't meddle in the affairs of his children like Ma, but he cared deeply for their happiness. Impulsively, Amy gave the old man a hug.

"I don't know if it's a good idea or not, but I'm going on a date with him tonight. I've missed him all these years, but maybe this is a bad idea. Maybe I'm just setting myself up to get hurt, and I don't want to go through that again—" She stopped, aware she was saying more than she'd meant to.

She hadn't told anyone about Armand, and frankly she didn't plan on doing it anytime soon. It was more than humiliating, and she wasn't ready to relive it.

Luckily, Pop wasn't the type to pry. He put a hand on Amy's shoulder. "Don't you worry," he said.

She wasn't sure if he meant not to worry about the date or her past pain or what, but it was fine not knowing. He probably meant all of it. Pop didn't need many words to be there for his daughter.

Amy turned back to the mare to finish grooming her. "How's the riding school going?" she asked, ready for a change of topic.

The old man puffed out a stream of air that made his mustache flutter. "Fewer kids every year, seems like. If it weren't for the rest of the ranch and the few stud horses we have, it wouldn't be worth the costs. Still, it's such a part of this place I'd keep it going if it cost me a small fortune. Your ma thinks I'm crazy, but there it is."

Amy hadn't heard her father say so many words in one go since the time he'd lectured her on the dangers of peer pressure when she was a teenager. She'd always known her pop was partial to the riding school, and even though she worried about his health, she had to love his loyalty to the horses and the children.

The mare under Amy's hand snorted and shook her mane, as if trying to get Amy's attention back on her where it belonged. Amy smiled. "I like this horse, Pop. What's her name?"

"Queen Bee."

Amy chuckled as the animal raised her head regally. The name fit her, certainly.

"Be careful riding her, though. She had a run-in with a snake a while back and spooks easy. I don't let the riding school kids take her out anymore."

Amy patted the horse like she was an old friend. "I can handle a skittish horse, Pop."

Jack drove back to his family's ranch in a state of disbelief. He had prepared himself for an ugly fight, or for no answer at all, but not this. A reconciliation? Maybe not quite, but it was at least a new chance for him and Amy.

He also hadn't been prepared for all the emotions he would feel when he saw her. He'd tried to be ready, but nothing he could have done would prepare him for the electricity that shot through him at the sight of her. She was as stunning as ever.

There was also a sliver of fear, as if she was going to disappear again before his eyes, as if she had never been real in the first place.

He drummed his fingers on the steering wheel, full of nervous energy. He didn't know what he could do to keep himself occupied until that evening, but he'd need to find something or he would go crazy waiting, wondering if it was all real, if she would be there when he arrived at the McNeal house at seven.

Once his truck was parked in front of Stuart Ranch,

Jack went immediately toward the barn, veering around the house. Indoors sounded stifling, and he knew it would be infuriating to pace around the living room watching the hand on the clock move with frustrating slowness, which he was sure would happen. Better to get onto a horse and do something under the clear cool sky rather than hole up inside.

As he approached the barn, his brother Tom walked out with a couple of horses on leads. Jack went up to him, seeing an opportunity for distraction. "How can I help?" he asked.

Tom gave him a curious look, as if he sensed something of Jack's emotions. "I'm setting up for a group of students. They'll be here in a half hour."

"Ages?" Jack asked, turning to go to the barn and get whatever else they might need for the riding lessons.

"Under sevens," Tom answered. "There'll be about four kids total," he added before Jack could disappear into the barn.

Jack sighed. He should have expected such low numbers, but it was always a little deflating to be reminded how much it had dwindled. With more than one school in this tiny area, and the drop in population over the past few years, having any students at all was a stroke of luck. His father and Mr. McNeal had started their riding schools years ago when the high demand for lessons meant both schools could prosper. When their father was, if not young, at least spry, they had kids driving in from towns over an hour away. He loved teaching children how to ride, and it showed in the flourishing school he ran.

Without his touch, the school had fallen off to maybe twenty students. If Spring Valley's population had stayed steady, maybe they would be afloat even without Dad's magic touch, but as the town dwindled, so did their business.

Now they were at the point that the only reason they'd manage to pay the bills was Jack's winnings from the rodeo and Tom's determination to stretch every dollar. If Jack didn't find a new partner soon, he didn't think even Tom's penny-pinching would save them.

Still, the ranch had to run. It was their mom's home— it was Jack's future. Tom didn't want the ranch, never had, but Jack always dreamed of turning it into a rodeo school when he retired with a good chunk of cash from his roping career.

If they could somehow last that long. Something would need to change, but what and how?

Jack pulled himself out of his reverie. It wasn't helping anything, and he'd gone over it all so many times, but it always led to nothing. Now was the time to work, not think, so he grabbed a couple more of their gentlest horses and brought them out to the paddock where Tom was standing with the others.

They looped the leads over a fence post and both went back for saddles. "Have a good drive?" Tom asked.

Jack could tell Tom wanted to ask what had happened, knew Tom saw a change in him. And even though there was no reason to hide his reunion with Amy, that their date couldn't possibly be a secret, he still felt a momentary desire to hide it, as if talking about it might make it all go away like a birthday wish or something.

Tom was watching him, though, and he knew he had to come clean. "I went to see Amy. We talked and decided to go out tonight."

"Like on a date?" Tom asked, sounding a little surprised.

"I guess so," Jack answered, not ready to clarify more.

He loved his brother, but talking had never been their strong suit, and it seemed strange to open up to him about the real history of his relationship with Amy and what this date could or could not mean. Heck, he wasn't even really ready to *think* about all that, let alone *talk* about it.

Tom seemed to understand, because he didn't ask anything more, and soon they were guiding little kids around the paddock, each one practicing squeezing their legs to make their horse go and pulling on the reins to stop. The two youngest children, identical twins, could hardly manage enough force to get the horse's attention, but the docile creatures listened to them with the patience of loving parents.

Jack watched the twins with interest. Zach and Carter, Brock's soon-to-be sons, had settled into Spring Valley comfortably and seemed more than ready to add Brock to their family. He'd seen the way their faces lit up around Amy's brother. They loved him and from what Jack had seen, Brock clearly doted on them. Jack had always wanted a family, and it made his heart swell to think that a child didn't need to be yours biologically in order to be family.

Like the McNeal clan. All four children were adopted, and their parents loved every one of them as much as any parent could. If a couple were unable to have children for some reason…

His mind balked as Jack realized he had drifted into territory he wasn't remotely ready for. He had only seen

Amy for a few minutes after ten years of complete silence from her—there was no way he should be thinking about them starting a family together. Heck, part of him was still dead sure dinner was a bad idea. The part that had never healed when she left the first time.

He wasn't ready to get hurt like that again, and thoughts like those would only make it worse.

Still, he couldn't help but watch the time tick by oh so slowly toward seven, and he did everything he could think of to speed it along.

He hadn't been this antsy for a date in a very long time. About ten years, in fact.

Chapter 3

Amy sat with Cassie, the two women shading their eyes against the afternoon light as they watched Brock play tag with the young twins, while the new cows lowed happily in the pen Brock had built over the past two months. If Amy hadn't been so preoccupied with thoughts of her date in just a few hours, the antics of the three males would have been hilarious. As it was, though, she was hardly able to even hold a basic conversation with Cassie, let alone anything else.

After the third time Amy had to apologize for not hearing what Cassie had said, Cassie gave her an intense clinical stare. "Is everything okay, Amy? You're almost as difficult to talk to as Brock was when he had a concussion. Did you hit your head recently? Who was the first President of the United States?"

Amy chuckled and shook her head. "I don't have a concussion, Cassie. I'm just…preoccupied."

"With what?" Cassie asked, her demeanor shifting from doctor to sister instantaneously.

Amy didn't have any sisters—well, didn't grow up with any, at least, she amended—so it felt odd to confide in Cassie like this, but she needed to talk to someone. Pop was a good listener but not one for advice and long conversations, and Ma would end up trying to play the ultimate matchmaker if she even got a whiff of an opportunity. Amy took a breath and spilled her thoughts to her soon-to-be sister-in-law.

"Do you know Jack Stuart?" she asked, knowing the answer.

"Sure," Cassie said. "He was at the riding school with Tom today for the boys' lesson. Zach said he is, and I quote, 'a really cool rodeo cowboy.'"

Amy agreed with Zach's assessment, but it didn't even scratch the surface of everything there was to say about Jack.

"He's also my high school sweetheart, my first boyfriend," Amy added. "He's taking me out tonight and I'm just a bit nervous. It's been a long time since we've seen each other and so much has changed and Jack—" Amy cut off the torrent of words, not sure what she wanted to say.

Jack was special.

Jack could be a chance to start over.

Jack didn't know who she was and what she'd done, and she wasn't sure he'd still like her when he found out.

Cassie seemed to have filled in the blank her own way, because she hopped up and grabbed Amy's hand, pulling her inside. "If you've got a date, we have much more important things to do than sit here watching three guys tumbling around the yard. Do you even have any nice clothes in that backpack of yours?"

Amy smiled as Cassie's enthusiasm calmed some of her worries. "Nothing but travel clothes, jeans and a few summer dresses. Jack won't care what I'm wearing but—"

"But you do, of course," Cassie said before Amy could finish the sentence. "I'm a bit shorter than you, but I bet a few of my things will fit. Want to go shopping in my closet?"

Amy nodded, relieved she would have something to wear that hadn't been tainted by her recent past. Amy cut that thought off before it could gain any more traction and followed Cassie. In a few minutes they were ankle-deep in discarded dresses. Each one had been pronounced too something for this date. Too conservative. Too risqué. Too formal. Too short.

Finally, Cassie clapped her hands in delight, and Amy had to agree. She was holding a knee-length dress in a shimmery navy blue with little cap sleeves that Amy loved. "Go try it on," Cassie urged, and Amy took the dress into the bathroom.

When she stepped back out, Cassie's squeal of happiness confirmed her thoughts: it was a beautiful dress.

"He's going to fall in love with you the moment he sees you," Cassie said dreamily.

The thought made her heart stutter. Did she want him to fall in love with her again? The thought sent a wave of fear through her, and she knew she wasn't ready to talk about anything resembling love.

"What's wrong, Amy? This isn't about the dress, is it?" Cassie asked, putting her hand on Amy's arm.

Amy sat on the bed, feeling sudden tears spring into

her eyes. Cassie sat beside her. "You can tell me anything, Amy. Doctor-patient confidentiality," she added with a smile.

"Are you a therapist?" Amy asked with a little laugh as she brushed a tear away.

"Not technically, but I can sure try, if that's what you need."

Amy sighed. "In Morocco, I met a man. Armand. He was—"

She searched for the right word while Cassie waited patiently. "He was incredibly charming," Amy finally finished, though that didn't really do justice to the pull he had over her.

"I gather it didn't end well?" Cassie prompted quietly.

Amy laughed. "That's the understatement of the century. He wasn't who I thought he was. He was married, for one thing."

Cassie pulled Amy into a hug, and Amy was grateful she didn't have to explain any more about her relationship with Armand. The way he manipulated her feelings, the way he'd treated her after he'd known she was hooked. How difficult it had been to get back her independence and leave.

"Anyway, I got away from all that and came home. And now I'm going on this date and feel like a complete basket case for even agreeing to it after all that," Amy said, trying to end the conversation and stop herself from becoming completely overwhelmed with still-fresh feelings at the same time.

Cassie gave her a look of concern. "You can still call off or postpone this date if it's too much for you, you know. This dress will wait, and I'm sure Jack would understand."

Amy only thought about that for a second before dismissing it. There was no way she was going to cancel this date. "I need this date, I think. It might help me get rid of Armand, but mostly…" She paused, struggling for words. "It's *Jack*," she finished, sure Cassie couldn't understand everything he meant to her. Heck, she didn't think she did, either.

"Well, if you're going on a date tonight, we need to figure out something for shoes, because I don't think mine will fit you," Cassie declared, shaking her head.

Amy smiled, glad the conversation had turned to less serious topics. She looked at her feet and knew instinctively what shoes she wanted to wear with this dress. "Shoes I've got taken care of. Thanks so much for the help, Cassie. And for listening. I promise next time we'll talk about fun things like your wedding instead of having a therapy session."

Cassie shrugged and started picking up the discarded dresses. "It's no problem. I mean, how can I ask you to be my bridesmaid if I'm not willing to be a shoulder to cry on once in a while? I'll probably need you to return the favor as the big day approaches and the inevitable wedding disasters occur."

Amy's eyes widened in surprise. "You want me to be one of your bridesmaids?"

Cassie looked up. "Of course I want you to be a bridesmaid. I was hoping to have three. Emma from the bakery, my sister who lives in Minnesota and you. I really *do* want us to be sisters, Amy."

Amy felt her eyes sting with tears again, but managed to hold them back. There had already been too much crying today.

"So, will you be my bridesmaid?" Cassie asked.

Amy nodded and the two women hugged.

A door slam and thumping footsteps heralded the entrance of Brock and the boys. "Momma, why are you hugging Auntie Amy?" Zach asked, looking concerned.

Cassie leaned down low and ruffled her son's hair, sending a pang through Amy's heart, just as it always did when she saw mothers interacting with their children. "Auntie Amy is doing me a favor, so I was saying thank you with a nice big hug. She's going to be in the wedding with us," Cassie explained.

Carter's face broke into a wide grin. "We're going to be in the wedding, too! We get to hold the rings and stand next to our uncles!"

Brock held out a hand for each of the boys to high-five. "That's right. Y'all are going to do me proud, I know it."

Carter and Zach both puffed with pleasure.

"So I know now's not the time, what with your imminent date and all," Cassie said, turning back to Amy, "but we need to get you fitted for your bridesmaid dress soon so there'll be time to alter it before the wedding. We're less than a month away at this point."

Amy nodded, taking her role as bridesmaid very seriously. "I'll be here for whatever you need," she said earnestly.

Brock cut into the sweet, sisterly moment. "Wait, you have a date? With who?" he asked, sounding almost protective.

Cassie gave Amy a worried look, as if she was waiting to see if she'd already slipped up as a sister and confidante. Amy gave her brother a steely gaze. "I'm going on a date with Jack Stuart, and you are not to say anything overprotective or big-brotherly about it."

Brock held up his hands in mock surrender. "I wouldn't think of it. Have fun, my adult sister who can make her own decisions."

Amy and Cassie both smiled in relief.

"But if he tries to get fresh with you—" he began, pointing a finger in warning.

He was cut off when Cassie shoved him out the door. "Sorry about that," Cassie said, grimacing.

Amy laughed. She'd forgotten what it was like to have a big brother around watching out for her. It was a little obnoxious, sure, but also nice in its own way.

"So, let's talk about the wedding," she said, filling the silence.

Cassie shook her head. "Nuh-uh. We're not done here. Next is makeup and hair."

Amy twirled a strand of her blond hair around one of her fingers as she was dragged into the bathroom. "How do you know how to do all this stuff?" she asked.

She'd assumed her doctor sister-in-law was just as clueless as she was, but it seemed very clear that she was wrong. Cassie shrugged as she opened a drawer of brushes and powders. "I have a sister. This is what you do when you're bored over summer vacation."

Amy had never felt like she'd missed out having only brothers, but now she wondered what it would've been like to grow up with a sister. She couldn't go back and change her childhood, but maybe she'd be able to have the closeness of a female sibling now, as an adult. The thought made her smile as she closed her eyes so Cassie could apply eye shadow.

* * *

Jack walked to the door of the McNeals' ranch house, a combination of nervousness and excitement turning his stomach into knots. He could well remember being seventeen and feeling that same emotion as he stood waiting for Amy. That was on the occasion of their true first date, when he had nearly convinced himself that it was all a hallucination or something. Or a cruel prank.

It was funny how history repeated itself, he thought as he quelled the sudden voice insisting Amy wouldn't be home. What if she'd changed her mind and taken off again, leaving him without explanation for another decade?

Jack took a deep breath and knocked on the door. It opened almost instantaneously, and he breathed a secret sigh of relief. Amy stood there in all her glory and then some.

"You look…" he began, but words failed him as he took in the sight of her.

Amy's long blond hair cascaded over her shoulders in wavy curls, and her dress was a blue that made her eyes sparkle. Or maybe they were sparkling because she was looking at him.

A man could hope.

When his eyes landed on her scuffed cowboy boots, his expression broke into a wide grin. "My girl knows how to dress for a night out on the town, that's for sure," he commented, chuckling.

For just a split second, Amy's smile faltered and Jack wanted to smack himself. He'd forgotten that this wasn't a decade ago, and Amy wasn't his girl anymore. But then the moment was gone and they were just two strangers standing awkwardly, unsure what came next.

"Is this okay? Since I wasn't sure where we were going, I didn't know how to dress," Amy said as she stepped out onto the porch and closed the front door behind her.

The old Amy would have put some attitude behind the words, teasing Jack for his insistence on making even the most mundane outings a surprise. This time, however, it was just an explanation, nothing more. "You look perfect," he said, earning him another nervous smile.

Jack suddenly felt like this date was a bad idea. She had always been feisty to the point of exasperation, and even a simple compliment rarely went unchallenged. Now she seemed timid, nervous, and he panicked at the thought that she had changed so much and he would forever lose the perfect picture of her he had in his mind. He told himself this was just a strange moment, and they were both acting a little odd because of it.

After waiting all day filled with too much energy, Jack was already exhausted trying to live each moment in the present and the past.

He made a declaration then and there to give up the constant comparisons. Tonight was about having a nice first date with a beautiful woman.

As if to prove it to himself, he held out his hand to shake hers. "Nice to see you again, Miss Amelia. Thank you for agreeing to go out with me. I know many women would hesitate at a date with a stranger, but I'm sure glad you accepted my offer."

The light in Amy's eye sparkled, and she put on a really terrible Southern Belle accent. "Well, I do declare that it was a might unbecoming of me to allow your advances while I was unchaperoned, but a girl of my age must defy the rules on occasion or she may live the rest of her days as an old spinster."

Jack tried to keep a straight face, but he was wildly unsuccessful, and soon they were both laughing.

"I seem to have come to the wrong house. I was picking up Amy McNeal, not Scarlett O'Hara," he finally managed once the bout of laughter had passed.

"Well, I have never been so insulted in my life!" Scarlett-Amy exclaimed, putting her hand to her heart so dramatically that it sent them both back into giggles.

Jack felt relief course through him. Some things had changed, certainly, but she was still Amy.

They walked down the porch steps, still chuckling, and Jack had to restrain himself from wrapping his arm around her and pulling her in for a kiss. If she wasn't ready yet to be "his girl" again, she probably wasn't ready for a make-out session in the driveway.

To be fair, he wasn't sure if he was ready for that, either. The flood of feelings just being near Amy was almost overwhelming; kissing her could send him right over the edge.

Instead, Jack rushed to the passenger side of his truck and opened the door for her, bowing slightly as he did so. She bobbed her head in appreciation and settled into the seat as he walked around to the driver's side.

"So, where are we going?" she asked the moment he was inside the vehicle.

Jack shook his head. "So impatient," he commented, starting up the vehicle.

"I was once trapped for three days in a shack in India during a monsoon so I could meet an ascetic monk for an article, only to be told that the weather was a bad omen and he refused to speak with me. I'm plenty patient. I just want to know where we're going."

Jack shook his head, not swayed by her story in the least. He turned his truck down the drive and pulled out onto the road. When she settled back in the seat looking resigned, Jack smiled. "You must've had some pretty amazing escapades out there in the world," he said.

Amy nodded. "It's been an adventure. Lonely, though," she said, the last part quiet, as if she was speaking to herself.

Jack knew what that was like. Out on the circuit, there were times when he felt detached from every important thing in his life. His brother, his mom, his home, the town he grew up in. And Amy. Always Amy.

As if she could read the direction of his thoughts, Amy asked, "Are you taking some time off from the circuit right now?"

Jack shrugged. "Involuntarily. My partner broke his leg at our last rodeo. He's decided to take it as a sign that his rodeo days are over, so right now I don't have anyone to ride with. Can't compete in team roping competitions without a partner," he explained.

Amy nodded her understanding. "Well, maybe it's for the best. I imagine there are plenty of people willing to ride with you, and Chester didn't seem all that hot anyway."

Jack was about to tell her that finding a new partner wasn't going to be quite that easy when something she'd said made him pause. How did she know he rode with a guy named Chester? They'd only been competing together for a few years. A glance in her direction made it clear that she'd realized the same thing.

"I keep up with the circuit online," she confessed.

"Including the team sports, huh?" he said, trying to make her blush an even deeper shade of red.

He succeeded, and she didn't need to answer with words—her expression said enough.

So she's been keeping track of me, he thought, feeling a little smug for just a moment, until he realized he wasn't exactly being fair. He knew he would need to tell her his own little secret.

"I read your articles, you know," he said. "Every one. I have for years. I even learned how to set up a filter so anything with your byline goes straight to my email."

He knew she was staring at him, but he couldn't bring himself to turn his eyes from the road in front of him. He didn't want her to know everything he was sure his eyes would say.

Luckily, they soon pulled up in front of Tony's Steak House at exactly the right moment. "I hope you're not a vegetarian or anything," he said as he parked the truck.

"No matter how much I've traveled, I'm still from Texas," she answered, as if that obviously settled the question.

Jack went around and opened Amy's door for her, but decided not to try to take her hand. Even after their giggles and confessions, she still seemed ill-at-ease. But that was fine—there would be plenty of time for that later. He hoped.

For now, it was enough to be walking with her into the "fancy" restaurant that a teenage version of himself had taken Amy to for her eighteenth birthday after scrimping and saving for months in order to be able to afford it.

"It's been a long time," she said, as if he'd mentioned that romantic dinner they'd had so long ago.

"It's not going to break the bank for us to eat here this time," he answered, though that might not be entirely true if he couldn't find a new roping partner soon.

"I remember I was too nervous to order anything on the menu because I thought it would bankrupt you. You had to finally order for me just so I wouldn't have a meal of table bread and water." Amy smiled at the memory.

Jack could remember every moment of that evening they'd had together, and the images it brought to mind sent zings of pleasure through him. If he wanted to go slow with Amy, start from zero, a walk down memory lane certainly wasn't going to help.

"I really wanted to impress the beautiful stranger tonight, so I thought this would be the best place to take her. It may not be the Ritz, but it has great steaks and happens to be the nicest restaurant within a fifty-mile radius."

"I bet you take all your dates here," Amy commented, playing along.

"Only the most interesting ones. And never on a first date. I'm not *made* of money."

She chuckled. "I guess neither of us are pulling in the big bucks, huh? Weekly dates here are still just a dream."

He remembered the "one day" conversation they'd had shortly after the birthday dinner, talking about when they'd have enough money to eat there all the time, after he'd become a star on the rodeo circuit. Teenagers with big hopes and very little real-world experience.

For Amy, though, he'd gladly take her to Tony's for every meal until he went broke, if it made her happy.

They stepped inside the dim, romantic atmosphere of

the restaurant and were quickly seated in a small corner booth. He took off his cowboy hat and slipped it onto a hat peg before holding her chair out for her. They settled in at their table, the candlelight flickering on the table.

After they looked at their menus for a few moments, Jack asked one of the many questions he'd been wondering about since he'd heard she was in town. "So, what made you decide to come to Spring Valley for a month-long visit when you haven't been home for that long in a decade?"

He tried to say it in a conversational tone, but he doubted it hid how curious he was in the answer.

"I thought we were doing the 'beautiful stranger' thing," Amy told him.

She sounded almost nervous, but Jack had to know. "How about we each get one nonstranger question?"

Amy sighed and looked at her water glass as if she suddenly found condensation to be very interesting. She was quiet for a moment, like she was gathering her thoughts. He waited, eager to hear what had changed.

"I was robbed at gunpoint about a month ago," she said.

"Someone pulled a gun on you?" he responded, shocked.

"Shh," she whispered urgently, ducking her head a little at his outburst.

It took Jack a second to realize how loud he'd been. Of everything he'd expected her to say, that hadn't been it.

"Someone pulled a gun on you?" he repeated, much quieter this time.

Amy shrugged. "I was walking around the Medina in Morocco at night and got pulled into an abandoned alley. It's fine," she added, placing a calming hand on his arm. "I wasn't hurt or anything, and all they got was a little bit of cash and my phone. Still, it was unnerving. I was in a bad place mentally for a while."

She paused, and Jack waited. It seemed like she was making some sort of decision, though what it could be, he had no idea. "Eventually I realized I needed to come home, see my family. And settle some unfinished business," she finished, her face grim.

He pointed to himself to check that she meant he was the unfinished business.

"Yes, you. And—you know, this is going way deeper than first-date conversations usually do," she said.

He was leaning forward with interest. What else could she possibly have left undone that would be changed by a near-death experience?

"And?" he prompted.

"And I figured I should meet my half sister. She emailed me a few months back, but I hadn't responded. I didn't know what to say. It took that gun pressed to my head to get me to realize I wanted to meet her. We're going to see each other next week."

Jack let out a low whistle and sat back. He'd always known Amy was adopted, but she'd never seemed curious about her biological family. The McNeals were enough, she used to say.

Before either of them could say anything else, their server arrived, and the moment she'd left with the orders—two steaks, of course—Amy turned to him. "Okay, I answered your one non-first-date question. Now it's my turn."

"Fire away," he said, wondering what on earth she might want to ask.

Chapter 4

Amy looked into Jack's eyes as he waited for whatever question she might throw at him, an open book. Guilt rushed through her.

She should have told him about what else had happened after the robbery, about Armand and the last push that finally sent her home to him, to this date. She just hadn't been able to make herself say it. Telling Cassie was one thing, but this was Jack. For the time being, Amy couldn't say the words aloud, see his reaction, feel the shame all over again.

"You okay?" Jack asked, putting his hand over hers. "You can ask me anything, Ames," he said, trying to reassure her.

Amy looked at Jack and resolved to tell him about Armand another time. For now, she wanted to have an enjoyable date with a man who was sweet and honest.

There was one question she could ask that might assuage her guilt a little, though, and she grasped at that straw. "What's your dating life been like since I left?" she asked, hoping to get answers to her real questions.

Did you forget about me? Have you loved others, even for a short time, since I've been gone?

She wouldn't have been able to say what answer she wanted to hear, but she had to know.

Jack gave her a little smile she couldn't interpret. "I've dated a few women here and there," he said.

Amy wasn't sure what to do with that, but before she could say anything he continued. "Nobody ever quite met the bar you set, so none of them lasted long. I think they knew as well as I did that there was always someone's shadow between us."

His blue eyes gazed into hers, and Amy felt gratitude and pain rush through her. She grasped his hand tightly, assuring herself that he was real, not just some wistful daydream. He squeezed back.

After a short silence, Amy let go and cleared her throat. This was getting too intimate for her comfort, and she decided it was best to change topics. "Do you have any prospects for your next roping partner?" she asked.

This set off a lively conversation of prospective candidates, and since Amy was, as she had confessed in the truck, up-to-date on the current competitors in Jack's field, they were able to both contribute to the discussion. They talked about it through dinner, between ordering food and being served their meals.

When the waiter cleared the dishes and they wrapped up rodeo talk, Jack asked, "Tell me more about what you've been up to, Ames. Is hotfooting it around the world as wonderful as you make it out to be in your articles? It always seems like even the disasters are once-in-a-lifetime adventures."

Amy ran a finger through the condensation on her water glass as she thought about what to share. Armand's face popped up once more, but she shoved it back down. Still not the right time. "It's not always as glamorous and fun as my writing suggests, no. Getting up at 4:00 a.m. when you're still jet-lagged because you need to move on to the next thing, even though you've hardly seen any of the cool new city you landed in two days ago, or typing on a laptop while sitting next to a toilet in a sketchy *alburgue* because you have a deadline and it doesn't care that you have food poisoning, or discovering that you were a few hundred yards away from a bombing in Istanbul. Having a strange man hold a gun to my head and shout in a language I don't understand."

A smooth talker getting what he wants from you, making you care for him, and then treating you like trash, she added silently. Amy cleared her throat, refusing to allow the tears stinging her eyes to fall. "Situations like that have made me wonder why the hell I'm not curled up in my bed with a book while Ma makes me a delicious meal," she finished.

Jack looked at her curiously, and she waited for the question she knew would come next. "Then why are you still doing it?"

She shook her head, knowing her answer wasn't going to do her experiences justice. "For every terrifying or awful moment I have, I get dozens of nuggets of perfection. The sun rising over Mount Fuji, or a stranger insisting they help you find your hotel and refusing any payment. A pickup soccer game with kids in South Africa."

It was a little disheartening, though not at all unexpected, for her to see that Jack didn't really understand what she meant. He had never felt wanderlust. Heck, up until she moved away to college, she hadn't, either. They had planned to honeymoon in Vegas to see the National Finals Rodeo and counted that an exotic trip to a far-off land.

Amy smiled at the memory, even though it made her a little sad. She had changed so much since she was a teenager. The past few weeks had made that clear.

Perhaps she'd changed too much to even be here, on this date with Jack. She didn't want to let herself think that through.

Luckily, Jack saved the conversation by picking up the dessert menu. "So, what do you want? The lava cake?"

Amy put a hand over her stomach and groaned. "I ate way too much to be tempted by dessert, and you have to bring up my biggest weakness? That's not fair."

He smiled at her. "How about I share it with you? Half a lava cake isn't too much for anybody."

She readily agreed, and soon they were dipping their spoons into the molten chocolate. Amy closed her eyes as the hot dessert melted on her tongue. "I've tried a million desserts in more countries than I can count, but this beats them all hands down."

"Maybe Texas deserves to be a regular stop for you from now on, huh? You know, since there's delicious lava cake to be had."

Amy wasn't fooled one bit into thinking Jack wanted her to come home more often because of a dessert, but she looked at the cake anyway. "Maybe I'll need to start making longer visits home a regular thing. For chocolate's sake," she said, glancing up into his eyes.

He gave her a smile that curled her insides and made her wish they were somewhere much more private.

Whatever else was true of the past decade, Amy knew that she had never quite gotten over her high school sweetheart, and here she was so close to him she could feel the heat coming off his skin. She knew she would be a fool to throw that away, no matter what ghosts tailed her.

Soon they were walking out into the brisk autumn air, and Amy only wished the date could have been longer. In fact, she didn't want it to end, to be left alone in her room with her worst thoughts and doubts. With Jack she felt safe, protected.

"I'd like to take you one last place before I drive you home," Jack told her as they settled into his truck.

Amy let out a silent sigh of relief. "Where?" she asked, curious.

"You'll see," he said mysteriously before turning his eyes to the windshield and the road before them.

Jack was always trying to surprise her when they were teens, so it seemed only fitting he would have another trick up his sleeve. Amy settled back and waited, knowing any attempt to learn more about his plan would be futile.

It only took a few minutes for her to realize where they were going, anyway, and a thrill went through her that she forcibly tamped down. He might be driving her to his house, but that probably didn't mean what her body wished it might mean. Even if it did, she knew it was too soon for her to get on that horse again, as much as Jack's presence sent her into overdrive.

"Taking me home to meet your mother? That's a pretty big step for a first date," she said, reminding herself to keep things light and slow.

Jack cocked a smile in her direction. "It's past eight, which means she's already in bed reading one of her mystery novels. A visit with her will need to wait."

Then what was his plan? She couldn't begin to guess, so she sat back and waited as Jack parked his truck in front of Stuart Ranch.

"Come on," Jack said as he opened Amy's door and took her hand, pulling her toward the barn. Amy followed without thinking, her mind focused on their hands. They hadn't made much physical contact throughout the date, and each time was purposely cut short, as if they'd both been avoiding something they knew to be dangerous. But now her hand was wrapped in his, and it felt as if it had never belonged anywhere else. Her heart thumped hard in her chest.

Then they were in the dark barn and Amy was distracted by the familiar sight and smells. She had spent countless hours in that barn with Jack doing all manner of things. Some innocent, but many less so, and those thoughts thrilled her.

Jack pulled her along until they were among the rows of horses, and then he reached up and pulled a cord to a bare bulb, illuminating a small circle around them. Amy looked at Jack, waiting for him to explain what exactly he was thinking, but he said nothing. He just pointed to a nearby stall.

Amy walked over, curious, and what she saw took her breath away. It was Bandit, *her* horse, the one that had died almost ten years ago. The same markings, the same shake of the head. Everything.

"How…" she began, but was unable to formulate her amazement into words.

"This is Maverick, sired by Bandit just after you— Just after we graduated," Jack answered.

She knew what he'd been about to say: *just after you left*. It stung, but she ignored it. The animal walked up to her and pressed his head against her just the way Bandit always had.

Amy could feel tears in her eyes yet again, for joy this time.

Jack watched Amy hug Maverick's neck and knew she was hiding her face so he wouldn't see her cry. Ever since the foal was born, Jack knew Amy would be shocked to see the likeness to Bandit, but for a long while he'd thought she would never have the chance. As soon as she'd agreed to go on a date with him, he knew that this would be an important part of the evening.

Amy leaned back from Maverick's neck and smiled, though her eyes were red. She patted the horse's neck gently. "It looks just like him," she said.

Jack smiled. "I know. Acts like him, too. I've always thought he has his father's spirit."

He didn't say that seeing Maverick every once in a while had helped when he missed her too much. Caring for the animal was, in a way, like caring for a little piece of Amy.

As they stood in silence together beside the horse's stall, a light pitter-patter on the roof told them it had begun to rain.

"Can I come back and see him again?" Amy asked, her voice so quiet Jack almost didn't hear her.

"Of course," Jack told her. "You're always welcome here, no matter what."

With that, she said goodbye to Maverick and they walked to the barn door. For a long minute, they stood watching the rain fall, glittering in the light from his childhood home. It was getting late, and those lights would go out soon.

His mind drifted back to long-ago hidden moments spent in this same barn with this same woman, and the urge to kiss her overwhelmed him. He turned to Amy, and as if she had been anticipating this exact moment, she fell into his arms with an almost desperate urgency.

With their lips together, Jack knew what heaven must be like. The lifting, soaring feeling inside him over-shadowed any possible worries about falling in love with Amy all over again. If this kiss was any indica-tion, he'd never managed to recover from the first time, whatever he'd told himself.

After what seemed like several lifetimes, their lips broke apart, though neither of them moved from their embrace. Jack rested his forehead against Amy's and tried to gather all his control for what he knew he should say. "My truck doesn't handle rain well, so I should probably get you home before the rain gets too bad and we're stuck out here," he told her.

"Would that be so bad?" she asked, still breathless from the kiss.

Jack groaned quietly. "If you're *not* suggesting we sleep together, you need to tell me now. I've only got so much self-control, and most of it is being used to have this conversation instead of kiss you again."

In answer, Amy put her hand on the back of Jack's neck and guided his lips back to hers. She seemed to almost be pleading for his attentions, as if she needed him right at that moment, and he could do nothing but oblige. He was sure she could feel his own eagerness for the connection he'd been missing for so long.

Everything about them being together was familiar and comfortable, yet new in surprising ways, and afterward they lay together on a makeshift bed of horse blankets.

Jack wanted to say something, but what was there to say? It had all been said already, everything except *I still love you*, and he wasn't ready to say that yet. The fear that she would leave all over again was still strong inside him.

Amy sat up, and Jack looked at her carefully. She seemed worried. Remorseful, maybe?

"I think the rain's stopped, and it's late," she said.

Jack sat up, too. Was that really how they were going to end this night—it's getting late, see you later? It seemed that she regretted how quickly things had progressed now that it was over, and the thought sent a pang through his heart.

After all, to him they were just continuing from where they'd been a decade ago, however much he tried to pretend this was a first date. He couldn't regret one bit of what they'd done, except if it hurt her, somehow.

They gathered their clothes in silence and dressed, then made their way through the inky darkness to his truck. Once they started on the road, though, Jack knew their night couldn't end like this. He wanted her to know that he didn't consider what had happened as just some fling in the barn. He may still have lingering worries about her disappearing again, but that wasn't going to stop him from pursuing some sort of relationship with her.

"What are you doing tomorrow? I was thinking we could take Maverick out for a ride. Maybe you can help me practice my roping skills if you're up for it. I need to keep sharp if I'm going to find a good partner," he said.

"I haven't competed in so long," Amy said wistfully.

"You were wonderful, you know. And some things are like riding a bike," he told her, only partly talking about horse-riding.

"That's true," she answered in a quiet murmur, and he saw out of the corner of his eye that she was smiling, but it didn't completely erase the lines of worry on her forehead. He wished that he could read her thoughts.

"I'm sure Ma has a big Sunday dinner thing planned for tomorrow," she said.

"Celebrating the prodigal daughter's return?" Jack asked, trying not to be too disappointed.

"Something like that," Amy responded. "Jose and Diego will be coming into town and everything."

Before Jack could suggest another time to meet, Amy added, "But I can be free for a while in the morning, if that's okay," saying it all in a rush, as if it was against her better judgment.

"Sounds great," he answered quickly, in case she might try to take back what she'd said.

He was already looking forward to the time when they'd see each other again.

Amy lay in bed later that night, staring at the ceiling, berating herself over all the rash decisions she'd made that evening and wishing she could go back and change them. She knew, though, that if she had the chance, she would do it all again. Her skin still tingled from Jack's touch.

Even though it was past two in the morning, Amy felt wide-awake. There were too many thoughts swirling around in her head for her to even consider sleeping. Was she just going to pick things up with Jack right where they left off a decade ago, despite everything that had changed? Is that what he wanted? Is that what *she* wanted? Even if it was, would that be enough?

She knew they shouldn't have slept together so soon, while Armand's shadow still loomed so strongly. Still, she couldn't regret it. Jack was such a comforting presence, and her body had begged for comfort. His touch erased some of the shame and guilt she'd felt the past few days, even if it added a little more in the process. After all, he deserved to know everything about her last few weeks in Morocco before she jumped into bed with him. And she resolved to not let it happen again until they had a long, honest conversation.

Finally Amy couldn't take it anymore. She needed to talk out her thoughts, and she knew who she needed to turn to for guidance.

"Morning, Queen Bee," Amy said softly as the horse snorted a greeting to her.

Amy felt a little bad about turning on the barn's light and disturbing the horses trying to sleep, but she needed to speak her mind or she'd go crazy.

Luckily, Queen Bee seemed to understand, because she nuzzled Amy's shoulder affectionately. Amy stroked the animal's neck, feeling comforted. This animal seemed like just the one to listen to the thoughts bouncing around in her brain. "I'm feeling lost right now, Q.B.," Amy started. "I just want to put Armand behind me and enjoy my time here, but I can't seem to. Not yet, anyway. And now there's so much to consider about Jack and me. I mean, I don't know what I want for us, or what's even feasible. Closure? A fresh start? To pick things up where we left off? It's…confusing, to say the least."

Queen Bee tossed her head. "You agree, huh?" Amy said, hugging the horse's neck. "If we try to start a relationship, is it just going to be a do-over of our past? I'm not sure that's even possible, with all that's happened. I've changed too much for that, I think. Or maybe I haven't, you know? Do I really *need* to hop on planes all the time to make a few bucks? I'm sure I could find a job writing articles right here in Spring Valley."

The large animal tossed her head again and snorted. Amy nodded. "You're right. I'd go crazy staying in Spring Valley for the rest of my life. Heck, I've only been here for two days and already I'm having conversations with horses. As much as I love it here, I'd probably go all *Yellow Wallpaper* in a few months."

Queen Bee tilted her head and stared at Amy, who gave an exaggerated sigh. "It's a story, Q.B. A famous one. Really, you should read more literature."

Amy laughed and sat down on a bench across from Queen Bee's stall. "I can't tell you how glad I am that you're a horse and can't tell anyone how insane I am, Q.B."

"Yeah, but if one of your brothers happened to drive home in the middle of the night and go out to the barn to investigate the light on there, you could be in trouble," a voice said from behind Amy, nearly giving her a heart attack.

She stood and spun to find one of her twin brothers standing not ten feet from her. "Diego, you scared me!" she admonished.

Even though her brothers were identical twins, she was sure she was speaking to Diego. Jose would have come roaring in with a big grin and a teasing laugh, not the quiet smile and kind eyes Diego always employed. As if to reinforce the difference, Diego sat beside his adopted sister and wrapped an arm around her. "Just be glad Jose's not showing up until midday tomorrow. He would have teased you mercilessly, then told everyone, just to round things out nicely."

Amy put her head on Diego's shoulder. "Yeah, he would. Thanks for not being a jackass."

Diego shrugged. "He's just getting through life the best way he knows how. Things haven't always been easy for him, you know."

Amy nodded, though her mind wasn't able to focus much on Jose and his problems, which she frankly doubted even existed. He was always the joker, the funny man. The life of every party, flitting from one thing to the next with the good luck of the lighthearted and carefree. She couldn't imagine what types of problems he could possibly have.

"So, do you want to talk about it?" Diego asked after a minute of silence.

"It depends. How much did you hear?"

"Not much, just the part about you going crazy if you move here for good. Is that suddenly a possibility?"

"Well," Amy started, not sure what her answer would be. "No, it's not. One date with my high school sweetheart can't change who I am—"

"You mean Jack Stuart?" Diego cut in, sounding surprised. "Are you two getting back together?"

Amy had forgotten that Diego and Jose, being a year younger, had still been home during her senior year. Diego at least was observant enough to notice how serious their relationship had been.

Amy put her head in her hands. "That's just it. I don't know. We only had one date, but it already feels serious, and I'm not ready for that."

There's still so much unsaid between us, she thought.

Diego squeezed her shoulders. "Hey, you don't need to make any big decisions if you don't want to. Just because you two dated a decade ago doesn't mean you have to start at square ten instead of square one."

Amy nodded. She knew all that, and Jack had said the same thing. So why was her mind insisting she make it so significant?

Because it didn't *feel* like they were at square one. Certainly not after what had happened between them just a few hours before.

But that didn't mean she couldn't slow things down and enjoy whatever it was they had without putting a label on it.

"Thanks, Diego," Amy said, standing. "I better get to bed. Jack and I are going to go riding in the morning."

Diego stood, too. "Just do me one favor—if you need advice, avoid getting it from horses. They're all a bunch of neigh-sayers," he said, giving Amy a big smile at his terrible pun.

Amy rolled her eyes. "Maybe you should leave the jokes to Jose."

Diego shrugged. "Fair enough."

Together they walked to the house to get some much-needed sleep.

Chapter 5

The next morning, Jack awoke at the crack of dawn, excited to spend the morning with Amy even though he'd brought her home past midnight and he wasn't expecting her to arrive for at least three hours.

Everyone else in the house was still asleep, enjoying their long, restful Sunday morning, so Jack crept quietly out of the house and down to the barn. Once there, he groomed Maverick until his coat shone, talking to him all the while. "Okay, boy, you treat Amy right, you hear? She's special, and I expect you to be on your best behavior."

Maverick tossed his head impatiently, and Jack chuckled. "Fine, fine. You know what to do. I'll stop beating a dead...well, you know," he finished, trying to spare the animal the insensitive idiom.

"Oh, and last thing," Jack said, looking Maverick

straight in the eye. "Don't let her know I spend so much time talking to horses. I don't want her to think I've gone crazy since high school."

Maverick dipped his head in what was an unmistakable nod and Jack patted his neck. "Thanks, boy," he said.

Once Maverick and Benny, Jack's favorite horse, were ready for riding, Jack went about the other chores of the ranch, desperate to keep himself occupied until Amy arrived. He mucked out the stalls, despite the thorough cleaning he'd given them the day before, fed the horses and prepared the paddock for roping practice.

After everything was done to perfection, Jack glanced at the time on his phone and groaned. It had hardly passed seven thirty in the morning.

What was he supposed to do for the next hour and a half? If he kept up at this pace, soon he would need to start breaking things around the ranch just so he'd have something to fix while he waited for Amy.

Even though it was a cool morning, Jack could feel sweat drying on the back of his neck, smell hay and horse on his skin, and he brightened a little. At least it was still early enough that he could take a shower before seeing Amy.

Jack went inside through the kitchen door of the old ranch house intending to cut through to the bathroom, only to find his brother Tom at the stove.

"I didn't figure you'd be out and about yet," Jack commented.

Tom seemed just as surprised. "What've you been up to so early this morning?"

Jack shrugged, trying to seem cool and relaxed.

"Amy's coming over for some roping practice, so I was getting everything ready."

Tom seemed about to ask more questions, but then apparently decided against it and went back to cooking. Jack was grateful to have his brother's penetrating gaze off him. "Well, I'm making plenty of food, so sit and have something. And after that, since you're up so early, you can help me muck stalls."

"Already done," Jack said, earning another curious glance from his brother. "What? I couldn't sleep, so I thought it would be nice to take care of a few things around here. You don't always need to be on the hook for everything."

Unfortunately, Tom didn't take the bait. He just raised his eyebrow further. "It's just surprising you have so much energy this morning, after how late you got home last night. That must've been some date."

Jack blushed a little and picked up his fork as Tom set a plate of eggs in front of him. "It went well," he said, trying not to picture the escapade in the barn in case Tom also acquired mind-reading abilities when he became so insightful and learned how to cook.

"Well," Tom said, sighing, "I'm happy you're having a good time."

Jack looked at his brother as he chewed his breakfast. When, exactly, did Tom stop being happy? Was it when he took over the ranch duties and started to see the bills stacking up, or when their dad died a year ago? Or had he gone sour even before then?

Whichever it was, Jack knew he should talk to his brother and try to find a way to make his life better. He'd sacrificed so much so Jack could live his life on the circuit and their mom could stay put on the ranch she'd owned her entire adult life.

Jack looked at his phone and cursed quietly. If he hoped to get a shower before Amy arrived, a heart-to-heart with Tom would need to wait. Under the time display was a new text from Amy:

Hope it's okay if I head over now. Excited to try my hand at roping again!

Jack sent her a quick reply and rushed off to the shower, leaving Tom alone at the table, smiling slightly at his older brother's disappearing form and determined to speak with him soon.

Washed and dressed, Jack hurried into the living room just as a truck pulled into the driveway. He didn't recognize the vehicle, but he certainly recognized the driver. Amy, her hair tied back and her cowboy hat on her head, looked as lovely as ever.

She may not feel like she belongs here, he thought, *but she is Texas through and through.*

Amy stepped out of Diego's truck carefully and looked up to see Jack standing in the front window of the sprawling ranch house, watching her. Her stomach gave a twist of excitement.

Despite the lack of sleep, she'd woken up early, unable to rest when she knew she'd be seeing Jack again so soon. She'd waited as long as she could until, feeling too impatient to wait any longer, she asked to borrow Diego's keys. He handed them over with nothing more than a smile and a reminder to be home by noon or face the wrath of Ma, and she was once again grateful that Diego, not Jose, had been the one to come home during the night.

Jack opened the door as she walked up the steps, and Amy could see he had just showered. He probably had to rush into the shower when she sent her text, and she wished she'd been more patient. Heck, she might've even woken him up. It was Sunday morning, after all, and they'd been up late the night before. "Sorry about getting here so early," she began, but he waved her apology aside.

"I've been up for a while," he said, running a hand through his damp hair. "Just needed a quick rinse after mucking out the stalls."

Amy made a face. She'd done that job enough times to know that a rinse afterward was more than welcome. He nodded his agreement and ushered her into the house. Amy looked around the living room, with its antique furniture and flowered wallpaper, and for a moment she felt seventeen again, coming over to visit with Jack and his family right after they'd started dating.

"Not much changes around here, huh?" Jack said, following her gaze.

Amy nodded but couldn't find the right words to say. She felt panic rise in her for a moment before she reminded herself that an unchanged living room couldn't suddenly suck her into the past, where she and Jack were practically engaged.

Luckily, Jack's brother walked in, and the erased years came flying back. He looked more than a decade older, careworn, with an air of anxiety about him. He smiled and held out his hand, grasping hers tight. "Amy. It's so good to see you. Would you like some breakfast?"

Before she could politely decline, her stomach grumbled. Tom nodded. "I'll take that as a yes," he said, leading her into the kitchen.

She and Jack sat beside each other at the table as Tom fixed her a plate of eggs and sausage. Jack already had a plate still half-filled with food, but he waited until she had her own before he resumed eating.

Amy put a forkful in her mouth and savored the flavor of eggs, bell peppers and cheese. If nothing else, Texas had great food.

As she ate, Amy kept her eyes on Tom—her conflicting feelings about Jack made Tom a much easier target for her attention, and his behavior gave her something to think about. While perfectly warm and friendly, he also seemed distant in a way. As if his thoughts were somewhere else.

"So Tom," she said, breaking the silence. "It's been a long time since I've seen you. What are you up to these days?"

Even though neither of the men moved, Amy could feel a shift in the air, as if they'd both stiffened.

"Not much. Just taking care of the ranch," he said.

Amy was no expert, but that didn't sound like his idea of a dream job from the way he said it.

"How about you? Brock told me you've been traveling all over the world," Tom said.

Amy nodded, forcing herself not to slide her gaze over to Jack. Did he and his brother ever talk about anything? If he was hearing about stuff like that from Brock, it seemed not.

Though maybe she'd been such a sore spot in Jack's life that he didn't talk about her. That thought brought with it the sour feeling of guilt, and she turned her attention back to Tom.

"Yes, I write for some different websites and magazines. Have you traveled much?"

Tom leaned back and sighed. "I did a fair amount back in college, but not lately."

She could hear the wistfulness in his voice. It seemed clear he was itching to get away from this ranch, do something other than run the riding school his parents started. Amy could empathize.

Before she could ask another question, Tom stood and gathered the empty plates. "Well, you two have fun today. I'll be working on paperwork a good part of the morning, so you'll have the run of the ranch."

With that, he disappeared, leaving Amy and Jack alone. They stood, Jack opened the back door and together they walked toward the barn, the scene of so many intimacies, old and new. As they walked, Jack said quietly, "He doesn't seem very happy, does he?"

Amy shook her head. "Any idea why?"

Jack sighed. "I think it's mostly the financial shape the ranch is in. We're pretty strapped right now and it worries him. He thinks everything's his responsibility."

Amy thought about what Jack said. That was probably a big problem for him, but she had a feeling there was something else to it. Still, she had to assume Jack knew more about it then she did. "Is the plan still for you to take over the ranch and turn it into a rodeo school?"

Jack nodded. "Spring Valley could use it, if I could just get the money together to make it happen. Tom wants to go off and do something else, I know, but until I land a few big wins, I don't know how to make any of that happen."

"What does Tom want to do when he leaves the ranch?" Amy asked.

"I'm not really sure, but he definitely doesn't want to be here. I know that much," Jack said shrugging.

They had stepped inside the shade of the barn at this point, and Amy leaned against the wall and crossed her arms, thinking about their predicament. "What does your mother think about the situation?"

Jack looked a little embarrassed. "I don't think she knows much about it, to tell the truth. Tom keeps it quiet so she doesn't worry."

"Your mother doesn't know the ranch is struggling and her son isn't happy?" Amy asked, surprised.

Jack gave her a sad shake of his head. "Mom's lived here for almost forty years. And she's getting older. We don't want her to be burdened with all that."

"It seems to me she deserves to know the truth about what's going on. And maybe if the three of you sat down and discussed some things, you could find a way to make everyone happy."

"I don't think it's going to be that easy," Jack said as he moved toward the stalls holding Benny and Maverick.

"At least it would open a dialogue and give her the chance to give her opinions. I know your mom—she's a smart woman."

Amy watched Jack seem to consider this, and then he nodded. "You're right. She deserves to know what's going on."

Amy felt relief. For some reason, helping the Stuarts figure out their difficulties made her feel like she might just be able to figure out her own.

Jack brought Maverick to her and Amy began saddling the horse, running her hands through his coat as she cinched the belt tight beneath him. He was so much like Bandit it made her heart skip.

"Now, on the topic of siblings, let's talk about yours. You have a sister?" Jack asked as he saddled his own horse.

Amy hadn't been expecting the topic to come up and took a moment to gather her thoughts. She still wasn't sure how she felt about the whole thing and hadn't talked to anyone else about it, so she didn't know what to say. "A younger half sister. Different fathers. Her name's Maryanne. She lives in California, but she's flying in to Austin and we agreed to meet for lunch there this Wednesday."

"Are you excited meet some of your biological family?" Jack asked as they both mounted their horses.

Amy had no real answer. Her whole life, Ma and Pop, Brock, Diego and Jose had always been plenty of family. As loving as anyone could want. What if her new sibling wasn't as wonderful as her adopted family?

And what if she was?

Jack seemed to realize she was struggling to respond to his question, because he turned his horse toward the barn doors. "How about we do some riding and talk about this stuff later? Benny is chomping at the bit to get some exercise."

Amy followed, glad for the reprieve.

Soon they were out in the cool fall sunshine, and Amy breathed in the autumn air. It smelled like rain and grass and animals, somehow distinctly Texas. It was a smell she hadn't even realized she missed in the deserts of Africa.

Soon they were riding at a trot through the familiar trails around the ranch, warming up the horses. It should have also been a chance for Amy and Maverick to become familiar with one another, but that wasn't really necessary. To Amy, it was like she and Maverick were old friends.

She took a deep breath, put away any worries she had about the next few days and weeks, and focused her attention on enjoying herself in this perfect moment.

Jack glanced back at Amy and felt his heart lift at the sight of her. She was sitting with her head thrown back, as if she was breathing in all of Texas. She looked so relaxed and comfortable riding on Maverick. Happy.

It was the same look he'd glimpsed a few times the night before when it had been just the two of them in the barn.

Benny shook his head and nickered, as if to remind Jack to stay in the here and now, and Jack turned his attention to the trail in front of them, patting the animal on the neck to show he got the message.

At that moment, Amy rode up beside him. "Should we get back to the paddock and do some roping before it gets too late?" she asked as Maverick and Benny matched strides.

Before Amy had arrived that morning, Jack had felt like he had the entire day before him, but now that she was here it seemed to be quickly disappearing. He nodded in agreement and together they turned the animals back toward the paddocks nearest the barn.

"Don't judge me if I'm terrible," Amy warned him. "I haven't lassoed anything in years."

"I'm sure you'll pick it back up soon enough," Jack assured her.

He'd never been longer than a week without a rope

in his hand for as far back as he could remember, and he couldn't even guess what it would be like to be so long out of practice. Roping was just something he did, a consistent part of his life, and he hoped Amy would remember how much she loved roping, too.

He tried not to acknowledge the part of him wishing she would remember all the things she used to love here in Texas, including him, and that maybe if she did, she wouldn't want to leave. The idea that an hour or two of rodeo exercises would make Amy give up her life and settle back in Spring Valley seemed crazy, he knew, but he couldn't stop himself from hoping.

In the ring, he gathered ropes from where he'd hung them on the fence and tossed one to Amy, keeping one for himself. He moved to the opposite end of the paddock to give them space to practice. "Do you want to dismount?" he asked, wondering if she was so rusty that lassoing while on top of a horse might seem intimidating.

In true Amy fashion, she looked at him with raised eyebrows and gave a sarcastic snort. "The day I can't handle a rope from the back of a horse is still a long way off yet, Jack."

Jack noticed with some amusement that her cowgirl twang, which had gone subtle over time, had grown in intensity now that she had a lasso in her hand.

Soon they were both working with the ropes, swinging them in wide circles over their heads and tossing them over various posts, tightening as the loop dropped over the target. This was child's play for Jack, a professional roper, but he thought it might be best for Amy to start with something simple. It quickly became apparent, however, that he had been right about roping being like riding a bike.

In no time at all, Amy was racing around the paddock on Maverick, roping her targets at high speeds and adding to the difficulty by aiming for more distant posts and turning Maverick at the last second, making the tosses more elaborate as her muscle memory took over. Soon, her face was flushed and she was giving Jack a wide grin.

"Not bad," he commented.

Amy rolled her eyes. "Not bad? I've still got it, Jack! Heck, I could give you a run for your money."

Jack shook his head, more to annoy her than anything else. "I'm going easy right now. Don't want to embarrass you with my superior skills."

Amy gave him a skeptical look, then blew a strand of hair back from her face. Jack urged Benny close to her and tucked the strand behind her ear. "You're fantastic, Amy," he said quietly, his hand lingering for an extra second on her cheek before he pulled it away.

She moved away, and although she tried to seem nonchalant, there was a hint of panic on her face. Had he moved too quickly, been too intimate for her comfort? That seemed odd considering what had happened between them the night before, but he couldn't deny her discomfort, and it cut at him.

For a brief moment there, he'd felt as if there was nothing between them, no past hurts or missing years. Now all that rushed back in, reminding him oh-so-clearly that this couldn't possibly be that easy. Jack prayed Amy wouldn't disappear from his life again before he had a chance to break through some of those walls. She truly was fantastic, in so many ways besides her lassoing skills, and he was sure life without her in it would go back to that grey, lonely place it had been for months after she'd left the first time. But this time, he might not ever find his way back. He was too old to fall out of love with her now.

Jack turned away from her and steered Benny toward the far end of the paddock. "Since we're warmed up, how about we try some team exercises?" Jack called over his shoulder.

He was answered with a clatter of hooves as Maverick galloped to catch up to him and Benny. Together, Jack and Amy surveyed the paddock and the dummy steer Jack had hauled out of the barn that morning. "No real stock to work with?" Amy asked.

Jack shook his head. "Not until I can get my rodeo school going," he said. "The closest place for real rodeo practice is an hour away. I know if I can pull together the money, it'll be profitable. There are so many rodeo hopefuls around here that could really use the opportunity to improve." Then, realizing he'd gotten off topic, he refocused on the dummy fifty feet away. "You want to take the header position?" he asked.

Amy seemed to consider a moment before nodding. "Sure, no pressure. Just roping my first steer in a decade with a pro as my teammate."

Jack laughed and leaned in for a quick peck on her cheek before moving away to give her room. If she was nervous, it didn't show, and she called and lassoed like a pro. They caught the dummy smoothly, their timing nearly perfect. Amy gave him a satisfied smile as she pulled her rope from around the horn and nose of the steer. "Not top marks, and it *is* a fake animal, but still, that wasn't bad."

Jack agreed. "Not bad at all. Should we try again?"

The second time around, they did even better, Amy's lasso falling squarely over the steer's horns. The third, her throw was long and missed the dummy completely. Even though Jack could see that Amy was getting sore and tired, she insisted on continuing and they went through the workout another five times, until Amy's throw was so bad that they both sagged on their horses in laughter.

"Were you trying to lasso the dummy, or me?" Jack asked, his eyes sparkling with amusement.

"If I was trying to get you, it was purely my subconscious. While there's a lot to be said for muscle memory, it seems being in shape is fairly important, too. My arm feels like a wet noodle."

Jack looked up at the sun. "It's probably best we stop now, anyway, if you don't want your ma in a tizzy."

They dismounted and walked the horses into the barn, and then brushed them down side by side in comfortable silence. Jack felt satisfied with the events of the morning; the only dark spot was that one moment when she shied away from him, but he tried to focus on the good parts. Anyway, he was sure she would come around if they spent more time together.

If only he could ride out with her like this every day...

"Will you help me stay in practice while you're in town?" he asked, hoping he didn't sound as desperate as he felt. "I could use a teammate to keep me sharp."

Amy rotated her shoulder and grimaced. "I don't think I'll be much help for the next few days as I recover from the workout today, but I'd like that."

Jack smiled. "Great. Come over tomorrow morning

and we can walk through the moves. I promise I won't make you throw anything."

Amy agreed, and then Jack walked her out to the truck she'd used to get to his house. After their hands and eyes lingered for a few extra seconds, he forced himself to let go and watch as she climbed into the vehicle and went on her way.

He knew she needed to leave, had family obligations, but damn, he didn't want her to go. As the truck disappeared around the corner, he could only console himself with the knowledge that he would see her again the next morning.

In the meantime, he had some matters to discuss with his family, and there was no time like the present.

Chapter 6

Jack walked back to the house, wondering if it was even possible to make everyone in the family happy. He would just need to try, he supposed.

Since nobody was in the kitchen or living room, Jack went in search of his mother in the place he knew he was most likely to find her: a guest-room-turned-sanctuary that she occasionally called her woman-cave. With bright sunlight streaming through the windows and light, happy colors everywhere, calling it a cave seemed a bit of a misnomer.

Jack's mother was sitting by the window in her favorite chair, reading. She looked so comfortable, so content, that Jack almost decided to forget the whole thing and not break the older woman's sense of peace. But then he thought of Tom's worry and knocked lightly on the open door.

"Mom, you got a minute?"

His mother chuckled as she closed her book. "For a person who used to be so busy, I seem to have all the time in the world since I officially became an old lady and my boys started taking care of things for me."

Jack didn't think they'd "taken care of things" particularly well, but only said, "I'm going to find Tom. I actually need to talk to both of you."

Jack's mom looked curious, but not worried. "He's out in the barn, most likely. I'll go fix up a few sandwiches and we can eat while you say whatever's on your mind."

Jack nodded and left for the barn. After a little searching he found his brother cleaning a horse's hooves, a frown of concentration on his face. Although, Jack corrected himself, it seemed like Tom wore that frown nearly all the time these days. Jack should have done something about this months ago.

Jack wondered if Tom ever told the horses his problems when he was in the barn alone, but he immediately dismissed the idea. Tom would never confide in a horse, which was one of the clearest indicators, Jack thought, that he shouldn't be running a ranch. Tom did what needed to be done, but he just wasn't a cowboy at heart. Though what else he wanted to do was anybody's guess.

Jack pulled himself out of his own head when Tom glanced up at him. "Why are you watching me like that?" he asked.

"Nothing," Jack said. "Just letting my mind wander. Mom's making us some lunch."

Tom nodded and quickly finished his task before

joining Jack on the walk to the house. "Did you have a good time with Amy today?" he asked.

Jack nodded but didn't elaborate. Now was not the time to get lost on the subject of Amy.

In the kitchen, their mother was just setting three plates on the table, and the two men took their seats. "So, what did you want to discuss with us, Jack?"

Tom gave Jack a surprised look, but Jack ignored it and spoke more honestly to her than he or Tom had in a long time. "Mom, we haven't wanted to say anything because we knew it would worry you, but the ranch is losing money. Badly. And Tom's been doing the best he can, but he shouldn't be carrying this burden all on his own when he doesn't even want to be here."

The older woman looked back and forth between her sons and Tom glared at Jack. Jack shrugged. "Sorry, but it's true, and Mom deserves to know. And you deserve to do something besides worry about bills constantly."

Their mother's eyes settled on Tom. "Are things truly that bad?"

Tom's glare turned to a look of apology as he turned toward his mom. "I just didn't have the heart to tell you I was running this place into the ground," he said quietly.

After a beat of silence, the older woman shook her head. "What is the matter with you two? I thought I raised you better than to hide something like this from me. Tom, you go get any paperwork you have right this instant and we're going to sort this all out right now."

It was Jack's turn to be surprised. He hadn't heard his mother speak to them like that since they were children. Tom slunk out of his chair and down the hall to the office. Soon he was back with a stack of paperwork and they ate their sandwiches as the true state of the ranch became clear to all three of them.

It was even worse than Jack had guessed. Once they'd gone through every scrap of paper, their mom leaned back and pushed her reading glasses to the top of her head. "Well, it seems we don't have many options, boys," she said finally. "We can keep losing money until we go bankrupt, or we sell the ranch and move on while we're still able. Tom, I know you've never wanted to live here—do you have someplace to go if we sell?"

Tom flushed. "There's a girl I met online a while back who I'd like to meet. She lives in Boston. I'd like to spend some time out that way, get a job and see where things go with her."

Their mother nodded as if this was the most normal thing in the world, though Jack was still having trouble absorbing it all. Tom wanted to move to Boston to be with a girl he'd met on the internet? Before he could reconcile all this with what he knew about his brother, their mom turned to him. "With my part of the sale I'm sure I'll be able to find a place in town that I can afford. So that just leaves you, Jack. I know you always wanted to buy out your brother's stake in this place and keep the ranch running, but I just don't see a way for us to hold out that long."

It broke Jack's heart to think of his future rodeo school being sold to some stranger while he went off to…do something. He could keep roping for a few more years, maybe, but after that? He'd never considered doing anything but come back here to Spring Valley for good.

Still, his mother was willing to give up her home without a complaint, and Tom had put his own life on hold for God only knew how long. He couldn't exactly ask them to fight to keep the ranch and risk bankruptcy just so he could keep his dream alive.

Jack nodded. "I'll land on my feet, whatever happens," he assured her.

The old woman stood. "It's settled then. We'll put the ranch up for sale. It's the only way," she said, looking at Jack as she said it.

She knew exactly how difficult this was for him, Jack was sure. He was also sure she was hurting at the thought of leaving her home, even though she didn't show a hint of her feelings. Jack gave her a small smile and nodded in agreement.

"I'll stay to help get everything settled," Tom said, his voice so somber that Jack knew he was feeling the loss, too.

Their mother agreed instantly, her hand hitting the table lightly, like she was a judge banging her gavel. "Then it's settled. Is there anything else you wanted to discuss with us, Jack?"

Jack shook his head and she stood up. He hadn't said anything for a long while, but he still kept his mouth shut. What was there for him to say, really?

His mom gave him one last curious look. "I tell you, I wasn't expecting *this* to be our topic of conversation at all," she said, waving her hand to indicate the house.

Jack finally felt his tongue unstuck from the roof of his mouth. "What did you think I wanted to talk to you about?" he asked.

"Oh, nothing," his mother said in a tone that meant obviously something. "Perhaps something regarding you and Ms. McNeal. But it may be a bit early for that, I suppose."

Before Jack could say a thing, his mother was on her way out of the room. "I'll get started on a list of Realtors," she said as she disappeared back into her woman-cave.

Tom gave Jack a quick grin before leaving the table himself. "I'm going to work out in the barn for a while," he said with a spring in his step.

Jack just sat there at the table, his brain trying to absorb what had happened, what he'd instigated. He tried to tell himself it was all for the best, but it was hard to believe.

Amy sat inside the truck, though she had parked in front of the McNeal house minutes ago, a nervous fluttering in her stomach. She knew she should get inside, that she was already late, but her mind was a flurry of activity and refused to settle down. What if they asked her about Jack once she got in there? She wasn't sure what to tell them. Heck, she wasn't even sure what to tell herself.

Everything had been going so well, and then Jack had pushed back a hair from her face and she'd panicked, and it frustrated her to no end that it was all because of Armand. He'd acted just that same sweet way when they first met, and it made her want to run from Jack as fast as she could. But she knew that was unfair. He *was* sweet and kind, and she knew it. So why couldn't her heart accept that and move on?

Amy sighed and leaned back. If only things could be simple, the way they had been when she was seventeen and in love with the nice cowboy. She still felt strong feelings toward him, along with a desire so strong it surprised her every time she laid eyes on him, but her head was so full of worry and doubts that she didn't know how to relax and accept any intimacy.

If her siblings asked, she would just say they were rebuilding a friendship. It wasn't exactly a lie, even if it didn't tell the whole story. Since she didn't even know what the whole story was, it would have to do.

As she unbuckled her seat belt, another concern occurred to her: Should she tell them about her scheduled meeting with her half sister? Would they be excited, or maybe a little hurt that she felt the need to find more family, like they weren't enough?

She stepped out of the truck, considering what to do on that account, and didn't even notice Jose barreling out the front door until he picked her up in a bone-cracking hug that made her give a loud, startled laugh.

"Big sis!" he said once he set her down and wrapped an arm around her shoulder. "There you are! Ma was about to have us send the dogs out to search for you."

Amy chuckled at the idea of Buster, Pop's old shepherd, searching any farther than his dog bed. Jose, Diego's twin, could be frustrating at times, but he was also the guy you wanted around if you needed to forget your worries. He led her into the house shouting, "Don't worry, Ma! I found her!"

Diego glanced up from his spot on the couch. "Where did he find you?" he asked.

Amy rolled her eyes. "In the driveway, climbing out of your truck. Thanks, by the way," she said, tossing him his keys.

He caught them with a nod. Amy waited for Jose to ask where she'd been, with whom, and what scandalous acts she'd done there as he mined for his next joke, but he said nothing. Amy guessed she had Diego to thank for that. He was the only person who could even attempt to keep Jose in line.

Soon Brock, Cassie, Jose, Diego and Amy were all sitting in the living room together, where they had been relegated when they, as Ma put it, "kept getting in her hair while she was trying to make a decent meal for all of them."

"Carter and Zach didn't get kicked out," Jose grumbled. "It's clear who Ma's favorite twins are."

Brock shrugged. "They're way cuter than you two."

Jose put on an offended air. "Excuse me, we're *adorable*."

"And they follow directions better," Brock added.

Jose grinned and nodded. "Well, that's true enough."

Amy listened to her brothers' banter, but a good deal of her attention was on her right arm. Now that she was relaxed, it was clear she'd pushed her muscles way too far, and her bicep ached like crazy. She kneaded it gingerly.

"Is there a problem with your arm?" Cassie asked, watching with her sharp doctor's eyes.

Amy stopped her ministrations. "It's fine. Just a little sore from exercising this morning."

Jose snorted in what was clearly an exaggerated attempt to start a joke, but Diego stepped on his foot and Jose's snort turned into an innocent cough. Amy gave Diego a quick glance of thanks, and he sent her a little smile. She didn't need Jose to start commenting on what "exercise" she could have been up to.

The moment passed and Diego turned to Jose. "Now that we're all together, will you tell us about your new secret girlfriend? He's been waiting all week to talk about her," Diego explained to the gathered siblings.

Jose held up his hand, and Amy could see he was enjoying building the anticipation. "I will talk about her when we are *all* together, including Ma and Pop."

"If Zach and Carter are in the room, you better keep it G-rated, little brother," Brock pointed out.

Jose gave Brock his widest, most innocent smile. "Come on, Broccoli, you know my stories are fun for all ages."

"What about the story about the night you spent in Atlantic City? That was definitely adults-only," Amy threw in, happy to be joking with her brothers.

Jose's smile became much less innocent. "Oh yeah, that was a crazy night. Cassie, you haven't heard this. So, I was in Atlantic City for the weekend…" Jose started, launching into his story.

Amy leaned back and looked at her brothers and soon-to-be sister. She hadn't realized how much she'd missed this part of being a family. Just sitting around, talking about nothing. She'd been home so rarely, and had always had Jack's cloud hanging over her, that it seemed ages since she and her brothers had talked like this.

"Time to set the table!" Ma called from the kitchen.

At the same time, two little whirlwinds rushed into the room balancing plates and silverware. Amy watched her young nephews hand out jobs, as directed by their grandmother. Cassie seemed grateful that Jose's story was left unfinished as she followed her children into the dining room.

"What are we having?" Amy asked the crowd as she sniffed the air.

"Sweet potatoes and okra and pork something. I forget. It's really yummy!" Carter told her all in a rush.

Jose gave the young twin a shake of his head. "You got to taste the food? I got kicked out just for suggesting I try a little. That's not fair!" he called into the kitchen.

Ma walked in with a plate piled high with pork chops. "You're not competing with a pair of four-year-olds, Jose," she said before giving Zach and Carter a big grin. "Let's go get you two some soda pop," she added, hustling them back into the kitchen.

Jose crossed his arms. "*We* never got soda pop when we were kids. It was always 'that stuff will rot your teeth.'"

Brock set the plates at each place while the rest of them took the other tasks. "She's taking her job as a grandmother very seriously. Soda pop, desserts, she even started up the candy bird thing."

Amy looked up, surprised. She could remember every trip to her grandparents including a visit from the "candy bird," a magical creature who left candy for young children.

"Ma said she would *never ever* do the candy bird. Remember how much she grumbled on the drive home while we ate our Tootsie Pops?" Diego said, sounding as astonished as Amy felt.

"Oh, I know," Brock said, "That didn't stop the candy bird from making an appearance a couple weeks ago."

Ma, Pop and the twins chose this moment to make their appearance in the dining room with the last of the food, the two young boys each carrying a cup of cola. As they sat down, Jose pointed a finger at his adopted mother. "So, the candy bird comes here now?" he asked, sounding a little more indignant than a grown man should about candy.

Zach and Carter immediately launched into the story

of the candy bird. "If we're really good and leave the window open, Nana Sarah says the candy bird will come again soon!" Carter finished excitedly.

Ma blushed. "Pop reminded me about the candy bird, and I thought it might be nice to—er...send her our address," she said, looking around significantly, daring any of her children to ruin this for her grandsons.

"Come on, guys, everyone loves the candy bird," Amy said as she piled food onto her plate. "Just look at the boys," she finished, pointing to the sparkly-eyed children.

The first bite of food overshadowed the gentle bickering, and Amy's heart felt full at that moment. Really, there was nothing like home and family. Even when they were all adults, things didn't change, and for that she was grateful. As much as she enjoyed her lifestyle, it forced her to be a grown-up all the time. Here, she could have an argument about the rightful existence of a fictional bird that brought children sweets.

"Fine!" Ma said, sounding exasperated. "I'll let the candy bird know you'd like her to bring enough treats for the rest of you lot, too. Ya happy?"

Jose settled back and speared a bite of pork chop with his fork. "Extremely," he said, looking very satisfied with himself.

The family settled down and ate quietly for a short while before Diego spoke up. "Now that we've cleared up important topics like the candy bird, we can move on to Jose's new girlfriend he's been dying to tell us about."

Jose looked up, all innocence. "Brother, I have been protecting my amour's privacy, not withholding information. It's actually quite gentlemanly of me."

Diego gave Jose a look and Jose dropped the act.

"Okay, her name's Kate and I met her at one of the ranches outside Dallas when I was looking at livestock out there. She's a riding school instructor."

Amy wasn't sure why Jose had built up this whole thing to tell them about a girl he'd met. She'd assumed the woman would be someone they knew or famous or something. Everyone else seemed to be confused, too.

"Well, she sounds nice. When will we meet her?" Ma asked.

"In a week," Jose said, looking straight at Pop. "She's going to interview to take over the riding school for you."

Amy let out a long, low breath. There it was.

They had all been concerned about Pop and the toll that running the riding school and ranch was taking on him at his age, but telling him that hadn't ended well in the past.

Pop slowly put down his fork and looked up at his adopted son. "What was that, Jose?"

Jose looked serious for one of the few times in his life. "In a week Kate's coming here to interview so she can take over the day-to-day riding school operations. She can live here and stay in Brock's old room, since he doesn't need it anymore. I'll pay her from my own pocket if I need to. And if you don't think you need help," he said pointedly, "the riding school and the kids are the ones who will suffer."

Pop and Jose stared at each other, and the rest of the family watched, quiet. "You've thought this whole thing out, haven't you?" Pop asked.

Jose nodded.

There was another second of silence before Pop nodded back. "Fine, I'll meet with her. But I'm not promising anything," he added.

The tension in the air seemed to dissolve and Jose went back to his usual smiling self. "I knew I was your favorite," he said.

Exclamations of protest broke out around the table, and the rest of dinner was spent arguing over which of the children was, in fact, the favorite.

After Brock, Cassie and the boys left that evening, Jose stood up and stretched. "I don't know about you two, but I woke up too early this morning. I'm heading to bed. And," he added, pointing to his twin, "I'm taking Brock's room tonight. No more bunk beds for me."

After he left, Diego commented, "I didn't know we could call Brock's room now that he lives next door."

Amy shrugged. "Jose beat you to it, fair and square."

Diego nodded in his usual good-natured way. "How was today at Jack's?" he asked.

Though Amy had been relieved she didn't need to discuss her activities with the whole family, the events of the day hadn't been far from her thoughts the entire evening. She looked down at the couch and picked at one of the faded roses on the upholstery. "We did some roping."

She didn't know how to express what it felt like to be so in sync with someone, or how much she wished she could just fall into his arms without thinking about Morocco and everything that had happened there.

Diego seemed to sense some of that, though. "You don't need to make any decisions right now. Just do what you enjoy and what makes you happy, okay?"

Amy nodded and Jose stood. "I'm heading to bed myself. See you in the morning."

Amy said good-night and slipped onto the bench that ran beneath the large front window of the house. She thought about all the times she'd sat there, praying Jack wouldn't appear and want to talk to her. Now all she wanted was to see him and hear his voice.

Amy glanced at her phone, briefly considering calling him before putting it away. It was late, and besides, she'd see him the next day. That should be soon enough to satisfy her.

But it wasn't.

She wanted to give herself over to her feelings like they'd done in the barn. Shut her mind off and allow her heart to accept who he was without her baggage from the past few weeks tainting the moment.

Just as she decided to call him despite the time, headlights flashed across her face as a truck pulled into the driveway, then went dark as it parked. She would know that truck anywhere, even in the pitch dark, and Amy hopped up and ran outside to see what Jack was doing in front of her house so late in the evening.

Jack put the truck in Park and killed the headlights, his heart jumping at the sight of Amy in the big window, her form outlined by the light behind her. He had been driving just to think, and had ended up at her house without even realizing where he was headed. He'd gone into the driveway so he could turn around—or at least that was what he told himself—when he saw Amy in the window, as if she was waiting for him.

He opened up the truck door as she ran down the porch steps, and without thinking about it, he wrapped her in a tight hug and pressed his lips to hers. She seemed just as desperate for the intimacy, and it was a long moment before they parted. Any hesitancy Amy had shown that morning was long gone, if her tight hold on him was any indication.

Once they could breathe again, Amy gave a little sigh. "I was just thinking about you," she told him, leaning her head against his shoulder.

He didn't respond, just held her close. He didn't know what had changed in the few hours since he'd last seen her, but he wasn't about to do anything that might ruin it. She wanted to be in his arms, and she'd been thinking about him. A thrill of love shot through his veins. If he was honest, he was *always* thinking about her, but he kept that thought to himself.

"What are you doing here?" she asked.

"I went out for a drive to clear my thoughts," Jack explained.

She lifted her head to look him in the eye. "What's the trouble?"

Jack tried to give her a reassuring smile, but he wasn't sure how well he succeeded. "I talked to Tom and my mother, and we've decided we don't have any choice but to sell the ranch."

Amy's eyes widened at the news, and Jack knew she understood how hard this was for him. His childhood home owned by some strangers, his rodeo school dream up in smoke.

He shrugged, trying to seem lighthearted about the whole thing. "We just don't have the funds to keep it going, and it's not likely I'll ever win big enough in competitions to get the money I'd need to renovate the place anyway, so really, this is for the best. I'll land on my feet."

Jack knew by her expression that she saw right

through his words, so he stopped talking and just hugged her close, gathering strength from her.

"Are you going to be leaving Spring Valley for good after that?" she asked, and he thought her voice caught in her throat for a second.

"I'm so sorry," she said in a whisper. "If I hadn't meddled—"

"Then we would have lost even more money and would end up with the same outcome, only worse," he told her.

He saw that in her eyes she still felt guilt over her part in this decision, and he lifted her chin until she was looking him in the eye. "This is what needs to happen, Amy. You didn't create our mess, and you shouldn't feel bad for pointing out that we were hiding from it. Thank you for stopping us from keeping our heads in the sand until we went bankrupt."

Then he leaned down and kissed her, and neither of them said anything for a long time.

"Any idea when all this will happen?" Amy asked eventually, her forehead pressed against his.

"It'll be at least a month," he answered, "and probably longer if the ranch sits on the market a bit."

Finally, after another long silence, they broke apart. "I better get home," Jack said. "But I'll see you tomorrow, right?"

Amy gave him a smile that looked slightly forced. "I'll be there," she said.

Then, with a little wave, she turned toward her house and he climbed into his truck. Jack waited until she was inside and the light in the living room was turned off, then started the truck's engine.

In a month, Amy would leave once again for her adventures. In a month, maybe a little more, the ranch he'd always thought of as home would be gone.

When the time came, there would be some very difficult decisions to make. But until then, he was going to enjoy this month for all it was worth.

Chapter 7

Amy awoke the next morning feeling light-headed. For the second night in a row, she'd gotten very little sleep and it was starting to take its toll on her. She rolled out of bed, had a quick breakfast with her parents, Diego and Jose, and then asked to borrow Diego's keys.

"What, you aren't going to stick around here and have quality time with your brothers?" Jose demanded.

"I'm helping Jack practice roping to stay in shape until he finds a new partner," she told him.

Jose seemed about to say something, but Diego put a hand on his twin's shoulder and Jose quieted down. Amy thought, not for the first time, that Jose really shouldn't be allowed out in the world without Diego nearby to balance him out. "You never let me have any fun, you know," she heard Jose whisper to Diego, who took no notice of his brother.

"I'll be back in a few hours, and we can do quality time then," Amy said, ignoring their interaction. Jose shook his head dramatically. "Too little too late, sister. And I was going to tell you where Ma hides the soda pop."

Diego rolled his eyes. "It's in the fridge. Have a good time, Ames."

Amy waved goodbye to him over her shoulder as she walked out.

Her morning at the Stuarts was much the same as before, except for two things: one, she could hardly lift her right arm to shoulder height and had to practice without an actual rope in her hand, and two, the mood of each person in the Stuart household had changed, though they all seemed to be taking pains to hide it. Tom was certainly happier, more relaxed, and Jack couldn't completely conceal how at a loss he felt.

Amy's heart ached for Jack. He'd always held tightly to his dream, had been so sure as a young man that he would be able to reach his goals. Now he was faced with giving them up completely, and Amy could tell it hurt him badly.

Amy also had a selfish reason for not wanting Stuart Ranch to sell. If Jack left Spring Valley for good, would that destroy even the tiny chance that they might be able to make something work between them? As it was, his time on the rodeo circuit and her travels, let alone the baggage and other difficulties that lay between them, made a relationship seemed laughably impossible. Take away Spring Valley, the one connection they really had, and it seemed there was no hope at all.

She tried hard not to think about it, but it was clear she and Jack were both preoccupied, and she almost felt relief when they finally called an end to the practice session.

As Amy and Jack brushed down the horses, Jack brought up a topic she hadn't even thought of since his news the previous night. "So, have you thought about how you're going to get to Austin on Wednesday?"

It took Amy a moment to remember why she was going to Austin, and then a burst of some combination of emotions too complex to name flowed through her. She was going to be meeting her half sister in just a few days. "I—I guess I'll just borrow Pop's truck for the day," she said, not really liking the answer.

If she borrowed the truck, she'd feel obligated to explain why, and Amy just didn't know if she was ready to talk about it with her adopted family yet.

"How about I drive you instead?" Jack asked.

Amy looked up at him in surprise, but before she could protest, he added, "I should go in anyway to get the property listed with some Realtors. And you never know, you might need someone around."

She was still about to insist she could handle it on her own when he looked into her eyes and made her arguments for her. "I know you've thought a lot about this, and I know you can take care of yourself whatever happens, but you shouldn't have to."

Amy closed her mouth, took a moment to let this thought settle in her mind. She was so used to relying on only herself in every situation that it seemed odd to need someone else, but it also gave her a sense of comfort. Finally, she agreed. "That would be nice. Thanks."

She grasped his hand and felt the familiar rush of electricity through her veins. She couldn't know where this would go, but she knew that for the moment she was happy.

When Amy arrived home a short while later, Jose and Diego were sitting in the living room arguing over something. They stopped when she arrived, but she could feel the tension between them. "What's going on?" she asked as she sunk into the old couch.

Jose rolled his eyes. "Diego has no vision and wants to keep us living at the poverty line instead of believing in me," he said.

Amy looked over to Diego, who seemed just as irritated, though without the sarcastic edge Jose employed. "Our business is just getting off the ground, and I'm sorry if I don't think now's the time to start putting what little money we've made into other ventures, even if some guy you know told you it was a 'sure thing,'" Diego retorted.

Amy felt a sort of guilty happiness that the twins were so caught up in their own lives that they would hopefully avoid asking about her own. Between her lunch with her half sister, guilt about Jack losing his ranch, and the confusing nature of her relationship with Jack, everything felt like a land mine she wasn't prepared to discuss. Better to talk about the two of them and their issues rather than hers. And maybe she could even help them somehow.

"What is this 'sure thing'?" she asked Jose.

"It shouldn't really matter," he answered, "at least not to a brother who's supposed to trust me."

With that, Jose stood and walked out of the room. Diego sighed and dropped back against the couch. "Sometimes he can be such a pain in the ass," he told Amy.

Amy shrugged. "Yeah, but I don't think that'll be changing anytime soon."

Diego nodded. "And, as usual, he's going to get his way. He knows I'll let him take the money if he pushes hard enough."

Amy agreed. They all knew Diego and Jose well enough by now to know how they worked. "How's your rodeo stock business going?" she asked, trying to understand the situation a little better.

He sighed again, making it clear that it wasn't exactly pleasant territory, either. "We're making enough to survive," he said.

That sounded like a big red flag to Amy. "Are you enjoying it?"

Diego didn't answer. Before Amy could ask another question, Jose was back with a cup of soda, his grin settled into its normal position on his face. "Sorry about that," he told both of his siblings. "This is something we can figure out later, Diego. I'm only here through tonight, and I don't want to spend it arguing when I can pry into my sister's life instead."

Before Amy could process what he'd said, Jose set his glass down on the coffee table, flopped onto the couch and put an arm around her. "So, Ames, how are things with you and Jack? Starting up the old flame? Is it love?"

Amy wasn't sure if Jose was teasing her, genuinely curious, or just trying to irritate Diego, but now she was stuck, and she knew Jose would refuse to take "no comment" as an answer. She shuddered to think of the mayhem Jose might cause if she didn't satisfy his curiosity at least a little bit.

"Jack and I," she began, choosing her words with

care, "are trying to find out who we are after all these years."

Jose looked unimpressed. "That's it? No declarations of love and lifelong happiness? At least tell me one of you has proposed a secret elopement in one of those weird foreign countries you love so much."

An image of her and Jack walking along a beach, her long white wedding dress trailing in the sand, made her heart jump before she quashed the thought.

If she let herself dream like that and it didn't come true, Amy wasn't sure she'd ever be able to recover. After all, she knew better than anyone that a good start to a relationship didn't mean things would end well at all. It was just best not to dream at all.

"Nope," Amy said, to both herself and Jose. "We're just dating. Kind of. *Casually*," she emphasized, even though she knew there was nothing casual about the way Jack looked at her.

Or about the way she looked at Jack, for that matter.

Amy wanted desperately to change the topic, but the only other thing in her mind was meeting her half sister, and—

And why couldn't she talk about that with Jose and Diego, her brothers *who were also adopted*?

They always felt like such close siblings to her, she often forgot they were adopted, too, despite their differences. Brock was technically adopted as well, but Ma and Pop were his biological aunt and uncle. He'd lived with his real parents until they died when he was eight. If anyone in the family would understand her situation, it would be the twins.

Suddenly, she was bursting to talk to them about what only minutes before she'd been carefully keeping to herself. She took a deep breath and went for it. "Hey, have you guys ever thought about your family?"

"If you're accusing us of not coming home enough," Jose answered, crossing his arms, "that's a lot of talk from a woman who only comes home—"

"No, Jose," Amy said, cutting him off. "Your *family*. Your biological family."

"Oh, that," Jose said, settling back into the couch and putting his feet up. "Nope. Who needs 'em?"

Amy felt a rush of disappointment. Was she the only one who was curious about her real parents, her other siblings?

"Jose," Diego said, his voice quietly disapproving, "This is Amy. We can tell her."

Jose waved a hand in the air, as if to say Diego could do whatever he liked, but he wasn't going to participate. Amy turned to Diego and waited.

"When we turned eighteen," he told her, his voice hushed, as if he was afraid someone was going to overhear, "we dug into our adoption papers and found our parents' names. We found them and tried to contact them."

Amy was nearly breathless, waiting to hear what they'd found. And amazed she didn't know about this. Where had she been?

But she knew the answer to that. She'd been away at college, hiding from Jack and dealing with the loss of her picture-perfect future. So focused on herself that she hadn't been around as her brothers grappled with growing up and finding out who they were, where they were from.

"Anyway, it didn't go well," Diego finished quickly,

leaning back on the couch himself to show his story was complete.

Amy waited another few seconds, sure he wouldn't just leave it at that. "That's all you're going to tell me?" she asked.

"What else is there to say?" Jose countered, standing up. "They didn't want us when we were born and they didn't want us as adults, except maybe as a way to get money, somehow." With that, he stalked out of the room for the second time in ten minutes.

Amy watched him go, not sure what to say. "He was the one who really wanted to find them," Diego explained to her once Jose was gone. "It hit him hard that they weren't interested in us."

Amy's heart broke for her little brother who always seemed so happy and carefree. Diego had warned her that he had difficulties of his own, but this was her first real glimpse at one. What other burdens was he carrying under that smile?

"Why did you want to know?" Diego asked, taking her attention from the empty doorway. "Have you been doing some searching of your own?"

"A woman from California emailed me," she confessed. "She's my half sister, apparently. I'm meeting her Wednesday for lunch."

Diego nodded encouragingly. "That sounds like a better start than we had. I'm sure it'll go well, and we're here for you if you need us, you know."

Amy hugged her brother tight. Then he stood. "I better go find Jose and tell him he can have the money for his 'sure thing' scheme. That'll put him in a better mood."

Before he made it to the door, though, Amy had one

more question for him: "Did you talk to Ma and Pop about looking for your parents?"

Diego shook his head. "I think they would've been supportive, but we didn't want to do that to them, you know?"

Amy nodded. She knew. Diego walked out of the room, leaving her alone with her thoughts.

Amy spent the rest of the evening, and the better part of the following day, only able to half focus on the people and places around her. The only time she was able to truly be in the moment were the few hours she spent on a horse roping with Jack.

Now that her meeting with her half sister felt real and was looming so near, it engulfed her. What if she had more family out there, a whole tribe of people she'd never met? What if she came away from all this as disappointed as Jose was? Or what if she found another family who was loving, who wanted her to be a part of their lives?

And she also had so many questions about Maryanne and the information she held. How were they similar, and what traits did Amy have that she got from her mother, their common parent? Did Maryanne know their mother, or was she adopted, too?

Amy suddenly wished she'd spent more time emailing this woman before agreeing to meet. She was going into this with so many questions.

Wednesday morning, as she buckled herself into Jack's truck, Amy had a quick moment of panic and started to think it might be best if she called the whole thing off. Before she could say anything to that effect, though, Jack leaned over and put his hand on her shoulder. "It's going to all be fine, I know it," he said, his voice quiet and soothing.

She looked at him and her heart calmed a little. So long as he was nearby, it would be.

Jack drove the two hours to Austin keeping up a continual stream of conversation, trying to keep Amy's nerves from getting the better of her. As relaxed as he sounded, he had his own knot of anxiety in his stomach. He could hardly imagine what a big deal this was for her, and his sympathy made him feel itchy with the need to make it better. But for the moment, there was nothing he could do but be there in the truck with her.

At last, they entered the city, and Jack thought with relief that it would all be over soon, for better or worse. He heard Amy's phone ding and watched her out of the corner of his eye. She stared at her phone for a long while, and it didn't take long for him to see that something was wrong. Jack pulled into a parking lot, cut the engine, and turned to Amy.

"She can't make our lunch," Amy said, still not taking her eyes from her phone. "Work stuff came up at the conference and she won't be able to get away. And she's leaving for California this afternoon, so we can't reschedule."

Amy looked up then, and the disappointment in her eyes cut him to the quick. "She says she's really, really sorry," Amy finished quietly.

Jack unbuckled his seat belt and pulled Amy tight against him. "She *should* be sorry," he said, angry on her behalf.

After a minute of silence, Amy pulled away and sat back in her seat. She wasn't crying, but she still seemed upset. "Things happen, I guess. I hope you don't mind me hanging around while you meet with Realtors," she said.

Jack shook his head as he started the truck's engine. "No, we're heading back to Spring Valley. I can do all that online."

For a second, he thought she would argue, or maybe if he was lucky she would say something sarcastic. Instead she just agreed, lay back against the headrest and closed her eyes.

The ride home was quiet, and even when Jack asked Amy if she'd like to stop for lunch, she did no more than shake her head.

As they got close to Spring Valley, Amy became more animated. "I'm feeling much better. Sorry about that back there. I was just startled and needed a little while to process the change. But really, I'm fine now."

Jack wasn't sure he believed her, but he nodded. "How about I take you home for a little while, and then we go out to dinner? I could use another lava cake, and I sure would like to see that blue dress again. Or something else. Or nothing at all, if you like," he said, hoping for a laugh or an eye roll.

Amy pinched her lips together, the only hint he got that she was at all amused. "Lava cake sounds good," she said, but she didn't sound very excited.

When they were parked in front of the McNeal house once again, Jack turned to her. "Would you like me to come inside with you?"

Amy gave him a small smile and shook her head. "I'm going to take a nap. I haven't been sleeping well, and I think a little rest is the thing I need most right now."

Jack watched her walk into the house, but didn't start his truck. He could see how disappointed she was, and he knew he needed to do something to help. He was pretty sure there was a way. There was the chance, of course, that it would blow up in his face and make her absolutely furious.

But he'd take that risk if it might give her some comfort.

Amy awoke slowly, feeling a little groggy but better. She was surprised how the loss of the chance to meet her biological sibling hit her so hard, and she told herself for the fiftieth time or so that she had plenty of family, and she could always keep emailing Maryanne to get answers to her questions. It didn't make the cloud hanging over her dissipate entirely, but she knew it would in time.

It took Amy several seconds to realize she was hearing voices downstairs, and that one of those voices was Jack's.

What's Jack doing here? she wondered. Was it already time for their date?

A quick glance at her phone confirmed it was still too early for that, so she got out of bed and went to investigate. Jack was sitting with Ma and Pop at the dining table, drinking coffee. When she walked in, they all looked up at her. She waited for them to explain what was going on, even though she was pretty sure she could guess based on the slightly guilty look on Jack's face.

It didn't take long. Ma and Pop both stood and engulfed her in a big hug. "We're so sorry about what happened today, sweetie," Ma said as she squeezed Amy so hard she could barely breathe.

Amy looked at Jack for confirmation that he'd told them. He gave her an apologetic shrug, but before she could process his decision to tell her parents without her permission, Pop spoke. "We think you should go to California next weekend and meet your sister. Get your questions answered. We'll help any way we can."

Ma nodded. "And I think I should go with you. For moral support and all. Or to break down her door if need be."

Amy hugged her family tight and, after a minute, threw Jack a look she hoped he'd be able to interpret. It was gratitude. She knew he was trying so hard to give her what she needed, even if it meant she left for days when they already had so little time together.

Fewer than four weeks.

Jack stood, tipped his hat at her and mouthed *be back at seven* before taking his leave.

Amy allowed herself to be shuttled into a chair and given coffee while Ma and Pop discussed precisely what would need to happen in order for this California trip to be a success.

"The first thing that we should do is email this Mary-anne to let her know we'll be there in ten days—you will, won't you dear?"

It took a second for Amy to realize a response was required of her, and she thought for a moment. Was this what she wanted?

The devastation from a few hours ago made the answer clear. She *had* to know. "I'll email her right now," Amy said decisively.

The excitement that had disappeared in such a flash a few hours before began building again. And it was all because of Jack.

After a couple hours of planning and an enthusiastic response from Maryanne to Amy's carefully worded email, Amy dressed for dinner and was at the door when Jack arrived, running down to him before he even had a chance to park.

As she climbed into the truck, he glanced at her sheepishly. "Sure you still want to go out with me?"

In response, Amy leaned over and gave him a big kiss full on his mouth. Then she smiled. "Thank you. Because of you, I'll be meeting my sister after all. What made you decide to talk to them?"

Jack looked relieved. "I was half sure you'd hate me for telling your parents about it, but I thought they could help you in ways I couldn't. And I was hoping you'd decide that they deserved to know and would forgive me eventually," he said.

Amy grimaced a little as she heard her own advice being used on her. "I should have told them days ago. I'm just embarrassed I needed you to do it for me. And while I'm not sure I like being saved, it's rather nice to have a knight in shining armor ready to rescue me."

"I don't think you've ever needed someone to rescue you. I was just trying to help in the only way I could," he told her.

Amy felt the tears prick in her eyes. How could he make her feel so loved and cared for in just a few sentences? Best of all, she knew he was being honest, that she could trust him. For the first time in weeks, when Armand's face popped into her head, she was able to shake him off as easily as a horse's tail shooing a fly. He had no place in this thing with her and Jack.

Jack cranked the engine, leaning back after it began to purr. "Should we go get some dinner?" he asked.

Amy agreed and settled back into the passenger seat, letting her feelings for this good, kind man wash over her.

On Saturday morning, Jack woke early, his mind immediately on Amy. Something had changed between them since their drive to Austin on Wednesday, and it filled Jack with hope. He didn't know exactly what it was, but all of Amy's little hesitancies and moments of worry seemed gone. The way she held his hand as they sat together at dinner that night, along with her tiny acts of affection during their roping sessions over the past couple days, made him think that maybe they could make this thing work. And by God, he wanted it to work.

They had spent so many hours laughing and flirting that for the first time, Jack wondered if Amy would be willing to change her life a bit in order to keep him in it. He wasn't ready to ask her yet—they still had time, after all—but he couldn't help but imagine that it was possible.

Jack pulled himself out of those memories and instead thought of the day ahead. He and Tom would spend the next several hours sprucing up the ranch a bit in order to help it sell, and then he was going to Amy's in the evening.

As he finished dressing and settled his cowboy hat on his head, Jack's phone started to ring. He looked at the number but didn't recognize it and couldn't think who would be calling him at such an early hour. He swiped his phone, wondering who it could be.

"Hello?" he prompted, putting the phone to his ear.

"Is this Jack Stuart?" said a voice he only vaguely recognized.

As soon as he answered in the affirmative, the mystery man exclaimed, "Jack! Sorry to call you so early, but this is important. You haven't gotten a new roping partner yet, have you?"

Jack's eyes widened as he realized where he'd heard that voice before. He'd gone to the NFR in Las Vegas as merely a spectator the year before and had met the second-place roping team. "Is this Sam Evans?" he asked, incredulous.

A chuckle came through from the other end of the call. "I was hoping you'd remember me. So, do you still need a teammate?"

Sam's words slowly worked their way into Jack's brain. "I sure do," he answered, trying not to let his excitement run away with him.

"Great! I need someone, and I think you and I could be great together. How about you come out here to Cheyenne next weekend? Unless you want to hold out for a better offer, of course," he said, sounding almost amused at the idea of a better offer.

"No!" Jack blurted out. "That'll be fine. I'll be there."

This was a chance of a lifetime, the chance to be great. His chance to save the ranch and his dream.

He and Sam quickly planned Jack's trip to Wyoming, "to see how they fit," in Sam's words. "I'm sure we'll be able to work together just fine, though," Sam added. "I've seen you ride, and you're damn good."

The two men said goodbye and Jack hung up, though he kept staring at his phone. He wasn't totally sure this was more than a fantasy.

With Sam as his partner, Jack might be able to finally

make some serious money. His old partner was fine, but Sam was a legend. Sam Evans and Jerry Isaacs were top five in the world last year, easy. Arguably number one.

For the first time, he wondered why Sam was no longer riding with Jerry, but dismissed the question quickly. Guys left the circuit for all sorts of reasons, from injuries to old age to just wanting to spend more time with family. A partnership breaking up, even one as successful as Sam and Jerry's, wasn't unusual.

Jack thought again what this could mean for him. A real possibility for his career, a possibility to win, to get to NFR, and maybe even become a champion. With that kind of money, he'd be able to keep the ranch running for the next couple of years, and then he'd be able to retire and start the rodeo school. His heart leaped at the thought.

A chance to fulfill his dream had just dropped into his lap out of nowhere. This could be it, his one opportunity.

He'd need to move to Cheyenne for at least the next couple years, though, and that realization gave him pause. Even though he'd already decided it made sense to move somewhere better suited to the rodeo circuit once the ranch sold, he'd never truly believed he would live anywhere but Spring Valley. And Wyoming was a good long way away.

And of course there was Amy. She would be in California while he was in Wyoming, but what would happen after that? He'd need to talk to her before he found himself so in love with her that he wouldn't be able to give her up if he had to.

Jack tried not to acknowledge the thought that it might just be too late.

As Jack and Tom replaced loose boards and old shelving in the barn, then did the regular work to keep the ranch running, Jack's mind bounced between Wyoming and Amy. After about an hour, Tom straightened and crossed his arms over his chest. "Are you really okay with all this, Jack?"

It took a few seconds for Jack to realize that Tom was talking about putting the ranch up for sale. He had been so preoccupied with Amy and the possibility that they *might* not need to sell after all that his mind had been nowhere near that topic. "Actually," he said, choosing his words with care, "I might have a way to save the ranch if things go right on the circuit this year."

Tom's face fell, and Jack knew he was wondering if Jack expected him to stick around and run the place for another year. "I'm not saying it's going to happen," Jack added hastily, "And I know that if it does, it'll be without your help because you'll be in Boston. I'm just saying that there's a possibility."

He couldn't ask Tom to stick around and run the place. Tom had his own thing to do. Not having anyone to run the ranch made this nearly impossible dream even more difficult, but Jack still couldn't give up on the thought. Not until he'd explored the option completely.

Tom looked skeptical, so Jack said, "I'm not asking anyone to stay on here, or even to stop trying to sell it. It's just something I'm looking into."

This seemed to satisfy Tom, and Jack felt it was time to change the subject. "Tell me about your Boston lady," he said, putting aside his own thoughts to find out more about his brother.

Tom looked awkward for a minute, as if he wasn't sure about the topic change, but then he couldn't suppress a little smile. "We've been talking for about six months. She's a dental hygienist."

Jack waited patiently, and finally his brother continued. "I can't wait to meet her. She's pretty great. We love each other."

"And you met online?" Jack asked, hoping he only sounded pleasantly curious.

"I know it sounds strange," Tom responded, "but we hit it off really well and we've been calling and texting for months. I know her better than any woman I've ever dated."

Jack slapped his brother on the back. He was happy for Tom. If there was any way Jack could save the ranch, it would definitely need to be done without his brother around, that was for sure. His heart was in Boston.

Jack thought of Amy. His heart was in Spring Valley, but for only a couple more weeks. Where would it go then? Would it be too far away to ever come back to him?

Chapter 8

Amy shook hands and sat down across from the freckled, red-haired woman Jose had introduced as Kate. Jose had gone off to find Pop, who was probably hiding in the barn now that it was approaching the time for him to meet this woman who might send him into retirement. Amy gave her a smile. "Thanks for coming out here. Pop might be a bit of a grump about it, but we all know how hard it is to keep the school running at his age, even if there aren't as many students as there used to be."

Amy tried not to think about the Stuart Ranch selling and giving Pop's school a much-needed influx of students.

Kate waved away the gratitude. "This is as much for me as for him. I've wanted to move for a while now, and Spring Valley seems like the perfect home for me.

I just hope I can convince your father that I'm the best candidate."

Amy couldn't help but laugh. "At this point you're the *only* candidate. I'm still shocked Jose managed to arrange this at all."

"Well, I'll do my best," Kate said sincerely.

Amy didn't know what to make of this woman. It wasn't that she didn't like her—she was actually quite sure they could become good friends in no time. It was what she was doing with Jose that was confusing.

She was sweet, honest, pleasant. Jose was loud, constantly kidding regardless of the situation, and could be more than a bit frustrating if you wanted anything other than a good joke. How on earth did they end up together?

"So, how did you and Jose meet?" she asked, hoping she didn't sound like she was prying too much.

Kate gave a little shrug and a smile. "He came by the ranch where I currently work to discuss stock with the owner and we just struck up a conversation. He has a great sense of humor."

Amy nodded. It was definitely true that Jose had a sense of humor. Was that really enough? Before she could ask any other questions, Jose came back into the room. "Pop's sitting at the table. Knock 'em dead," he told Kate. "Not literally, though. He's an old guy and we're not afraid to sue."

Kate laughed and gave a little roll of her eyes to Amy before gathering a few papers from her bag and walking out of the room. Jose took her spot. "What do you think?" he asked Amy.

She didn't know what to say, so she stuck with the

most honest thing she could think of. "She seems like a very nice person," she answered.

Jose nodded, though he didn't appear very in awe of her kindness. "Yeah, and she has a great smile. Did you notice? Athletic, attractive, low maintenance. My kind of woman."

Amy doubted Kate would appreciate Jose's list of her most important attributes but said nothing. They were both adults, and who was she to give anyone dating advice?

Speaking of…

She looked at the clock on the wall and her heart thumped hard. "I should go get ready for dinner," she said, standing quickly.

Jose grinned. "That's right, Jack's invited to tonight's meal. You, me, Kate, Jack and the parents. That won't be awkward at all."

Amy pointed a finger at Jose. "It doesn't *have* to be awkward, if you can control yourself and be polite," she warned him.

Jose shrugged in his noncommittal way that drove Amy nuts. "I'll see what I can do," he said.

Amy knew she wasn't going to get anything better from him and left the room, nearly skipping at the thought of what she was going to wear that evening. That morning she'd gone with Cassie for her final wedding dress fitting, and while they were out they'd done a little shopping to fill out Amy's wardrobe. Even though Amy reminded herself again and again she'd be back on the road in a few weeks, she couldn't help but buy a few new pieces of nontravel attire, and she couldn't wait to see Jack's reaction to one piece in particular.

Amy closed her door and smiled at the dress spread

out on her bed. Knee length and turquoise blue, the dress was neither very extravagant nor revealing, but it had caught her eye immediately at the store. It was a nearly identical version of her favorite dress from high school, which she'd worn to all their most important occasions: their first date, her eighteenth birthday, graduation, the first time they…

Well, it was a significant part of their history, that was for sure.

Amy dressed and brushed out her hair, laughing every time she looked in the mirror. A decade had fallen away, leaving her the sweet, carefree girl she'd been in high school. And just like back then, she glanced at the time over and over, her stomach a flurry of nerves as she anticipated Jack's arrival.

Once she was ready, Amy went downstairs to talk with Jose and Kate, though she really just wanted to sit at the window and wait for her boyfriend to show up.

Amy wasn't sure if it was just this blast from the past or her finally labeling whatever she and Jack were doing, but she reveled in the word *boyfriend* for a few minutes, even if she'd only said it inside her own head.

When Jose saw Amy, he gave her a big grin. "I know I'm your most beloved brother and pretty much the favorite child around here, but that doesn't mean you need to dress up special every time I come over for dinner, Ames."

She almost stuck her tongue out at him, but she hadn't reverted back to her teenage self *that* much. "I bought a pretty dress today and we're having guests over for dinner, Jose," she explained. "I think that's enough of a reason to look nice."

"Ya hear that, Kate?" Jose said, squeezing his girlfriend's waist with his arm, "Amy already likes you enough to dress nice for you. Isn't that sweet?"

Amy and Kate exchanged amused glances, but before either of them could say anything, Pop entered the room. "Stop teasing your sister and my new employee, Jose, or you'll be eating in the barn with the horses," he grumbled.

Amy gave Kate a big smile. "So, you're moving to Spring Valley?"

Kate nodded with a contented air. "Seems so. I'll be starting mid-November."

Even though that was only a month away, it seemed long to Amy, who had been measuring her life in days since arriving home. By that time, she'd be finishing with the lantern festival in Thailand, her next big adventure. After that, who knew where she'd be going?

She could feel her mood start to drop as she thought that far in the future, so she forced her mind back into the present moment. Luckily, Jack chose this moment to drive up in his old truck, and Amy went to the door to meet him out on the porch, someplace private and away from Jose's prying eyes and runaway mouth.

As Jack closed his truck door, he spotted her standing at the top step of the porch, waiting for him, and the look on his face made her blood rush inside her. He walked up to her slowly, a smile playing on the edge of his lips. "Nice dress," he said, looking her up and down slowly.

"Thanks," she responded, sounding out of breath. Something about the way he was sauntering up to her made her lungs stop working correctly. "I bought it today."

"Strange how something brand-new can stir up so

many memories," he said, so close now that his voice wasn't much more than a growl reverberating through her body.

Amy could guess exactly which memories he was thinking of, and she could feel herself blushing. She gasped lightly as his arm wrapped around her and pulled her tight to his body, and then his lips were on hers, hard and urgent. She pushed back with all the desire she had to give, kissing him for all she was worth.

When they broke apart, they were both gasping with the rush of electricity, and they kept holding each other tightly, as if they might not be able to stand otherwise. "I know it would be polite to go in and say hi to your folks and all, but I might need a minute before I'm in any sort of condition to do that."

Amy, pressed so close to his body, was well aware of what he meant, and it didn't help her calm down one bit. "Wait here," she said, nearly running the few feet to the door and cracking it open. "Jack and I are going for a short walk before dinner!" she called to Jose, Pop and Kate, who were still sitting in the living room.

Jose gave her a smirk, but the other two behaved as if nothing was amiss, so Amy took it as a good sign and closed the door behind her. She might get some looks from Jose for the rest of the night, but it would be worth it.

Amy's dress wasn't made for the cool evening, but she hardly noticed as they made a beeline for the barn, Jack's arm wrapped around her waist. Her blood was on fire, and even if it wasn't, there was more than enough heat emanating off Jack to keep her warm whatever the weather.

In the barn, they turned toward one another and

kissed again, feeling like the teenagers they used to be who needed to enjoy a few stolen minutes alone whenever they could manage it. Jack's touch on Amy's skin was explosive, and it wasn't long before they were taking full advantage of their privacy.

Afterward, as they resettled their clothing, Jack said, "I don't know if I said this yet, but I *really* like that dress, Amy. I mean, wow."

Amy laughed. "I think it's pretty 'wow' my own self," she replied, falling back into his arms for one more long kiss before they made their way to the door, holding hands.

"Let's just hope Ma hasn't put food on the table yet, or we might be in for a scolding," Amy said as they made their way back toward the lights of the house.

When they passed in front of the large front window, Amy could see Pop, Jose and Kate still talking in the living room, so at least that wouldn't be a problem. As she reached the door, she felt Jack fall behind her, and she turned, curious. He was standing there, looking nervous.

"Is something wrong?" she asked.

"No," he answered, though he didn't move. "It's just—this is kind of a big step, you know. Dinner with the family."

Amy's amusement must've shown on her face, because he nodded as if she'd said something. "I know, I know. I've met your parents a hundred times. Still, this feels serious to me," he explained.

"And that's bad?" she asked, her amusement turning to concern.

He gave her a smile and kissed her nose. "Not bad.

Never bad," he said before taking one last breath and walking through the door.

Amy wasn't sure what to make of all that, and something about Jack's manner made her think something had changed since they'd last seen each other, but now wasn't the time to think about it, and she dismissed it as aftereffects of a difficult day preparing the ranch for potential buyers. Soon they were immersed in greetings and introductions between Jack and Kate, and almost immediately Ma called for them to come to the dining room for dinner.

Jose gave Amy several significant glances, but said nothing about her and Jack's disappearance, and nobody else acted at all curious, for which Amy was very relieved, and she settled in to enjoy dinner.

Once dinner was finished and Ma and Pop excused themselves for the evening, Amy sat with Jose, Kate and Jack, unsure what to talk about. Luckily, Kate seemed to have a knack for starting conversations, and she quickly turned her skill on Jack. "I hear you're a roper on the rodeo circuit, Jack. When is your next competition?" she asked, looking at him with wide, curious eyes.

"I'm not sure," Jack answered. Amy expected him to explain that he didn't have a current partner, but instead he turned to look at her as he added, "I might be getting a new roping partner next weekend, so we'll need to see what rodeos are coming up that we can enter."

"You found someone?" Amy asked, curious. When did this happen?

Jack nodded. "I got a call from Sam Evans this morning."

Amy stared at him, amazed. "Sam Evans, one of the best ropers in the country?"

Jack nodded. "He's looking for a new partner. We're going to meet up next weekend, when you're in California, and see if we're a good fit together."

Amy could see the excitement in Jack's eyes, and she grabbed his hand, squeezing it hard. "That's wonderful!" she said.

This could be Jack's chance to achieve his dreams. Be a real big shot on the circuit.

Before Amy could ask any more questions, Jose said, "If you two need to run off for another walk, Kate and I won't stop you."

Kate slapped his arm lightly, looking embarrassed, but it was too late to get back the moment, and soon the conversation turned to other things.

Amy had trouble focusing enough to say much, however. She was bursting with curiosity. If Jack could work with Sam Evans and make some big purses, he'd be able to save the ranch and open his rodeo school. She didn't know what it might mean for the two of them, but she knew it was the best thing for Jack's career.

As Jack drove home that night, he felt a strange mix of emotions: he was excited about the new possibilities for being a real contender on the circuit, still euphoric from his and Amy's secret encounter in the barn, content with the pleasant company, stuffed with a delicious dinner. And, though he didn't like to admit it, a little worried.

He didn't know if he and Amy would be able to survive such a fragmented relationship, with her flying all over the world and him in Wyoming and on the circuit, doing what it took to become a champion.

As he settled into his room for the night, Jack opened

the drawer of his bedside table and dug into the far back, pulling out a small, ornate box. Sitting on his bed, he raised the lid of the box and looked long and hard at the ring it held inside. The ring that had been waiting in that drawer for ten years.

The ring that had been waiting for Amy to come back to him.

After a long, long while, Jack placed the box back in the drawer and closed it carefully. He would ask her before she left for Thailand. After Brock and Cassie's wedding. By then, he hoped she would be as sure as he was that this was what they wanted.

Even though there were so many things unsettled, he and Amy would be able to sort them out together. As a team. As partners. As husband and wife.

Amy breathed in the cool, wet air. It had rained that morning, and the scent of it was still fresh and sweet. It was hard for her to explain what it meant to be back on a horse again, riding almost daily, and she regretted that she wouldn't be able to see Maverick for the next few days while she was in San Diego and Jack visited Wyoming.

It soothed her soul in a way she'd almost forgotten was possible, and she knew there was no way she could spend another decade away from these amazing animals. Her feelings about Jack were similar, she thought as she looked at him riding beside her. How had she spent a decade without him in her life? His humor, his heart, his eyes, all gave her a feeling of comfort and home. The wall that had built up around her heart over time, girded and strengthened by her experience with Armand, had crumbled a little more each day they were together.

"You up for a race, Ames?" Jack asked, looking over at her with a sideways smile that made her want to lean in to give him a hard kiss.

Instead she winked and gave Maverick the signal to let loose. The horse didn't need much urging, and soon they were flying along the path, Maverick's hooves churning up the fresh ground. Amy let herself savor the moment, the sound of Jack and Benny close behind them, the rush of adrenaline pumping through her.

She tried not to let her worries for the future taint these mornings she spent with Jack, but as each one passed and the number of days they had left together dwindled, she found herself dreading her flight to Thailand.

As much as she told herself they would be able to work out some sort of plan that could keep them together, the logistics of it seemed staggering. If she cut her time out of the States, she would still need to be gone several months of the year in order to make enough money to keep herself afloat.

And then there was Jack on the circuit. If everything worked out on his trip to Cheyenne, he would move there, meaning she would need to give up any time she hoped to spend in Spring Valley so she could be with him.

Amy slowed and looked around. Now that she had found Spring Valley again, her home, it hurt to consider spending as little time there as she had during the past few years.

Jack pulled up beside her and slowed Benny's gait to

match Maverick's. "Everything okay, Amy?" he asked, looking at her with concern.

Amy gave him a smile. This wasn't the time to talk about all that. Right now, she wanted to enjoy the time they had together before they parted ways for the next few days. "Just fine. What do you say we go do some roping?"

Jack agreed and they turned their horses toward the paddocks.

Jack watched Amy as Maverick slowly trotted toward the paddock that contained the roping gear. Far too soon for Jack's tastes, the day before his trip to Cheyenne had arrived, and he wasn't ready to say goodbye, even for a couple of days. It felt as if the moment they went their separate ways, everything would change. He tried to tell himself that it was silly, that they would pick up on Monday right where they left off on Thursday. It didn't ease his worries.

As Jack and Amy finished a series of roping exercises, the question that he'd been bursting to ask her since he'd dug out the ring nearly a week before finally became too strong to hold back. He had to know what she was thinking, now, before anything had the chance to change. "Do you think we have a future, Amy?" he asked as they guided the horses back to the barn.

Amy pulled on the reins, stopping Maverick's progress. Jack stopped Benny, too, and they sat looking at each other for a long moment. "I want us to," Amy said, and Jack's heart twisted at her sincerity.

But when she didn't elaborate, he sighed. He'd hoped she would have enough confidence for both of them. "So after the wedding, when you leave…" he prompted.

She shrugged. "We'll keep in contact, and I'll try to fly back a few weeks later for at least a couple of days. I can go out to Cheyenne if that's where you are. After that, we can take it a day at a time."

"A day at a time," Jack repeated.

This wasn't what he wanted to hear, but did it change anything?

Once he proposed, she would come around, he was sure. He loved her, and even though she hadn't said it in nearly a decade, he was sure she still loved him, too.

In silence, they urged Maverick and Benny into the barn. Jack dismounted and started turning toward Amy when he heard her stumble. It was only by the tiniest of margins that he managed to move in time to stop her fall, his arms wrapping around her as her legs folded. "Are you all right?" he asked, looking her over carefully in his concern.

Amy grabbed her head with one hand and his arm with the other, keeping her weight off one ankle. "I think so," she said, though she sounded shaky. "I got dizzy for a second as I was swinging my leg over and landed wrong on my bad ankle."

He watched her put weight on her foot and steady herself a bit. "I'm better now. Just a weird head rush thing, I guess."

Jack looked her up and down carefully. "All the same, I'd prefer if you sit while I take care of the horses."

She really must have been feeling strange, Jack thought, because she nodded and sat down without an argument. As Jack quickly unsaddled and groomed the horses, he kept one eye on Amy, wondering what could make her stumble like that. She'd never been clumsy or prone to fainting spells. Heck, if someone ever implied she couldn't handle herself, they would live to regret it. So to fall while dismounting seemed more than a little weird.

After the horses were both settled in their respective stalls, he came back to where Amy sat. "Maybe you should talk to Cassie about what happened," he said, offering her a hand up.

Amy rolled her eyes and ignored the proffered hand, standing up under her own power. "I don't need to see a doctor for momentary wooziness. I probably just need to drink more water."

Jack wasn't so sure, but Amy really did seem back to normal, so he said nothing about it as he walked her to her father's truck parked in the driveway. "I'll see you for dinner, right?" she asked, and he knew she was thinking of his trip to Cheyenne. He wondered if she felt the same worry he did, that a few days apart might be enough to break whatever fragile thing they had built together over the past couple weeks.

"Dinner," he agreed.

"And before you say anything, I'm fine to drive," she said, giving him a wide grin he knew was at least a little false.

He said nothing and watched her leave, not taking his eyes off the vehicle until it was gone from sight. Even then, he watched the spot where it had been.

He knew he needed to go to Wyoming, that even if he didn't go, Amy would be off to California for the weekend. Still, Jack ached to stay.

Amy drove away from Jack's ranch slowly, trying to absorb everything that had happened in those last few minutes, from Jack's question about their future to her near fall. The woozy feeling worried her more than she'd let on, as did the heartrending look on Jack's face when she admitted she wasn't sure about what would happen next in their relationship.

And really, she didn't have a clue what they could do to make this thing between them work. As comfortable as she'd gotten with Jack again, as much as she enjoyed his company and—yes, she could admit it, if only to herself—*loved* him, their lives were so different that the decision to stay together seemed terrifying, whatever her feelings for him.

And in the back of her mind, as much as she hated it, she still kept a little piece of herself hidden from him. She hadn't told him about Armand despite all her promises to herself, and every once in a while, the fear popped up again: the fear that all of Jack's sweetness and affection was a con, that one day not too far from now, he'd show his true colors and hurt her like Armand had.

No matter how often she told herself that it wasn't true, she couldn't entirely rid herself of that feeling.

Amy parked her pop's truck, but hesitated before going into the house. She couldn't do anything at that moment about her relationship with Jack, but she *could* relieve her worries about that moment of light-headedness, and that was better than nothing. Plus, she'd be able to spend a little time with Cassie, which might just make her feel better.

Amy turned her sights on Cassie's house next door and began walking through the scrub grass that sprouted up between the two properties, following a trail most likely worn down by Brock's frequent visits between the houses over the past several months.

As she approached the door, Amy wasn't sure what she planned to say to Cassie besides *I felt dizzy for a minute, what do you think it could be?* She didn't even have enough time for that, however, because the moment Cassie opened the door she said, "Just the person I wanted to see! My dress is steamed and hanging up in the bathroom and I desperately wanted someone to gaze lovingly at it with me. Come in," and Amy was inside and being hauled down the hallway before she could say a single word.

Amy and Cassie both looked at the dress hanging from the shower rod in Cassie's bathroom. It was long and white, with simple, delicate ornamentation. Perfect for a ceremony on the ranch, which Cassie insisted was everything she could ever hope in a wedding. Even though Amy had been with Cassie at her last fitting just a few days before, she couldn't help but look longingly at the dress.

"It's beautiful." Amy sighed, running her fingers along the silky hem.

Cassie's eyes sparkled as she stared at the dress, and Amy could tell she was close to tears. It seemed this was going to be a wedding-themed visit instead of a doctor's visit, and Amy didn't mind one bit.

"When does your family arrive?" Amy asked while they left the bathroom, wondering how big of a part Cassie's mother and sister had in the wedding preparations.

Cassie rolled her eyes. "Oh, you'll know when they get here. I'm pretty sure you'll be able to hear my mom from your parents' house. They fly in a couple days before the wedding."

"Are you…excited to see them?" Amy asked, unsure

if she was giving Cassie an opportunity to talk or over-stepping her bounds.

Cassie threw her hands in the air in exasperation as she walked over to the bed and sat down. "I have no idea. I love my family, but my mother hasn't always been the easiest person to be around, and I think she's still uncertain about this whole thing. I just don't want to be in charge of corralling her through the entire reception to be sure she doesn't say anything insulting about us deciding to live 'in the middle of nowhere' instead of with 'civilized folks' in the city."

Amy laughed at Cassie's depiction of her mother. She really did sound like quite a handful, and Amy felt a rush of gratitude for her opinionated-but-ultimately-supportive Ma. "Why don't you put Ma in charge of her?" Amy asked as the thought struck. "She'd love a job, and if anyone can convince a person about how great Texas is, it's Ma."

Cassie's eyes lit up at the idea. "That might work," she said, sounding excited. "I can tell my mom that the two of them are in charge of Zach and Carter."

"If Ma gets to be with the twins and browbeat someone into loving Spring Valley at the same time, she might die of happiness. The rest of us will have a hard time following that act," Amy said.

"That's perfect, Amy," Cassie said sincerely. "I'm so glad you came over. Speaking of, I never asked you why you were here. If you were looking for Brock, he and the boys are busy in town for a couple of hours."

"No, I came to see you, actually. I had a weird dizzy spell earlier today and I wanted to check with you about it. You know, as my doctor and all," Amy said, feeling a little silly.

Cassie immediately shifted into doctor mode. "Has this ever happened before? Do you have any other symptoms?"

Amy thought carefully. "It could be period-related, now I think of it. I'm a bit late and my breasts are a little tender. Probably just weird hormones or something. I've never gotten woozy like that before."

"Well, I have one guess," Cassie said immediately.

"I can't be pregnant, Cassie," Amy explained, knowing what Cassie was thinking. "A doctor told me that a decade ago."

Cassie nodded, though she didn't look convinced. "Well, will you take a test for me? That way we can rule it out entirely and move on to other diagnoses."

Before Amy could say anything, Cassie was already back in the bathroom, scrabbling in a cupboard under the sink. After a few seconds, she popped back up with a pregnancy test.

"Whoa," Amy said, "I didn't think you'd have one quite so handy. Are you and Brock planning on growing your family already?"

"I keep some on hand for patient use," Cassie explained, but when Amy didn't break eye contact, she blushed. "But yes, we've talked about giving Zach and Carter a sibling before they get too much older. Now will you go take the test, please?"

Amy took the small object from her soon-to-be sister's outstretched hand. "Okay, but after it comes back negative, will you please let this idea go for now? And really, the whole thing was probably just a weird moment that means nothing. I shouldn't have even bothered you about it."

Cassie held up her hands in promised surrender, and

Amy closed the bathroom door behind her. After a minute, she opened the door again, allowing Cassie to re-enter the bathroom. The test sat beside the sink. "How long does it take?" she asked Cassie, not even trying to hide her skepticism.

"Just a couple of minutes," Cassie said, looking at her watch.

Amy turned her attention back to the white dress that took up so much of the bathroom. "So, are you hiding this somewhere so Brock won't see it, or are you two not bothering with all that?"

"Oh, we're bothering, all right," Cassie answered. "I was actually hoping we could sneak it over to your place before he and the boys got back from their errands. I'm sure the McNeals would be able to keep it safe, and Ma invited me to get ready over there. I bet if I didn't, she'd be bringing half the house over anyway, just in case we might need something."

Amy chuckled. Ma wasn't about to leave anything to chance for this wedding, Amy was sure of that. Guessing it had probably been long enough by now, she glanced down at the pregnancy test on the counter.

Amy was silent for a long moment before uttering a quiet "Oh."

Chapter 9

At dinner, Jack watched Amy carefully to see if she was still feeling off from her earlier dizzy spell, and it seemed obvious that she still wasn't feeling herself. He didn't say anything at first, not wanting to make her roll her eyes and insist she was fine. Besides, they were going to be saying goodbye for a few days, and he knew that was enough to make him act oddly.

It seemed silly for a weekend apart to be such a big deal, but it really was. By the time he got back from Wyoming, his career could be back on track, but their relationship might not be able to survive the time and distance that a real shot on the circuit would require.

Finally, though, Jack could tell that Amy was very distracted by something, and it wasn't just her being worried or nervous about the weekend.

"What's going on, Amy? You don't seem like you're

actually here with me," he told her, leaning in and grabbing her hand.

For the first time that night, she really seemed to look at him. He waited patiently to see what she'd say.

After a long silence, she finally opened her mouth. "I'm pregnant," she said, in little more than a whisper.

The words rang in his ears as if she yelled them. She was pregnant? How could that be?

"But you can't—" he started, but was unable to finish the sentence.

"I know," she answered, her eyes wide with her own emotions.

He still couldn't make his brain understand what she was saying. "You're—"

"Pregnant," she said again, even quieter.

Then it finally clicked. He broke into a huge grin and pulled her into a tight hug, almost lighting himself on fire when he leaned too close to the candle sitting on the restaurant table. "This is fantastic!" he said, not letting go of her. He couldn't think anything beyond that.

Amy pulled away and searched his eyes with hers. He could see she was barely holding herself together. "Really, fantastic?" she said, shaking her head. "What about you moving to Wyoming and my job and I don't even have health insurance and…"

Her voice drifted off and a tear slid down her cheek.

Jack wiped away the tear with one hand, his palm settling on her neck protectively. "We'll figure it all out, Ames," he said steadily, his blue eyes capturing hers.

He suddenly felt no doubt. Just pure joy. He was finally going to have the family he'd always wanted. Amy and their baby.

"Will you dance with me?" he asked, pulling her onto the dance floor and holding her close, his heart bursting with happiness.

I have to tell him, Amy thought as they danced, but she couldn't force herself to open her mouth. He was just so delighted that the words wouldn't come out.

It would crush him to hear he might not be the father. This was what he'd always wanted, and the moment she said those words, she wouldn't be able to take them back. So instead she held him close and wished with all her might: *Please, please let this baby be Jack's.*

For the rest of the evening, every time she got her courage up enough that she was about to tell him, she'd see the smile on his face or feel the squeeze of his hand on hers and she would fall silent again. By the time he suggested dessert, she was so exhausted from her internal struggle that she told him she wasn't feeling well—which was true, but not for the reason he thought—and they left shortly after that.

"I wish we could spend more time together this evening, but you probably need some rest, and I have an early flight tomorrow," Jack told her as he settled behind the wheel of his truck.

Amy nodded, but she must have looked anxious, because Jack gave her another big smile. "Don't worry, Ames. I know it seems overwhelming right now, but we'll get everything sorted out as soon as I get back Tuesday."

Tuesday. That was when she'd tell him about Armand and the possibility that he might be the baby's father. She *needed* to tell Jack the truth. But she couldn't tell him right before they parted ways for the weekend. He would have to be at top form if he was going to do well with Sam Evans in Cheyenne, and that was too important to put in jeopardy.

She couldn't tell him this possibly devastating information and risk him being so hurt that he screwed up his chance to pursue his dreams.

After a quick goodbye, Amy was relieved to see Jack leave. She felt guilty about keeping this secret, but it was for the best. Amy sighed and went to her bedroom, but she knew there was no way she'd be going to sleep anytime soon. After a few minutes of aimlessly wandering around the tiny room she opened her laptop and checked her email as a desperate bid for a distraction, hoping she could find something to keep her mind busy.

And she found it, though it wasn't at all what she'd been hoping for.

Amy stared at her computer in disbelief, clicking on the top email robotically, hoping the article wasn't what she thought. The title splashed across the top of the webpage finally brought her out of her stupor and she grimaced.

Married Prince of Monaco Caught in Moroccan Love Affair.

She read the first sentence with mounting disgust.

Prince Armand of Monaco, married father of two, was photographed in an illicit relationship while on a diplomatic visit to Marrakech, Morocco.

After that, she could only skim, unable to read in depth the words that publicized one of the biggest regrets of her life. The tabloid seemed to revel in pointing out again and again that the man in question was married, and the woman an American travel writer by the name of Amy McNeal. They didn't seem very interested in how the woman in question had been duped into thinking he was single and had dumped him as soon as she discovered the truth.

And he could be the father of her child, she thought, appalled. It *had* to be Jack's.

The fact that Armand was a prince only made her annoyed. He'd mentioned his "royal blood" as if she should know what he meant, but she'd been too wrapped up in her loneliness and desperate need for affection to care, and now she only saw it as a cause for this article. If he'd been anybody else, she wouldn't be reading this internet tabloid right now.

As Amy scrolled, she saw with a sinking heart the pictures mentioned in the first sentence. She stared at the photos and groaned, her hand slamming against the desk in anger. Damn Armand and his smooth talk. There were three photos, each one as suggestive as the last. Armand's arm curled around her waist as they ducked into a cab, Armand's lips to her ear as he whispered his beautiful lies, a kiss captured at just the right moment.

Or wrong moment, in Amy's case.

Amy's head filled with if-onlys.

If only she had known he was married.

If only she hadn't been feeling so alone when he approached her.

If only she'd seen through his handsome face and sweet words.

Then her phone buzzed and she read the text, only to add another if-only.

If only Jack hadn't found out this way.

She read the message again:

I'm coming back over. We need to talk.

He had told her on their first date that he'd created a filter to email him when one of her articles posted—it seemed it worked on anything with her name on it. And her name showed up in the article several times, painting her as a sexy seductress. He must've driven home and checked his email to find this piece sitting in his inbox.

He could be coming over for an entirely different reason, she thought, before shaking her head at her own wishful thinking. There was no other possible reason for him to drive back so soon after dropping her off, she was sure of that much.

Amy sent a text back telling him she'd be waiting outside, then steeled herself for whatever might come next.

He'd understand, right? These photos had been taken weeks ago, before they had reunited. Why the tabloid had waited until now to print them, she couldn't say, but they were still before her time with Jack. She was sure he hadn't been some monk waiting for her for the past decade, so he couldn't expect that of her.

But the baby. She hadn't meant to sleep with Armand and then Jack so close together, hadn't *planned* for any of this, and now she needed to come clean and let him know the baby might be someone else's. Would he reject her and the baby in disgust? She couldn't blame him if he did.

Amy stopped the train of thought and walked into the cool evening. No point in arguing against phantom accusations. She needed to give Jack the benefit of the doubt, hope he would take it all in stride.

When his truck pulled up beside her in the driveway, though, Amy's heart sank. Any hope for a sympathetic response to the article disappeared at the sight of his face. She'd known him long enough to be able to tell when he was angry or frustrated but trying to hold it together. From the looks of things, he wasn't managing it particularly well.

Jack held up his phone, the picture of her kissing Armand covering the screen. "What's this about, Amy?" he asked, his voice calm enough that the irritation was only a sharp edge on her name.

"It was before I came home," she said, hoping that would be enough to help him relax. He had to know that, right?

"How long before?" he countered, as if he already knew the answer.

So he'd read the article and done the math. He'd realized she had been seeing Armand almost up until the day she left for Texas. Amy sat down on the gravel and waited for him to say what she was sure would come next.

"How long after you slept with him were you and I together in the barn? Days? Maybe a week?"

He was right, of course, but he didn't even realize the half of it, and it was her responsibility to tell him. Before she could explain, though, he slumped onto the gravel beside her while leaving enough space so they wouldn't touch. "Am I just your rebound while you get over this guy?"

"No!" Amy exclaimed automatically. After a moment, though, she realized that wasn't entirely true. "That first night we were together," she admitted, the words sticking in her throat, "I was still hurting from Armand's betrayal, and I don't know if things would have…progressed so quickly otherwise."

She felt him slump beside her. "But after that," she added quickly, "every close moment we had was just you and me. Armand was gone, and all that was left was my affection for you and my shame that I ever bought into his lies when such a good man was waiting for me here."

He didn't answer, didn't say anything. Didn't even move. So Amy just kept talking, hoping she could say something that would make Jack understand. "Right after I was robbed, I was feeling so alone and unhappy, but I hadn't gotten up the guts to come home. Then this guy comes up to me with his flattering words, and I fell for them out of desperation. I was stupid and he was manipulative. I didn't know he was married at first, and I never realized he was a prince."

Amy paused again, but Jack said nothing. She wanted to look at him, but kept her eyes on the gravel. It was safer at the moment. "We were together for a couple of weeks before his true colors started to show. He was… not a nice guy," she said, knowing she couldn't do justice to the way he'd treated her. "It was only when I found out he was married that I wised up and bought my plane ticket. I flew home the next day."

Jack gave a low whistle, and Amy blushed. She knew Jack had done the math again, and it definitely didn't put her in a good light. This was when she had to say the rest. "And the baby—"

Before she could get out the rest of the words, Jack gasped and threw his face into his hands. It broke her heart to see him that way. "It's not mine," he said, his voice full of despair.

"I don't know," she responded, her voice quiet.

They sat there in silence for a long while, until she couldn't take it anymore. "I didn't plan for it to be like that, you know. I didn't plan for any of this. But I don't want to lose you, Jack."

Her story done, Amy waited.

And waited.

Still, Jack said nothing. Just when Amy didn't think she could take the silence any longer, Jack stood. Amy could hardly see him in the dark, but she watched carefully for any sign of his feelings. He didn't seem angry, but he wasn't looking at her, either. "You should probably get inside," he told her, his voice flat. "It's too cold to be out without a sweater."

"What about you?" she asked, meaning so much in that sentence.

"I just…need time to think, okay?" he answered.

What could she say to that? "Okay," she responded quietly.

"I'll talk to you on Tuesday," he said as he walked to his truck without a backward glance.

Her skin was goosebumped and she'd begun to shiver, but she waited until long after his truck disappeared before she went back inside.

Jack drove away, but not toward his family's ranch. Instead, he turned his truck toward open country, driving until he was surrounded by little more than grass and hills.

After a long while, he pulled over and got out of the truck, ignoring the brisk air. He opened the tailgate and sat on it, staring into the darkness that surrounded him.

Amy hadn't cheated on him, obviously, but he couldn't help but feel betrayed. The idea of their first night together being about more than just the two of them hurt. It explained her reaction after, and he could understand what that felt like—if there'd been some way to soothe the pain after she'd disappeared from his life, he was sure he would have jumped at the chance.

He also felt angry at the man that had done all this to Amy. He could feel the embarrassment almost emanating off her as she told her story, though he'd been too wrapped up in his own thoughts to think much about it in the moment. Now, he realized how she must have felt coming back to Texas, her heart and soul battered and broken from first the robbery and then the betrayal from someone she trusted.

Knowing that the baby might not be his, but instead be a product of an encounter with that manipulative liar was a painful blow.

But dammit, that guy would never be the child's parent. Even if he was the biological father, Jack knew Amy well enough to be sure she wouldn't ask the man for a dime. And she was strong enough to raise this kid herself.

But she shouldn't need to. Jack gripped his truck's tailgate and shook his head. Even if the child wasn't his, did it change his feelings for Amy?

That answer was obvious enough. He'd always loved her, had never stopped loving her, and he already loved the child that was half her, even if the other half might not be him. They could still be the family he'd always wanted.

And his last but very real problem was finally clear to him: Would he ever be enough for her, or would he one day come home to find she'd disappeared again, taking her child with her and leaving him alone?

That thought scared him more than anything else.

Jack sighed and lay back into his truck bed and stared at the stars for a long while, ignoring how uncomfortable the cold metal was on his back, trying to figure out what to do next. He could play it safe and break things off with her before it went any further and save himself more pain when it all fell apart somewhere down the road.

But Jack thought of the ring and the baby, and he knew there was no safe place for him to hide his heart. It was too late for that. Amy and her child already had it, and stopping things now just meant he would miss out on all the possible wonderful moments he might have. The truth was, he wanted that family. So badly that he couldn't imagine running from this opportunity, as complicated as it might be.

Finally, Jack sat up and rubbed his back. There was no question about what he would do, of course. And he needed to let her know before he left for Wyoming the next morning.

Jack got back in his truck and started driving back the way he'd come. When he arrived at Amy's house everything was dark except the living room, which was lit by a single lamp. He could see Amy sitting in the window seat, the light spilling around her, as if she was waiting for him. He rushed out of the truck, and she had just stepped out the front door when he pulled her into his arms, kissing her with all his might.

She kissed back, and they held each other for a long, long time.

Amy sat on her bed in the hotel room she and Ma were sharing in San Diego, not sure what to do with herself. Jack was already working with Sam in Wyoming, so she didn't want to bother him, as much as she'd like to call and get assurance once again that he was still a part of her life despite everything with Armand. She had an article to write that she'd been putting off for two weeks, but she doubted she could do much of anything, as distracted as she was. Sitting and doing nothing was only making her feel stir-crazy.

Amy stood up and began pacing. She was having a *baby*. It was still impossible to wrap her mind around it. After all, she'd spent the past decade expecting to never be pregnant. It was just a fact of her life. And now that was turned upside down and here she was with a little one on the way.

Amy wished she felt euphoric about it, like Jack had when he first found out. But instead she felt nervous. And scared.

Now that she had finally accepted the truth of the matter, it left her with so many questions. How would she be able to continue the life she'd created for herself and raise a child? What would the next eighteen years look like? Would she and Jack be able to make all this work?

She didn't have answers to anything, and felt lost. At sea without a life raft. Jack's steadiness and confidence were the only things keeping her afloat, and she had no idea how much longer that might last.

Ma came out of the bathroom shaking her head. "I tell you, dear, this ain't half-bad. The lounge, the airport and now this hotel. Maybe I should convince Howie to see a bit of the world with me."

Amy nodded, though she hardly heard the older woman. After a few moments, Ma came up to her and put a hand on each of Amy's cheeks, staring into her daughter's eyes. "I'll be here for you whatever happens with Maryanne, Amy. Don't you worry."

Amy felt tears welling in her eyes, and she almost spilled the truth out to her kind adopted mother, but she stopped herself. Ma's entire life had been focused around her children, and Amy just couldn't confess her fears and risk being told to give up everything important in her life for this baby. So she kept silent.

Amy would tell her soon, possibly even before they returned to Texas, but first she needed to sort out her thoughts on her own. Ma patted her cheek gently and smiled encouragingly.

Amy hadn't even been thinking about the reason for their trip to California, and only now considered what it might be like to meet her half sister the next day. As if Amy's phone knew she was thinking of Maryanne, it pinged with a new text message from her:

My son just reminded me he has a birthday party tomorrow at a bowling alley.

Amy's heart sank. They were supposed to meet tomorrow. Was her sister canceling on her again? It didn't seem like she really wanted to see Amy after all. Then the next message showed up:

Are you up for some bowling? I can drop Devin off with his friends and we can get our own lane as far from the party as possible. Your adopted mother is welcome to join, of course.

Amy felt a sense of relief. So Maryanne wasn't begging off from their meet-up. Amy looked over at Ma, who was carefully unpacking her bag into the chest of drawers. "You interested in going bowling with Maryanne?"

She wasn't sure what she expected Ma's reaction to be, but she certainly didn't expect her to clap her hands with excitement like a child. "I haven't bowled in years!" she exclaimed.

That decided it, and Amy texted Maryanne back. Soon everything was planned and Amy set her phone down. Before she could go back to wondering what to do with herself, Ma was picking up their hotel key card and her purse. "Get up off your behind, dear. We're going to see the ocean."

Amy gave her mother a confused look. "Don't you think it's a bit cold out to go to the beach?" she asked.

Ma shook her head. "I haven't seen the Pacific Ocean in more'n twenty years, and I intend to go right now so we can be there when the sun sets. Grab a sweater so you won't be chilled."

Amy hopped up immediately, threw on her jacket and followed her mother out the door. In no time at all, they were standing on a beach, sitting with their toes in the cold sand despite the temperature, watching the waves crash against the shore.

"I love Texas with all my heart and soul," Ma said quietly, almost as if she was speaking to herself, "but there's something about watching the sun set over the ocean that lifts my spirit. I shouldn't have waited so long to see it again."

Amy said nothing, just watched the rolling waves as the sun touched the horizon. Brock had grown up here, and this place must hold special memories for Ma and her sister, Jeannie, Brock's mother. It certainly was beautiful, and she loved this time with Ma, but her mind kept drifting back to Jack in Wyoming. If everything worked out there, he would be incredibly busy for months, years even, as he pushed to make it to the top. Even if he wanted to be a part of the baby's life, how could that work?

Even these few hours apart were hard—she couldn't imagine what it would be like when she was in Chiang Mai and he was on the circuit. Even if she loved him and he loved her, she would be very, very alone. Could they make it work without constantly tearing themselves apart?

Amy stared at the water as the sun went down, wishing she had answers to everything. Ma patted her hand, catching Amy's attention. The older woman smiled kindly at her. "Don't you worry, dear. You two will figure it out."

It took Amy a moment to realize what Ma meant. "How did you know what I was thinking?" Amy asked.

"Are you ever *not* thinking about Jack Stuart these days?" her mother responded.

Amy didn't know what to say to that. "Love is difficult," Ma continued. "You will find what's right for you."

Amy wanted those words to reassure her, but she couldn't help but be skeptical. Sometimes things just didn't work out. She knew that well enough.

And wishes couldn't change facts here. She would try to have a lasting relationship with Jack, and they might try to raise a child together, but would it work? Or would the facts be so strongly against them that wishes wouldn't matter?

The sun dropped below the horizon with a last tiny flash of light and the two women sat in the sand for another moment before standing. "Dinner and then bed," Ma announced as they brushed the sand off their feet. "Tomorrow's a big day."

Amy's heart jumped. Tomorrow she would spend some quality time with her half sister. She would learn about where she came from, at least a little bit. It was time to put Jack and the baby aside for the time being, as hard as that seemed to be, and focus her attention on the here and now.

Chapter 10

Jack woke early, his eyes bleary from getting so little sleep. With everything on his mind, from his upcoming roping session at Sam's to Amy and the pregnancy, it was hard to quiet his brain enough to rest.

Still, he was satisfied that he'd come up with the best plan for his new family. It would hurt to give up on his dream for the Stuart ranch once and for all, but he'd finally had to admit to himself that he couldn't put every cent into the place, which was what it needed to make it work. No, there was something more important now. The child in his arms would be the only thing that mattered.

He also needed to decide how to propose to Amy. He'd been planning to wait until her trip to Chiang Mai, but with the pregnancy, all that had changed. Putting it off until after Brock and Cassie's wedding seemed silly now.

Jack pulled himself out of bed and splashed some water on his face. He needed to be at his best if he was going to turn these few days with Sam into a lucrative career move, and that was more important now than it had ever been.

A couple of hours later, Jack wiped the sweat from his face. Even though the air was cool, he was burning up. Almost the moment he'd gotten onto Sam's property he'd been put to work running drills, showing his abilities as best he could. Sam was watching him carefully, and Jack felt like everything he did was being scrutinized, and he hoped he wasn't coming up short. He needed this. For Amy. For the baby.

Jack looked around beyond the practice arena he was currently working in. He hadn't yet had a chance to look around the ranch much, but from what he'd seen, it was pretty fantastic. Everything a rodeo cowboy could possibly want. Jack's heart longed for something like this back in Spring Valley, and he could almost picture what he'd need to do to Stuart Ranch to make it a reality. Before he could get too lost in that old pointless dream, though, Sam rode once more to the starting position. "Come on, Jack, let's go at it again. And pay attention this time."

Jack bit his lip and turned his horse toward where Sam was waiting. He was starting to understand why Sam's old partner might've quit. While the man was a great roper, one of the best, he was also a frustrating person to work with. Even after such a short time, Jack could tell that Sam was a rigid taskmaster who spoke to almost everyone with brusque condescension, including his teammates.

It was clear that for this to work, Jack would need to

keep his mouth shut and do everything asked of him, no matter his opinion. That would be the only way to set his career on the right path and do what was best for his family.

"Focus, Jack," Sam said, cutting into his thoughts. "I expect better this time."

Sam waved his hand in the air and a steer was released into the arena. Jack gripped his rope and rode in time with Sam toward the animal. In just a few seconds the steer was immobilized and Jack felt a grin of triumph spread across his lips. It had been a great ride, first place in most any rodeo.

Sam pinched his lips together and shook his head as they let the steer loose. "You turned a little slowly at the end there. Wasted a quarter second. Let's try again."

By noon, Jack was exhausted and his nerves were frayed from Sam's constant criticisms. Jack's partners had always been supportive and excited to ride together. They'd been a team but also friends. Sam, however, seemed to be making it very clear that he didn't want a friend.

Jack dismounted and rotated his roping arm slowly, feeling the burn of the muscles beneath the skin. Sam walked over to him and held out his hand. "I think we'll be able to do great things, Jack," he said with a small smile.

Jack shook the proffered hand, though he found it difficult to return the smile. It had been a long work day, and not exactly the pleasantest in recent memory. But this was his chance and he had to take it.

Amy stood in front of the bowling alley, unable to make her feet move. This was the big moment, and now that it was here, she wasn't sure she'd be able to do it. Ma, however, seemed unfazed by the momentousness of the occasion. "Hurry up, dear. For a woman who travels around the world constantly, you move slow as molasses sometimes."

With that, her mother set a brisk pace toward the entrance, and Amy could do nothing but hurry to follow. Inside was dim compared to the bright sunlight, and it took a moment for Amy's eyes to adjust. Before they could, she was engulfed in a hug. "Amy, you're here!" said a woman who Amy couldn't see but assumed to be Maryanne.

The woman stood back and, sure enough, she matched the picture Maryanne had sent. Amy's same nose and mouth set into a different, darker face and surrounded by dark wavy hair. "I'm sorry for attacking you the moment you walked in. I'm just so excited that you're here. Thank you for coming," she added, turning to Amy's adopted mother and grasping the older woman's hand in both of her own.

After brief introductions, the three of them settled into a lane and started lacing their rented shoes. "Thanks for agreeing to meet at the bowling alley," Maryanne said over the din of balls hitting pins. "I would hate to disappoint my son when he'd been looking forward to this for weeks. I can be a bit scatterbrained."

Amy smiled, but before she could say anything, Ma was already reassuring Maryanne. "I think this'll be a hoot, dear," she said as she went to choose her bowling ball.

"Your adopted mother seems wonderful," Maryanne told her while the older woman was out of earshot.

Amy had to agree. "I've been very lucky."

Maryanne seemed to know what Amy was thinking, because she pulled a picture out of her purse. "This," she said, handing one to Amy, "Is our biological mother. She… Well, she's a difficult woman to explain."

Amy stared at the photo, trying to absorb that this was her mother. Maryanne kept speaking, and Amy listened intently. "I don't know much about your adoption, just that Mom was young when she had you and wasn't ready to have a kid. Not that she was much more prepared when I came along a few years later."

Maryanne gave a sad little laugh that tugged at Amy's heart, and Amy squeezed her sister's hand. Maryanne shrugged, as if to say the past was the past. "I bounced between her and my dad a lot when I was little, but didn't see her much by the time I was a teenager. I'm sorry to tell you that I don't know where she is now."

Amy still said nothing, staring at her mother. The woman in the photograph was thin and pretty, with a wide grin, but the characteristic that caught Amy's attention more than anything else was her eyes. Those were Amy's eyes. It was such a strange feeling, holding a picture of the woman who had given birth to her almost thirty years ago, then put her up for adoption.

A loud crash of pins broke Amy's concentration, and she looked up to see Ma standing triumphant as the screen above their lane announced a strike. "Who's next?" Ma asked, sitting down.

"I didn't know you were bringing a ringer to bowling," Maryanne commented before standing.

Amy shook her head. "Me neither," she said.

After several games of bowling, each one ending

with Ma soundly destroying the other two women, the birthday party wrapped up and Amy drove to Maryanne's home while Ma went back to the hotel to "rest on her laurels," as she put it.

Amy sat at Maryanne's table as her half sister pulled out a box of pictures and a photo album. "The box is full of random pictures—some from my father's side and some from Mom's, but the album is all Mom and other people related to you. I brought it with me to Texas. I'm still so sorry about that, Amy."

Amy waved away the apology and opened the album. Her mother stared out at her from the pages, looking young and happy in most of them. She looked friendly and outgoing. Amy turned to Maryanne, remembering the way she'd spoken about their mother at the bowling alley.

"Tell me about her," Amy said, pointing to the woman in the pictures.

Maryanne sighed. "She…loves her life. Every time I was around her, she'd tell me about the things she was doing and the exciting people she'd met. And she was very extroverted, always the life of every party."

Amy waited a moment, but Maryanne seemed reluctant to go on. "But…" she prompted, knowing that would be the next word out of Maryanne's mouth.

"But she didn't really want children, and I always felt like more of a hindrance than an actual part of her life. She didn't have the time or patience to care about anyone but herself, and she was flighty. Here one day, off on her newest adventure the next without a word of warning. We lost touch when I grew old enough to resent it and stopped pushing us to have a relationship."

Amy took in all this information, staring at the photos in front of her. Their mother hadn't wanted a child, hadn't been prepared for a child, and Maryanne suffered because of it. Amy felt a twinge of fear run through her. Was she going to be like her mother in that way?

Maryanne turned the page and pointed out an older woman, explaining that it was their grandmother. Amy could hardly listen.

After a few more minutes, Amy left her sister's house, thanking her for the information, but insisting she needed to go. Maryanne gave Amy a concerned look. "I'm sorry if I've said anything that upset you. I really would like us to have a relationship, Amy."

Amy hugged Maryanne and assured her that they would stay in contact, and then she hopped into her rental car and drove toward the hotel. Once she was parked in the lot, however, she didn't make a move to leave the vehicle.

The truth about her biological mother worried Amy more than she liked to admit, and she couldn't seem to get it out of her head. All her fears about her ability to be a good parent while still living her life and traveling shot to the surface. Would she end up having the same kind of relationship with her son or daughter as Maryanne experienced?

Maybe it wasn't worth the risk. Maybe setting up an adoption with a good family before the baby was even born would be the best thing for everyone involved.

Jack would be devastated, she knew. He would never forgive her for ruining his chance to have the dream family he'd always wanted. But, Amy reminded herself, that dream was unrealistic anyway. It didn't include her job taking her out of the country or him being away on the rodeo circuit for months at a time. What he had was a vague wish that couldn't possibly match up with the reality of their lives.

Perhaps it was better to hurt him with the truth now.

Amy shook her head in exasperation. She didn't know what to do and it frustrated her to no end. Before she'd come back to Spring Valley, life was simple. Even if she didn't know where she was going to be in two weeks, she didn't worry about it. Now she was panicking over events that wouldn't occur for eight months or more.

Amy sighed and finally climbed out of the car, walking mechanically toward the hotel elevators.

When she arrived back at their room, Ma looked uncharacteristically nervous. "How did it go?" she asked, almost timidly.

Amy shook her head, unable to explain.

Ma said nothing, just walked toward her adopted daughter and pulled her into a tight hug. Amy hugged her back, all her panic and worries crashing on her like waves at the beach, one right after the other. In a whisper, she said, "Thank you, Ma. For giving me a home and a family."

Ma hugged her with all her might.

Jack waited impatiently with his phone to his ear, wanting so badly to hear Amy's voice on the other end. After the day he'd had with Sam, he needed a bit of a pick-me-up, and this phone call was sure to be that if it went the way he expected.

"Jack," she said, her voice almost a sigh.

"Hey Ames," he answered, feeling suddenly relaxed, at ease. He loved the sound of her voice.

"How's Wyoming?" she asked.

"It's great," he told her, trying to put enthusiasm into his voice.

He had already decided not to tell her about Sam's difficult personality. It was something he would no doubt get used to after a couple weeks, and she was already worried enough without his adding more to the pile. His job at the moment was all about easing her doubts, not adding to them.

And he was bursting with news on that front. "Amy, I found us a house," he blurted out, excited to share the news.

"A house?" she said, sounding unsure.

He'd known she would react like that—after all, they'd never talked about a house before. He launched into an explanation. "Well, a neighborhood, really," he said. "I don't have the money right now, but once the ranch sells and I make a couple big purses we'll have enough for a down payment. We'll need to rent until then."

He waited for a reaction, but there was only silence from the other end of the line, so he continued, "It's in the suburbs of Cheyenne, near to Sam's ranch. The whole area is filled with three-bedroom tract homes, just the thing we'll need for a family."

He smiled to himself, sure he'd just eliminated so many of their problems. With a home all their own, Amy and the baby would be settled and comfortable while he was on the circuit, and he'd have a place to come back to. They could start living the life they needed to live.

Amy finally spoke, her voice hesitant. "I thought you wanted to save the ranch and put all your money toward the rodeo school," she said.

Jack grimaced. "I hate giving up the ranch, but it's the only way I can get enough money together for the baby."

He could tell she was dwelling on the loss of the rodeo school, and it was starting to dampen his spirits. He wanted her to be excited about all this.

"How about you come out here with me after Brock and Cassie's wedding? You can look at the houses first-hand, and if the ranch gets an offer by then, maybe we'll be able to make one of our own," he told her.

"I'm going to Thailand after the wedding. My flight's a couple days later. I won't have time to go to Wyoming," Amy told him.

Jack knitted his brows. "Is your ticket nonrefundable? If you call the airline and tell them you're pregnant, maybe they'll waive the cancelation fees."

"No, I have trip cancelation insurance. I wasn't planning on canceling it."

"You weren't?" Jack asked, genuinely surprised. "But you're pregnant. Don't you need to stay home and go to doctor's appointments, relax, that sort of thing? Aren't you worried about going to Thailand and catching some kind of bug that might affect the baby?"

Jack was incredulous. It was as if Amy didn't understand that everything had changed.

"So I'm supposed to turn my entire life upside down because I miraculously got pregnant a couple weeks ago?" she asked, sounding angry.

Jack wished they were having this conversation in person instead of over the phone. He would be able to explain it so much better in person. "Well…yeah," he said as calmly as he could. "This is our family, Ames." He willed her to understand how important this was.

"I need to go pack for my flight" was all she said in response.

Before he could say anything else, she was gone. He briefly considered calling her back. But what would he say? It was best to let her calm down and see reason, and when he was back in Spring Valley the day after tomorrow, they could talk about it again. She'd have a clearer head by then.

Amy stared at the phone, shaking her head. How could Jack sacrifice so much, his ranch and home and dreams, for a tiny little baby who wasn't even born yet?

Was she the one who was being ridiculous in this situation?

It bothered her to think that might be true. Her conversation with Jack seemed to be one more example that she was too much like her biological mother.

But maybe she could fake it. Go to Wyoming and live in a nice house in the suburbs. Do all the mom things. And maybe someday she'd find a way to be happy living that life.

Really, what were her alternatives?

After sitting and thinking for a long time, Amy opened up her laptop and looked up her airline ticket to Thailand. After only a last brief hesitation, she moved her cursor over the words "Change/Cancel Reservation" and clicked.

Chapter 11

The moment Amy stepped out of Pop's truck back at the ranch, she made a beeline for the neighboring house. She knocked on the large wood door, praying Cassie would be the one to open it. She loved Brock, but didn't think she could face her big brother right now.

To Amy's relief, her sister-in-law opened the door, took one look at Amy, and folded her into a hug. It was exactly what Amy needed, and she grasped onto Cassie with all her might. When they finally let go, Cassie led Amy inside the door and shut it. "Do you need a doctor's office or a sister's shoulder?" she asked.

Amy laughed a little. "Sister, though I do feel like I'm going to throw up."

Cassie nodded and rushed off for a moment, asking her to wait there. Seconds later, Amy could hear Brock and the twins leaving the house through the back door in a noisy storm of boots and voices. Then Cassie was back, ushering Amy into the kitchen. "I sent the boys out for a while so we could have our privacy. Something to drink?" she asked, moving to the cupboard.

Amy shook her head, but Cassie was already pouring hot water into a mug. Soon Amy had a cup of tea on the kitchen table in front of her, and she grabbed it with both hands, as if the heat could rid her of some of her swirling emotions. "It's ginger tea," Cassie said, "so it should help with the nausea."

Amy nodded her thanks and took a sip. "I'd prefer a rum and Coke, but considering the situation, this is perfect. Thank you."

Cassie sat down across from Amy with her own cup and waited quietly while Amy drank another sip of tea. "Did something happen at your sister's?" Cassie asked when Amy put the cup down.

Amy shrugged. She didn't want to get too much into what she had learned about her biological mother. "I came over to tell you I won't be at your wedding. I'm so, so sorry, Cassie."

Cassie looked stricken, and Amy flushed with embarrassment. "You won't be there?" Cassie asked, sounding so upset that Amy had to bite her lip to keep from crying.

"I changed my flight to Thailand. I'm leaving first thing in the morning. I just need to get out of the country," she said.

"Before Jack gets back from Wyoming," Cassie said, a statement rather than a question.

If Amy hadn't already been blushing, she would have done so now. She felt the heat emanating from her face. "If I see him, I'll cave," she whispered.

She knew she would, too. She'd never be able to hold out against his determination to do what he thought was best for her and the baby. He would convince her to move to Wyoming and then what? She'd spent the last decade making a life for herself, and then she'd just throw it away. And if she regretted it in one or two or five years, what would she do then?

No, she needed to leave again. Jack would be able to pursue his dreams and she… Well, she'd need to figure out what she was going to do next.

"I wish you wouldn't go," Cassie said, breaking into Amy's thoughts.

Amy stood. She needed to get to her room, where she could lie on the bed and privately cry for all she was leaving behind. Even though she felt this was the better choice for both Jack and herself, the thought of giving up her chance with Jack was killing her.

Ma's reaction hadn't helped any, either. The older woman was devastated. Amy couldn't bring herself to explain why, not when she was still so confused about what to do with this pregnancy and everything. She wanted to curl up like a child in Ma's arms and hear her comforting words, but she and Pop had gone out to dinner, most likely as a chance for him to talk her out of her depression at their daughter's sudden decision to leave without warning.

Once Amy left Cassie's house, giving her sister one last hug and trying not to notice the tears in the other woman's eyes, she went home and curled up in her bed, alone. It was only then that she let herself cry. She cried for the future she and Jack could have, the poor baby that didn't ask for any of this, and a dozen other things. She fell asleep with tears on her eyelashes.

On the airplane the next morning, there were no more tears, but Amy still felt raw and tired. She tried to blame it on the pregnancy, but she knew it was more about the decision she'd made. She told herself over and over that if she wanted Jack to pursue his dream instead of settling for a house in the suburbs, she needed to force his hand the only way she knew how. As much as it killed her, they couldn't stay together and both be happy, so it was up to her to keep them apart.

Even so, she felt incredibly selfish. Whatever she said, she knew that she was leaving mostly because of her own fear, her own desire to keep the life she knew and loved.

Amy willed the plane to move faster, to get her to Thailand. Maybe if she was far enough away and surrounded by a world different enough from her own, she'd be able to forget the way Jack's cornflower blue eyes sparkled when he smiled at her.

Jack awoke with a warm feeling of expectation running through him. Soon it would be time to catch his flight, and then he'd be in Spring Valley, where Amy was waiting for him. Even though their last phone conversation hadn't gone the way he'd wanted, Jack knew that a good talk in person would sort everything out, and before too much longer, they would be moving into a house together in Cheyenne, settling down and preparing for the arrival of the baby.

The image brought a smile to Jack's face, and he let himself enjoy it for a few more moments before getting up and packing his things that he'd scattered around the tiny room where he'd been staying the past few days.

Normally he was a somewhat tidy person, but the

rigor and demands of working with Sam Evans, along with spending every spare moment searching around the area for a decent place to rent and various other details that came with moving to a new place, had made him careless, and things were scattered everywhere.

He was relieved to be leaving Wyoming, not just because he was excited to see Amy and his home, but also because he was ready for a break from Sam. The man had only gotten more harsh and constantly critical once they'd agreed to be partners, and working with him was more difficult than Jack had imagined. He was sure they'd settle into each other's personalities eventually, and once they won a few purses together, Sam would probably calm down a bit.

Jack looked around the room, ensuring he hadn't missed anything, then checked the time on his phone. He still had a few minutes before he needed to leave, so he sat to glance through his email. One message caught his eye first. Something from Amy. He opened it.

I'm going to Thailand, Jack. My flight leaves at 6am, so I'll be gone before you get back to Texas. I need some time away. I want you to have your rodeo school and your dream, and I don't think that's possible with me in your life.

I'm sorry.

That was it. Jack couldn't believe it. It was past seven already, but he called her phone anyway, just in case this was some kind of a mistake.

No answer. She'd really left him again. Jack slumped forward, not sure what to do next.

After a two-hour flight that seemed to take forever,

Jack went straight to Amy's parents' house. He refused to believe she had really gone until he saw proof for himself.

As soon as Amy's mother opened the door, though, he knew it was true. The woman looked so crestfallen that she didn't need to say anything. "She really left," he said, mostly speaking to himself.

The woman nodded. "Would you like to come in, Jack?" she said, her voice soft and sounding as though she had a cold.

Jack shook his head. He needed to be alone, away from everything that screamed out Amy's absence. He got back into his truck and drove away, hoping a long drive would soothe his anger and sadness, but even his truck smelled faintly of her. Soon he was walking along a dirt road, trying to get as far from Amy as he could.

Like a ghost, she followed him.

Jack sat in the dirt, unable to go any farther. She'd run away from him again, just as he'd feared she would. And now he didn't know what to do. He was sure he couldn't just forget about her, or about the baby that he planned to raise, but what could he do? He couldn't force her to allow him into her life.

Finally he drove home. He didn't know what he would do there that could keep his mind off all this, but he hoped to find something better than just sitting around thinking.

As soon as he walked in the door, though, it became clear he wasn't going to be done with the topic anytime soon. His mom was sitting in the front room, and it was clear she'd been waiting for him.

"I'm guessing you heard," he said, sitting down heavily on the couch.

She leaned toward him. "I spoke to her mother today. I know this must be very difficult for you, Jack."

Jack shrugged. He didn't want to talk about it. Of course it was difficult. He felt abandoned. Rejected. Betrayed.

Again.

"I know there's nothing I can do to help," his mother continued, "But I hope you can find some way to move past this. You deserve someone who won't run away from you when things get difficult, and I know she's out there somewhere."

With that, she patted his knee and stood, leaving him to his thoughts. After a few minutes, Jack stood and stalked to his room, his bewilderment and pain turning into anger. He walked directly over to his bedside table, grabbed the ring box sitting on top of it and dropped it back into the back of the drawer where he'd found it, shutting the drawer so hard that the lamp on top nearly toppled off.

Jack knew what he needed to do. He needed to pack and get ready to leave for Wyoming. It was time to get the hell out of Spring Valley.

Amy braced her body as the open-back truck careened around a corner, the driver apparently trying to hit every pothole he could find. *If riding horses is bad for pregnant women, I can't imagine this is good,* she thought.

Amy banged on the window to get the driver's attention and hopped out, even though she could still see her hotel behind her and was nowhere near her next destination. After a short argument and paying the equivalent of about fifty cents, Amy watched the red truck continue down the street, followed by three similar vehicles. Amy pulled out her phone, hoping one of her car service apps would work in this country, since the taxi system apparently left a lot to be desired.

A couple of months ago, a bumpy ride on a bench bolted into the back of a truck would be hardly worth noticing except as an interesting cultural phenomenon, but now things were different. There was a baby to think about.

An image of Jack's silver truck, old but with an unmistakable feeling of security built into it, enveloped her, and she longed for home. Amy could feel tears prick her eyes, and it was difficult to see her phone screen for a minute. Finally, she was able to request a car to pick her up, and she leaned against a wall while she waited for it to arrive, trying to stay out of the sun.

The moist heat of the air filled her lungs, and she wished for a cool rain. Like the one that had trapped her and Jack in the barn after their "first date."

Amy bit her lip in frustration. She had been in Chiang Mai for twenty-four hours, and she'd spent almost all of that time wishing for Jack and home, or else feeling nauseated and wanting food from home, which was so completely different from the ubiquitous Thai offerings that she'd already broken down and visited a Mexican restaurant for food that tasted exactly like she should've expected food at a Mexican restaurant in Thailand to taste like.

Amy stopped the flow of negative thoughts and tried to pull herself together. Since when did she complain so much about the little difficulties that came with travel? She was here to have adventures, experience a new culture and see the lantern festival, something she'd wanted to do for years. Then she would write an article about it and get paid. Anyone would love to have this opportunity.

It upset her to no end that she was absolutely miserable.

Before she could dig into everything that had changed and what that meant for her, Amy's ride, a sleek black car stopped in front of her and she hopped in, determined to at least give this city a chance. She directed the driver to the temple she had planned to visit, then leaned back against the cushions and soaked in the air conditioning. Without thinking, her hand crept to her stomach, as if she could feel the child growing inside her.

The child whose future depended completely on her decisions, even though she felt more lost and confused than she ever had in her life. She didn't feel like she was remotely capable of making decisions for anyone, let alone an innocent baby.

Amy repeated the mantra she'd started as soon as she arrived in Thailand: If she could just make it to the lantern festival, everything would sort itself out somehow. She knew it was illogical, stupid even, to assume that she would magically know what to do after that, but she had to hold on to some sort of hope. Unfortunately, the lantern festival was weeks away still, and Amy had no idea how she would survive until then.

But this was her life, right? If she wasn't willing to give it up for Jack and the baby, then she better find some way to enjoy it.

Maybe by the time the festival was over and she moved on to the next place, her heart would hurt less. Then she could broach what to do about this baby. Right now, she missed Jack so deeply it was hard to think about much else. After two weeks, hopefully she would have healed enough to think about life without Jack and not feel pain.

Amy tried to believe that, but couldn't quite manage it.

She arrived at the temple and walked past the statues and worshippers half-heartedly, taking pictures and notes for her article, but not actually seeing much of the scene before her. Her thoughts were so focused inward that it was impossible for her to do much more than wander aimlessly. Finally, she sat down on a bench in the shade as out of way as she could find and sighed.

What was she doing? Where had the spark of adventure gone?

Amy didn't know, and that scared her. She pulled out her phone and glanced through her email, hoping Jack had written back to her. She wanted so badly to hear from him, even if it was an email telling her off. Anything written by him would be a comfort in its own way. But there was nothing from him, not a single word. There was, however, another message that made her sit up. It was from a website editor she'd written for several times, the subject line Important Opportunity, Respond ASAP.

Amy opened it. She read it through once, then again.

Hi Amy!
I saw those pictures of you in The Sun—seems like you're having an exciting time out on the road! I was actually trying to figure out a writer for a series we want for our site: Winter in the Alps. We'd want write-ups of at least four different locations, details about the ski-

ing opportunities and holiday festivities, etc. etc. This could be anywhere from four to as many as ten articles, if you can make them unique enough, and if anybody can do it, it's you. We'll pay expenses and your usual fee per article. Please let me know if you're available and interested as soon as you can!

Amy leaned back and closed her eyes. This was an amazing offer for her, an opportunity to go to a great location with a sure purchaser for her articles about it. And it killed her that she wasn't at all excited about the prospect.

It wasn't just the pregnancy, either, and she knew it. She could easily find doctors in Swiss hospitals for checkups, and she didn't *need* to ski to write about the slopes. She should be jumping at the chance to take this job, baby or not. And now that she'd broken things off with Jack, there was nothing holding her back. How could she say anything but yes?

She closed the email, not sure how to answer.

As Amy sat there, watching the temple-goers pass, there was one person she wanted to speak to, one woman whose advice and voice she most wanted to hear.

Her mom.

Not the biological one—the mom that had gone to every track meet and junior rodeo competition, who'd bought her prom dress, and who'd cried every time she left home.

Amy tapped her phone a few times before putting it to her ear. It rang several times before Ma answered with a very sleepy "Who on earth is calling at this hour?"

Amy almost slapped her forehead. It had to be after midnight in Texas. "Sorry to call so late, Ma," she said.

The voice on the other end suddenly sounded much more alert. "Amy? What's wrong? Did something happen?"

"No, nothing happened," Amy said in her most reassuring voice. "I just forgot about the time difference. I'll call back at a better time."

"Oh, no, dear," Ma said, and Amy could hear her moving around. "I'm awake now, so I expect you to talk to me for a good long bit. Make getting up worth it. What's bothering you, dear?"

Amy smiled. She was sure that Ma wouldn't rest until she found out why Amy had called. "There are a few things going on that I haven't told you about, Ma," she confessed.

At first, Amy had only planned on telling her about Jack and the pregnancy, but as soon as she started everything poured out: the robbery in Morocco, her affair with Armand, her fears about being like her biological mother. All of it. By the time she was finished, tears were streaming down her cheeks.

Her mother was silent on the other side of the line for several long seconds after Amy finished. Then she said, "Oh dear, you *have* had a difficult time of it lately, haven't you?"

Amy laughed through her tears.

"How can I help with all this, Amy?" Ma asked, her voice earnest.

Amy shrugged even though she knew the other woman couldn't see the gesture. "I just needed you to know. I've never felt so lost. Should I move to Wyoming? Keep traveling? Give up the baby or keep it? This is all so confusing."

"Do you remember that book you read in high school, *The Bell Jar*?" Ma asked.

"I remember it," Amy answered, with no idea how Ma was planning to connect this to her life.

"Do you remember the fig tree thing?"

Amy's class had spent almost a week talking about that part of the story, and Ma's meaning became clear in a flash. "She sees her life as a tree and all her different options as figs on it, but she can't decide which thing to pursue," Amy said, digging the scene out of her memory. "Because she doesn't pick one, the options wither and fall around her as she starves."

"Good girl," Ma said. "I can't choose for you, but I can tell you that you best make a choice. Don't wait until it's too late."

Fear still held Amy back. "I'm so scared I'll be a bad mother," she admitted, almost in a whisper.

Ma's voice came to her like a warm hug. "Sweetie, if you're so worried, you'll do just fine. It means you care and you want the best for your baby, and that's what being a good mom is all about."

After another few minutes, Amy hung up the phone and used her app to request another car. Since she had a few minutes to wait, she settled back on the bench, trying to get comfortable.

Her mom was right—she needed to make a choice. It was time to grow up and stop acting on momentary whims and selfish desires that just made her more miserable in the long run.

So what did she really, truly want, for herself and her baby and the other people around her? Amy closed her eyes and created images of her future, trying to assess her feelings about each one. An image of her in a Swiss ski resort, taking pictures and writing articles as it snowed outside, an image of her in Spring Valley with her family, an image of her in Jack's arms, the background a mystery. The baby in her arms, the baby being taken away to another family.

In all that mess, all those lives she could live, what did she want?

Amy opened her eyes and sat up. As afraid as she might feel, or unsure or whatever, she knew what she wanted. And now it was time to put it into action.

Then she stood and went to meet the car waiting for her, hurrying her steps a little. She needed to get back to her hotel room and her computer—she had some flights to book.

Jack slammed another bag into the back of his truck. He wasn't sure what was in it, and frankly, he didn't care much. He just needed to get the stuff into the vehicle so he could get out on the road and away from this damn town as quickly as he could.

The past two days, ever since he'd arrived home and learned that Amy was actually gone, had been a blur of cramming everything he owned into duffel bags and working as much as he could on the ranch. His body desperately needed a rest, but he couldn't manage to sit still. It was better to work and keep his mind blank, stay angry. If he wasn't angry, he'd be hurt, and he couldn't deal with that anymore.

As he tossed the last two bags in with the others, Jack heard a truck turn into the driveway. He turned and felt as if he was hallucinating. Amy pulled up beside where he stood, stepped out of the truck and ran toward him. Without thinking, he opened his arms wide and caught her up in them, holding her close.

She was here, back in Spring Valley, back in his arms. He didn't know how or why, and for the moment he couldn't think of anything beyond the feeling of her in his arms. "You left," he said, trying to process what was happening.

Amy nodded, not removing her face from where it rested against his shoulder. "I got to Thailand and realized the only place I wanted to be was wherever you were. Here or Cheyenne, a ranch or in the suburbs. As long as I'm with you, Jack."

He squeezed her close, trying to absorb her words. She continued speaking, her voice a little muffled by his shirt. "I'm not scared anymore, Jack. I know that I love you and I want to have this baby with you."

Jack held Amy tight for another second before forcing his arms to break their hold on her. Amy backed up a little and looked into his face. Her cheeks were stained from her tears. "I love you, Jack," she said again.

"I love you too, Amy," he told her.

She stepped closer, but he moved back, keeping distance between them. He felt so much pain in his heart that he had to stop himself from rubbing the skin above it. He focused on his anger instead.

Her expression grew confused as they looked at one another. He knew what he needed to say next, but it took him a moment to get out the words. Angry, he reminded himself. He was angry. "But I can't do this, Amy."

Shock flooded her face and Jack looked away. He needed to say it all. "When you left the first time, it about killed me. And this time...well, I just know I can't put myself through that again. It's too hard. I love you and I'll always love you, but I can't risk my heart like that."

"I won't run again," she said, her voice a whisper.

Jack shook his head, holding tightly to his fury. "I can't let myself believe that." He thought of his mother's words. "I deserve someone who I know won't disappear when things get difficult, Amy."

He stopped talking, but Amy said nothing else. "I still want to be a part of the baby's life and help any way I can. I'm happy to be your friend, Amy," he said stiffly, knowing it didn't sound sincere.

But it was all he was capable of at the moment, dammit.

Jack finally risked a glance up and felt his anger dissolve in one quick swoop. She wasn't crying, but her expression spoke of the agony she felt. Jack wanted to say something to help, but there was nothing left to say. He knew what he'd said was right. Now he just needed to get away before he caved.

Jack gestured to his full truck and where Benny was waiting nearby, ready to settle into the horse trailer for the long ride to Cheyenne. "I better go. I'll see you at the wedding, Amy."

With that, he turned and walked away, not risking a backward glance until he heard her truck driving away. Once he did, however, he watched until it disappeared, only able to keep himself from chasing after her with the hardest effort.

When she was gone, Jack turned again and continued walking toward where Benny was waiting for him. He hugged the horse's neck tight for a moment, telling himself he'd made the right choice no matter how horrible it made him feel at the moment.

Benny snorted in commiseration. Or maybe in disappointment. Jack couldn't be sure.

Chapter 12

Cassie opened the door, nearly squealing in her excitement when she saw that Amy was on the other side. "You're back!" she shrieked as she gave Amy a giant hug. "This means you're going to be here for the wedding, right?" she asked, leaning away and looking into Amy's face.

Amy nodded, but Cassie's face fell immediately. "What happened?" she asked, looking concerned.

Amy felt the tears she'd managed to suppress at Jack's coming to the surface, but she held them back. This was a time to stop being so selfish. Cassie was getting married in a week, and she deserved Amy's attention, not Amy's sadness and tears. "It doesn't matter right now. What matters is that I shouldn't have left. I'm sorry for the way I treated you, and if you don't want me to be your bridesmaid, I understand."

Cassie pulled Amy into another hug, this one full of sympathy instead of excitement. "Of course I want you to be my bridesmaid. You're my sister," Cassie said.

In a flash, the two women were inside, sitting at the kitchen table. "You sure you don't want to tell me what's wrong?" Cassie asked again, looking into Amy's eyes.

Amy wanted to sob into her sister's shoulder about her heartbreak and shame at causing a sweet man like Jack to feel so hurt and angry, but she held it all back. "I've just made a lot of mistakes the past couple of weeks—years, actually—and they're coming back to me," she said, chiding herself. Before Cassie could say anything, Amy added, "But I'm going to try to be better. I want to be a stronger, more selfless person. For my baby, if nothing else."

Cassie gave her an encouraging smile. "It sounds like you did some soul-searching in Thailand."

Amy tried to smile, but failed. "You could say that."

Amy wanted to curl up and cry about Jack, beat herself up over all the pain she had caused him with her selfishness, and mourn the loss of the man she loved. Now that she'd said what she needed to and apologized to Cassie, her strength felt sapped. She stood up slowly. "I should get home," she said.

Cassie stood and grabbed Amy's arm. "I don't know what happened, but I'm here if there's anything I can do to help. Same with Brock. And your entire family."

Amy nodded, though she hardly heard the words, and walked out and toward her parents' house. It was only when she was at the midpoint between the two ranches that Cassie's words really sunk in. She had so much family and so much love around her. She needed to remember that.

When she arrived home, Amy fell into Ma and Pop's arms, apologizing for her disappearance. Then she told them about what happened with Jack. "You were right, Ma," she said at last. "I didn't make the choice I really wanted, and by the time I realized it, I was too late. I've lost him."

Pop shook his head. "Are you going to give him up that easy, Amy?"

Amy looked up at her father, not sure what he meant. Her mother nodded in agreement. "Why, if I had let Howie go when he told me I was too stubborn to date, you wouldn't be sitting on this couch with us," she said.

Amy looked to Pop in surprise. He nodded and wrapped his arm around his wife. "She convinced me to give her another chance, and I haven't let her go since. I just thank my lucky stars she was smart enough to see what I couldn't."

Amy had to smile at the couple. They'd been married for nearly forty years, but they were looking at each other like newlyweds.

When Amy went to bed that night, she felt a new emotion: determination. She wouldn't give Jack up just yet. She had to try once more, give it another shot. If he still didn't want her, she would accept his decision, but she wasn't going to throw up her arms and let him go without a fight.

Now she needed to figure out what she could do to prove to him that she was in for the long haul, and it better be good.

"Dammit, Jack, pull it together!" Sam yelled across the paddock.

Jack took a deep breath and looked down at the rope

in his hand. He was just a second too slow, a second off, but it was enough. The difference between winning and losing.

And Sam wasn't going to let that slide. He rode up to Jack, getting close enough to his face that Jack leaned back, away from him. "I don't know what your problem is, Jack, but you need to pull it together. I expect to win this year, and if you don't, you should just get the hell out of here."

Jack bit his tongue, holding back the torrent of words. Sam was the best there was, and it wouldn't do to piss him off any more than Jack already had. Instead, Jack turned Benny to get back into position. "Let's do it again."

They went through the process again, but Jack's throw was even worse than before.

"What are you doing, Jack!" Sam yelled, throwing his hat to the floor.

Jack watched as Sam's face turned red, but he forced himself to remain calm. He'd already learned not to react to Sam's little tantrums or they only got worse.

To be fair, Jack was a little frustrated with himself, too. For the past couple of days he'd been missing throws he could make in his sleep ever since he was a teenager. His mind was somewhere else, and it was driving Sam crazy.

"If you don't want to be here, you damn well better not come back after that wedding, Jack. I expect to win a purse in two weeks, not be a laughingstock. And with you throwing like you are today—"

Sam stopped talking and turned his horse. He rode away, still seething.

Jack didn't say anything, just sat on Benny and

watched Sam ride away. He was sure if he said any of the thoughts swirling in his mind, it would mean the end of his time working with Sam already, and he didn't want that. Sam was the way to the top. If he could pull together his own performance, of course.

It was no surprise to Jack that he was roping so badly. It seemed like the closer it got to the wedding, the worse he got. And with the wedding the next afternoon, this was by far his worst session yet. He was glad he'd be leaving in a couple hours, if only to get away from his terrible riding.

He would be seeing Amy again, trying to be a friend instead of what he'd expected and hoped they would be. Lovers, partners, parents. It killed him to think of that.

He'd considered skipping the wedding, almost called his mom in Spring Valley a dozen times, but at the last minute he'd held himself back. He needed to go home anyway. For one thing, his mom had told him that they were expecting to get an offer in the days after the wedding, and Tom was planning to leave for Boston then, too. He had to be there.

And he'd told Amy the truth when he said he wanted to be part of the baby's life, which meant he needed to be able to spend time with her, as much as it hurt.

He could only hope that it would hurt less over time.

Jack brought himself back to the present, where he was sitting on Benny in an empty paddock. Sam was nowhere to be seen, and Jack was glad of that. He would call and apologize, assure Sam that he'd be in the right headspace when he got back from the wedding. If he spoke to Sam in person right now, there was a chance he'd say something he would regret. Sam was angry enough that Jack knew it would be nearly impossible to have a rational conversation with him.

Jack slid off Benny and walked him into the barn. Once the horse was settled in his stall, Jack drove to his new apartment to pack. Even though he'd been in the apartment for several days, he hadn't done a single thing to settle in. It still felt too new, too temporary, whatever he told himself about how he was planning to be here for the long run.

Soon it was time to go, and he only hesitated once more before locking the door.

"Where does this go?" Amy asked, lifting a large pot of flowers and tilting it toward Brock.

"How many times have I told you that I'd get the heavy stuff?" Brock demanded as he grabbed the pot away from her.

Amy rolled her eyes. "It weighs about five pounds, Brock. I'm pregnant, not dying."

Cassie smiled at her from where she stood, decorating an arch for the wedding that was scheduled for the next day. Ever since Amy had told her family about the pregnancy, everyone had been treating her as if she was made of glass, despite Cassie's assurances that Amy was fine.

Amy walked up to her soon-to-be sister. "What can I help you with?"

Cassie shrugged. "Are you sure you have the time? I know you've been busy planning your own thing like a madwoman."

Amy had been spending every spare moment on her computer or her phone for the past several days. If the wedding was her last chance to win over Jack, she wasn't going to take it lightly. At the same time, she had to make plans for herself and her baby. There was insurance to get, a doctor to find, and so many other details they made Amy's head swim.

But at least she felt as if she was being productive instead of living life by the seat of her pants, basing her decisions on her selfish feelings at any given moment.

It was time for her to be a grown-up now.

To Cassie, Amy said, "I've done everything I can do. Now I just need to wait until after the wedding and hope it's enough."

"And if it isn't?" Cassie asked, so quietly Amy almost didn't hear her.

Amy had considered that, too. "If it isn't, I have a life I want to live, and I'll do the best I can with it."

Even if she couldn't win Jack back, Amy knew she had to work hard to give her baby a good life, and that meant she couldn't sit around feeling sorry for herself. She would make it work.

It would be hard to get by without Jack in her life, but she had the confidence in herself now to know she would survive.

But she couldn't think like that. Not yet, anyway. She had to hope.

Amy settled into a spot beside Cassie, helping decorate the arch. "I've got to hand it to you, Cassie, this is going to be a beautiful wedding."

Cassie laughed. "The 'beach in Bali' girl is coming around to my country wedding, huh?"

Amy looked at the wide blue sky then across the ranch, decorated with white chairs and pots of flowers. "I'm more Texas than I used to admit," Amy confessed.

* * *

It was the morning of the wedding, and Jack sat at his family's kitchen table, slowly drinking coffee. He wasn't ready to see Amy again in just a few hours, and the fact that it would be at a wedding, something he'd hoped the two of them would have one day, only made it worse.

It had been nearly a week since they'd seen each other, but the pain of it all was still fresh and raw. He was almost thankful that Sam had been working him so hard right up until the day he left because it gave him less time to think. He didn't want to think. Whenever he did, his mind settled on Amy, and it stayed there until he got so busy or tired he couldn't focus on anything.

But now here he was, watching the sky lighten over the home he'd soon be leaving for good, and he had nothing to do but sip his coffee.

He could picture every moment of the last few minutes he'd spent with Amy. The devastation on her face when he'd rejected her. It made his heart ache.

"Morning," Tom said, walking into the kitchen and getting himself some coffee. "You ready for the wedding today?"

Even though Jack had only seen his brother for a few seconds since his encounter with Amy, the way Tom spoke made Jack sure he knew something about what had happened between them. Jack just shrugged. It wasn't something he was ready to talk about.

Besides, there were other topics that needed to be discussed. "Are *you* ready for your big move?" he asked.

Tom was finally leaving for Boston in three days. It made Jack nervous to think his mother would be left on this ranch by herself, but she'd already assured him that she was organizing plenty of help and she didn't need him to worry about her.

Tom looked at his coffee cup and smiled to himself. "I'm ready," he said, not elaborating.

He didn't need to. It was obvious from his expression that he was chomping at the bit to meet this woman from the internet and settle into his new life in Boston. Jack could tell that Tom was over-the-moon in love.

He was happy for his brother, but it also made him wonder if he'd ever feel that way about anybody again.

As if Tom could tell where Jack's mind had gone, he asked, "So, you and Amy are really done for good, huh?"

Jack nodded, as much as it hurt to do so. "If she left again, I don't think I'd be able to take it. It's just safer to stop things now," he explained.

Tom turned toward the stove, away from his brother, and started making breakfast. "So you're happy living in Wyoming, then?" Tom asked over the sound of cracking eggs.

Jack wasn't sure what to say. He didn't want to lie to his brother, but there was no point complaining about the choice he'd made, and if he could make a big purse before his mother accepted an offer on the ranch, then maybe he could still make his rodeo school dream come true. "I'm starting to settle in," he said carefully.

Tom nodded, and Jack thought for a moment that the conversation was done. "And Sam? Is he a good partner?"

Again, Jack chose his words cautiously. "He is an incredibly skilled rider and roper. And he's very dedicated."

Tom turned from the stove and looked at his younger

brother. "So long as you're happy with your decisions, that's all that matters," he said before turning back and pouring eggs into a sizzling pan. "You want some breakfast?" he asked over his shoulder.

"No thanks," Jack said.

He felt antsy, like he needed to go do some thinking. He stood and walked over to the back door, where he had a view of the barn and paddocks. The chances that he could keep this place, especially with an offer coming in over the next couple of days, according to his mom, were slim to none. If he couldn't save the ranch, what would he do with any big purses he won while riding with Sam?

Jack knew it was time to be realistic about his future, and the more he looked at it, the less he liked what he saw. But he needed Sam, didn't he? Otherwise he'd just be a failed roper with a few dollars to his name and no prospects.

Jack walked to the barn and went up to Maverick, who seemed to be looking over Jack's shoulder for someone. "She's not here, boy," Jack told the horse.

Maverick seemed crestfallen. Jack knew how the animal felt. After a minute of brushing the sleek black horse, Jack started talking. "There's not much chance working with Sam will get me the ranch, Maverick, and I can't ask my family to hold off living their lives while I try to make enough money to have it happen, but without that, what do I have?"

Jack had no idea, and Maverick didn't seem forthcoming with any alternatives, either. Jack kept brushing the horse, wondering what kind of a life would make him happy.

Nothing came to him. Maverick snorted and tossed

his head, and Jack patted the animal once more before turning back toward the house.

Amy looked over the crowd from her vantage point of Cassie's bedroom window, a bouquet in her hand. There were nearly three hundred people taking their seats: an interesting mix of Spring Valley residents, Brock's rodeo buddies and Cassie's family from Minnesota standing out among the sea of cowboy hats. Even among all those people, it only took her a second to see Jack sitting with the rest of his family.

She wanted so badly to rush over to him, but managed to hold herself back. This was Brock and Cassie's wedding, and she had a job to do. At the reception, they would be able to talk. That was when she would have her chance.

And if it went wrong or he just decided not to be with her, well, she'd handle it. Amy put a hand to her stomach and said a little prayer, then turned to where Cassie stood with her two other bridesmaids, her sister from Minnesota and Emma, who ran the local bakery. Cassie was brushing her hands along the skirt of her wedding dress, looking a little nervous.

"Are you ready, sister?" Amy asked her, putting a hand on her shoulder.

Cassie nodded and Amy gave her a brief hug. "Let's go get you married, then," she said, and the four women trooped out of the room. Soon they were all walking down the aisle toward where Brock, Jose, Diego, Zach and Carter stood, the younger twins looking especially proud in their suits.

Amy tried to keep her mind focused on the ceremony, but she couldn't stop herself from glancing at

Jack every few minutes. Every time she did, her heart thumped hard and painful against her chest. Twice, their eyes met, and it only made things worse.

Did he miss her, or was he truly satisfied with just being friends? She couldn't tell by his small smile or the look in his blue eyes.

When it came time for the vows, though, all off Amy's attention was on the bride and groom. Brock held Cassie's hands in his and said, "Cassie, you are everything I could imagine in a wife, and you make me a better man. I feel so honored that you would let me into your life and become a part of your family. I love you more every day, and I want to be with you always."

Tears streamed down Amy's face. She was so happy her brother had found someone to love who wanted to spend her life with him.

Amy could only hope to be so lucky. She risked one more glance at Jack, but his eyes were on the couple.

Soon the wedding was over, and the guests moved toward the barn, where scattered tables circled an open area that was clearly meant for a dance floor. Even though it was late October, the air was almost warm and the flowers scattered everywhere gave it a summery atmosphere.

Amy started walking toward Jack. This was it. She would be able to speak to him before the reception truly got started, and then she would know, for better or worse. On her way, though, she was waylaid by Jose and Diego, who had arrived after she'd gone to stay over with Cassie and the bridesmaids the night before the wedding.

Jose picked her up and squeezed her in a tight hug.

"Congratulations!" he shouted so loudly that several guests turned to stare.

Amy would've felt embarrassed by Jose's outburst, but he'd done something like that to her so many times that it had ceased to be surprising. Right now, she was just a little annoyed. She was a woman on a mission.

"Set me down, Jose," she said, hitting him on the shoulder to show she meant business.

Jose set her down and Diego said, "We heard about what's going on. Good luck, Ames."

The endearing nickname made her heart twist. If Jack rejected her once more, she wasn't sure she could stand to hear anyone call her that again. "Thanks, Diego. I'll come talk to you two and Kate when I'm done," she told them.

"Kate couldn't come," Jose said, "but I expect a long sincere conversation with my sister about why she doesn't let me in on all her interesting gossip."

Amy nodded. If things didn't go the way she wanted, it might be hard to have normal conversations, but she had vowed to be less selfish, and this would be the perfect test.

Then she left her brothers and continued on her way. As she closed in on Jack, it became hard to breathe. Part of her wanted to run away, but she held fast. She was done running from her problems.

Jack could hardly keep himself still as the wedding guests moved around him, finding their seats and chatting with friends. He knew Amy was walking toward him, her eyes focused and unwavering. She looked different, somehow, than the last time he'd seen her. There was a sense of calm around her he couldn't explain.

* * *

"Jack," she said in a sighing breath that made his heart ache. "Can I speak to you for a minute? Privately?"

Jack agreed and followed her toward Cassie's house, though he found it difficult to make his feet move. There was so much unsaid between them, and he wasn't sure if he was ready for this even though he'd known it was coming.

Before they could get too far, however, Amy's ma walked up with a woman about her age and Cassie's young twins in tow. Based on the fact that she was a nearly identical older version of Cassie, Jack guessed this must be Brock's new mother-in-law. She had on a sour expression that made Jack wonder how hard she'd fought to stop this wedding.

"Amy, Jack!" Amy's mother said with a big smile. "I'm showing Cassie's mom around the place, giving her a chance to see all that Spring Valley has to offer to these young'uns and their parents."

Jack turned to Amy. He saw her hesitate and knew she wanted to keep going, but then she gave the women a big smile. "Spring Valley is home, ma'am. I've traveled all over the world, but there's no place else like it."

Her gaze turned to Jack as she finished, and he knew her words were for him as much as for Cassie's mother. He watched her, speechless, as she quickly extolled the virtues of Texas, gave the young boys hugs and then continued on their path to the house.

Who was this woman? It was Amy, but with a new demeanor he couldn't understand. He didn't know if it had to do with the pregnancy or his rejection of her, but he watched her closely as they walked through the ranch home's back door that led them into the kitchen.

"I want to buy the ranch," Amy said the moment they were through the back door of the empty house.

"What?" Jack asked, sure he hadn't heard her correctly.

Of all the things he'd guessed she might say once they were alone, this was a complete surprise.

"I want to buy your family's ranch. I have some cash saved up, plus a loan from my parents. It's enough to get a mortgage on the place. Tom would get his fair share, and your mom would like to continue living on the ranch and put her portion into helping me turn the place into a rodeo school. With help from Jose and Diego I can get the stock, and Brock and my uncle Joe will gladly help get rodeo hopefuls out here."

Jack stared at her, uncomprehending. What was she saying?

"I can make your dream a reality, Jack, and I want to do it. I want to live here, on a ranch with horses and family close by. Brock and I can manage the place as long as you're on the circuit. I'll still be able to do some writing for magazines I know would love to hear about Texas life. And I'll be here with the baby when you're ready to take over. I'm not running again, Jack. If I get on a plane, I want you to be there by my side," she finished, handing him a stack of papers.

Amy took a deep breath, as if she'd just given a speech she'd been preparing for a long time. Which, it seemed, was pretty accurate.

Jack quickly rifled through the pile of documents. It included an offer for the ranch, a purchase order of rodeo stock and a passport application with his name already filled in.

He didn't know what to say. Jack looked up at Amy, who was shifting nervously. "Are you really ready for all this?" he asked, gesturing to the papers.

Amy nodded with conviction. "I think all these years I've been traveling, I've been looking for something. A home, a place to be, something. When I was in Thailand, though, I wasn't looking for that because I'd already found it here, with you, on your ranch. I was miserable so far from the people, the person, I love. I know what I want now, and this is it," she said, gesturing toward the documents.

Jack didn't need to hear any more. He tossed the papers onto the table and pulled Amy into a long, tender kiss that left them both breathless. After, he pressed his forehead against hers, taking in her sweet flowery smell and staring into the endless depths of her eyes. "I love you, Amy McNeal," he said softly.

Amy sighed and closed her eyes. "No 'but' this time?" she asked, as if she couldn't be sure this was real.

He shook his head while still leaning it against hers so hers shook as well. "No 'but,' Ames," he said softly. "Never again. I have a ring for you back at the ranch. A ring that's been waiting for you for ten years. Will you marry me?"

Amy let out a long sigh that was all the answer he needed. They shared another deep kiss. "I want to be the woman you deserve," she told him.

Jack felt his heart go tight with love for her. "You're everything and more," he reassured her, giving her a last squeeze before realizing it was probably time to go back out among the other guests.

As they walked back to the wedding together, Amy leaned against Jack. "When do you need to go back to Wyoming?" she asked.

Jack smiled. "I don't, actually, except for a quick trip to get Benny and my things," he said.

When she stopped walking and gave him a look of confusion, he explained, "I called and quit this morning. Wyoming isn't where I want to be. I want to be here in Spring Valley. I always have. Money might be a little tight for a while, but—"

"But we'll make it work," she finished for him.

He planted one more kiss on her lips, unable to stop himself. "Let's dance," he said with a smile as they threaded through the wedding guests toward the dance floor.

They had so much to celebrate.

Epilogue

Amy watched the paper lantern lift into the sky, the small fire beneath it propelling the entire thing up to join the others, thousands of them looking like so many stars in the darkness. She leaned close to Jack, staying silent until she could no longer see which lantern was theirs. "So, what do you think?" she asked him as she looked across the throng of people celebrating the festival.

Jack gave her a little squeeze. "Way better than Bastille Day in Paris."

Amy nodded in agreement, her eyes still on the sky as her thoughts drifted to their daughter and son, so far away.

"You're thinking about Spring Valley, aren't you?" Jack asked her, his cornflower blue eyes studying her face.

She smiled. He always knew when she was missing home. "Darcy would love this," she told him, picturing their four-year-old daughter shrieking with delight as the lantern flew away, her blue eyes sparkling just like her father's were.

"She would," Jack said, "and we'll definitely need to bring her and Archer when they're a little older. For now, I'm sure they're perfectly content getting spoiled rotten by all three grandparents. Remember how happy Archer was when we did that video call this morning?"

Amy knew he was right, but she was still itching to see them. Archer had only been adopted the year before, and it still felt odd to leave him for a few days, no matter how good of hands he was in. "You don't think they're jealous that Jessie got to come?" she asked, putting a hand on the small swell of her belly.

"By the time we've given them all their gifts, I'm not sure they'll even remember we were gone for any reason other than to buy them stuff. It's a good thing the rodeo school is doing so well or we might need a second mortgage on the ranch to pay for this trip."

Amy knocked him playfully with her shoulder. "Those are business expenses. I'm going to write a great article series on how to haggle."

They stood silently as another hundred lanterns joined the rest, then Jack asked, "Should we get back to the hotel?"

Amy nodded. "My feet are exhausted. Just one last thing," she said, diving into the crowd.

She was back a minute later with at least a dozen more paper lanterns piled in a big stack. "Now we can have our own little festival in Spring Valley," she explained.

Jack gave her a wide grin. "The kids will love them," he said.

Amy agreed. "Everyone will have a great time lighting them off. That, or someone will burn the house down. Either way, it'll be a good story. And we have insurance that covers paper lanterns lit on fire, right?"

Jack laughed and shook his head at his wife's silly sense of humor. "I love you, Amy McNeal-Stuart," he said, wrapping his arms around her.

They kissed, and the noise and crowds of the festival faded away as they held each other.

* * * * *

**WE HOPE YOU ENJOYED
THIS BOOK FROM**

⊕ HARLEQUIN
**SPECIAL
EDITION**

Believe in love. Overcome obstacles. Find happiness.

Relate to finding comfort and strength in the
support of loved ones and enjoy the journey
no matter what life throws your way.

6 NEW BOOKS AVAILABLE EVERY MONTH!

*An explosion ended Jake Kelly's military career.
Now his days are spent alone on his ranch, and his
nights are spent keeping his PTSD at bay. But the
ex-marine's efforts to keep the beautiful Skylar Gilmore
at a distance are thwarted by his canine companion.
Every time he turns around, Molly is racing off to the
Circle G looking for Sky. Maybe the dog knows that two
hearts are better than one?*

*Read on for a sneak peek at
The Marine's Road Home,
the latest book in Brenda Harlen's
Match Made in Haven miniseries!*

"Actually, I think I'll try a pint of Wild Horse tonight."

She moved the mug to the appropriate tap and tilted it under the spout. "Eleven whole words," she remarked. "I think that's a new record, John."

He lifted his gaze to hers, saw the teasing light in her eye and felt that uncomfortable tug again. "My name's not John."

"But as you haven't told me what it is, I can only guess," she said.

"So you decided on John...as in John Doe?" he surmised.

She nodded. "And because it rolls off the tongue more easily than the-sullen-stranger-who-drinks-Sam-Adams, or, after tonight, the-sullen-stranger-who-usually-drinks-Sam-Adams-but-one-time-ordered-a-Wild-Horse." She set the mug on a paper coaster in front of him. "And I think that's a smile tugging at the lips of the sullen stranger."

"I was just thinking that next time I'll order a Ruby Mountain Angel Creek Amber Ale," he said.

"Careful," she cautioned with a playful wink. "This exchange of words is starting to resemble an actual conversation."

He lifted the mug to his mouth, and Sky moved down the bar to serve a couple of newcomers, leaving Jake alone with his beer.

Which was what he wanted, and yet, when she came back again, he heard himself say, "My name's Jake."

The sweet curve of her lips warmed something deep inside him.

Don't miss
The Marine's Road Home *by Brenda Harlen,*
available August 2020 wherever
Harlequin Special Edition books and ebooks are sold.

Harlequin.com

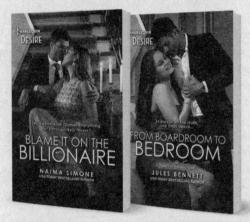

*Successful architect Rani Gupta has sworn off all men.
So when she begins working with hotelier Arjun Singh,
India's hottest bachelor, she vows to keep it professional.
But he won't ignore the attraction they share, especially
when she needs a fake fiancé…*

Read on for a sneak peek at
Marriage by Arrangement *by Sophia Singh Sasson*

Rani's pulse raced. *Is this really happening? I'm going to lead a big contract?* The best she had hoped for was to get the promotion to senior architect and be allowed to work on this high-profile project. She wasn't prepared to manage a big client like Arjun Singh. Arjun's eyes sought her out and he lifted his chin. *Is he asking me if I'm okay with this? Can't be!* Wealthy Indian men didn't ask permission; they took what they wanted. Panic seized her. Could she really work with a man like Arjun? While she had legally freed herself from Navin, the scars from his verbal assaults still tore at her soul. Would Arjun be a reminder of what she'd worked so hard to leave behind?

She met his eyes and gave a slight nod of her head, trying to look nonchalant, as if she was asked to lead big projects every day. *I'm not going to let Navin get in my head. I can do this.*

"I'm willing to do a limited contract with your firm for the construction of the owners' suites, plus blueprints and a 3D interior design for the lobby that mimics the one Ms. Gupta presented for the owners' suites." Arjun stood and left the room without even a goodbye handshake.

Rani slipped out and caught up with Arjun at the elevator banks, her heart beating so hard she was sure he could hear it.

"I look forward to working with you, Mr. Singh." She held out her hand and he looked at it for a second before taking it. Her hand felt small enveloped in his firm grip and a delicious current danced through her body. She was five foot four and wearing two-inch heels but had to tilt her head to maintain his gaze. She met his eyes and her legs turned to Jell-O.

"Call me Arjun." His lips twitched. "Is it okay if I call you…Rani?" He said her name slowly, like it was a sip of fine wine tantalizing his tongue.

"Um, sure." She tugged on her hand and he let it go, but his eyes stayed on her. The man vibrated with sexual charm. *Careful, Rani!*

"How much of the owners' suites did you personally design?" he asked.

Rani resisted the urge to look back at the boardroom. "All of it."

He smiled. Not the clipped polite smile he gave when reporters thrust a microphone in his face or the fake one he gave at the meeting. This one was wide, revealing a tiny dimple in his right cheek. Rani's stomach flipped, and then flipped again. She'd looked at hundreds of photos of this man in the course of her research and there wasn't a dimple in any one of them. *Oh my God. Can this man get any hotter?*

"I've been meeting with architectural design firms for months and no one has come close to what I wanted. You're quite talented, Rani. I can't wait to see what you come up with for the lobby."

Now it was Rani's turn to smile.

"I already have your lobby designed. I think you're going to like it."

His lips twitched. The elevator doors dinged opened and he stepped through, then turned to face her and smiled. A full-watt smile with the little dimple. "I think we're going to work really well together." He joined his hands as the elevator doors closed. "Namaste, Rani," he said in a silky voice that melted her insides.

Namaste, temptation! Rani stared at the closed doors.

Don't miss what happens next in
Marriage by Arrangement *by Sophia Singh Sasson.*

Available August 2020 wherever
Harlequin Desire books and ebooks are sold.

Harlequin.com